The Net Around Joan Ingilby

A Chief Inspector Pointer Mystery

By A. E. Fielding

Originally published in 1928

The Net Around Joan Ingilby

© 2014 Resurrected Press
www.ResurrectedPress.com

Published by Resurrected Press

This classic book was handcrafted by Resurrected Press. Resurrected Press is dedicated to bringing high quality classic books back to the readers who enjoy them. These are not scanned versions of the originals, but, rather, quality checked and edited books meant to be enjoyed!

Please visit ResurrectedPress.com to view our entire catalogue!

ISBN 13: 978-1-937022-82-2

Printed in the United States of America

Other Resurrected Press Books in *The Chief Inspector Pointer Mystery* Series

RESURRECTED PRESS CLASSIC MYSTERY CATALOGUE

Journeys into Mystery
Travel and Mystery in a More Elegant Time

The Edwardian Detectives
Literary Sleuths of the Edwardian Era

Gems of Mystery
Lost Jewels from a More Elegant Age

Anne Austin
One Drop of Blood
The Black Pigeon
Murder at Bridge

E. C. Bentley
Trent's Last Case: The Woman in Black

Ernest Bramah
Max Carrados Resurrected:
The Detective Stories of Max Carrados

Agatha Christie
The Secret Adversary
The Mysterious Affair at Styles

Octavus Roy Cohen
Midnight

Freeman Wills Croft
The Ponson Case
The Pit Prop Syndicate

J. S. Fletcher

The Herapath Property
The Rayner-Slade Amalgamation
The Chestermarke Instinct
The Paradise Mystery
Dead Men's Money
The Middle of Things
Ravensdene Court
Scarhaven Keep
The Orange-Yellow Diamond
The Middle Temple Murder
The Tallyrand Maxim
The Borough Treasurer
In the Mayor's Parlour
The Saftey Pin

R. Austin Freeman

The Mystery of 31 New Inn from the Dr. Thorndyke Series
John Thorndyke's Cases from the Dr. Thorndyke Series
The Red Thumb Mark from The Dr. Thorndyke Series
The Eye of Osiris from The Dr. Thorndyke Series
A Silent Witness from the Dr. John Thorndyke Series
The Cat's Eye from the Dr. John Thorndyke Series
Helen Vardon's Confession: A Dr. John Thorndyke Story
As a Thief in the Night: A Dr. John Thorndyke Story
Mr. Pottermack's Oversight: A Dr. John Thorndyke Story
Dr. Thorndyke Intervenes: A Dr. John Thorndyke Story
The Singing Bone: The Adventures of Dr. Thorndyke
The Stoneware Monkey: A Dr. John Thorndyke Story
The Great Portrait Mystery, and Other Stories: A Collection of Dr. John Thorndyke and Other Stories
The Penrose Mystery: A Dr. John Thorndyke Story

The Uttermost Farthing: A Savant's Vendetta

Arthur Griffiths
The Passenger From Calais
The Rome Express

Fergus Hume
The Mystery of a Hansom Cab
The Green Mummy
The Silent House
The Secret Passage

Edgar Jepson
The Loudwater Mystery

A. E. W. Mason
At the Villa Rose

A. A. Milne
The Red House Mystery

Baroness Emma Orczy
The Old Man in the Corner

Edgar Allan Poe
The Detective Stories of Edgar Allan Poe

Arthur J. Rees
The Hampstead Mystery
The Shrieking Pit
The Hand In The Dark
The Moon Rock
The Mystery of the Downs

Mary Roberts Rinehart
Sight Unseen and The Confession

Dorothy L. Sayers

Whose Body?

Sir William Magnay
The Hunt Ball Mystery

Mabel and Paul Thorne
The Sheridan Road Mystery

Louis Tracy
The Strange Case of Mortimer Fenley
The Albert Gate Mystery
The Bartlett Mystery
The Postmaster's Daughter
The House of Peril
The Sandling Case: What Would You Have Done?

Charles Edmonds Walk
The Paternoster Ruby

John R. Watson
The Mystery of the Downs
The Hampstead Mystery

Edgar Wallace
The Daffodil Mystery
The Crimson Circle

Carolyn Wells
Vicky Van
The Man Who Fell Through the Earth
In the Onyx Lobby
Raspberry Jam
The Clue
The Room with the Tassels
The Vanishing of Betty Varian
The Mystery Girl
The White Alley
The Curved Blades

FOREWORD

The period between the First and Second World Wars has rightly been called the "Golden Age of British Mysteries." It was during this period that Agatha Christie, Dorothy L. Sayers, and Margery Allingham first turned their pens to crime. On the male side, the era saw such writers as Anthony Berkeley, John Dickson Carr, and Freeman Wills Crofts join the ranks of writers of detective fiction. The genre was immensely popular at the time on both sides of the Atlantic, and by the end of the 1930's one out of every four novels published in Britain was a mystery.

While Agatha Christie and a few of her peers have remained popular and in print to this day, the same cannot be said of all the authors of this period. With so many mysteries published in the period, it is inevitable that many of them would become obscure or worse, forgotten, often with no justification than changing public tastes. The case of Archibald Fielding is one such, an author, who though popular enough to have a career spanning two decades and more than two dozen mysteries has become such a cipher that his, or as seems more likely, her real identity has become as much a mystery as the books themselves.

While the identity of the author may forever remain an unsolved puzzle, there are some facts that may be inferred from the texts. It is likely that the author had an upbringing and education typical of the British upper middle class in the period before the Great War with all that implies; a familiarity with the classics, the arts, and music, a working knowledge of French and Italian, an appreciation of the finer things in life. The author had also traveled abroad, primarily in the south of France, but probably to Belgium, Spain, and Italy as well, as portions of several of the books are set in those locales.

The books attributed to Archibald Fielding, A. E. Fielding, or Archibald E. Fielding, are quintessential Golden Age British mysteries. They include all the attributes, the country houses, the tangled webs of relationships, the somewhat feckless cast of characters who seem to have nothing better to do with themselves than to murder or be murdered. Their focus is on a middle class and upper class struggling to find themselves in the new realities of the post war era while still trying to live the lifestyle of the Edwardian era. Things are never as they seem, red herrings are distributed liberally throughout the pages as are the clues that will ultimately lead to the solution of "the puzzle," for the British mysteries of this period are centered on the puzzle element which both the reader and the detective must solve before the last page.

A majority of the Fielding mysteries involve the character of Chief Inspector Pointer. Unlike the eccentric Belgian Hercule Poirot, the flamboyant Lord Peter Wimsey, or the somewhat mysterious Albert Campion, Pointer is merely a competent, sometimes clever, occasionally intuitive policeman. And unlike, as with Inspector French in the stories of Freeman Wills Croft, the emphasis is on the mystery itself, not the process of detection.

Pointer is nearly as much of a mystery as the author. Very little of his personal life is revealed in the books. He is described as being vaguely of Scottish ancestry. He is well read and educated, though his duties at Scotland Yard prevent him from enjoying those pursuits. His success as a detective depends on his willingness to "suspect everyone" and to not being tied to any one theory. He is fluent in French and familiar with that country. He is, at least in the first two books, unmarried, and sharing lodgings with a bookbinder named O'Connor, in much the manner of Holmes and Watson, though this character is absent in later works. In *The Net Around Joan Ingilby* we discover that not only was he a professional footballer playing for England before joining the police, but that he is also a capable pilot, but the real private Pointer remains obscure.

In reality, there appear to be two Chief Inspector Pointers. One is a stolid, somewhat characterless detective who solves cases through the routine of police work, the other is a dashing figure of international intrigue willing to cross over to the continent in his search for justice. Fielding alternated between the two Pointers, particularly in the early books in the series. *The Net Around Joan Ingilby* definitely involves the second of the two Pointers.

One intriguing feature of the Pointer mysteries is that they all involve an unexpected twist at the end, wherein the mystery finally solved is not at all the mystery invoked at the beginning of the book. I leave it to the reader to judge whether Fielding is "playing by the rules" in this, but it does keep the books interesting up to the last chapter.

The Net Around Joan Ingilby is the sixth book in the Pointer series and published in 1928 four years after *The Eames-Erskine Case* the book that introduced Chief Inspector Pointer to the world. What it lacks in maturity, it makes up for with a certain flair, and resembles in that aspect some of Christie's work from the same period.

The Net Around Joan Ingilby centers around the death of a Mrs. Amcott who is found asphyxiated in a charcoal burning hut. After a rather incendiary article appears in a newspaper, the governess to the dead woman's daughter, Joan Ingilby, becomes the prime suspect. The author of the article, however, becomes smitten with Ingilby and becomes determined to prove her innocence. The cast of suspects is rounded out with a dissolute brother-in-law, his unsavory foreign companion, a young widow with a foreign title, the dead woman's cousin, the local clergyman who has secrets of his own, and the dead woman's husband who may or may not be in the Sudan. Each has a motive more or less, and each has an alibi, but of these there is plenty of doubt. All in all, the makings of a proper British mystery. It is into this environment that the chief inspector finally descends to investigate the case. And, in true Fielding fashion, the mystery at the end of the book bears little resemblance to the one in the first few chapter.

Despite their current obscurity, the mysteries of Archibald Fielding, whoever he or she might have been, are well written, well crafted examples of the form, worthy of the interest of the fans of the genre. It is with pleasure, then, that Resurrected Press presents this new edition of *The Net Around Joan Ingilby* and others in the series to its readers.

About the Author

The identity of the author is as much a mystery as the plots of the novels. Two dozen novels were published from 1924 to 1944 as by Archibald Fielding, A. E. Fielding, or Archibald E. Fielding, yet the only clue as to the real author is a comment by the American publishers, H.C. Kinsey Co. that A. E. Fielding was in reality a "middle-aged English woman by the name of Dorothy Feilding whose peacetime address is Sheffield Terrace, Kensington, London, and who enjoys gardening." Research on the part of John Herrington has uncovered a person by that name living at 2 Sheffield Terrace from 1932-1936. She appears to have moved to Islington in 1937 after which she disappears. To complicate things, some have attributed the authorship to Lady Dorothy Mary Evelyn Moore nee Feilding (1889-1935), however, a grandson of Lady Dorothy denied any family knowledge of such authorship. The archivist at Collins, the British publisher, reports that any records of A. Fielding were presumably lost during WWII. Birthdates have been given variously as 1884, 1889, and 1900. Unless new information comes to light, it would appear that the real authorship must remain a mystery.

Greg Fowlkes
Editor-In-Chief
Resurrected Press
www.ResurrectedPress.

CHAPTER ONE

SO THICK was the fog that sky and sea and deck were all one and the same—all mystery.

A long blast came out of the grey wall quite close beside the Dover Queen. "I'm heading to starboard," some ship, too small to carry wireless, was calling aloud.

Martin Blair caught the far-off, continuous ringing of a bell. The hoots that preceded it had passed him unheard. A fishing smack was telling the world that she had been surprised by the thick mist with all her nets out, and would other craft kindly keep well away?

He watched the face of his companion in the little deck retreat that he had tumbled on by accident. She seemed to be still asleep. Just as she had been when he had taken the empty seat beside her. He recognised her at once. That was why he had slipped into the chair. He had collided with her on the gangway, and as a reward for his abject apologies, had had a faint smile from eyes which he thought were the most wonderful that he had ever seen.

How lovely she was as she lay in her chair, her slim length vaguely outlined under her rug, He frowned as he studied that rug. It was supposed to be a tartan, but it would have puzzled a Scot to tell the clan. Its quality, too, struck the young reporter, whose livelihood depended on his sharp observation. It was the shoddiest affair. Almost guiltily he looked down at his own. His mother had given it him when he went to Norway one year, and it was the warmest and lightest that she could buy. The first was her choice, the latter because otherwise it would have had short shrift from Blair.

Suppose he changed the rugs? The thing she had across her knees was not fit for a church bazaar, and the winds of earl' September can be shrewd ones. He lifted it off her and laid his own in its place. It would keep out some of the creeping mist, for the sun was in a lazy mood to-day, shrinking bad under his blankets at any excuse.

The girl opened her eyes suddenly as Blair stooped over her. They really were beautiful eyes. Her gaze fell on the rug, the on the make-believe plaid on the deck.

"You'll catch cold." He spoke almost crossly to cover the awkwardness which he felt. "That thing's no good."

"This is!" she said with a friendly smile. "Aren't we there yet?"

He was nearing the seventh heaven, but she doubtless meant Dover. Women are apt to be matter-of-fact, though she looked poetry itself—a living sonnet. He told himself that life, which had not been over-kind to him in his twenty-six years, was not more than making amends by sending this fog, by keeping the Channel boat, which should have been already in Dover or Folkestone, still floating outside harbour.

"Aren't we nearly in?" she asked again.

"The captain's afraid of entering while this fog lasts. And quite right too," Blair said firmly. The mere idea that the captain might be going to be rash enough to endanger all their lives—and his chance to talk to this divine creature—by rushing the ship into port gave Blair a distinct tremor. "One can't be too careful in a fog," he repeated.

She smiled again. Her smile was faintly elfin.

"I shouldn't have taken you for such a careful boy." She spoke vaguely, as though the matter did not interest her much. As how could it? Blair was doing well as a journalist, thanks to brains, grit, industry, and the good luck that these three always bring; but even so, how could he ever hope to interest such as she? He studied her covertly. Her head was turned a little away, her profile coming up against the fog like a flower against a cloud. How perfect she was—the loveliest thing ever! And how perfect was everything she wore, in a soft, quiet monotone, with only one knot of gold that matched her hair to strike a gay, rejoicing note.

"What would you take me for?" he asked, greatly daring. She looked sleepy still. Her thick white lids almost covered her eyes. Suddenly she flashed them open.

"I think you are kind." She spoke more soberly than he had expected. "Kind and energetic."

"Isn't everyone kind to you, Fairy Princess?" he asked gently, but there was no question in his voice. He knew the answer.

"Yes," the girl beside him said drowsily. "Yes, I've never known what it was not to be petted."

"Tell me," he said, "we shall never meet again, and I like fairy tales, Princess, tell me about yourself!"

"There is nothing to tell," she murmured, her eyes now quite closed. "There's my home, of course—I think you'd like the garden. I've never seen one quite like it. Do you like gardens?" she asked.

"Rather!"

"So do I. I love it more than the house, I think. Though that too... It's a quaint old parsonage."

Yes, he would have guessed her father to be something like a parson—a wealthy parson, king of his little realm.

"And father's too busy with his books to do much more than wander round and tell me about each flower and bird. He knows them all. And they know him. Then mother—mother's wonderful!" She opened her eyes wide for a second with a child's look of rapture. "She's more like my sister in looks. But she's the dearest mother in all the world. The very dearest. Only she does spoil me."

"They both do," he said gruffly.

"I suppose so." She smiled contentedly. "But I spoil them. We all three love each other and our wonderful old home. We all think nobody is so dear or so wonderful as each other and it. I come up to town now and then..."

"For the dentist?" he asked gravely. "Every well conducted young person I. ever heard of comes up for him."

"Not in my case," she said firmly, "but if there's anything very good on in the way of a lecture or a play, father brings us, of course. Otherwise we just live and are happy." Her voice dwelt on the words and caressed them lingeringly.

"And work?" he asked suddenly. "Don't you ever feel like work?"

She opened her gold-flecked eyes. What colour were they? Hazel? Brown? Or clear amber?

"You've forgotten the garden, and how much work it takes to keep it as it likes to be kept. Even with a gardener I do a lot. Then there're the bees and the two dogs."

"Rabbits? Guinea pigs?" he asked gravely.

She dimpled, and her eyes sparkled, just as a brook will in the sun.

"I don't think I like guinea pigs, and I know I don't care for rabbits. Now hares—but you couldn't keep a hare in a garden, could you? Once, after a visit to the Zoo, I thought of an otter, but it's cruel to have only one. And two otters..."

"Doves, of course?" he went on.

She shook her head.

"I can't bear the lumps, nor the noise they make. But there's a bantam cock and his two wives. They're darlings. They play on the lawn with the kitten. But now about you—doesn't all this seem very silly to you? Your life must have so many interests. I feel sure of that."

"It has! Rather! Absorbing interests, too, such as bread and butter, rent and clothes."

In a few sentences he told of his struggles, struggles that he made quite humorous, and which were beginning to be easier now. As he finished, the boat started to turn. Vague outlines of what might be docks began to show through the grey walls.

"We're in!" someone called triumphantly.

Martin Blair woke up. "In"—that meant "over." Done. Finished. Never again would he see his fairy princess, except perhaps at a function which he might be sent to report.

She began to slip off his rug.

"Not yet," he begged. "This thing of yours really isn't warm enough."

She looked at it soberly.

"It belongs to a poor girl who lent it to me." She fingered it gently. "Don't despise it so. She bought it with such pleasure. I'm glad she can't know how bad it is. I fancy"—she raised her eyes to his—"I fancy she isn't too well-off, and if you've got to make sixpence do what a shilling will hardly reach—I suppose it must be difficult." She seemed to ponder.

"That's not a task you've ever had to tackle," he said almost grimly. Oh, spoiled fairy princess, whom he was never to see again!

She smiled once more, that faint smile of the lips, that laughter of the eyes.

"I've never known what it was to think of money," she confessed, and as she turned, the scent of damask roses reached him, vague but delicious. Even Blair knew that only the most expensive perfumes can so exactly copy nature. He could have sworn that the wind blew off a rose bush on a summer evening after rain.

He folded up her rug and picked up her bag.

"Let me see you to the train," he begged.

But she shook her head, though her young eyes said to his young eyes that she too was sorry to part.

"There'll be a car to meet me. But thank you"—she said as an under-steward picked up her luggage—"especially for lending me the rug."

"And you—especially for giving me a memory," he said softly. "Good-bye, Fairy Princess."

For a moment he stood watching her as she followed her luggage, watching her off the gangway and into a waiting car. A vague impression of size and splendour of fittings penetrated his brain, but all except the girl was 'a blur. Then it silently glided away, and the fairy princess was gone out of his life.

He shook himself and tramped off for the train, and town, and his daily bread. He still had her plaid rug on his arm. He had managed to hand his own to the steward. His name was on it. You never knew...

For days he kept a sharp watch on society functions. For weeks he "did" smart gatherings as well as his own work, but the weeks became months, and still Blair had not seen again that lovely face.

It was now mid-December, the fifteenth to be exact, and he was in a train bound, so he had thought, for Elmhurst in Sussex, where there had been a railway collision early this morning. But he found to his great annoyance that both the train he was in and the ticket he had taken would fetch him up at Elmhurst in the New Forest unless he changed at once and got back to Waterloo.

Elmhurst... It was a pretty name, he thought. He had never heard it before. New Forest...

He was a free lance, though getting to be a very busy one. It was a glorious morning, cold and bright. He had not had an hour off for weeks, not since a return journey in September. He had a sudden longing to hear the ring of hoofs on a frosty country lane, to tread crackling leaves underfoot, to look up at bare boughs overhead. He decided to go to the place which the booking clerk had assigned to him. At least, he thought then that it was that humdrum official, but he realised later that it was one greater than any railway official who had thrust that little strip of cardboard into his hand.

He knew the New Forest slightly, which meant that he only knew it badly. He had merely motored through it, and Nature is a true socialist. Her treasures are for the man of simple ways. You must walk a land to have it for a friend. Yet even he knew it as a world apart, this hundred square miles of ever-changing woodland. He had heard much of the commoners who lived in it. Blair decided that he would spend a few days in their midst, and write an article on them for one of the reviews to which he contributed more and more frequently.

He little knew that, though he was about to spend several days amongst them, his interests would be fully occupied with something much more absorbing than feudal remainders. That, sharply though the coming hours were to be etched on memory, not one new fact concerning the people of the soil would be included. That, as far as they were concerned, might have been staying on the moon.

At the station he made his way to the telephone. A word was due to the paper in which he blew off a good deal of froth on six days of the week, and which was expecting him to send in an account of the railway mishap in Sussex.

His message sent, Blair picked up his bag and walked to the inn close at hand. All Elmhurst was close at hand. You could settle down for life in the place, be married, call on each of the villagers, and be buried, all within ten minutes of the station.

In the coffee room he found a long table set for a larger number of people than he expected. There was a subdued hush and yet bustle about the whole place. It might have been busy Sunday. Somewhat to his surprise he was conducted to the upper end of this board.

"Is it a market day?" Blair asked the inn's only waiter. The man looked scandalised, and then so taken aback that he broke out in his own dialect.

"'Tis for the 'quest as you'm come down, I doubt, sir?"

Then on Blair's stare and "What quest?" he went on:

"The inquest on Mrs. Amcott, as was found dead this morning. The coroner is holding it this afternoon. A bit quick like but he's due on that find of Saxon coins over to Beaulieu to-morrow, and the next day there's the 'quest on that porter here. So Mrs. Amcott is to be done to-day.

You see 'tis just a form like. We all know how it happened. The poor lady fell asleep in a charcoal shed, to wake in heaven. We made sure as you was come from Lunnon, because of it. Shall I set you at one of the smaller tables?"

"No, no!" Blair liked being in the midst of things. "Who is Mrs. Amcott?"

Again scandalised surprise filled the elderly face bending over him.

"Why, Mr. Ralph Amcott's lady, sir, to be sure! Wife of a brother of the squire of Elmhurst. A gentleman as be abroad in the Sudan, putting the fear of God into them as killed Gordon. This table is for the jurymen."

Blair decided to claim all the rights of the Press, and was accepted as a London reporter who had rushed down in some miraculously fast way to be present at the inquest. Which was only as it should be, thought the man. It wasn't every day that a lady went out for her usual walk at nine of an evening, was silly enough to enter one of the sheds which covered in a charcoal pit, and was found asphyxiated by the fumes in the morning.

The men agreed that only, an "up-country furriner" could have done such a thing. Though, considering that Mrs. Amcott was married to a Forester born...

After lunch, a charabanc took the jurymen, and, of course, Blair, who was the guest of honour, out to see the place where Mrs. Amcott had been found. In winter the Forest is as full of activity as in summer. Beech leaves are being gathered, firewood for hauling collected, furze-tops, dear to the palate of the hardy forest ponies, are cut. Charcoal burning has no season. To an ever diminishing extent for over a thousand years this trade has been plied under the trees. The sheds were but loose structures of boards nailed together, but roofed, and with a door fastened by an ordinary padlock. The charabanc stopped beside one.

"Be ye come to see the pit?" a grey-bearded man asked them. With his bent shoulders, and reddened lids, and brown, seamed face, he looked like a forest gnome on a large scale.

"Burned charcoal in the time of the Conqueror, we did, said Mr. Gull. "I be the only charcoal burner hereabouts. Ye can't teach burning. Mr. Grimshaw, he may think this or that but deary me, tiddn' so. Many a tell we'm had together, but he's old for learning. Nor charcoal burning can't be taught. Father to son and son's son be the only way. It takes four days to finish a lot. Two tons to one burning. I cut un four foot long, hard woods to one pit, soft woods to another, stacked in a circle, leaning innards, covered wi' bracken and litter. I fires un from the top wi' a torch, and waters un when need be. And there lies the skill."

Mr. Gull evidently thought the jurymen wanted a dissertation on his art.

"But what about the lady?" one man asked.

"Poor soul! I found her dead." And Mr. Gull forthwith would have dismissed her from the conversation.

"But why did she come into the shed, that's the question?" the man persisted fussily.

"Now, 'tis no manner of use standing in a fairy ring a-staring at I," Mr. Gull said crossly. "I'm in a terrible rout this morning, and as only the Lord above could tell you why she done it, I hope you'm haven't interrupted me at work for that sort of a tell!" he went on, as one who puts childish things behind him. "Then when 'tis burnt out, 'tis covered wi' turf or ashes. Then I lets un cool. Three to four days maybe...

Blair touched the mound of brown turf. It was pleasantly warm to the hand on this cold day. The other men followed his example, and, giving up the attempt to get Mr. Gull to talk about the dead woman, they returned to the charabanc and home to the inn. A few drops were falling, but they assured Blair that "'Tis not a rain; 'tis only a smizzle," and they were right. It had dried by the time they reached the village.

Going and coming, Blair learnt what he could of the dead woman. It was not much, and not at all interesting. She was the wife of the second son of the late squire of Elmhurst. Her husband was in the Sudan Government. Mrs. Amcott, during her husband's absence, had come down last month for the winter, taking a suite of rooms in a wing of the manor house, her brother-in-law's house. The conversation drifted to her looks. Most of the men considered her plain. Her age they believed to be around thirty.

"Like to have a sight of the manor house?" the townsman asked Blair. "The inquest isn't for another hour. There's her electric bath-chair as I'd like to see. I'm an electrician by trade."

The two strolled on together, followed by the major part of the jurymen, who were at a loss how to kill time.

"Her electric chair?" Blair queried.

He learnt that Mrs. Amcott had hurt her back in a recent motor smash, and though she was practically cured, she still used this bath-chair constantly. It was propelled by an electric motor beneath the seat, and only needed guiding by the occupant inside. Strictly speaking it should have gone on the road, but she was tacitly allowed to trundle it along the pavement, as it never went faster than a perambulator. There was an electric foot warmer and warmed cushions, so that even in the coldest weather whoever sat inside was comfortable.

Blair found the manor house to be a very beautiful unspoiled example of the Tudor period. The ivy that clung to the mullioned oriel windows and ran up the ornamental Tudor chimneys must have been first trimmed when Elizabeth and Mary were children. Now it was close as crinkled velvet. The butler took the visitors around to a little door in a side wall and unlocked it.

"The children used to keep their bikes here in the old days," he explained. "Here's the chair. The rooms over this are those the poor lady used. Her bedroom's just above." Everyone looked up at three long windows to which the butler pointed. Blair was bored. So were most of the jurymen. At a glance the chair seemed the usual kind, barring the fact that it was perhaps roomier than usual. It had the ordinary waterproof hood, supplemented by a roll-down flap with a mica window for bad weather. As Blair tried to enter into the electrician's very complex explanations of how the thing worked, a man was pacing a gravel path not far off. His face, apart from his collar, would have marked him as a priest of some kind. It was of the ascetic type; for the rest, it was rather an arbitrary and passionate face, with features at once complex and self-contained. In age he looked around thirty, with a spare, wiry, athletic frame.

"That's Mr. Grimshaw," whispered one juryman to another. "Always on the lookout for flies and 'skitties' and all they things that do creep about wi' too many legs on un. Worse nor an old woman he be for wanting to know what they'm doing wi' their spare time and where they bide o' nights. Onnatural curiosity, I calls it. Though I don't deny as he'm rare clever."

"I dunno about clever," the other grumbled. "He looks at my lil' Maudie, and he says, 'Less potatoes for that child and more apples.' And we done it, and she'm lost a pound a week. Fattest child in the Forest she were afore, and now she'm like any of the other lil' deurs, iddn' she?"

"Eh, and he says to I, when I speaks to un about my game leg, ''Tis the years, Mister Fletcher,' he says, ''tis the years.'"

Another put in warmly, "Years indeed! T'other leg be the same age, iddn' it? And nothing wrong wi' un. If so be as 'twas years, how could that be?"

"The interest he takes in charcoal burning, you wouldn't believe," a third murmured. "Many a time he goes the round of those huts. He was away this morning, or he might have found the poor lady himself."

Blair, who was too far off to hear this idle talk, chanced to look up—at the Elmhurst parson, as he rightly guessed. Handsome chap, he thought, in an autocratic,

imperious way. Bit of a volcano, he judged. Not the usual
"squarson" by any means. Just now the face wore an
expression which Blair had seen many times on lads
going into an examination room, running over in their
minds some last, all but forgotten tag. He had seen it, too,
on the faces of inexperienced actors standing in the wings
before they went on for the first time.

At that moment the rector turned and nodded to the
electrician, who stepped forward to speak to him, Blair
beside him. The man introduced the two. "This gentleman
is a newspaper man come down from London about Mrs.
Amcott's death," he finished.

"Indeed? Why this interest of a recording angel in our
secluded hamlet? Can't we even die in peace nowadays?"
Mr. Grimshaw asked coldly.

"Not in charcoal sheds," Blair retorted. The electrician
stepped back to the chair again. Blair and Grimshaw
walked on. It was nearly time for the inquest.

"It seems to have been an accident, due to
carelessness," the clergyman said thoughtfully, and then
spoke of the weather and the scenery until they reached
the room off the police station where the coroner was
already chatting with the Police Inspector. The coroner
was none too pleased to have to summon a jury at all. But
new-fangled red tape, as he called it, made it necessary
even where, as here, he was certain, everybody was
certain, that death was due to the merest misadventure.

The doctor was first called.

He briefly identified the body as that of his late
patient. He and another medical man from Salisbury had
carried out the autopsy together this morning. There was
no shadow of doubt but that Mrs. Amcott had died of
carbon monoxide fumes, a peculiarly deadly gas owing to
its absence of smell, of premonitory symptoms. It was the
dreaded "miners' damp," that used to account for so many
a life underground. It was the poisoning agent in all
deaths from charcoal fumes. As to the time when Mrs.
Amcott's death had occurred, he pointed out that that

would depend on when she was last seen, for this particular gas had a way of upsetting usual computations.

The Salisbury doctor's evidence was to the same effect, with the addition of unimportant details.

The coroner then explained to the world at large that the news of the dreadful accident had been at once wirelessed to the lady's husband, Mr. Ralph Amcott, Civil Secretary at Khartoum. A reply had come already, saying that Mr. Ralph Amcott had been taken ill only yesterday, and could not be allowed to return to England for some time. The squire of Elmhurst, Mr. Ralph's eldest brother, Sir Christopher, was, as everybody there knew—except Blair—away big game shooting. There only remained the youngest of the three brothers, Mr. Hilary Amcott, who, like his sister-in-law, had been staying at the manor. Incidentally, Blair learnt from a local confrere that Ralph Amcott, alone of the three brothers, was married. Mr. Hilary was next called. He was a very dissipated-looking man, who appeared to be around twenty-seven or eight, with weary, red-rimmed eyes that seemed unable to look at any one thing for long without closing.

His tale, corroborated by all the servants, was that Mrs. Amcott had gone out as usual last night about half-past nine a stroll with the Airedale, and, seeing the dog back by ten, had unfortunately been taken for granted that she had returned as usual, and was safely upstairs in her own rooms. It was now only too evident that Mrs. Amcott had not returned. Hilary Amcott explained that "Laddy" had the strongest objections to those with whom he was out going inside anywhere. Nothing was more likely than that, if Mrs. Amcott had entered one of the charcoal sheds, the dog would have returned home. He was a peculiarly unintelligent animal except where guarding the house was concerned.

No explanation could be given of how Mrs. Amcott came to enter a charcoal shed, let alone sit down, with the door closed, the warm turf inside, except that of fatigue and chill. Both were considered sufficient reasons in the case of someone who, like the dead woman, was only just recovering from a recent motor accident, and knew little about the dangers of charcoal fumes.

As to her being near the shed so late in the evening, it was explained that Mrs. Amcott never omitted a quick turn out of doors at that hour. It was the doctor's orders, she had said. Dr. Pearson, recalled for a moment, explained that the celebrated specialist, who had had charge of Mrs. Amcott after her accident, had advised a brisk stroll of about ten minutes every night when possible before going to bed, as helping to limber up the spine for the next morning. The charcoal shed where her body had been found was about fifteen minutes' walk from the gates of the manor, and last night had been unusually fine. Mrs. Amcott was without a maid for the time being. She had let her own go, and then found that the new maid would be unable to come for a couple of days yet, owing to a death in her family. There was one person, however, who might have been able to tell more of the last evening, had she been at the manor, and that was the governess of little Doris Amcott, but she had left on Saturday with the nurse to take her charge to an expensive children's sunlight home outside London. The child had been suffering from a bad cold. The governess was not expected back until to-morrow, Thursday. A telegram and a telephone message to the hotel where Mrs. Amcott and she always put up, and where she was believed to be staying, had brought the information that Miss Ingilby—the name of the governess was Joan Ingilby—had only inquired for letters on Monday morning. She had not stayed at the establishment.

A query to the home showed that she had left the child and nurse there for a fortnight's treatment as arranged, so it was believed that Mrs. Amcott and she must have settled that on this occasion Miss Ingilby should stay at some different hotel to the one usually patronised by the dead woman.

The charcoal burner, when his turn came, was inclined to scout the idea that he could have left any of his charcoal sheds unfastened. But the jury were men of the village, and a series of questions as to this date and that soon reduced him to a confession of at least two lapses in the past.

"But only twice times, and I never 'ave agained. So don't you pert me, John Boon!" he finished, eyeing the young foreman belligerently, "or I could up wi' a few things as you'm forgotten."

The coroner smoothed him down, but it was only from between his assurances that the doors had all been padlocked last night that an account of how he had found Mrs. Amcott lying was drawn out and pieced together. She had apparently been overcome by the fumes while resting.

Blair was sorry, of course, for the dead woman—in that unthinking way in which we are sorry for those who have died—but he stifled a yawn with ever-increasing difficulty.

He had not seen her yet. A constable in the hall of the manor house would not allow him in until the official identification was over. He must in due course take a photograph of her, for he intended to send in a word picture of a New Forest inquest, larded with local customs, and laced with their quaint expressions. He looked about him, mentally photographing the village types. Then he caught sight of the rector's face as he was asked a few questions; more from civility than from any idea that he could add to the facts already known, Blair fancied, when he learnt that Grimshaw was a great friend of the dead woman's absent husband. What a mobile subtle mouth he had, the reporter thought, and a jaw like a prize-fighter's.

Yet Blair had a sudden conviction, as their eyes met, that the man was nervous. If so, he did not make the mistake of being too talkative. When he sat down after a few unimportant queries and answers, Blair had another certainty about the rector, and that was that he had not liked the dead woman.

The verdict was as expected—death by misadventure. A couple of riders were added, the first expressing sympathy with Mr. Ralph Amcott, the second reprimanding the charcoal burner for his negligence about the lock.

Mr. Grimshaw was just ahead of Blair as the hall cleared. He looked like the younger brother of the man who had paced the gravel path but an hour ago. Blair noticed that a young girl passed on the outskirts of the crush of people pouring out of the room. She bowed to Grimshaw, who was very close to her. Grimshaw did not stop, did not apparently see her, and the girl's face lost some of its brightness. Her colouring made Blair think of the girl on the boat.

Where in the wide world was his fairy princess? The meeting with her seemed to have brought him luck. It was after it that he had broken through into the ranks of those writers who, in some mysterious way, seemed to count. If he found her again now... it might not be so absolutely impossible to think that in a few years' time... He pulled himself together and walked to the manor house. The constable was still there, but had changed from a helmeted, one-headed Cerberus into affability itself.

Blair entered a pretty bedroom reverently enough, but still inwardly very bored. He was not bored when he came out a few minutes later. He had had the greatest surprise of his life so far.

Mrs. Amcott lay on her bed, dressed as when she had been found just before daybreak this morning. She had a face that did not attract him, but after one cursory glance at it, his eyes became riveted on her pretty little black shoes. The feet faced him as he stood at the end of her low couch-bed. The soles were painted black too, but they were as free from any, marks of forest litter, let alone charcoal, as his own had been when he had stepped out of the train this noon—not at all like his shoes now, or those of anyone who had visited the sheds. He passed his hands over them. They came away practically unsoiled. He asked a few casual questions of the policeman before that worthy hurried off. The answers told him that nothing on the dead woman had been altered, or could have been changed or cleaned.

That being so...

Blair had not obtained the position that was his because of any slowness in jumping to the right conclusion. And when he jumped, he jumped with both feet, as he would have said. There had been foul play here. Mrs. Amcott had been carried into that shed—carried some distance. He had noticed that you had to walk about five yards to get to the hut from the path, and walk across rotting leaves and charcoal debris.

.

CHAPTER TWO

BLAIR unslung his camera and took two portraits—one with the soles pointing straight at the camera, the other the usual portrait of the head and shoulders. That done, he walked carefully around Mrs. Amcott's rooms, which were cut off by a door from the central landing. Her own bedrooms and the governess's room communicated through an intervening bathroom with each other. The little suite had its own boxroom, and a staircase leading down into the garden beside the place where the bath-chair was kept.

Blair spent some time in the governess's room, and a moment or two in the boxroom. Passing slowly down the stairs at the end, he looked at each tread, then he inspected the bath-chair again very closely—the door had not been relocked yet. There were charcoal and leaf-mould stains on the carpet inside the chair and on the india-rubber tyres.

After that, Blair sauntered around to the back of the house. Here he knocked at the kitchen door, and asked whether there were any uncovered beams, or possibly even a Tudor stone fireplace in the servants' hall, which he might photograph.

He was shown a fine example of the latter in the kitchen. While using his camera, he found out that the cook was a Frenchwoman, a Niçoise, and enchanted her with his appreciation of *Pissaladiera* and *Pan Bagnata* and heaven knows what other tasty, popular dishes of that gay town, for he had only lately returned from a trek through the Côte d'Azur on a missing company promoter's heels.

After quite a long and rambling chat about Mrs. Amcott's last days, he searched inside and outside the kitchen parts of the house for any "bits" that took his fancy—searched for them in some very funny places too. Then only did he leave the manor, walking slowly down the drive, with a pause and backward glance at the windows of the house.

Blair quickly developed his films at the inn, and then made for the police station.

"Want you to initial these snapshots of Mrs. Amcott."

"What's the idea?" asked the constable on duty.

"The rule. Saves faking. Proves we've been on the job," Blair said wearily. He held out his two prints. The policeman laughed aloud at the first.

"Look here! You're never going to send that one in? Why, it's all feet. This, now, is quite good."

"I have to account for every film used," Blair murmured sadly, and, surprised at the parsimony of London papers, the man stamped films and prints with the official dated stamp. Blair next asked and obtained the address of Dr. Pearson, the local general practitioner.

He found the doctor more than willing to talk of Mrs. Amcott's death to a duly qualified listener. Blair left him quite convinced that there had been no struggle, no marks of binding or gagging, that death had been due to nothing but charcoal poisoning—carbon monoxide, as Pearson would insist on calling it. Pearson was young and clever, and had by no means neglected to think of more sinister explanations for the lady's end than carelessness. Blair made many discreet inquiries after he left Dr. Pearson.

Back in town—he did not arrive till past midnight— he typed the article on Mrs. Amcott's death which he had written in the train coming up.

The night editor glanced it over and then looked at him.

"Sure of the ground under your feet?" he asked laconically. It was well known that the *Daily Comet* would run any risk except that of big cry and little wool.

Blair nodded. He had put all his energy into his pen. He felt drained. The sub-editor re-read a line here and there. Then he raised his eyebrows.

"Grand slam, eh? It's the last word of yours we'll ever print if you've over-called your hand." He gave the orders for the article to be rushed in. Blair had already telephoned to reserve sufficient space. The article was headed *Who Killed Mrs. Amcott?*

Beneath its daring headline it set forth soberly enough the facts that made the writer—he signed his name—hold that what the jury and the coroner considered an accidental death was in truth a cunning and carefully planned murder. Blair burnt his boats. He stated that Mrs. Amcott's shoes proved that she had been carried into the shed where she was found early this (Wednesday) morning. He maintained that, as she had not been gagged nor bound, nor seemed to have struggled in any way, she must have been already dead when carried in.

As to the death itself, the medical evidence showed that she had been killed by charcoal fumes, but Blair denied that they were those of the charcoal pit where she had been found. His idea of the instrument of death was this:

In a kitchen outhouse he had found a portable charcoal stove about the size and roughly the shape of a man's top hat, and but little heavier. It was a type that is to be found in every concierge's rooms along the Riviera. A tall bag of charcoal sticks stood beside the stove. It was impossible to tell whether any had been recently taken, just as it was impossible to say whether the stove had been lately used or not. The ashes were merely shaken out, more or less carefully—chiefly less.

Blair, after mentioning the stove, proceeded to detail the clues that he had found.

The bath-chair tyres showed marks of having been wheeled close up to the hut across the charcoal and forest debris. On the treads of the staircase leading up to her room, beside the carpet runner, were some marks left by charcoal-soiled shoes. The stairs had been cleaned on Tuesday morning as usual, the wooden margins polished. One of these shoes had undoubtedly been a woman's pointed shoe. "See inset, photograph," said the article.

In the bedroom of the governess was a gas stove with a little concealed gas-ring on the top. In the centre of this ring Blair had found—and left—a very fair-sized piece of charcoal, the same charcoal as that in the bag downstairs. He went on to explain that method of lighting charcoal stoves when there is gas available, which is to hold each piece with a pair of tongs over a lit gas jet until well caught, and lay it in the stove until a handful of glowing sticks is built up; then to fill up the stove, leave the damper open, and set it outside in the open air to draw well, unless a special funnel is used. On the window ledge of the governess's room was a black smear, a smear of charcoal, and charcoal that evidently had scorched the paint of the sill where it had fallen.

Blair maintained that whoever had killed Mrs. Amcott had waited at night in the boxroom belonging to her suite for the right moment. A trunk showed marks in the dust which even in his photograph supported this theory. When all was quiet, this someone had come downstairs, taken the charcoal stove, set it going, and placed it noiselessly in the room of Mrs. Amcott, who sometimes took veronal. Blair had seen little a veronal bottle lying out on the table beside her bed, as though used by her for her last sleep.

Mrs. Amcott would have been dead long before morning—she slept in winter with her windows closed—supposing that the little stove had been filled to the uttermost. In the dark her body had been carried down the staircase of her suite and placed in her bath-chair in the lock-up below, which was fitted with an electric light. Mrs. Amcott kept the key hanging in the boxroom.

But since dead bodies cannot be shifted in daylight without comment, and since a bath-chair cannot be trundled at night along newly gravelled paths that loop backwards and forwards in front of quite a number of bedroom windows without causing a noise, many noises, which would have been fatal to the success of the plot, Blair held that the crime had been carried out in parts—a little at a time. So that only when daylight came, and a suitable hour, had the self-propelling bath-chair passed out of the gates as so often before, but this time to be hidden in some secluded part of the Forest until it should again be dark, and Mrs. Amcott's body be able to be finally carried into the nearest charcoal shed, and placed in a position as though she had been overcome by the fumes while sitting down. A couple of turves had been taken off the still hot wood to account for the deadly effect of the fumes. The body from the chair would by this time be stiffened into a sitting position. It would look, as it did, perfectly natural when found by the charcoal burner.

Here Blair pointed out that his reconstruction of the crime meant that since the body had been found on Wednesday morning before daybreak, it had been hidden all Tuesday, and that therefore the actual murder must have occurred during the night before (Monday night). In other words, according to him, the figure seen throughout the Tuesday, but—as he cleverly pieced together—never spoken to, could not have been Mrs. Amcott, for Mrs. Amcott, he maintained, was by then dead.

He went on to show that this was possible. While breakfast had been laid in her sitting-room on Tuesday— Mrs. Amcott took no early cups of tea, and when, as now, without a maid, would turn on her own bath—the maid had heard music played on the piano in an adjoining room—music at which Mrs. Amcott had been working for some days. She had knocked at the door as usual under those circumstances, a discreet knock, not loud enough to interrupt, but loud enough to catch the player's ear, and had heard later on, while downstairs, Mrs. Amcott walking about the room.

She had heard the impersonator of Mrs. Amcott throughout Tuesday, Blair felt sure, heard her both at the piano and walking about, heard the woman who—before the maids had come upstairs to clear away the breakfast table or start on the rooms of her suite, which were never touched until nine—had slipped down these convenient stairs, dressed in Mrs. Amcott's clothes, and got into the roomy bath-chair, which already held another, a very slender, silent, and cold occupant. The hood had been up, and the mica shutter down—it was a vile morning—when the chair had passed the woman at the gates. The woman had curtseyed, thinking that it was "Mrs. Ralph," and indeed it was that lady's hat.

Blair believed the impersonator to be a woman, but at the charcoal shed itself, he reasoned that a man must have helped in the final placing of the body, as in carrying it down the stairs and lifting it into the bath-chair; and a man might well have forced open a padlock while waiting for the chair with its double burden to come creeping up, just before nine, probably, from its temporary hiding place in the Forest.

The body disposed of in the charcoal shed, the woman had returned alone in the chair to the manor, and gone up to the murdered woman's rooms, leaving those marks on the stairs that he had found. In the evening a maid had heard the bath chair being rolled into its lock-up about nine. This meant, she had thought, that Mrs. Amcott had returned, either from Salisbury, or from town, by one of her favourite trains, one to which a restaurant car was attached. For on Tuesday Mrs. Amcott was often away from the manor house all day long and always all morning and evening. On that day, from five to eleven, at Salisbury, "Teapot Row"—the generic name for the wives and daughters of the army men stationed there—had a bridge drive and a friendly dinner, and cut off as she was this winter from dances and hunting, the dead woman had become a regular visitor, generally putting in the morning as well in the quaint old town, and lunching there.

She had not been to lunch or bridge this last Tuesday. Indeed, an inquiry at the railway station had told Blair that she had not been anywhere by train since Saturday.

A little later on this last Tuesday evening, the same maid had seen, from the other end of the large outer hall, the supposedly Mrs. Amcott coming down the stairs that led to and from her rooms, her well-known fur cloak around her, a felt hat pulled low over her face, according to the fashion of the moment. A very useful fashion, Blair said.

Blair had learnt in the kitchen that "Laddy" had behaved oddly all Tuesday, appearing uneasy and restless. In the light of Wednesday's discovery of the dead woman, the servants were inclined to think that he had some sort of intuition of what was coming.

Blair did not refer to the dog's restlessness in his article, any more than he tried to explain why Mrs. Amcott had kept so much to herself. His point was only this: if, as he maintained, the dog's companion this last Tuesday evening had not been Mrs. Amcott, who was she?

It must be someone who knew all her habits thoroughly; who knew all the habits of the manor house extremely well; who was friends with the by no means effusive Airedale; who was roughly about Mrs. Amcott's height and slender build. And Blair wound up with regretting the apparent inability of everyone to get into touch with the governess, the governess who was supposed to be in town. Where was this Miss Joan Ingilby?

He asked the question ostensibly by way of gaining light on various obscure points, but he showed how this woman, in whose room the broken bit of charcoal still lay, whose window bore the smear of a glowing charcoal cinder, could have come back at any time after she had left the child at the home.

With great skill he pointed out, without seeming to do so, that she fitted all the requirements of his theory. In short, his whole conclusion was an indirect accusation against the absent woman.

It was a brilliant piece of writing. Short and temperate and deadly. But no paper except the *Comet* would have printed it

He read it himself with approval when the sheet was brought to him at the breakfast table in his comfortable rooms near Victoria.

Half-way through it he raised his head from the page. He had unusually good ears. Or, rather, he had the faculty, of instantly and accurately cataloguing what he heard. There was scuffle going on just outside his door.

Suddenly it was jerked open and then shut in the same instant—shut as one shuts a sanctuary in the face of imminent and deadly peril.

And there, her back against the door, her eyes wild with terror, her breath coming in swift jerks, leant the girl of the boat, the girl of his dreams, his fairy princess.

He jumped to his feet.

"You!" It was a cry of rapture.

She put her finger to her lip in a gesture of fear. The sleeve of her coat was torn at the cuff.

"Look out quickly. Someone attacked me just as I was going to knock."

Instantly Blair switched out the light and peered on to the landing. He caught but the merest glimpse of a man's dark figure on the stairway below—of a grey felt hat. He jumped the stairs three at a time, but when he reached the front door no one was to be seen in the dark December morning, for it was not yet nine.

Upstairs he bounded again, his whole being in a turmoil. What did it mean? His fairy princess and that lurking figure on the stairs!

When he entered his sitting-room she was standing out of sight until the door was shut.

"Lock the door," she whispered tensely. "He must have been outside your rooms, watching them. I know I wasn't followed."

"Followed—he—who? Why on earth—"

"I'm Joan Ingilby, Mr. Blair. Perhaps that's why."

Joan Ingilby! He stared at the pretty young creature before him, the colour moving back inch by inch from his pale but healthy face. Joan Ingilby! Mrs. Amcott's governess! Whom he had...

"I only read the paper just now. The one with your article in it," she managed to articulate. "If they find me they'll hang me—because of what you wrote. But they'll never think of looking for me in your rooms—after it. You don't mind my coming?" She scanned his face with a timid glance. She was trembling—the whole lovely, slender figure of her.

"Mind!" he jerked out. He was appalled, dazed. He felt like a surgeon whose knife had slipped and cut a vital part. He had been so certain that he was right. But, thank God, in spite of her terror, the blunder he had made was not irreparable.

"You will help me?" She was not sure of even that much from the writer of that article. Though she had staked everything on it, she was not sure. "You can, without doing wrong. For *I* did not kill Mrs. Amcott, Mr. Blair." She spoke with a sort of pitiful dignity.

He could only look at her. Help her? He would die to put right what he had put wrong. She read his ardent, horrified eyes, and her face lost some of its tension.

"I need help." she said simply, "as I don't think many people have needed it in this world." And suddenly she put her hands to her face and broke into low, smothered sobs.

Dropping on a chair, she crouched there, crying under her breath with the terrible insistence of despair. He was on knees beside her. That soft, heart-broken weeping wrung his very heart's core.

"Had I known or dreamt that you were the governess—" Blair said hoarsely. His tone told how differently in that case he would have read the mystery of Mrs. Amcott's death. "But we'll soon put it right—about my article and you, I mean."

"How?" she asked without looking up.

"Haven't you an alibi?" he demanded, a sudden cold chill touching him.

"Not the ghost of such a thing. Nothing but my word. Not for Monday night nor Tuesday. Nor for last night." For a second she turned so white that he thought she would faint, but she forced herself to speak on.

"Mr. Blair, Mrs. Amcott wasn't killed." She spoke with certainty. "You are wrong about its being a crime. I'm sure of that." The conviction in her voice was almost catching. But Blair shook his head.

"There's no possibility of its not being a crime," he to her honestly and definitely.

"Yet you were wrong about who did it," she said timidly "Indeed, *indeed* you are."

"You don't need to assure me on that point. God forgive me for the blunder I've made. But there's no question but that Mrs. Amcott was murdered. None whatever. I know it—and the police know it now. But we'll soon put right any mistake caused by that article. We'll clear you at once, fairy princess."

"You will if you can," she breathed, "but can anyone? Can you really clear me?" she turned towards him The light fell fill on the pale oval of her face. Blair thought that she had the softest, most trusting eyes that he had ever seen.

'You see," she went on nervously, in the whisper of a whisper, "I have no alibi except for Monday afternoon. Usually I stop at a little hotel in Kensington, but I didn't quite care for the people there when I was by myself. They were so off-hand to me, I didn't speak of it, but I went to a much cheaper, and to me much more civil, house. I'm afraid it will prove dear economy and pride, for it's the sort of place where no one knows whether you are out or in."

"But surely someone saw you on Tuesday? You talked to some person who might remember that you were in town?" He pressed her confidently.

She almost wrung her hands.

"No. I got up late. It's a treat nowadays to get the chance to sleep long, and I didn't do anything in the afternoon but stroll through the shops. I lunched at the A.B.C. in the midst of a fearful crush. I didn't dine anywhere either on Monday or Tuesday. I wanted to save up for my winter coat. I put some of my own money to the cheque which Mrs. Amcott had given me, and to make it stretch I had some chocolate and cakes both days, again at a fearfully crowded bun-shop. Oh, I couldn't have done it better if I'd been trying not to have people know where I was! Then I changed and went to the theatre, alone."

"Still—the lack of all motive...," he said with determined hopefulness.

"But there is what some people might twist into a motive," she murmured brokenly. "Her brother-in-law, Mr. Hilary Amcott. He—he drinks," she murmured in a distressed whisper, "and I'm so sorry for him. I tried to help him, and Mr. Amcott chose to think, and to say on Saturday, that I was trying to catch him. She gave me notice—I think that's the word. Poor, poor, Mrs. Amcott!" She lifted eyes on whose lashes the tears still hung like diamonds. "In spite of our last parting, I liked her. And I loved the child—little Doris. Mr. Blair," she breathed, "if you were clever enough to write that awful article that could only apply to me, be cleverer still and see the truth, the real truth. Find out the real criminal!"

He would! he told himself. He would. But meanwhile, what of his fairy princess? A noose was circling around that innocent head, and his was the hand that had flung it.

"What step to take first," he muttered. "An immediate recantation goes to the paper, of course."

"First of all, I need a disguise," she said practically.

"Oh, come, it's not so bad as that," he began, and then stopped. His article rose before him—the noose that he had knotted. If there was a motive, however slender... if she had no alibi... if the police chose to act on his thinly veiled accusation of the governess... something cold and heavy seemed to be labouring inside his breast.

She gave him a pitiful travesty of a smile.

"If the police get hold of me, it couldn't be worse, so I must have a disguise first of all. My portrait will be in the evening papers." She flushed. Blair felt that that stung her to the quick, and for a second her eyes showed full of indignation

"Oh, to be dragged into this! To be considered part of crime! To be thought a murderess! Why, I can't drown a trapped mouse! I always let them run. And now, now—if the police find me—because of what you wrote..." She stopped and turned to him again.

"Forgive me! Of course, you had to write what you thought the truth! But my picture will be out everywhere soon, I'm afraid. I acted in the Elmhurst church theatricals only last week, and everybody took snapshots of everybody."

"Yes, you're right. You must have a disguise. I'll get you one at once." He forced himself to speak in a business-like, practical tone.

"Oh, will you?" Her voice and eyes thanked him, and Blair had to bite his lip.

"I've written on this paper a list of things I shall need. Thank goodness, I'd just bought a new coat and hat. The coat was to be Mrs. Amcott's Christmas present to me." She turned her face away, and Blair saw her hand—such a little hand—go up. Then she faced him again. "Luckily I put them on this morning to go down to Elmhurst, and luckily I came to you!"

"But the risk!" His mouth was dry. With no alibi—
with a motive of revenge—after—he could not deny it to
himself—after his article!

'It was my one chance. My one chance for my life." But
there Blair could honestly contradict her.

"Not a bit of it! In spite of my article, in spite of no
alibi, not a bit of it!" he protested stoutly. "You mustn't
get the wind up like that. But now I'll hurry off with this
list."

"Don't go to any theatrical agent," she put in swiftly.
"The police may inquire if any wigs have been bought of
them lately. Will you take my purse, please. I want a wig
bought at Harrods. I saw one there only yesterday in
their hairdressing rooms that would do splendidly—black
and curly. But if it's been sold, get any dark, bobbed kind.
Say it's for a small-sized head, to cover Eton-cropped hair.
Fortunately I had them cut mine extra close. Ask the
woman to pack you up the right kind of face cream or
lotion to go with it to make up an Italian type of face.
Liquid powder that won't rub off, either; and the right
colour rouge, and lash pencils, and lipstick, and, oh! a
bottle of belladonna. They'll give it some ridiculous name
such as Eastern Delight, probably." She all but pushed
him towards the door. "Oh, hurry, and hurry back! I'm"—
she gulped —"I'm frightened," and she looked at him with
distended eyes.

"Lock the door after me," he told her. "When I come
back I'll rub gently along a panel." And with that he was
gone.

To the girl he left in his rooms every second was sixty
separate intervals of terror. At first she walked the floor
like a person all but demented. Could Blair save her?
Could anyone save her? The article which he had written
was terribly logical. Anyone reading it must think her
guilty. Then she calmed herself, and told her reeling wits
that Blair would somehow undo what he had done. That
nowhere was she safer than here—here, in the house of
the man who would be supposed to be against her, on the

hunt for her. She must keep up. She must not crash now. Glancing with almost unseeing eyes down into the street from behind the lace curtains she stiffened. It was daylight outside, and Blair had switched off the lights and pulled up the blinds. As she stared, the little colour which she had rubbed into her cheeks left them in a wave of almost green pallor. There was a man standing in the shadow of a doorway opposite. He had not moved since she had looked out. He did not move now. It was too dark still, too far off, to see his eyes, but his face was turned towards the rooms where she was. Joan clutched the back of the nearest chair, and, frozen with horror, stood looking at him. For fifteen minutes by the clock she watched him. He was still there, still facing the house which was her only refuge. So she *had* been followed! She pulled herself together by a violent effort. She felt certain that the man opposite was a police watcher. If so, that meant? Her head swam. Let her be arrested, after that damning article, and she would have no chance at all— absolutely none. Except, perhaps, that of insufficient motive. Perhaps!

A step came running up the stairs. One man's step. There came a rub. She unlocked the door without a sound.

It was Blair, and only Blair, a packet in his hand.

"Got everything," he murmured after he had closed and locked the door. He stooped and looked hard at her. There was something about that tense little figure.

"What is it?" he asked hoarsely.

"There's a man across the street watching this house. I think he's from the police. I think they've found out where I've got to."

Blair peered out in his turn. It was still foggy, but he could see the burning end of a cigarette far back in the doorway.

"I'll saunter over and see what he looks like near at hand," he murmured. "Don't do anything rash."

"I—I haven't the ghost of a chance if he's from the police. If they have found out that I'm here..." Her face quivered convulsively.

"You mustn't feel like that!" he scolded gently. "The ghost of a chance indeed! You've a fat certainty even if the police were the dunderheads they aren't. But I'll soon find out about that man."

Again she locked the door noiselessly behind him. He came back quickly and smiling.

"So much for nerves," he said gently in a very low voice. "He's a chauffeur waiting for his employer to come out. Something has gone wrong with the car at the garage, and he's funking telling him."

"Sure?" she quavered.

"Absolutely."

For a moment Joan thought she was going to faint after all, then, with an immense relief, she took the parcel and ran into his bedroom. She was away a full half-hour, during which he walked figures of eight over his floor. It was all very well to deny it to her, but his heart was sick with dread. His very soul was afraid for her. That article... and she without an alibi... and with a motive of sorts.

When she entered he would not have known her. She was lovely always, but now her make-up showed a dashing quality—Joan intended it to show it. She looked a handsome, artificial girl of the day, lipsticked, rouged, with glossy black hair hanging in an Egyptian mop around her ivory face. She had a certain Eastern, Byzantine beauty that made Blair marvel at how a woman can change her appearance. Then she looked at him, and he found his fairy princess again.

"I can face the world now," she said more cheerfully than she had yet spoken. "It was because I couldn't, daren't even buy a disguise, and yet had to have one, that I was so panicky."

"How did you know where I lived?" he asked. So many questions were thronging within him that he took the first that cropped up.

"Your name was stitched on the rug you lent me. Do you remember? I didn't know where to send it to. But when I saw your name heading that article this morning, I telephoned to your newspaper office, and learnt where you lived. You see, as I said, I felt at once that, apart from a hiding place and apart from the fact that I needed someone to get me a disguise and daren't turn to anyone, apart altogether from those things, you alone could save me—if it's possible to save me."

There came a pause of terrible emotion. Blair hurried in with another question out of his thronging host.

"The man outside my rooms—when did you see him? What happened?"

"I thought I felt someone pass me on the stairs before he caught hold of my arm on the landing, as though to pull me away from your door."

"Did he say anything?"

"Nothing. He only made a grab as I stepped past. I don't think he had heard me come up the stairs, and it was dark outside."

Blair had noticed that the light had gone out when he came down to his breakfast.

"You don't think you've ever seen him before? Not that that would make it less amazing."

"I couldn't see enough of him to be sure." She seemed engrossed in some more pressing thought. Suddenly she looked up.

"I'm going down to Elmhurst. Now that I'm disguised, and well disguised too."

He thought that he could not have heard right.

"Yes, to the manor," she repeated. "I shall go as Lucy Ingilby, Joan's sister, it won't seem quite so much of a lie then. Besides, my voice..."

He would have made some wild demur, but she faced him with the alert, intelligent look of one who under all her prettiness has brains. There was character in that lovely mouth, whether lip-sticked or left to its own wild rose colour.

"Of course I'm going down. I must go. Do you suppose I can rest with such a story as that out against me and not try to find out the truth?"

He felt as though she distrusted his powers to help her. She saw the hurt, and a very sweet look came into her own face.

"I want you to come down too. You're appointed my own private investigator, but I must help. I can find out lots of things no one else can—about that charcoal in the gas-ring in my room... lots of things... and minutes count. Whoever did the murder will be able to do away with all the traces if I'm not quick. And I can't get down in much under three hours!" She looked desperate.

"I want you to telephone at once to the nearest garage for a car, a good one, to get me down as fast as possible. Tell them to meet me at Victoria. Don't give any name. I'll settle with the driver before we start."

"You can't go!" he protested, with no pretence of her not being in danger. "You're playing, not with fire, but with..." He could not finish.

"With a rope." She said it for him very quietly. "I know I am. But I must go down. I must clear up this dreadful thing. I owe it to Mrs. Amcott, and I owe it to Joan Ingilby."

"You can do it faster by train. There's one that leaves Waterloo in an hour that gets down quicker than any car could. It's not a good road for hurrying along. Too many police traps."

He pulled a timetable towards him and showed her. She nodded finally.

"A whole hour to wait. I feel as though I were burning up, and yet I only hope I shall be able to stick to my resolve when hour's gone by! I'm an awful coward!" she half whispered the words to herself. "But I mustn't be one now!"

Blair would have liked to take her hand. He would have liked to draw her into his arms. But he was very conscious that it was his doing she had no refuge save with him, and that a refuge which only her daring had given her. Also, there was something about the girl herself that checked him. She seemed to him like Britomart, clad in shining armour.

"What to do when I get there—how to start," she was murmuring thoughtfully. "You say someone was in those rooms of Mrs. Amcott's, hiding... They're sure to've left some clues behind them if so. Clues that only I could see. For you wouldn't notice anything strange in the room as I should."

"Look here," he said urgently, "haven't you any suspicions yourself?"

"Suspicions? Of murder?" Her tone was a negative in itself.

"Yes, but now," he persisted, "now that you know a crime has been committed."

He saw her hesitate, start to speak, then check herself. "I mustn't drag other people down just because I'm drowning," she said a little wearily. "After the experience I've had as to where circumstantial evidence and very accurate reasoning—judging by what seemed the truth—can bring a clever man, am I likely to repeat it?"

Blair flinched, but he persisted.

"What sort of a person is Mr. Hilary Amcott, for instance?"

"He's a man who has no interest in life beyond learning recipes for cocktails, and drinking them. I suppose when he's away—I believe he's been shunted to some place in Asia—I suppose he now and then does work out there, though I can't believe it. He certainly had no hand in any murder. Neither the brains nor the energy."

"And the eldest brother? The Squire, as they call him, at Elmhurst. The one who's big game hunting in Uganda or Rhodesia. What's he like?" he queried.

"I've hardly met Sir Christopher. I only came to Mrs. Amcott in September, just after you and I met on the boat. I didn't know it at the time"—her lip quivered—"but I was sent for because my father had died. It killed my mother. She only survived him two days. And then I found that things were quite different to what I expected. My poor father had believed some account of a gold mine that only needed money to work it. Somewhere in Peru it was, and every penny had gone into it. He was so sure it was a—well, a gold-mine." Blinking, her eyes hard, she managed to smile. "But about the Amcotts, you see I don't know very much of them or the house."

"Nor of Mrs. Amcott's husband?"

"I've never seen Mr. Ralph Amcott."

She stopped, or, rather, she started, made a sign to him to unlock the door noiselessly, and herself crept across the floor to the room beyond. A knock came. It hurt Blair intolerably to see the look in her face as she turned to him for one pallid second before she slipped into his bedroom and closed the door behind her without a sound, just as the maid opened the one from the landing.

"Gentleman to see you, sir."

In came a smart-looking, keen-faced man, who bowed politely.

"Mr. Blair? I'm Police Inspector Armstrong from Elmhurst. I saw you yesterday, down at the inquest. Well, Mr. Blair, a pity you didn't tell us your very interesting theory of Mrs. Amcott's murder last night. We'd have got Miss Ingilby then. As it is, she's escaped. Got away—for the time being. We shall get her in the end, of course. By the way, are we alone?"

"We are," Blair said promptly. He was sorry, but this was no place for George Washington. "Let's go out for a stroll, however. There's always the chance of a maid eavesdropping."

His one idea was to get the Inspector away from Joan's neighbourhood.

"We shall be quite safe if we talk low, Mr. Blair." The police officer was glad of a rest. "Now, what I've come about is this: the Chief Constable doesn't suppose that you want to leave the case where it is. We would like you to work with us, sir. We think you're too good to lose."

Blair offered him some cigars before he replied. His thoughts were with Joan, with his poor, hunted fairy princess, for he knew, what she did not, that in a few minutes the maid would start doing up some rooms on the ground floor, and then attack his own bedroom. Ellen was always punctual to the minute. Joan would very likely be seen when she tried to slip out of the house, unless she got away at once.

"Yes," the Inspector repeated, "much too good to lose, Mr. Blair. Though I don't mind saying that we weren't the blind mice you perhaps thought us. In fact, we think, and thought, very much along your lines, though we hadn't linked up with the governess as quickly as you did. Clever idea that, and the right one. Oh, undoubtedly the right one!"

"Hold hard!" Blair said lightly. He kept his head from swimming only by an effort as he lit up. "That idea about the governess was only a newspaper scoop, you know."

"Merest column filling as far as she is concerned. Newspaper stuffing," Blair said firmly.

"You're too modest, Mr. Blair. Much too modest. Even the cook bears out your idea of the governess having been the one to use that stove," the Inspector went on pleasantly. "She says Miss Ingilby was the only person for miles around except herself who knew how to light it."

Blair told himself that he must seem casual enough for the conversation to be dealing with a stranger.

"No, no!" He spoke contemptuously but lightly. "The steps in the murder are, I think, more or less rightly outlined. But as to connecting them with the governess..." Blair shook his head. "It was the best I could do for something sensational on the spur of the moment. But the real facts of this crime, Inspector, are much harder to solve than that; much more recondite than my little fantasia. I have a theory—it's only vague as yet—but it's a very different theory from that article of mine as to what really happened." He finished on a mysterious note.

"And that theory?" the Inspector asked quickly.

Blair shook his head, as well he might. He had no other theory than the terrible one that had brought Joan Ingilby to him, seeking a refuge in the lion's den itself.

"I must wait and see whether anything turns up to support it."

Again there came a knock at his door, a quick, firm tapping.

He called "Come in!" and then jumped to his feet.

A girl stood there with a magnolia-like complexion and eyes like big black coals. Her lips marked two double wings of carmine against the creamy velvet of her skin. Two little waves of black hair showed beneath the trim hat.

The Inspector rose hastily.

"Are you Mr. Blair?" Joan Ingilby asked Martin, coming into the room with a haughty, head-up carriage.

He bowed, too overcome to speak. The grit of her! Again her only way out had lain through the lion's den.

"I'm Lucy Ingilby, a sister of Mrs. Alcott's governess," Joan said coldly, eyeing him as though he were a cockroach, "and I would like to speak to you for a moment."

CHAPTER THREE

BLAIR'S exclamation was a mixture of amazement and consternation. It was a genuine let-off to some of his emotions. He stared at her wildly.

"But how—how..." He could not think of anything to say.

"Miss Ingilby's sister?" The Inspector looked very pleased. "We've been trying to get into touch with that young lady all morning." He mentioned his name and position. "Can you give me your sister's address?"

"No." Joan spoke even more coldly than before. "She is not at her usual address. I do not know where she is. Hiding in some spot until this terrible accusation you have brought against her is cleared up." She turned to Blair.

"I'm most awfully sorry about it," that young man said earnestly. "I deeply apologise, Miss Ingilby, for having written that article. It was only meant for what we call a newspaper scoop, and was based on a very hasty judgment of the facts of Mrs. Amcott's death, on what I now believe to be a quite wrong assemblage of them."

"And what good does your regret do my sister, do to Joan?" she asked with a forlorn note in her voice that wrung young Blair's very soul. "That 'scoop' of yours, as you call it, will cost my sister every friend she has in the world; it will leave a life-long stain on a girl who has to work for her living; and who has always as I know, kept her reputation untouched until you have smirched it. It was a cruel article." Joan spoke passionately; in truth, she could hardly trust herself to think of it. "Cruel and most utterly untrue!" She could have burst into tears as she finished. "I demand a public retraction of it from you."

"You shall have it," he said promptly. "I was writing it when the Inspector arrived."

"Yet, you're clever. You might help us, Joan and me," she said after a pause.

"Just what I've been suggesting, Miss Ingilby," the Inspector, who had been patting his neat moustache as though it might drop off, said quickly. "What we all want is the truth. That's what we want, isn't it? By the way, how did your sister come to go to Mrs. Amcott? No one quite knows."

Joan did not reply. She stood looking down at the table, her head a little on one side. Blair thought the line of her temple and cheek made the most entrancing Greek-vase curve that he had ever seen.

"I do not intend to tell you anything about my sister," she said at last, very quietly and collectedly.

"Mistake, Miss Ingilby," the Inspector said pleasantly. "A good character is worth a lot in a case of this kind."

"The last thing my sister would want is to have her past dragged along into this terrible present." Joan spoke with certainty. "Her old friends are all that she has left now, I'm afraid. No, Inspector, it's no use asking me for any information. When she is cleared, Joan herself can tell you what she likes. I shall be absolutely dumb about her, and about myself too, therefore."

She had read his next question in his eyes.

"Mistake, Miss Ingilby," the police officer repeated, not quite so pleasantly.

Joan's chin went up into the air. She shook a very determined little black head.

"The last thing I should do would be to give you any addresses," she said crisply. "Joan can at least hope that that terrible article won't reach some of our friends and relatives. Your inquiries would drag them all in."

"They would be made very guardedly," he said coaxingly. "A past such as I don't doubt your sister could show goes a long way in a case of this sort, as I said before."

"My sister's past makes any idea of a crime on her part quite silly," Joan said confidently, "but, all the same, it's her past, Inspector! I'm on my way to Elmhurst Manor now to see what threads I can pick up."

Blair stopped her.

"A moment. I'm working on this case too, Miss Ingilby, to repair, if I may, the harm I've done. Now, as the sister of Mrs. Amcott's governess, you must have heard a good deal about the house and its inmates. Haven't you any clue to give us?"

"You both believe it was a murder?" she asked as before, in a low, agonised tone.

"Most certainly a murder," the Inspector this time assured her, "and two people in it. One at least, if not both, must have known Mrs. Amcott closely and intimately, and known the house, and been known to the dog—more than known to him. That Airedale wouldn't have gone out with anyone but an actual member of the household. That will be our greatest help."

"Our greatest pitfall," she retorted with spirit.

"That person was probably a woman," he went on unmoved.

"A woman!" she repeated incredulously.

"Altogether, Miss Ingilby," the police officer threw in casually, "you really would be doing your sister a good turn to advise her to come forward. Your sister leaving just before the crime..."

"Saturday morning! Mrs. Amcott wasn't murdered until Monday night at the earliest, according to Mr. Blair's article," Joan reminded him.

"Even so. Sticking to Mr. Blair's idea that she was killed Monday night—I think you still hold to that, Mr. Blair?" the Inspector asked.

"I see no reason to change that part," Blair agreed.

"Your sister left the Saturday before," Inspector Armstrong continued. "Now, Miss Ingilby, taking it that she had nothing to do with Mrs. Amcott's death, have you any idea who first suggested that she should go up to town? It's odd that she should have been sent away just then."

Joan reflected a moment.

"Mrs. Amcott sent her up because of little Doris going for a fortnight's violet ray treatment. As for Joan, she would have infinitely preferred to come up to town on Monday. Saturday and Sunday were so many lost days for Christmas shopping."

"You take my advice and ask her to come forward," the Inspector repeated.

"I'm not by way of seeing my sister, as I told you, Inspector," Joan said quietly.

There was rather a constrained silence.

"And now what about telling us where you think of looking first?" Blair urged. He had an idea, an impression, that Joan had some line of action mapped out in her mind. That she was going down to Elmhurst to see if some theory of hers would hold water, would work.

"You might think that I was trying to lead you astray," she said bravely, looking at the police officer.

"We should sift anything we hear," was the prompt reply from Armstrong.

"Well, I happen to know that Joan intended to go to Scotland Yard this morning," Joan began unexpectedly. "Of course, that newspaper article must have prevented her. But what she was going to tell them has nothing to do with Mrs. Amcott's murder."

"How do you know?" the Inspector asked immediately.

"Because the man about whom she was going to— well, ask advice I think would be the best word—was in full view of us both at a performance of The Craven at the Royalty, Monday night—the night when, according to you, that awful crime took place." Joan looked at Blair. "And the next night, last Tuesday, when we went to the Gaiety, there he was again. That was when my sister told me about him. She believed that he was following her about. She intended to go to the police this morning, I know."

"Why? Because the man followed her about?" asked the Inspector.

"Oh, no! But Mrs. Amcott has a wonderful emerald necklace. Joan thought it the most beautiful thing of its kind that she had ever seen—not that that means much! But she says that this man whom we saw at the theatre twice running, a Monsieur Waddy, who is staying down at the manor house, acted in what she thought a very suspicious way about it."

Monsieur Waddy... Blair remembered the name. The cook had said that the charcoal stove, which was her own property, was in almost daily use since the arrival of a friend of Mr. Hilary Amcott's, a Monsieur Waddy, a gourmet who agreed with her that in dishes prepared with olive oil charcoal should be the fuel used.

"Ah-h!" The Inspector nodded emphatically. "That is one of the things I intended to find out first of all—whether Mrs. Amcott had any valuables in her possession."

"Joan, at any rate, thought the necklace immensely valuable. So did Mrs. Amcott, I feel sure. My sister was quite worried about it and this man. She got it into her head that he is after the necklace, staying down at the manor house for that purpose only."

"She didn't say what made her think that?" Armstrong questioned.

"I don't think she could give actual facts, but I know she was so nervous about it that she had begged Mrs. Amcott to send it to the bank or to her solicitors. I understand that, acting on Joan's advice, she did finally send it out of the house. Joan fancied that it was this that set this man, this Monsieur Waddy, against her, for she told me that lately he never missed a chance of being perfectly horrid and most offensive when they were alone. I don't doubt the necklace is safe and sound, or someone would have spoken of its loss at the inquest." Joan's voice suggested that anything else was too good to be true. "But as it happens, Mrs. Amcott had Joan get it out of the bank for her only this last Saturday."

"What bank was that?" the Inspector asked quickly.

Joan thought that she had better not know its name. He could easily find out this point.

"So you think Mrs. Amcott had this necklace in her possession when she was killed?" he asked.

"That, of course, I don't know, but Joan gave it to her before they all drove to the station, and she and the child and the nurse went on up to town."

"What about the nurse? Was she in the car?"

"I asked that. Joan said she sat in front."

"You don't know if Mrs. Amcott took the necklace out and looked at it at all?"

"Joan said she undid the sealed paper and just snapped the case open and shut to see that it was all right."

"Do you know why Mrs. Amcott wanted the necklace on Saturday last?"

Joan said that she had not the faintest idea.

There was a silence of a few seconds.

"Do you think Mrs. Amcott shared your sister's distrust of this man?" the Inspector asked.

Joan had no idea.

"I know my sister told Mrs. Amcott that she thought he was too interested in the necklace."

"But for your having seen this man on Monday and on Tuesday evening..." Blair began thoughtfully. The Inspector shook his head imperceptibly. He did not approve of discussing theories of crimes before sisters of very-much suspected persons. But Blair went on.

"My theory, first and last, presupposes an impersonator of Mrs. Amcott, but not necessarily that it was a woman. That idea was only—forgive me, Miss Ingilby—because of the note of the unusual, the startling fact that it introduced. But a man could have worn a disguise, supposing he knew the dead woman, and the house, and was well known to the dog, and could impersonate a woman's voice." Blair was desperately trying to upset his first theory and at the same time paddle on in a fresh one.

"Hard supposition that last, Mr. Blair," murmured the Inspector.

"But a possible one—to some men. And murderers don't like partnerships. Such a man as you tell us of could have done the whole thing off his own bat—carried the body downstairs, taken it off in the bath-chair, and laid it in the charcoal shed. But for the fact that you say you saw him at the play..."

"From first to last, on both nights," Joan said with a rather despairing catch in her voice.

The Inspector gave her an unofficial look of sympathy. She had scored with him by refusing to snatch at Blair's idea, by crushing it as utterly impossible.

Joan rose. "In any case, what I have told you both is in strictest confidence, of course."

The two men assented at once.

"I take it we shall all three meet again very shortly then," and with a grave bow apiece she let Blair open the door for her.

"How did you know where to find me?" he asked. It struck him that this had better be cleared up in front of the police officer.

"I telephoned to the newspaper for the address of the Mr. Blair who wrote the article about Mrs. Amcott's death. I said I knew something about Miss Ingilby and wanted to speak to you."

"I'll see you to the front door," Blair murmured. On the stairs she stopped.

"One thing more," she said in his ear. "Be very careful. This man Waddy is awfully clever. He doesn't look it, but he is!" And with that she was gone.

Blair re-entered his sitting room.

"Whew-w! That was a dreadful interview!" he said frankly. It had been a nightmare to him—lest she make some slip.

"Plucky young, lady," the Inspector said. He had an eye for a pretty girl. "Let's hope—but there's no use hoping the impossible. I'm always sorry for the relations of criminals. There's luck if you will. Yet some people don't believe in luck. As to what Miss Lucy has just told us about those emeralds—well, there's a possible motive for the murder! Joan Ingilby admired them tremendously, she says. As for that about Monsieur Waddy—of course, the sister probably believes it, and, of course, we'll look into it; but this Monsieur Waddy is a great friend of Mr. Hilary Amcott's. He's hardly likely to be a jewel-thief. Particular people, the Amcotts. None of your hail-fellow-well-met sort."

There was a short silence.

"I've questioned all the servants, and the nurse at that children's home included, and learnt nothing, though, of course, you never know... But if they're hiding anything, time will tell."

Joan sat in the train taking her to Elmhurst, and with mixed feelings watched the world fly past. She was not naturally brave, and the effort that she had just put on herself this morning, first to go to Blair's rooms, then to meet the Inspector in order to get away from the newspaper man's room without arousing suspicion, had made a heavy call on her determination. She was glad that she had seen the police officer. She knew now that he was absolutely sceptical of Joan Ingilby's innocence— until proof of that innocence could be furnished. She had to conquer a desire to get out at the first station and run for shelter. Now that she was disguised and perfectly disguised, she could hide. She had money enough to tide over the next weeks.

But that might mean permanent hiding, for, thanks to Blair's article in this morning's *Comet*, until Mrs. Amcott's murder was definitely brought home to someone, a sword dangled over her own head, and not by a hair, but by a spider's thread.

She sat alone in her compartment, every nerve tingling. Could she do it? Could it be done? Could she ever pass herself off successfully as Joan Ingilby's sister among people who knew her? Her safety would, she knew, lie in the fact that, like the Inspector just now, no one would easily assume that the practically accused girl would dare, or want to, return to the scene of her alleged crime.

She thought over all the people she would have to face at the manor house. There would be Baroness de Maricourt for one—Felicity Maricourt. "'Ty Maricourt," as her family called her, a young widow, was Mrs. Amcott's cousin and next of kin. She would be sure to be there, staying until at least after the funeral. She had very keen eyes, but Joan believed that the Baroness liked her. She might, she thought, be counted as a friend.

Then came Hilary Amcott, the dead woman's brother-in-law... Joan thought a great deal about him. He had tried to start a very hectic flirtation with her shortly after her arrival, then, finding that Joan ignored him, had made love to her of a more discreet, apparently more genuine kind. He might be safely considered as a friend too; at least, as much so as one could count a drink-sodden, weak-willed man as anything. As to his constant companion, Monsieur Waddy, who had expected to stay at the manor till the New Year, he would, she knew, be an ever-present danger. How much of a one time alone would show.

Dangerous too, though for other reasons, would be the rector and the servants and the villagers. Let her make one slip and betray her real identity, and she might be arrested. Joan thought that not a possibility, but a certainty. And once arrested, she would be the victim of the ruthless logic of an article written—oh! irony of things!—by a man who she had known on the boat, had for her one of those dream-passions which, given a chance, can lead to the most enduring love. But not all his efforts could save her if she blundered. Well, she must not blunder. But she did intend to search the manor. She would be on the look-out for any clue that had been left behind.

That charcoal... she must make some inquiries at once about that. Probably, or at least possibly, many people could have helped themselves to it and to the stove.

She spent many minutes trying to think of every possible explanation of the known facts that could account for a crime. Groping for any motive on the part of those at Elmhurst that could be considered adequate for a murder. She found nothing.

At last Elmhurst was reached. She saw Blair and the Inspector get out further down. She hurried out and took a fly to the manor. She was in a fever to see how her disguise worked. So far it seemed perfect. A parlourmaid opened the door. The butler was busy for the moment with the undertaker.

Joan was so deep in her own thoughts again that, to her horror, she all but smiled at the girl as one does at a familiar face. The oversight was a warning to her to be more on her guard.

Hilary Amcott was out, she learned, but was expected back any moment.

The maid, who eyed Joan excitedly when she gave her name, went over the top as far as the rules of decorum were concerned.

"Oh, miss!" Her face worked. "Oh, Miss Ingilby!" she said in a low but warm voice, "if I may make so bold, please tell your poor sister that we none of us in the hall believe that wicked stuff in the *Comet* this morning."

The approaching butler heard, but he was human after all. He pretended not to notice the interlude. As for Joan, it seemed to her a good omen. She smiled gratefully at the maid.

"If you will let me know when Mr. Hilary Amcott comes in, I would like to wait in my sister's room."

Again Joan had to catch herself up, or she would have turned into the right passage before her guide.

In the room, the familiar room, her eyes brimmed. How little she had thought when she last left it that the next time she entered it would be with an accusation of murder hanging over her head—all but in the hands of the police—doomed if she took one false step—as good as hanged if she gave herself away.

She stared at the smudge on the window-sill and the marks in the dust of the trunk in the boxroom. She could have screamed. For these, and such as these, she was being pilloried, her very life put in jeopardy. It was monstrous. She had to fight down the feelings that threatened to swamp her.

Pulling herself together, she searched the rooms inch by inch. There was nothing of any interest as far as she could see.

She went through the bathroom into Mrs. Amcott's room, where lay a silent form covered with a sheet. Blossoms stood about it. Their presence a reminder that that which lay in their midst was kin to them—was but earth and air and water in another combination; a combination that, no longer of use, would shortly be dissolved to bloom afresh in the flowers, blow again in the summer breezes, rise and fall once more in the deep blue sea.

In this room, too, Joan found nothing that could be of use to her. Also, she heard nothing. She might have done so, for, watching her every movement through a crack in the old door' hinges, flattened against the wall till he gave an idea of a slug, or a centipede, or anything foul and flat, was a man, eyeing her with malignant closeness. Not a glance of hers, not a touch of those well-kept little hands but he saw it, noted it.

Suddenly he detached himself from the door, and, stepping softly, so softly that he seemed to barely touch the carpet, he slipped round a corner.

Joan, who was in Mrs. Amcott's sitting-room, only heard two women's voices—it was their owners that had alarmed the watcher—as they entered the room where she had just been. She knew them both. One was the Baroness de Maricourt. The girl with her was Octavia Dallas. The two were by way of being friends, as childhood's playmates always are, however far apart the poles of character may lie...

Joan cautiously set the door ajar. She must know if anything were taken from the room. Apparently the two intended to go over the contents of a tallboy near the window. Leaving the door ajar, she stood back and watched them. Their backs were to her. They talked of the arrangements for to-morrow's funeral.

"Hilary wants me to check off Doris's locked-up things, as she's without a maid of her own. I think I know all her belongings." The Baroness took out a jewellery box.

"Can't think why people use these things," she said impatiently as the lock refused to open. "They're no good. 'Pon my word, Otto, the thing acts as though it had been all but forced. There's a trick about how you press the key in, you know."

The box opened at that moment, and the Baroness forgot her suspicions. Standing at the table, she glanced over its contents.

"They're mine now, so Doris always said. I shan't wear them, of course. I hate wearing other people's choosings." She bent down and looked at the box closer.

"The lining's fearfully scratched up, and it's a new case too. Doris must have tried to open the top pocket with her nail scissors! Have you a top pocket in your case, Otto? I have, just like this one." She moved as she spoke a little gold embroidered, padded cushion, and, pulling, drew open a hidden pocket in the lining.

"For love letters and bills," she said lightly; "at least, that's where I keep mine. But poor Doris's is empty, I see. And look at the lining behind it, cut to ribbons. How funny!" She locked the case again. "I shouldn't say that that pocket's always been empty of late, would you?"

"Didn't you think Doris's soul was rather to the fore since her accident?" 'Ty asked, smiling. "Mr. Grimshaw's awfully fetching. I adore those strong, silent men myself."

This time Octavia did smile.

"My dear 'Ty! He doesn't know the difference between Charleston and a banana glide!" she scoffed.

"He could be taught."

"I don't think he'd take dance lessons, not even from you."

"Maybe, but when he looks at me as though I were somewhere in the handle of the Dipper, I feel as if I could follow him anywhere," gushed 'Ty. "That North Pole, glacial air of his is awfully fetching. Makes you want to thaw it at once, or, at least, it makes me. You never seem to be taken with such fancies. And it made poor Doris feel that way too. I wonder if she did succeed in thawing him a bit?"

Octavia's answer was pointedly to look towards the bed room where Doris Amcott lay, colder than any air of Grimshaw's. 'Ty flushed a little.

"Poor Doris! It seems utterly impossible to think of her as having no further interest in clothes. To remember that she's dead, let alone that one silly paper is trying to make out she was murdered. I think the man who wrote such a thing must be mad."

"I think he wrote the truth," Octavia Dallas said firmly. "I was tremendously impressed by his reasoning. I mean that she must have been killed. Oh, poor, poor Doris! Not about.... Joan Ingilby having had a hand in it, of course. That's monstrous."

"But Doris wasn't murdered! You have to have a reason to murder people!" 'Ty Maricourt said hotly.

Octavia Dallas said nothing for a moment.

"Did you read the article in the *Daily Comet*?" she asked in a low voice.

"Yes. But Hilary said it was all stuff and nonsense. He went off raging about it to find Waddy. Of course it isn't true. It simply can't be true."

Again the other said nothing.

"You believe it!" 'Ty spoke as though accusing her companion of a crime. "Yet you know what it will mean to us here! How people will talk, and pry, and gossip! I know one thing. If there was a murder, then that article is right in its conclusion too, and Joan Ingilby had a hand in it. If there's a murder at all, she's in it. I always disliked her. I always knew that there was something sly and—oh—wicked about her. I could feel it through all her put-on sweetness that took me in too at first."

Baroness de Maricourt's face flushed, then it paled. She seemed to speak with a great deal of emotion. An emotion that sounded uncommonly like hatred.

"Oh, 'Ty!" remonstrated the other, "don't say that of Joan Ingilby! It's cruel. I'm sure she's innocent. And she must be in awful danger after that article. And she's only a girl—a helpless girl—"

She stopped. The door had opened, and the rector stepped in. He had a prayer-book in his hand, and seemed surprised to find the room occupied. Octavia Dallas left the two together.

"I—I only came to say a short prayer," he began, turning away.

"Don't go, padre," 'Ty said at once. "We shan't be a minute. We were just talking of the article in the *Comet* this morning. I don't suppose you've seen it though, as you never read anything but the leaders in the papers."

"I shall certainly read the article as soon as I get home," Grimshaw said promptly. He had a harsh voice for so young a man. "But I've heard all about it. Everyone is talking about it. I need hardly tell you, Baroness, how very sorry I am about it—about the possibility, I mean, that anything even suspicious is connected, or can be connected, with the death of-Doris Amcott."

"It's too utterly mad for words," 'Ty said indignantly. "I think it's positively indecent to increase the sales of the paper in that sort of a way. Murder down here at the manor house. Murder of Doris! No, don't go, Mr.

Grimshaw. This is the last drawer." She jerked it open as she was speaking. "Oh, only Doris's diary for the year. It's very nearly full, I suppose; though it's locked. How dreadful death makes personal things seem. She was sensible enough to only write about other people and what she thought of them." The Baroness laid the little book, bound in purple alligator skin, back again and turned away, running her hands over her shingled hair.

"Don't you think so too, padre? I mean that the idea of anyone having harmed Doris is quite ludicrous. Who would? Why?" She was staring out of a window.

"Why, there's the Police Inspector up here again, and a young man with him. What on earth..." She looked hurriedly around. Her face was rather pale.

"Do be so kind as to lock the door when you've done. I must go down and see what it all means."

She was gone on the instant.

And then the parson did a very strange thing. Without moment's hesitation, as though he had come into the room for that rather than for the prayer of which he spoke, he stepped to the tallboy and opened the drawer which 'Ty Marl de Maricourt said contained the dead woman's diary. In another second he had slipped the purple-bound book into the pocket of his coat. It was a flat book, though of a fair size.

Joan, who was watching intently, had taken a swift step forward, but, quite unprepared for the rapidity of the book's disappearance, was too late to save it.

"Oh!" she gasped, then remembered that she was only the governess's sister. "Oh! ought anything to be taken from these rooms? I'm Joan Ingilby's elder sister. I've come down because of that awful article in this morning's *Comet*—come down to clear her. These rooms must be left just as they are." She finished on a very resolute note.

The rector had wheeled at her sudden appearance, but otherwise he showed no perturbation.

"The rooms are left just as they were," he said stiffly. Then he went on in what seemed a very kind and genuine

tone, "Of course you'll clear your sister! But I trust that
she will need no clearing." Kind though the voice was, he
kept trying to step past Joan and out of the room.

Joan made no effort to move.

"Come down with me into the gunroom. It's always
deserted these days, more's the pity." The rector was still
speaking very sympathetically. "We'll talk it all over. I
am sure we can think of a dozen facts that will prove,
what, of course, we know, that your sister could have had
nothing to do with Mrs. Amcott's death. I have met Miss
Joan often, and formed the very highest opinion of her
character."

Joan was in a cruel dilemma. What ought she to do?
The rector was a very important person in Elmhurst,
naturally, and she needed every friend she could muster,
yet she could not suffer anything to be whisked away
from here without having at least seen it.

"But I—I saw you take something from the drawer."
She said it most unhappily.

The rector had bushy eyebrows above resolute eyes.
They drew together now, but he said nothing.

"I—I shall have to mention it," Joan went on
desperately. "I can't let anything be taken away from
these rooms. It might be something that would clear Joan
from that awful, unspeakable suspicion. I mean Mrs.
Amcott's diary. I was in there waiting till you should all
be done in here. I didn't want to intrude."

"Miss Ingilby"—something cold and resolute was in
the harsh voice now, though he spoke very low—"that
book I took was my own property, a book lent by me to
Mrs. Amcott and intended only for her. If her diary has
gone, which of us would he the more likely to take it? You
or I? I am the rector here. Pray understand that I am not
accusing you of having taken it. I know better. But if such
a book should be missing, your being here alone would
make it look as if you must have taken it. That would be
a very unfortunate debut for you efforts down here.
Believe me, I am almost exceedingly sorry for your sister.

Please believe that." He finished on a very warm, earnest tone.

Joan moved away from the door. She could not prevent Mr. Grimshaw from leaving the room. But she did not believe him, not for a moment. He did not look the kind of man to have books bound in purple leather. Also, the gilt edges of the book itself, the tiny lock... no, she felt sure, though, she had never seen the book herself, that the dead woman's cousin had not been mistaken when she had said that the book was a diary.

"Oh, may I look at it?" she breathed. "Surely, for my peace of mind, you would let me just glance inside it."

"It's locked," he said briefly, making no effort to produce it. "My dear Miss Ingilby, I don't think you quite realise what you are saying. Small wonder, after the terrible shock you must have had. But let me point out to you again, that if a diary of Mrs. Amcott's is missing, there is only one person who would be suspected of having taken it. Ah, I hear someone coming up the stairs," and, saying that, the rector opened the door, just as a servant knocked to say that Mr. Hilary Amcott had returned and would like to see Miss Ingilby. The rector stayed behind.

Joan, still trembling with amazement and indignation, was shown into an oak-panelled room, where Hilary Amcott hurried forward.

"Miss Ingilby? Miss Joan Ingilby's elder sister?" His voice sounded as flat as ever, but he was smiling broadly. Yet some people—Blair, for instance—might have thought that his smile seemed only on the surface.

"I should never have guessed the relationship," he went on, "though there is a likeness in a way, especially in the voice. How is your sister? What a terrible shock to her and to all of us, that dreadful article in this morning's *Comet*! It certainly was to me. Luckily I am able to prove it the merest rubbish. But come into the Indian room. The Police Inspector is there. We will settle this preposterous idea of a crime once and for all. It's a pity that it did not come up at the inquest yesterday. I could have proved it impossible there and then."

Joan followed with her head whirling. This was indeed unexpected, and most marvellously welcome. Was it possible that her peril was to pass almost as soon as it had come? The two men waiting turned at their entrance.

Blair held his breath as he saw her. The grit of her! And the danger! Hilary shook hands with the Inspector, a limp, clammy handshake...

"And are you a member of the police too?" he asked, turning to Blair.

"I'm sorry to say I'm only the writer of an article in this morning's *Comet*," Blair said hurriedly, while the Inspector murmured his name.

Staring hard at Hilary, Blair thought what a temper the chap had. For a second there had been a sort of frozen fury in his bloodshot eyes. Almost, Blair thought, they had glared like the eyes of a madman. Certainly the eyes of a fanatic. Then the red lids drooped again until they all but met as Blair hurried on.

"I'm afraid my wind-up must have been very painful to Miss Ingilby and her friends. I want to make it quite clear that I retract the concluding words as far as she is concerned. On more careful analysis of the facts of Mrs. Amcott's death: I see that any theory which includes the governess is grotesquely improbable."

"The article is grotesque from start to finish!" Hilary Amcott said, biting his pale lips, around which deep lines ran lines of ill-health and worse living. "I've just posted a reply to your paper that will settle any idea of a murder having been committed. I talked to my sister-in-law Tuesday after noon in Salisbury; about four or five it must have been, at a time when, according to that damned silly concoction of yours, she was already lying murdered."

"You talked to Mrs. Amcott, Tuesday afternoon?" Blair was not prepared for this. In so far as, by making his sketch of the crime impossible, it helped to clear Joan, he rejoiced exceedingly to hear it; but he had not expected his reconstruction to be blown sky-high quite so promptly and so completely.

"You saw her face?" the Inspector asked.

"I did. She talked to me for quite five minutes, about some Christmas arrangements for the village children. I wanted to see the Chief Constable early this morning and get him to drop the whole thing. I tried to get hold of you, Inspector, but you were both away."

"You actually saw Mrs. Amcott's face?" the Inspector persisted.

"Naturally, in talking to her."

The Inspector patted the centre of his moustache several times.

"I'm afraid I must look over the house just the same, sir. For Mrs. Amcott was murdered, whether murdered Monday night or Tuesday night or just before she was found yesterday morning. Mrs. Amcott didn't walk into that charcoal shed, sir. She was carried. Her shoes prove that. And that being so, she was probably dead when so carried."

"But my dear Inspector, shoes, eh? Suppose Mrs. Amcott wiped her shoes on a bit of turf, automatically, you know?" Hilary Amcott suggested feebly.

"Then where did those charcoal stains found on the carpet of the bath-chair come from?" the Inspector countered. "Not from Mrs. Amcott's shoes, which are new, and had only been worn indoors a few times, I fancy. They couldn't have made those marks. So the question is, whose could?" He carefully refrained from looking at Joan.

"But, frankly, your whole evidence seems to be absolute rot." Hilary poked a glowing log with his foot. "At any rate, I spoke to Mrs. Amcott late on Tuesday afternoon around four or a little later."

He eyed Blair as much as to say, "So that's that!" before he turned away.

Joan rose. She felt dizzy with all that she had gone through, was still going through.

"I think I will see about a room at the inn," she said faintly.

"You are staying on in Elmhurst? It must be very painful for you." Hilary spoke sympathetically.   .

"Very painful indeed!" Joan agreed with a catch in her breath. "But I can't leave this village until it is known who killed Mrs. Amcott. Joan didn't kill her. She was devoted to her. She thought her all that was dear and kind." Her voice trembled.

The door opened.

"That you, Waddy?" Hilary Amcott looked around, as though pleased to see the new arrival. "This is a sister of Mrs. Amcott's governess. She's come down about that article in the paper which you thought so damned funny. Mr. Waddy—Miss Ingilby. And this is our Police Inspector, and this is the Mr. Blair who wrote the article in question."

Raoul Waddy bowed as a Latin bows, from the hips; in fact, he almost seemed to bow from his supple knees. His figure was perfection. His movements had a grace and a spring that made one think of a Greek god in the flesh. But there was nothing Greek nor godlike about his singularly small dark head, and still more singularly small dark face. Yet he was handsome in a bizarre way, except that the narrow little forehead sloped back from the uncurving slant of brows beneath which the light, opaque eyes were set so high that they had the effect of a cobra's brows. The eyes themselves were the smallest that Blair had ever seen.

As Hilary Amcott muttered Blair's name the newcomer turned and gave him what would have been a stare from another man. Blair felt as though a rattlesnake had lifted its head and was regarding him. In Hilary Amcott's glance he had read a cold rage. Here he read stark murder for one second.

Blair in his turn looked at the man openly, steadily. He was so conscious of intense animosity on his own part that, apart from the singular flash of hatred which he had caught, it could but be mutual. He could well understand that a girl like Joan Ingilby felt this man's presence as evil. She had said that Waddy was clever "though he did not look it" But Blair did not think that Waddy looked in the least stupid. The face was too peculiar for that. Those strange eyes, so small, so dull, so much the colour of the sallow skin that you had to look very closely to see whether they were open or shut, gave an extraordinary effect of secretiveness to the face. Standing now with his back to the light, Blair was certain that they were closed. Then they moved, and he saw that they were open and staring at Joan.

CHAPTER FOUR

"A SISTER of Miss Joan Ingilby's?" Monsieur Waddy had a husky voice that suggested immense capacities for all the animal passions. His English was perfect, except for a faint evenness of accent which suggested a Frenchman. He turned his back on the room, as though to pull a chair forward. Blair saw that he was laughing, laughing silently, but with a hilarity that shook him for one brief second. Then he faced around again as Joan put her hand to the door, he opened it with a kind of solicitous gallantry.

"I trust I have not driven Miss Joan Ingilby's sister away. As a great friend of Miss Joan Ingilby's permit me to accompany mademoiselle down to the hotel and to express my..."

The shutting door drowned the rest of the sentence. Blair was strongly tempted to take his leave at the same time, but he decided, that he could better serve Joan by staying.

"Now, Mr. Hilary, was there anything in Mrs. Amcott's possession which might explain a murder? Did she have any jewels down here with her, for instance?" The Inspector had risen.

"Not to my knowledge."

"She didn't own anything uncommon in the way of stones or pearls?" the Inspector persisted.

"I think you had better ask my brother. A wire to him as soon as he is better would settle that." Hilary spoke as though bored by the police officer's insistence

"I should like to look over the house, sir," was the Inspector's only comment. "I'll try and not to inconvenience anybody more than I can help. And will you let me have another word with you when I've finished?"

"I should expect it," Hilary Amcott said with his silly grin. "Of course, I should expect to hear if you find anything that bears out your terrible idea, though to me it's still a most fantastic one."

"Maybe you'll hear and maybe you won't," the Inspector murmured to Blair as they closed the door of the now empty suite behind them, after the police officer had sent away the constable who had accompanied him to the house, and who was sitting on guard on the landing. Armstrong explained the latter move.

"No use keeping Higgins dangling around. Anyone who wanted to take anything away has had days enough in which to do it. I saw Mr. Grimshaw at the window in here as we came in. Not that he would tamper with anything," Armstrong added hurriedly.

"I don't know about days..." Blair said, looking around him keenly. "It's possible that the murderer or murderers thought themselves quite safe until this morning."

"Until they read that article of yours," mused Armstrong. "That's possible of course. Unholy looking chap that Frenchman is," he went on, examining the writing-table as he talked. "Do you think he really is French?"

"From Devil's Island possibly," Blair conceded. The Inspector laughed.

"I don't wonder the governess didn't like him." The police officer worked swiftly. "But as to his being a criminal and connected with those emeralds—I'm not so sure. A man with a face like that is bound to keep straight. It keeps him straight. He couldn't hope to get away with the dog's biscuit unsuspected. When I served with the Norfolks during the war we had a chap like that—a thorough wrong 'un. Always trying to do you, and never getting a chance. It really was pathetic. There was poor old Shirty, as we used to call him, ready and anxious to do any dirty trick he could play, and not the youngest lad out from home letting him get near him. One look at his face, and everybody felt for their money belt and counted the grub. He never had a look in. I'll wager he got through the war without a stain on his character. Yet as capable a crook, I do believe, as ever went unjugged. Hard lines that!" He rose from the writing-table. "No motive for murder here."

"Was Mrs. Amcott a wealthy woman?" Blair asked.

"Well-to-do. Her lawyer told the Chief Constable—he flew up to town this morning to have a chat with him and a glance at the will—that she had spent a good deal of her fortune. She was a gambler, like all the Norreys. Their place is quite close to us, you know. It's in their blood. Now, in spite of Mr. Hilary, the Amcotts are careful with money."

"In spite of Mr. Hilary Amcott? What's his character, then?"

"Light. They thought him no end clever as a lad, but he bitterly disappointed his brother in Egypt, they say. He was sent home in disgrace; too many pegs; too many little games like *Petits Chevaux*, I fancy, as well. Nowadays, since his return—on extended leave, as he calls it—he cares for nothing but night clubs. He and Mrs. Amcott's cousin, a Baroness de Maricourt, and that Monsieur Waddy you've just met go off to Salisbury night after night, and to some very queer houses, too—houses that we suspect of gambling as well as dancing. Suspect, but can't prove, mind you."

"How about Mrs. Amcott's will?"

"All her jewellery and personal belongings go to the Baroness, everything else to the child."

"And she was alive Tuesday afternoon, and Hilary Amcott talked to her..." Blair drummed his fingers on the window pane. "That staggering fact means an absolute reconstruction of my theory of the crime from start to finish. But, at least, it also means that Miss Joan Ingilby can come forward now."

"I only wish she would!" The Inspector spoke fervently. "I would arrest her on the spot. Do you mean to say that you believe Mr. Hilary's statement about seeing his sister-in-law the day before yesterday in Salisbury? Why didn't he mention it at the inquest? The coroner asked a lot of questions about her last day. Not a cheep from Mr. Hilary then about their supposed meeting."

"You don't think he's speaking the truth?"

"I don't, Mr. Blair. Not a bit; I think he's trying it on, hoping to quash a murder investigation. Though I must say I'm surprised..."

"Inspector"—Blair came up to him—"don't let my initial mistake mislead the whole inquiry. It's quite possible that he was speaking the truth just now and did see and did talk to his sister-in-law herself late on Tuesday. It's quite possible that not only my suspicion that the governess had a hand in the murder, but also my whole idea of how it was committed, is wrong."

The Inspector shook a stubborn head.

"No, Mr. Blair. I'm as certain that you've got hold of the truth as though I'd been there myself. I'm finished here, if you are. I came up at once, of course, as soon as I'd read my *Comet* and secured that piece of charcoal and the flake of paint with the scorch mark from the window-sill."

Armstrong and Blair went downstairs. The Inspector paused at the telephone. Blair opened the door of the room where he had been. He saw an extremely pretty girl with a lively skin and a pair of hot, devastating black eyes, and hair so satin-smooth in its waves around her head that it looked as though painted on wax. He guessed her rightly to be the Baroness de Maricourt. She was warming her hands at the fire, little hands like carvings of rose ivory. Blair watched them with a curious feeling.

Had those dainty fingers lit a charcoal brazier—a brazier which was to bring death to a sleeping woman? For the first time, there, in that beautiful old room a horror of the whole affair, quite apart from Joan's danger, came to Blair. Up till now it had been academic except where she was concerned. Even though he had seen the dead woman's body, it had in reality been an affair of the mind. But now, could it have been this girl? Some one intimately connected with the household it must have been to account for the dog... But this lovely girl.

She looked up. He introduced himself.

"The author of that frightfully clever article in the *Comet*? I heard you had come and rushed down to meet you. For you're right in that awfully brilliant guess of yours. There's no use mincing matters. If my cousin's death really is a murder, who else could it have been but the governess? As your article said, it must have been someone who knew Mrs. Amcott, knew the house, and whom 'Laddy' knew. I was at the big ball at the French Embassy given in honour of the President's arrival. There isn't anyone else but Miss Ingilby whom it could have been."

Blair marvelled how he could have thought Baroness de Maricourt pretty. The girl was a ghoul, he told himself, a vampire.

"But Miss Ingilby may have a perfectly good alibi too," he said equably. "I have already absolutely retracted everything in my article which suggests that the governess was implicated in the crime."

The Inspector entered.

"I can't think why you should want to undo all your article," she said swiftly. "It loses its point without your conclusion. It's the climax of your whole argument surely."

"My opinion exactly!" the Inspector agreed.

"But Mr. Hilary Amcott spoke to his sister-in-law on Tuesday afternoon," Blair said almost triumphantly. "That knocks the bottom out of everything—down tumbles the whole theory."

"Mr. Hilary said..." 'Ty Maricourt seemed positively to gape.

The Inspector quoted what Mr. Amcott had said, and ended with:

"I think he may have mixed two days up. Confused Tuesday with, say, the day before, Monday."

"Mr. Hilary would try to be wrong if it would help Miss Ingilby at all," Ty said coldly.

"Meaning?" The Inspector bent forward.

"Miss Ingilby used to flirt with him whenever she got a chance. That was why she was leaving. Mrs. Amcott had learnt about it. That's quite confidential, by the way. My cousin told everyone that it was because she needed a better trained governess now that the child is getting older. Whatever Mr. Hilary says, I know that you were right in your first idea, Mr. Blair, and that Joan Ingilby killed Mrs. Amcott. It's a terrible thing to think and to say, but, between ourselves, strictly between ourselves, of course, I know it was the governess."

"You know?" The Inspector was startled.

"I feel sure of it."

"Oh-h!" The Inspector's eyes lost their gleam.

"Miss Ingilby once showed that she was perfectly familiar with the use of charcoal stoves," she went on to the Inspector. "It was when little Doris was ill, and had to have a poultice in the night. The gas ring wouldn't act, and Miss Ingilby brought up the stove and lit it in exactly the way you described in your article."

"You were in the room?" Blair asked thoughtfully.

"I was." The reply was brief.

So supposing her story to be accurate, or even true, after that night she herself would know how to light that stove.

"Anyone else in the room with your ladyship?" asked the Inspector.

"Miss Dallas. There was a dance on. Mrs. Amcott was away in town, but Miss Dallas and I did what we could."

There was a short silence.

"Your ladyship thinks it is the governess," the Inspector broke in to say musingly. "It certainly remains my own belief, except for the lack of motive. That's the great obstacle to going by that theory."

'Ty Maricourt drew a deep breath.

"Mrs. Amcott had a very valuable necklace," she began in a queer, hurried voice. She paused as Monsieur Waddy and Hilary Amcott came in.

"Dismissed!" the former said with a lift of his eyebrows. "Miss Ingilby would have none of me. You were saying, Baroness?"

She did not seem in a hurry to speak.

"The Inspector is certain that Doris Amcott was murdered," she said at last in an almost propitiatory voice.

"Absolutely certain," Armstrong said curtly, watching her curiously.

"It's only that there seems no motive," the Baroness went on, still in the same odd voice. "But I've just had a most frightful shock."

She did not look it. She looked very excited and very nervous, Blair thought, but not as if she had had a shock of even a slight kind.

"Better go to bed in that case," Waddy said, turning his head slowly towards her.

"By Jove, yes!" Hilary agreed, jumping up as though to open the door for her.

"Mrs. Amcott's emeralds are missing," 'Ty Maricourt announced with a certain defiant lift of her slender neck. "I mean the Norreys necklace."

"Oh, rubbish!" Hilary said after a glance at his friend Waddy, his friend, who sat very immobile on his seat. "Absolute rot, 'Ty. You've not looked in enough places. Why, they're at the Bank."

"They're missing," she repeated angrily. "They're not at the Bank, for I found the empty case."

The police officer now joined in the conversation.

"And what is the Norreys necklace, my lady?"

"An heirloom in our branch of the family, an emerald necklace from Peru—Inca work. It was the Duke of

Parma's ransom when Sir Peter Norreys took him prisoner after the Armada. It's mine now, of course, as I'm the last of our branch. I've just telephoned to the Bank, and found that it was handed last Saturday to Miss Ingilby. She had a note from Mrs. Amcott, and as they knew her, and she had often cashed Mrs. Amcott's cheques, they handed her the box after trying to get Mrs. Amcott on the 'phone and not finding her."

"By Jove!" muttered Waddy, thoughtfully. "Those stones were worth £500 merely as stones, and historically the necklace was worth—well, I've heard the rector, who's as well up as you, Hilary, in such things, say that they would fetch eight thousand any day at a London auction."

Hilary Amcott nodded. Blair thought that he looked relieved.

"Well, now they're gone. Stolen! Miss Ingilby has them!" 'Ty Maricourt finished almost shrilly.

Blair's heart felt as though it were lead.

"Evidently the theft of the necklace was but the first step in the murder of poor Doris," 'Ty Maricourt went on. "Doubtless she missed them and perhaps suspected Joan Ingilby at once." She stopped with a little exclamation like a crow of satisfaction. "Why! I remember now. Mrs. Amcott"—she was speaking to the Inspector—"once caught Miss Ingilby trying the lock of her trunk in which she kept the necklace within a couple of days after her arrival."

Blair held his tongue, but with difficulty. He was prepared to put up with unpleasant facts, but unpleasant lies were a harder matter.

"When was this?" the Inspector asked 'Ty.

"Oh, months ago now. Mrs. Amcott was frightfully upset about it."

"It's a pity to confuse a clever argument," Waddy put in softly, "but Miss Joan Ingilby could not have played the role in Mrs. Amcott's death that you, Baroness, suspect, and which you, Mr. Blair, so cleverly sketched for her, for the very good reason that Mr. Hilary Amcott and I saw her Monday night at the Royalty. Again on the Tuesday night, at the Gaiety, who should be sitting in the front row of the dress circle but Miss Ingilby! And there she continued to sit, as on the night before, throughout the whole performance, so certainly she could hardly have been waiting in the boxroom for a chance to kill Mrs. Amcott. Yet undoubtedly those marks show that someone was sitting here."

"Was Miss Ingilby alone at the theatre?" asked the Inspector.

Monsieur Waddy said that he had not noticed. Hilary Amcott said that he, too, could not say.

"But," the Frenchman went on, "though I know that she was not the murderess of Mrs. Amcott, I am sure she is the thief of her necklace, and that is why she dare not come forward. I am right in assuming that she has not come forward, am I not?" He asked the question of Blair with a leer that made the newspaper man's blood run hot and cold—hot for himself, and cold for Joan.

He would dearly like to close those dots of eyes still more completely.

"Besides, who is this Miss Ingilby?" Monsieur Waddy asked of the room at large. "No one seems to know. Her sole reference you, Baroness, think, was a lady living abroad. Oh, these ladies living abroad!" He shrugged his shoulders. "Several times she asked me questions in the short time I am here which struck me as over-curious about those emeralds."

Hilary Amcott was grinning as though something amused him. It was a silly grin, and yet Blair thought that it held a touch of covert malice. 'Ty Maricourt looked sullen.

"You two may have mistaken someone else for the governess," she said now. "My cousin was parting with her, and of course, her disappearance since Mrs. Amcott's death is a very suspicious thing."

"I'm afraid that seeing my article in the paper of this morning, she can't come forward until she is cleared," Blair said heavily.

"And I'm afraid in that case she'll have to stay hidden a long time!" The Baroness spoke with an upward tilt of the chin that used to be called a toss of the head. "But I shan't prosecute. About the emeralds, I mean. I only want you Inspector, to know, the facts."

"Thank   you,"   Inspector   Armstrong   said noncommittally.   "About   the   Squire;   is   he   still unreachable?"

"As I told you, Inspector," Hilary replied negligently, "Southern Rhodesia is the last address we have—if you can call that an address. The Mounted Police are trying to get into touch with him."

"So, as Mr. Ralph is ill, you're the head of the family for the time being?"

Hilary promptly refused even temporary rank.

"Count me out, Inspector. I'm on a much-needed holiday, and I don't intend to get out of my depths. I should like to help, of course, in this terrible business, but I should be no good. Amateurs had much better stay out." He shot a vindictive glance at Blair.

Armstrong rose.

"I think I'll have a last look round, for the time being, in Mrs. Amcott's rooms. Of course, I shall have to be out and in a good deal until this tragedy is cleared up, which won't be long."

"And Miss Ingilby found," 'Ty Maricourt put in sharply. How plainly she hated Joan, Blair thought. Poor Joan, who needed friends so badly, so desperately.

The Inspector made no reply, but took his leave.

"Funny thing," he muttered as they shut the door of the suite behind them again. "It's a funny thing that Miss Lucy, the sister of the girl who is as good as accused—for as far as I'm concerned she is that—and this here monseer Waddy should both swear that Joan Ingilby was at a theatre on a night that puts your idea of how the murder was done quite out of court. Makes me wonder, that does."

"What does, Inspector?" Blair asked quietly. He could have bawled the words in passionate anger. He guessed what was coming.

"Why, that both should hurry to give her an alibi!"

"Why not? If it's true?"

"Does Mr. Waddy strike you as a gentleman to care about what's true and what isn't?" the Inspector asked duly.

"Hilary Amcott agreed that she was there too," Blair pointed out.

"Ah, Mr. Hilary, I'm afraid, will agree with everything that Mr. Waddy chooses to say. Apart from pity, or a penchant for Miss Ingilby, it looks to me as if the Frenchie had a hold over him, which is likely enough. They say in the village that more times than not this winter he comes home the worse for drink. He used to be out with the hounds three times a week at the least, but not this year, not since that monseer has come to the manor. But this alibi of Joan Ingilby's, it doesn't make your theory of the crime impossible, Mr. Blair. I mean, the governess could have got down here afterwards and done it."

"She would have been seen at the station, or if she hired a car it could be traced. I think those two men told us about the theatre because they were seen there by someone who knew Miss Ingilby too. So knowing that any appearance of Miss Ingilby's on the night on which, according to my article, she had killed Mrs. Amcott, would in time be reported, they've spoken at once to give an appearance of honesty to any later declarations of theirs."

The Inspector listened with an unconvinced look.

"Maybe so, Mr. Blair. Quite possible, of course. But to me this alibi of Joan Ingilby's looks as if she and this Frenchie were the two criminals, and have to stick it out together, each saying they saw the other."

"You think Miss Lucy Ingilby..." Blair queried sarcastically.

"Is Joan Ingilby's sister, Mr. Blair! Of course she would do what she was asked to do. The more I think it over, the more certain I feel that the governess and this monseer"—the Inspector could speak very good French indeed, but his pronunciation was meant to mark his contempt for the man—"fill all the chinks. The sister may think Joan disliked the man; that would be bluff on the sister's part, of course. But—" He shook his head. "And the motive for the crime, so far, looks like the emeralds."

"The emeralds?" Blair still kept to his tone of sarcasm.

"Why not?" asked the Inspector. "It looks to me as if the governess had got 'em, and Monseer Waddy had been double-crossed, which naturally would make him like to put us on to her and their track. He gives the girl an alibi for the murder because he's in it, and he throws suspicion on her where he's not in it. Simple enough, I think."

"And Miss Lucy Ingilby throws suspicion on her sister too"—Blair managed a superior smile with difficulty, for his lips were stiff—"when she first—first, mind you, Inspector—told us about the emeralds?"

"No, I think she's acting honestly about the necklace, and hasn't an idea that her sister took it. So far Miss Lucy strikes me as a very nice and straightforward young lady. So far." Armstrong's guarded tone told of an instant readiness to change his opinion should he see fit.

Blair wheeled on him.

"And you think that interview that we've just had down below was straightforward?"

"Ah!" The Inspector tapped his moustache. "I wouldn't go so far as to say that, not by a long chalk. Sounded to me as if the family band was playing a very odd tune, a tune they hadn't rehearsed together, a tune I mean to find out—and shall in time."

Apparently with the Inspector detection was always merely a matter of time.

"It's a simple enough one." Blair's voice was scathing now. "It's merely *The Devil take the Governess,* as sung by Baroness Maricourt, with an obligato by Monsieur Waddy, and accompanied by Mr. Hilary Amcott."

The Inspector laughed.

"It's a pity the Squire isn't here. Straight as they make 'em, like most of the Amcotts. Got brains too, he'd be a tower of strength in all this. For the trouble is the emeralds do belong to the Baroness now. Like you, I think there's something fishy about her story and her way of telling it. She knew well enough that Mr. Hilary, for one, didn't want anything brought out to confirm the idea of murder; nor apparently, by the way she looked at him, Monsieur Waddy either. Certainly she's got her knife into Miss Joan Ingilby right enough. Jealousy is what it looks like—that sort of heat. But there's one thing, whoever she's attacking, she didn't kill her cousin for the sake of a necklace. The Norreys aren't criminals. As I said, gambling is in their blood—but not criminals. Besides, in her case, she has about six thousand a year under her husband's will as long as she doesn't re-marry. She can't have needed to murder for money. But Miss Ingilby now, as that Monseer says, who are the Ingilby girls?"

"Oh, don't waste your patrician feelings on them, Inspector," Blair fumed. "They're probably not even 'County'. They're doubtless only some penniless parson's children."

Again the Inspector laughed. He was a cheery young man, and found Blair in a peppery mood very amusing.

"You know, you're like the writers of these detective stories some people read—I can't stand the drivel in 'em myself—who want you to suspect everyone near and far. The writers can't help themselves, I see that, or how could they fill their books; but it's not true to life! In a real case," the Inspector went on confidentially, "of course, you look up everybody's time-table and keep an eye on 'em—but there are some people you're certain aren't criminals. You've known 'em for years. You can leave 'em on one side—in your own mind. And there are others—well, you know they're crooked at a glance, and you concentrate on them."

"Do you mention your feelings in your reports?" Blair asked. He had regained his good humour.

"Well, no." Armstrong shook his head. "It mightn't read well if you wrote that it was no use Blank's saying a word in his own defence, for you had taken a violent dislike to him the moment you clapped eyes on him, and therefore didn't believe a syllable. But it's what happens nine times out of ten. And nine times out of nine the chap you suspect is the one who did it. Character—like murder—will out, Mr. Blair; only it takes time. I'm talking, of course, of people like us who aren't biased by being friends with anyone in the crime circle, and yet know them. And as a policeman, I wish I could get into touch with the Ingilbys' people. Her sister says Joan Ingilby's past is her own. It shouldn't be. See if you can't coax Miss Lucy to be a bit franker. Of course, we shall get at it in time, but she may help us to a short cut. You may get a chance of a talk with her, since she's putting up at the inn where you say you intend to stay."

Blair had refused an offer of a room in the Inspector's pretty house. Blair thought it as well to point out that it was highly unlikely that Miss Ingilby would condescend to be even aware of his existence, but that he would do his best.

"We know, it wasn't an outsider who committed the crime, thanks to the Airedale." The Inspector was harking back to his own thoughts. "Nice dog, 'Laddy.' Though I don't deny he's a bit dull-witted. Pity of it is he used to belong to a medical man who went in a lot for dissection. I think that's why he didn't howl at Mrs. Amcott's dead body. But he's a good dog, belongs to Mr. Ralph Amcott. He came from the Elmhurst kennels; his lordship gave me a pup from the same litter. First-class watchdogs, one and all."

Lord Elmhurst was Octavia Dallas's father, and had a well known kennel.

"I haven't seen the dog so far," Blair said indifferently.

Inspector Armstrong dropped the article which he was examining, and spun on his heel. "Why, that's true!" he said, as if to himself.

"I do sometimes speak the truth when I'm not thinking. But why this blind confidence in your fellow-man?"

Armstrong did not smile.

"'Laddy'... I haven't seen himself to-day. I don't doubt it's all right, but I'll ask if I can borrow him for Farmer Ryan's haystack."

But downstairs the Inspector learnt that the dog had not been seen since just before lunch.

"Hope he isn't poaching," the butler said anxiously. "He does love a rabbit hunt. And in the Christmas holidays so many young gentlemen are just learning to handle a gun that it isn't safe to let even a cat out of sight."

"I'll have a look around the grounds," the Inspector said as, followed by Blair, he turned down a path.

"This leads to his kennel. He and I are old friends. He comes to my house for a game with his brother at least once a day. Both use their kennels as larders. Ten to one 'Laddy's' still burying a bone or a bunny." He stopped short, and seemed to listen for a moment, then with a gesture of caution he stepped lightly and cautiously to a summer-house that backed in their direction.

"I don't doubt!" Blair, joining him, heard the Baroness say with a sneer in her voice, "what gallant cavaliers you and Waddy are to be sure! Both protecting that poor lamb. I don't care what you say. If there was a murder, she did it, and the Inspector says there was a murder."

"From now we must do exactly as Waddy says," came in Hilary Amcott's silly drawl. "He has the brains of the outfit. I agree with you about Armstrong's pig-headedness. That damned newspaper article started it all," Hilary went on with a note of surprising menace in his voice. "I'd like to wring the neck of the fool who wrote it."

"He's right about that girl in spite of all of you." 'Ty Maricourt's light, hard voice threw in.

"Why, you and she seemed no end of friends." The sneer was now in the man's voice.

"Not at all!" Baroness Maricourt spoke coolly enough. "I don't deny that she hoodwinked me too at first. But it didn't take me long to do what you've never done, Hilary, and that is to see through her."

The desire to wring necks seemed to be in the air. Blair had it very badly just then, and it was such a pretty neck that he felt like wringing.

"She tried her best to catch you when she saw you were interested in her, but it was Waddy she really hoped for. There's no reason why I shouldn't say what I think when we're alone," 'Ty Maricourt finished, with an attempt at a careless laugh.

"No reason why you shouldn't say what you think..." repeated the man. "Some of your thoughts might be interesting, 'Ty. Those about the emeralds, for instance."

"Nothing to those about your talk with Doris on Tuesday afternoon!"

Blair could see Hilary's face through a crack in the wood. It was convulsed for a second. But all he said in reply to this last sally was:

"Possibly, my dear kitten. Your claws are always sharp as needles. But you'll find that mine are longer, sharper."

Hilary was speaking in a muffled but very disagreeable voice. Evidently a family row of grade A quality was on. "And now let's cut along to the house, there's a good kid. Heart-to-heart talks might be misunderstood by our peerless police."

The two left the shelter and walked up towards one of the long windows.

"Funny little scene that!" Blair murmured as he and the Inspector stepped around some laurels.

The police officer threw him an eloquent glance.

"Like a couple of crooks, eh? I told you he was pulling my leg with that speech about having seen his sister-in-law on Tuesday afternoon. But this way to the dog show." He led on for a couple of hundred yards. At the kennel he stooped down and peered inside. "He's there right enough," he said in a low, sharp whisper, "but he's dead."

Together they dragged out the stiff body. The Inspector tightened his lips.

"I wonder if this might be the reason that you hadn't seen him? Poor old chap! Poisoned, by the look of him. He was in perfect condition yesterday. Shut up when the jury came to look at the body merely because his barks didn't seem seemly just then. Poisoned... That looks as if something were afoot at the house that isn't finished yet..."

"The family tune," Blair murmured. "Part of the quarrels over the rehearsal of which we heard in the summerhouse."

The Inspector only looked very grave. He was still peering into the kennel when his torch gave out.

"Mind you," he went on, straightening up, "the Elmhurst dogs won't touch food from a stranger or eat anything lying around. So if not from a stranger..."

"Yes?" asked Hilary Amcott's tired voice close beside them. "If not from a stranger, Armstrong, then what?"

He and the rector had stepped from behind some bushes. Both now stood gazing down at the dog.

"Dead, eh?" Hilary said indifferently. Grimshaw said nothing. He seemed to draw a little apart from the others.

"Poisoned probably," Inspector Armstrong said shortly. He was remembering that Hilary Amcott was credited with having objected to Mrs. Amcott's bringing the dog down with her. The animal belonged to her husband. It had taken a cable from the squire to make him give way about "Laddy."

"I came down to tell you," Hilary went on, turning negligently from the dog, "that, on thinking things over, I shouldn't wonder if I had made a mistake about Tuesday afternoon. I mean my talk with Mrs. Amcott. I rather fancy you are right, and that it took place on the day before, the Monday. One day goes by so like another in this God-forsaken hamlet to which the doctor banishes me that really—" Yawning, he moved off. The rector had already turned on his heel and left them.

The Inspector tapped his moustache.

"I don't like the look of this," he confided to Blair. "Do you mind staying by the carcass, Mr. Blair, while I go for the vet? I don't want to leave it alone."

In a short time a couple of men came hurrying up with a covered handcart. The dog was laid in and wheeled out of the garden. The Inspector hurried off, and Blair made for the inn and a room under the same roof with Joan.

CHAPTER FIVE

IT seemed to Blair that the gods of misfortune and bad luck laughed that morning. The death of the Airedale might have been used as a proof that other hands than Joan Ingilby's were stirring in this case. For Joan had been in the train when the dog was killed. But since the girl in the train was called Lucy, poor Joan could still be suspected by the Inspector of this new act of cruelty. Blair had a feeling that the Inspector so read the riddle of "Laddy's" poisoning.

The inn, whose outside was apparently built of thatch and ivy, had a bedroom which he could have. The landlady looked at him rather sharply.

"We've got Miss Ingilby staying here with us," she announced pugnaciously, "the sister of that poor young lady as you hinted at in this morning's *Comet*, sir. At least, I'm told as you wrote that article?"

Blair acknowledged the authorship and waited.

"We're all on Miss Ingilby's side in the village," the landlady went on in a tone that suggested that Blair might not care to stay in the place even overnight.

Once again he explained his present opinion of that article. Her face softened.

"Well, of course, newspapers have to sell, don't they?" she murmured. "I'm from London myself, and what with the police wanting promotion..." She seemed to think that any further explanation of covert remarks was needless.

Blair found Joan sitting by the fire in the empty drawing-room. She looked a very forlorn little figure to him as he stood a moment in the doorway watching her. She was wondering about that diary—and the rector. On the whole, she decided to be silent about the extraordinary affair—for the present. She might have a chance of getting the book back again. In any case, there was probably nothing to be found within its covers that would throw any light on the murder.

Just then she glanced up, and a vainer young man than Blair might have felt his heart leap at the look that came over her face.

"I thought you were never coming! That awful Mr. Waddy walked all the way here with me. I thought I should never get rid of him. I hope he doesn't suspect that I'm not Joan's sister?" she whispered. They were not only alone in the room, which was at one end of a long wing of the building, but it was approached by a passage whose boards would have creaked even under the feet of a ghost.

"I'm sure he doesn't!" Blair reassured her. He was sure that Waddy had a certitude, not a suspicion, on that point. That silent laugh could have meant nothing else; but there was no need to tell Joan that, at least not yet awhile. He had so much else that would be a shock to her to tell her. He gave her a very frank account of the conversation after she had gone to the inn.

Joan bounded from her chair.

"He—this Monsieur Waddy accuses me of having stolen those emeralds?"

Blair wished that it had been possible for the Inspector to see her at this moment. Truth now and then speaks with an accent, a look which even the most prejudiced cannot but recognise. It so spoke here.

"Oh, it's too monstrous to speak of!"

Joan was seething, boiling, bubbling, yet she looked alarmed too. This was a second and distinct accusation. If persisted in it might prejudice people against her; people who even after the accusation of murder had remained her friends. There was, to anyone who had ever seen her, let alone talked to her, a certain grotesqueness about suspecting her of the worse crime. But those emeralds—.

She turned to Blair with imploring eyes.

"You're so clever, can't you see any light? Have you no idea on which we can work? It seems horrible to talk like this about people with whom I've lived for months, but I must! What motive can there be which would account for a crime? That's what staggers me. If one could only think of a motive, one could think of someone to whom it would point. But no one, no one gains anything by Mrs. Amcott's death."

"As far as we yet know," he corrected. "That's what Armstrong would say if he could hear you. And, after all, this is only the first day, remember!"

"The first day!" she repeated in a tone of horror. "The first day of my back to the wall—of wondering from second to second whether I've been discovered and am about to be arrested." She spoke with a fierce passion.

Her hand was on the arm of her chair. Stooping, Blair suddenly kissed it.

"And, of course, that dreadful man won't say that he saw me at the theatre, saw me on both evenings!" she went on in a tense voice.

Blair told her that both Monsieur Waddy and Hilary Amcott had owned up to this. She looked very surprised.

"Then there's a catch in it somewhere!" Still, she looked relieved.

"What about this Baroness de Maricourt, what's she like herself?" he asked after a pause.

"At first I thought her a jolly good sort. But latterly"— Joan bit her lip—"it's too utterly silly, but latterly I thought she was jealous of me, and because of that awful man!" Joan's look of scorn was eloquent.

"What's the relationship between her and Waddy?" was Blair's indiscreet question.

Joan's answer was, "Heaven knows!"

"You don't know anything about him? His antecedents? His family?"

"Nothing. I don't think I've spoken to him more than twice all told. And he dared to say that he admired Joan Ingilby!" Her finely-cut nostrils dilated with anger. "He claims to've been a friend of the late Baron de Maricourt. She says so too. Says that's how he became such a friend of the Amcotts. Certainly in town he seemed to know plenty of the right people."

"Satisfactory testimonial to his banking account, but to nothing much else, in the case of a good dancer, and a bachelor. Did Mrs. Amcott care for him? Before you spoke to her about him and his interest in the emeralds?" he asked.

"I don't think she liked him. But he tried tremendously to ingratiate himself with her—for the sake of the emeralds, I'm certain. It used to make 'Ty Maricourt, as they call her, furious."

"She was jealous?"

"I thought, so, though it was only an impression. Outwardly she and Mrs. Amcott were the closest of friends, but I used to think sometimes that secretly she hated Mrs. Amcott—as much as she apparently now hates me."

Blair thought again of those rose petal hands. Had they carried in that charcoal stove, the instrument of a slow but certain death?"

"And Mr. Grimshaw, the rector, was he a great friend of Mrs. Amcott's as well as of her husband?"

Joan hesitated.

"He was constantly in her sitting-room, and I often met her coming away from the rectory. But I think she was in some trouble of mind. Mr. Grimshaw is wonderfully popular in the village with everyone who knows him, and I always thought he fully deserved it."

"Don't you still?" he asked quickly.

She hesitated. Should she or should she not speak of that diary? But she had a plan by which to get that back; she would try that first.

The creaking of the floor outside announced the waiter, who wanted to know if he should bring the lady's black coffee into the room where they were. Blair asked for a cup for himself as well, and when they were alone again told Joan of the death of "Laddy." She gave a little cry of pity.

"I searched the kennel with my torch," he went on, "and found something that I don't suppose will be of any use. But you never know where a clue will turn up."

Hardly in a kennel, Joan thought, with some inward amusement at the idea. Blair caught her look, and agreed ruefully.

"I'm afraid so, especially as it seemed to be only a ticket of some kind—Spanish, I think."

The door opened, and the waiter brought in a tray with two cups on it.

"I must show it to the Inspector, of course," he went on, watching the man set it down near them, "though it is probably only a dud. However, I sent it on in my attaché case by a constable to the station. I'll drop in after this and see what Armstrong thinks. You might care to have a look at it too."

The door had closed, but opened immediately again. This time it was a message. Mr. Blair was wanted on the telephone.

He found it was from the sub-editor of the *Comet*. That paper utterly refused to print Blair's recantation of his theory of how Mrs. Amcott had been murdered, a recantation handed in just before Blair caught the express down to Elmhurst. Blair did his best, but it was no use.

Joan came out finally. Long telephone messages made her nervous just now, she said.

They had barely returned to the room and seated themselves again, when another telephone call came. This time it was she who was wanted.

"A kind message of sympathy from Dr. Pearson and his wife. The dears! They believe in Joan," she explained as she returned once more to her chair. "Our coffee certainly won't be too hot now. How nice for you to have waited for me."

She picked up her cup. The first taste went into her handkerchief.

"Mr. Blair, don't touch yours!" Her voice was hoarse with terror. Her face had blanched. It was twisted with fear. Her eyes had widened until the whites showed all around the big, distended pupils. Even her lips were white.

"It's been tampered with!" She stared at him as though stupefied. "Poisoned!" She gave a rattling gasp. "Oh, have you drunk any?"

He had not.

"Ask Mrs. Black, the landlady, for an empty bottle. She's down in the coffee-room, I know." Joan was recovering her nerve. "Ask her to have it well washed, and we'll pour this into it. It must be examined. I know it's been doctored in some way."

Blair could taste nothing amiss, though he took care not to swallow any of it. He thought it merely the local idea of black coffee. However, Joan's face was too ghastly to be argued with. He returned with a bottle, into which she carefully poured both their cups, corked it, and suggested going with it at once to the Inspector.

"What had we better do with the cups?" she whispered. "Suppose they poison the water in which they are washed?"

Blair thought her nerves were getting the upper hand, and no wonder! But he promptly settled that question by dashing both cups on to the stone hearth, where they lay pieces.

At the police station Blair found that the Inspector did not pooh-pooh Joan's terrors. For one thing, the girl was too obviously shaken by at least a conviction of a very close shave for that.

"We'd better let Dr. Pearson have a look at your bottle. Sensible of you to've brought it." Inspector Armstrong held it against the light while Blair was busy getting his attaché case out of the safe. He opened it, and hunted for the tag of paper found in the kennel. He was right that it was of no importance. It proved to be only a stall for some Spanish play got up and produced by the

Anglo-Spanish Society in London some two months before, which obviously must have lain for nearly that time in the kennel, and equally obviously could be of no use in assisting to solve the murder of Mrs. Amcott.

Joan could have told them, now she knew what it was, that Mrs. Amcott had taken the ticket intending to go, and then, on something better turning up, had thrown it away. But she must not seem omniscient.

She and Blair hurried to the doctor's house, where Blair handed in a note from the Inspector as well as the bottle. They had rather a long wait before Dr. Pearson returned, looking very grim, and gave Blair a note for the Inspector, adding that he was telephoning as well. Apparently he was unwilling to discuss the contents of the bottle.

"Let's hurry back," Joan begged. "I must know what was in that coffee. Whether I was right or, as you thought me, absolutely ridiculous."

Blair protested all the way to the police station that under no circumstances could such an idea ever occur to him.

The Inspector tore the letter open, though he knew its contents already.

"Was I right? Was there something in our coffee?" Joan asked, moistening her lips before she could speak.

"There was, Miss Ingilby. Same stuff as killed the dog. Arsenic. Good job you had your suspicions and didn't swallow that mouthful you took. I don't suppose it was meant for you, though I'm bound to say that the doctor says there was enough for three people. You must evidently be very careful. If it was meant for you, it looks as though you knew something or were in possession of something that might be dangerous to, or is wanted by, the murderer." He eyed her keenly.

Joan shook her head. She had closed her eyes with horror. She was still badly frightened.

"Perhaps it's something you're not aware of yourself?" he persisted.

But Joan declared that this was impossible. The Inspector thought a moment.

"The coffee may have been poisoned when it was first brought in," he thought. "But more likely something was dropped in when you and Mr. Blair were both out of the room at the telephone. Some distance away, as I happen to know. Now, who was in the inn at the time? There are strangers there. Just now, except some reporters, and they were at the coroner's, as I happen to know. They all lunched with him"

Blair thought of the rector, whom he had met, looking very grim, talking to Mrs. Black in her parlour, or rather listening, with an obviously absent mind, to Mrs. Black's cheerful chatter, but he did not bring down on himself the Inspector's ridicule by mentioning that now. Instead, he offered to see Joan back to the inn, but she refused.

She wanted quiet and a walk in the open air, she said. So Blair reluctantly saw her leave. He had a feeling that some danger hovered over her, not over him, and that it might strike any moment, even. in a well lit main street, even though he knew that a constable would follow her.

"Here is the report from the vet," the Inspector said as soon as they were alone.

Blair learnt from it that the Airedale had been poisoned by arsenic inserted in, or scattered over, liver. The dog must have swallowed it about noon, and crawled into his kennel to die.

"Extraordinary thing, this attempt on your lives. Or, rather, it was probably only meant for you, and an over dose put in. And yet—is it possible that Miss Ingilby knows something? If so, is she keeping it dark?"

Blair could only say that if Miss Ingilby knew anything that could help the case forward, obviously she would have told it.

"It's really her terror that frees her from the suspicion of having herself tried to poison you just now. But that wasn't acting; she's fairly sick with fright," the Inspector muttered.

Blair kept his seat by an effort.

"You see," the police officer went on, quite unconscious of the emotion rioting in Blair's every nerve, "if the two sisters aren't really in touch, Joan Ingilby wouldn't know that you've changed your point of view. I haven't. I still think that article of yours points straight to the truth. She might imagine that you're still of the same opinion."

Blair clenched his hands. He must seem academic in his manner. He must remain impersonal and calm.

"Damn that article of mine!" was his way of achieving these desirable ends.

The Inspector looked surprised.

"Sorry! Nerves," Blair explained, "and having it rubbed into me what a fool I made of myself in that final paragraph."

"From beginning to end," Armstrong said quietly, "I still maintain that yours is the best, most probable theory of how the murder was done that we've hit on so far. And there's another thought, though linked to the first. Miss Joan may be trying to sweep both you and Miss Lucy out of the way. Her sister's efforts to clear her may be the last thing that she wants; she may be embarrassing some further project of hers. And it was you who wrote that article, you know! Joan Ingilby will never forgive you that we may be sure. If she poisoned the dog, she may have tried to poison you two, singly or doubly. As long as Miss Lucy is down here, there's a risk that she may give her sister's whereabouts away. I only wish the risk were bigger than it seems to be!"

Blair checked an hysterical laugh. Joan trying to poison Lucy!

"Joan Ingilby is not the answer to this puzzle, Inspector. It's not any governess, but a much more subtle and dangerous combination."

"Possibly," the Inspector agreed politely. "Strange case this. Frankly, I don't like its looks, unless your theory of the governess is the right one, Mr. Blair. But for it, I see nothing but bog, and bog isn't my idea of a neat job."

"What about Mr. Ralph Amcott... was he ever entangled with any woman before or during his marriage?"

"I don't know about entangled. He was engaged to Mr. Grimshaw's sister before he married Miss Doris Norreys, as she was then. Miss Grimshaw turned him down after a very short trial. He's got a rare bad temper and she's none so meek herself either. She used to keep house for her brother in those days; since then she's taken to living with her people in Yorkshire."

"So she's free to marry him now, should she change her mind about his temper," Blair said ruminatingly. "This rector of yours interests me, Armstrong."

"So he does the ladies," chuckled Armstrong. "Oh, not his fault. He never gives any of 'em a second glance unless they come about church matters. He believes in celibacy. Some say he's half-way to Rome."

"Yet, a man at the inquest said he's always in hot water with his bishop because he's so High Church."

"Because he's so high-handed," Armstrong said at once. "Mr. Grimshaw will only follow Mr. Grimshaw's rules."

"Apart from that sort of thing, what's his personal rating in the village?"

"Nothing could be higher. You're not speculating on his having killed Mrs. Amcott, are you, Mr. Blair?" Armstrong spoke with all but open derision. "That's what I say about you newcomers, clever amateurs, or even Scotland Yard men. You all have to begin at the beginning as far as the characters of the people are concerned, while we can take things up where the crime commences."

"No, I'm not suggesting that the rector is a murderer," Blair said after a long pause, "but I have a feeling that he suspects someone. And, more than that—that he knows something which he doesn't want to tell."

"That's quite an idea," ruminated Armstrong. Suddenly he jumped. "By Jove, Mr. Blair, I shouldn't wonder if you're right again! Mr. Grimshaw has taken to confessions lately, and, being Christmas time, has rather made a point of them. It's amused most of the women immensely. There's nothing they like better, high or low, than a chance of 'a tell,' as they call it hereabouts, and especially when they can bring in all their neighbours' sins as well. Half the village has been to confession this last fortnight, and I understand that what's told in the confessional is dropped into the sea. Awkward for us, that. And there's nothing Mr. Grimshaw would like better than to be hauled over the coals for it. He loves a fight with his fists or his tongue. Oh, first-class boxer is our rector! And you should see him batting!" The Inspector was in the village Eleven, and glowed with admiration.

"How about the people at the manor? Do they go to confession?"

"I'll ask Hobbs, the verger. He's as great a gossip as any of us. That's one thing in this sort of a place—you can't stop to pat a kitten but all the village knows of it."

"Yet you can commit a murder and all but get away with it."

"For the time being," conceded the Inspector; "only for the time being."

Blair made no reply as he watched the lights shine through the window.

"I suppose Ralph Amcott really is ill, and in Khartoum?"

"He is. Very ill. There's no doubt of that whatever."

"And his character?"

"Clever. Very high-and-mighty manner. Supposed to have the devil of a temper, as I said, and altogether not to be over-pleasant to live with."

"Oh, don't weaken on the local gentry!" begged Blair.

"Surely an Amcott of Elmhurst can do no wrong."

The Inspector only looked amused.

"Well, I don't think they've done much wrong here, Mr. Blair. Not for all of Mr. Hilary Amcott's knuckling under to that French friend of his and lying to keep his family's name out of the papers; and also the account of how he spends his time."

"Waddy is a very queer friend, Inspector. Like draws like."

"Queer he is," the Inspector agreed. "The Chief Constable has been trying to look up the facts about him. We can't get hold of anything wrong—as yet. He lives the life of an ordinary man of means about town. Seen everywhere with the Baroness. He's her dancing partner. They seem to think no end of his dancing and skating at all the places where he goes. He first came to London—as far as we can find out—two years ago as a friend of Baron de Maricourt. He was a Baron all right—fine old French house." The Inspector had unlocked a drawer while talking, and now drew out a number of long slips.

"What are you doing?" Blair asked.

"Looking up the time-tables of the different people connected with Elmhurst."

The Inspector placed the long slips in a row. Blair came and looked over his shoulder. He noted that Mr. Grimshaw had been spoken to by one of his constable parishioners on Tuesday night about midnight in a lane which led away from the manor house. He pointed it out with the stem of his pipe now.

"He had been working late at the. Boys' Institute over at Welldene. He has the keys of the manor gates, given him by the squire, they say, when he appointed him to the living. He might have seen something.... but in that case, not being a confession... still, Mr. Grimshaw is a law unto himself. Anyway, I'll get it out of him in time if he knows anything."

Blair was deep in his own thoughts, too deep to cast any doubt on the Inspector's ability to bring forth that which the rector preferred should remain hidden.

"Sure there's no gossip linking Mr. Grimshaw's name with Mrs. Amcott?" he said finally.

"None whatever as far as I know, and I hear everything sooner or later. Some do say that he was thinking of taking her along with him over to Rome. But only spiritually, Mr. Blair, only spiritually!"

The two parted on that. On the way back to the inn, Blair ran into the very man they were discussing. The rector stepped forward eagerly.

"What good luck to meet! It's about that article of yours in this morning's *Comet* that I wanted to see you. I didn't want to talk before Armstrong. Are you sure of your facts?" He flashed a knife-like look at Blair.

"The presumed facts? Possibly, though I've learnt something that shakes my belief even in them. But my theorising, my final winding-up"—Blair laughed carelessly—"utter rot! Purest rubbish!" was his verdict.

Mr. Grimshaw still eyed him.

"The reporters, who all rushed down here after it came out, are all convinced by it. So, I understand, are the police..."

"A second examination of the witnesses' statements has made me absolutely certain that the governess had no hand in the murder, as I hinted in the conclusion of that article," Blair said patiently.

"A second glance at her face would have told you as much, and been quicker." Grimshaw seemed to speak with genuine heartiness. "Though. I'm bound to say you made that article very convincing, statements and hints alike."

"Trick of the trade," Blair muttered contemptuously.

"Yet you still believe Mrs. Amcott was murdered?" Grimshaw seemed now to find a sudden interest in his pipe. "There's no doubt of that, none whatever; and in somewhat the way I mentioned."

"Do the police still agree with you? About Mrs. Amcott's death, I mean?"

"Absolutely."

There was a silence.

Mr. Grimshaw's face seemed to stiffen.

"Terrible thought. She's gone, but the crime remains. What is the motive supposed to be?" The tone was casual enough, too casual, Blair thought, to go with the brightness of the eye.

"Motive is the deuce and all in this sort of a case, isn't it?" he said vaguely. "Nothing adequate has turned up so far—to my knowledge."

"It's a dreadful thought... I mean the possibility of any human being committing such a sin." Grimshaw spoke in a low voice, though they had the road to themselves. "A man —called to the high destiny to which men are called... 'Which was the son of Adam. Which was the son of God.'... Perhaps the murderer has repented already. That would make a great deal of difference... Instant repentance..."

There was a pause. Blair said nothing.

"I wonder, too, what poor little Joan Ingilby, is feeling. You didn't know her, of course?"

"Heaven forgive me!" Blair said fervently, if a trifle incoherently. "Fortunately her sister came at once to me about my article. She read into it what I meant clearly enough."

"Like everyone else," Grimshaw threw in.

"Naturally she was—well, more than indignant. I'm doing what l can to atone, if one can atone for such a blunder. She is staying down here until the murderer is found and her sister cleared."

"Jolly plucky of her," murmured the parson appreciatively, yet absent-mindedly. "So you think that no motive has been found yet? It's rather early to tell, isn't it?"

"I suppose so. I wondered if you could help us." Blair shot a swift glance at his companion under cover of suddenly relighting his pipe.

Again came that stiffening of the features. This time more clearly to be seen. There was a wary look in the parson's eyes as he turned them on Blair.

"I? In what way?"

"You were out late on Tuesday night. Did you happen to see anyone moving about in or near the manor house as you passed it?"

"Surely you do not suppose that if I had I would not have told the police as much this morning?" Mr. Grimshaw looked at him with an effect of great surprise, a rebuking glance.

"You might have kept silence because of—many reasons," Blair said stubbornly. "You parsons have to keep so many things to yourself, that you might—might—have kept one more."

"I think the poisoning of the dog may help us all on to the right track," Grimshaw went on as though the other's question had been answered and done with. "His having been killed looks as though that outsider wanted to be sure that he would be unmolested, for, of course, 'Laddy' would go for any outsider."

"And would not go for any insider, which might have been equally betraying."

"You mean?"

"That he's as likely to have been killed by some friend who didn't want him following him around as by some outsider who wanted to prevent his barking," and Blair shook hands and turned back to the inn.

The rector was deep. Something lay behind that carefully careless questioning. The point was, what?

Blair knew, of course he knew, that not one of us is snatched suddenly from our complex modern lives without leaving a host of ragged ends behind us. In his own mind he placed Hilary Amcott's sinister-faced friend as the chief criminal, even though, in some cunning way he had avoided being actually in the place when the crime was committed. Could a fuse have been laid? Could Joan have mistaken some brother or disguised friend for

Waddy? But why should Mr. Grimshaw want to shield Waddy?

To his surprise he met Joan coming towards him. She was now feeling better, and had been for a stroll, she said. She did not add that it had been to the rectory, where she had rung, and, finding that Mr. Grimshaw was out, had boldly asked for the "purple-bound book that belonged to Mrs. Amcott." She had described it well, with its gilt edges and gilt lock. The maid, though quite without any suspicion of her, had first replied that she had never seen such a book, and then that she knew every one of her master's books, as they were always all over the place. "Purple leather, you say? I never saw such a book here in the rectory, never. If you're sure it wasn't some kind of a prayer-book? Mr. Grimshaw gets them given him of all colours."

Joan assured her it was not a prayer-book, thanked her, and walked away. She had failed. However, like the Inspector, she hoped that, given time enough, she might yet get that purloined book back, with its possibly invaluable contents, and possibly damning ones, else why had the rector taken it away? But if so, what on earth was his motive? She did not turn in at the little hostelry, a fact which greatly disappointed young Blair. But Joan wanted to see Baroness Maricourt without delay and question her about the alleged missing emeralds. She found, however, that the young widow and Waddy were both out. Then could she see Mr. Hilary Amcott?

She was shown into the same room as before. It was the study of the absent lord of the manor, a room that Joan had always disliked for its darkness and bareness and the number of slaughtered deer heads and masks and brushes that "decorated" it.

Just now Hilary was standing by the huge fireplace; as he turned she wondered if it was the play of the flames that for a second gave his face something vaguely menacing, secretly malignant, even, it seemed to her, unappeasingly hostile. Another moment and she wondered how she could have imagined such nonsense, for as he stepped into the full light she saw only his usual silly grin and vacant eyes that blinked at her out of a puffy, pallid face.

He greeted her with the empty cackle that she knew so well.

"At a loose end already?" he asked in a voice that sounded very unsympathetic.

"It's about Joan," she said, taking a chair with its back to the light like his own, instead of the one he placed for her. "Of course—in strict confidence—I have ways of letting her know about things down here. Now she's frightfully distressed for fear people should get to know about the trouble she had on Saturday with Mrs. Amcott."

"Indeed!" was Amcott's only and very indifferent reply.

Joan stiffened. She stared at him. What had changed him so? He had always acted as though devoted to her. She must know where she stood with him.

"It was about you," Joan said bluntly. "Mrs. Amcott thought that Joan and you had been seeing too much of each other."

Hilary gave a rather fatuous grin. Joan longed to shake him.

"Can she be sure that nothing will be said by you about that?" she went on instead. "As far as she knows, only you know of it."

She looked at him closely. Had he talked about it? Did Monsieur Waddy know of that rift between herself and her late employer that might be twisted to her detriment? Did the Baroness know?

"Your sister's been pulling your leg," Amcott said rudely. "We all think that Mrs. Amcott let her go because she wanted a Roedean girl as governess for the child. If I were you, Miss Ingilby, I shouldn't try to suggest anything else. It might only lead to trouble, like the dog being loose down here."

"Like the dog..." she repeated, bewildered.

"He was evidently one too many. Somebody thought they could bear to do without him apparently," was the callous reply. Or was it something more than that, much more?

Suddenly Joan felt afraid of Hilary Amcott—a formless, and as far as she knew, baseless fear.

"Joan thought you were a friend of hers!" she said in a low voice.

"Very kind of her." Hilary gave his silly giggle. "I'm afraid I can hardly presume to that position." He glanced patently at his French novel.

"'You mean you're not on her side?" the girl pressed. She wanted some explanation of the amazing change in the man. "You see, Mr. Amcott, that article in this morning's *Comet* practically accused my sister of the crime."

"Well, I said I saw her at the theatre," he said as though dismissing the subject—and the sister. "Jolly decent of me to volunteer that much!"

"But it was the truth! Naturally you'd tell the truth!" There was amazement and indignation in her voice.

"Anyway, it saved her. You tell her to be content with that."

"But—but—it's not a question of your doing anything for her; it's merely that she wants to know who thinks her innocent and who doesn't."

"Look here," he said reaching for his book. (What a boor the, man was, she thought.) "You tell your sister that Monsieur Waddy and I will stand by her as long as she keeps quiet—and hidden! But she's not to come down here and stir things... up, or she'll find she has to settle with us." His puffy lids lifted to let him give her a cold glance from pale grey eyes all criss-crossed with red veins—a glance that sent a shiver through Joan. It was a menace.

"Us?" she asked, rising, but he seemed not to hear the low; perplexed repetition.

"Anything I can do to help my friends," he said lightly. "Monsieur Waddy I mean by that, see?"

"And Joan thought you liked her! She thought she could count on you," the girl murmured.

"Let her count on Waddy and she can count on me." Hilary Amcott said succinctly. "But remember! No coming down here herself to rout things out—and stir the police up!" He spoke... very low, but with remarkable firmness for him.

"You mean that you wouldn't help her if she came herself and appealed to you?" she asked gently.

Hilary Amcott was at the door.

"Better not try it!" he said with a silly chuckle. Something in it drove the colour from her cheeks. She passed on through the hall without another word. The man was an enemy. Open and yet secret. "Acting on instructions received," as official papers said. Acting on Monsieur Waddy's instructions without a doubt.

As she walked away the man she so loathed and Baroness Maricourt were discussing her. They had returned while she was in Sir Christopher's study.

"You go too far in accusing the governess of Mrs. Amcott's murder," Monsieur Waddy was saying for about the tenth time, and with vigour. "You'll get yourself into trouble if you don't look out."

"What trouble?" snapped Ty.

He only looked at her.

"Oh," she shrugged pettishly, "you and your anxiety over Joan Ingilby! If you dislike her as much as you claim to, why do you care what I say about her?"

"Because I care about you," Waddy said, trying to take her hand, but she pulled it away, and began to set out on a table a little roulette wheel.

"The servants won't know, and as we can't go to any clubs for a few evenings we'll do as last night and play here. Heaven be on my side tonight." She spoke as though heaven were not always to be found there. "I can't afford to be unlucky again. Hilary won seventy pounds from me."

"You'll win it back from him at cards," Waddy said consolingly.

She nodded.

"Judging by his cards, he must be the luckiest man in love in the world, I should think," she said lightly as she left the room.

A minute later the door was flung open and Hilary rushed in. His eyes, like his hair, were wild.

"I've just seen Ralph! What the devil does he mean spying on me like this?"

"You've seen your brother?" Waddy's face went white, or rather pale yellow. "You're drunk!"

"I'll thank you not to be insulting," Hilary said with a weak man's sputter. "He was just slipping down the east corridor away from my room."

"And towards mine!" Monsieur Waddy was out of the room in an instant. He was away some time. When he came back he stood frowning and clenching his thin fingers and muttering to himself until Hilary hurried in again, still looking very much upset.

"I all but caught him! What the devil does he mean slinking around like that and spying on me? Did you see him?"

Waddy nodded. "I did. *Shi mahul!*" he muttered under his breath. And when Waddy broke into Arabic, or rather Cairene, he was indeed perturbed. "I thought he was ill in Khartoum." He turned his face towards Hilary, and seemed to stare hard at him.

"So did I!" echoed Hilary. "That, of course, is what he wanted me to think! But why should Ralph slink around like a burglar? Here, let's question the servants!" He strode, not oversteadily, towards the bell, but Waddy stopped him with a leap like a panther's.

"Don't be hasty. This is a serious matter. Your brother found hiding in the house where his wife was murdered!

This needs thinking over. I wonder if the rector knows... he's your brother's great friend, isn't he?"

Hilary's mouth opened, and stayed open, as he nodded feebly.

"Good lord!" he muttered, "you don't think... oh, rot! Ralph's spying on me, that's all. And as for Grimshaw... you think he's putting Ralph up at the rectory and letting him lie low there? It's only just across the park... but that's tosh. I think..."

"I think your brother is the answer to the riddle that's been puzzling us," Waddy said darkly, "if he's over here and not in the Sudan."

"How can Ralph be an answer to a riddle?" Hilary tittered foolishly.

"The riddle of your sister-in-law's murder," snapped Waddy. "The point is, what should we do?" He bit his nails deep in thought.

"But Ralph... why should he hurt Doris..." Bleated Hilary, goggling.

"Jealousy, you fool!"

"Not so much fool, if you please." Hilary again attempted, with marked unsuccess, an air of dignity. "I think you forget sometimes..."

"Oh, cut it out!" Waddy said shortly. "The point is your brother's secret arrival. I thought he was ill. There was a notice to that effect in *Al Mokattam* last week. They wrote of him as all but at death's door."

"I wish he were!" came unfeelingly from Hilary. "But you did see him, didn't you?" He asked this last a little shamefacedly. "It wasn't imagination on my part?"

"No, it was your brother," Waddy said between his teeth. "I saw his back."

"And I his face. He glared at me like a devil." Hilary touched his forehead, as though it were suddenly wet.

"Damn him!" came from Waddy, and was followed by some Arabic curses.

"I say!" Hilary bridled, "I can swear at my brother, for I've cause to. But you haven't any cause to curse him. And I don't..."

"If he's after you, that's quite enough for me, Hilary." Waddy spoke with a heartiness that went ill with his eyes. It seemed to touch Hilary.

"You're a good chap, Waddy," he murmured gratefully.

"There's no doubt he murdered his wife," Waddy went on. "I say, there's no doubt," he repeated as Hilary opened a protesting mouth. "The point is, shall we try and get hold of him ourselves, or shall we put the police on his track?"

"I think I see myself doing either!" muttered Hilary. "You don't know Ralph! He's a devil when he's in a rage. Doesn't care what he does. And he's as strong as an ox. Staying with Grimshaw you think... Look here, I'm off! He's come home because of that bill I told you of, the bill I—eh—had to get accepted. Anyone whom Ralph has it in for is a fool to stay. We'll go to Mentone. Jack Thynne's yacht is still there, and it's only ten minutes from Monte. I'll 'phone to Cook's for tickets now. Air, I suppose?"

"I'm not going to be frightened away by your brother," Waddy said in a none too steady voice. "I'm staying on. You asked me down here till New Year and I shall stay till then. If not here, then at the inn. I've made all my plans, and I don't intend to shift them. And as for you— you can't leave, my dear fool. Not till it's been found out who did the murder. Not till your brother's been caught, in other words."

"And have him tell them out that bill?" Hilary snapped. He was shaking in his chair. "Besides, he would kill us before the police could get to him. I know Ralph. I—I think we must say nothing about his being here and just slip away ourselves —fade out."

"I've said that I'm not going." Waddy spoke with an effort, but doggedly. "I promised 'Ty to get her emeralds back for her, and I won't fail her."

"What a good chap you are, Waddy!" Hilary said again. "I don't know what we'd do without you. If you stay—well, I'll stay too. But"—he looked very frightened—"I wish I knew what Ralph was up to. His face—you see I saw it—wasn't the face you like to meet in a dark passage, brother or no brother!" He broke off at Hilary's air of listening to something. "What is it? Do you hear him coming this way?" Quite patently Hilary looked around for cover

"Who's ringing like that? Has 'Ty's bell stuck?" Waddy asked sharply, opening the door. But before he could step into the hall the ringing stopped. A moment later 'Ty Maricourt came running downstairs looking extremely indignant.

"Is this supposed to be a joke? Which of you two locked me into my bedroom just now? The servants had their hall door shut. I thought I'd never make them hear me."

"Locked you into..." began Hilary with round eyes.

His friend laid a hand on his arm and pinched it hard.

"I did it, 'Ty," he confessed. "Hilary and I had a bet on as to who could run down the east wing and round by the loggia and back here first. I didn't want to collide with you and break your or my legs on the stairs."

"Winning that bet must have been easy money for you," 'Ty said with a glance at Hilary's shrunk figure, "though a couple of years ago you might have found your match. But Hilary's shockingly out of condition, from these late hours we all keep. Nearly as much as out of pocket. But now let's have a few minutes' amusement for goodness' sake." She moved towards the table, and the two others followed her.

CHAPTER SIX

AS a sleeper counts time, it was that same night, though in reality it was just before dawn next morning, when Blair was waked by something being pulled over his head. It was a felt bag with an elastic edge that gathered in tight around his neck, stifling his shouts and all but smothering him. He had no chance to do more than touch it with startled fingers before a noose of furniture-webbing was slipped over his body—he had sat up in bed with the first shock of surprise—down to his elbows and drawn tight. An end went round his knees. Within the minute he was neatly and completely, trussed.

He tried to shout louder. Instantly another piece of felt on another stout elastic was slipped over the bag and the whole held so close against his mouth that for a second he was smothered. A pair of short quills were thrust from the outside into his nostrils. He could breathe now, but make no sound. This was not a first performance. He was in experienced hands. He listened as best he could. His room was being searched, more than that he could not tell. After what seemed to him nearly an hour he himself was searched with the utmost care by hands that seemed made of smooth steel. Then he was hoisted on to the carpeted floor and his bed evidently minutely examined.

Finally he heard the key put into the lock, fumed, and then a snap of what must have been razor-edged shears cut through one strap around his legs. The next instant the door was shut, and he heard the key turned from the outside.

It took Blair at least half an hour to get his arms free and to fling off the gag and felt bag. Then he jumped for the switch; it refused to connect with his lights.

He pressed the bell, it did not ring. He shouted and pounded on the panels. No one seemed to hear. He and Joan were the only visitors in the inn as far as he knew.

Some reporters had tried to get rooms, but the landlady had declared that she had none to let. Joan had begged her not to let them stay in the house, and had accompanied the begging by a handsome "make weight," as Mrs. Black called it. There was a door at the end of his corridor, probably it had now been shut. Blair had chosen his room because he could see Joan's windows from it— she had been put in the corresponding wing—and also because it offered an easy descent to the ground if need be by means of a thick trunk of ivy just beside his casement.

He was half way across to that particular window now, intending to use nature's ladder, when he saw something dark slip from Joan's window, something dark—it was a man—let itself down by the brick work and creepers, and, as he jumped to his own window ledge, something dark melt like a solid shadow into the garden, and be instantly swallowed up in the blackness. At that moment his foot found the key of his bedroom door. It had been tossed onto his window ledge out of sight behind a curtain. The intruder must have had his own pass key.

As he grabbed it, he heard the faint click of the garden gate. Instantly Blair had his door open and was out in the corridor. He would have liked to catch the man, but first of all he must know if Joan were all right.

He hurried down the corridor that led to her room. There was no light in it, as there should have been, no light under her door either. He listened; all was silent. He tapped gently until he heard a low "Who is there?" It sounded reassuringly sleepy.

"Me—Martin Blair. Are you all right?" he whispered through the crack. She opened at once and peered out at him, rubbing her eyes as though he might be a dream.

Another moment and she came out wrapped in her green dressing-gown. He whispered to her what had happened. The whole affair was too grave, in his opinion, to hide things from her. She darted back into her room with a gesture that asked him to wait. She came out again in a moment or two looking disturbed.

"Someone's been searching through all my things. Not that they're many," she whispered. "To think of that dreadful man in my room! At this hour! Turning over my dressing-case!" Blair did not wonder that she gave a little choked exclamation. He felt choked too. "Luckily I keep my wig on even at night," she murmured after looking up and down the little corridor, but all the house was asleep.

"What man? Who was it?" he asked.

"Waddy, of course. Monsieur Waddy!" she answered with., out a second's hesitation.

Martin was not so sure of his visitor's identity. For one thing, the monsieur did not look as if he had muscles of such steel as those wrists that had knotted the webbing around Blair; for another, just as the bag went over his head, in other words, just as he waked, he now remembered a scent of peat-smoked Harris tweed, and a smell of an old pipe and of a very fragrant tobacco. Now there was nothing about Waddy to suggest any of these things. Harris tweed is not a French fashion, and Waddy did not look like a pipe smoker.

"And what would Monsieur Waddy be after?" he asked Joan slowly.

"The emeralds of course."

"But I thought you believed that he had stolen them?" Blair expostulated.

She nodded. "So I did. But from his words this afternoon, and now this visit to me and to you—makes me sure that they've been stolen from him again. He thinks evidently that I have them, or have perhaps given them to you to keep. And as I'm absolutely sure that he stole them, there's no other explanation that will reconcile the two."

Joan shivered, not from the cold, for it was a warm corner where they stood by a heater. Even country inns have heaters in their halls in this year of grace.

"You're cold?" he asked solicitiously. He himself could have stood talking to her in a snow storm and not felt it.

She shook her head.

"Frightened," she said, and fell silent. And that silence rammed the word home as no additional explanations would have done.

"Of him?"

She made a very helpless gesture and crept closer.

"I have an idea that he knows I'm Joan Ingilby," she whispered. "It's an idea that's been growing stronger the more I think it over. And if he hasn't denounced me to the police, it's because he's waiting for a good chance or for something. That something can only be to get the emeralds from me." She closed her eyes and leant half against the wall, half against his arm. "It would be no use swearing to him that I haven't got them, that I don't steal." She gave a little half sob.

"It's fixed in his mind that I've got what he wants, and, in my belief, unless he learns where they are, he'll go to any lengths to make me give him what I haven't got.

"Oh, why did I ever come to this horrible manor house? Why did I ever take the post with Mrs. Amcott? I should never have met him then, never have been dragged into this awful position! I know he's planning something, and if he thinks I have the emeralds he'll stick at nothing. Oh, Martin, I'm so afraid of him. I'm bound and gagged because of..." She swallowed a sob.

"Of my article!" Blair finished her sentence to himself. It was true.

"I feel as if he would sell his soul for that necklace!" she muttered.

"Sell his soul?" Blair tried to raise a smile on her pale cheeks, a pallor not entirely due to that stuff in the bottle which he had bought for her. "Chaps like that don't have souls to offer!"

"I'd give mine to make him slip up on whatever it is he's planning!" she said with sudden fire, and on the instant was gone.

In the morning he asked casually about the house dog. He was told by Mrs. Black that "Hero" was reliable, but a glutton that no amount of training could teach to pass food by.

"But he evidently went the rounds all right last night," that unsuspecting woman wound up, "for he's snoring like a house a-fire this morning. Won't even wake for breakfast, and he loves porridge and milk, does 'Hero.' Mr. Grimshaw told me I ought to leave some mustard done up in liver around to give him a lesson," Mrs. Black went on. "He found 'Hero' dreadfully sick one day when he called in after a day with the hounds, but as I told him, what's the good? It would take more than mustard to stop 'Hero' from gobbling up anything he found, short of poison there's nothing would cure him," and with that she moved off.

Blair had already decided that 'Hero' had had a free supper last night provided by someone who knew of his fondness for good things.

The funeral was at eleven. Blair went by himself; so did Joan.

When it was over Miss Norreys touched her on the arm. Miss Henrietta Norreys was the dead woman's aunt.

"Get into my car; I want to talk to you," was that lady's peremptory yet somewhat kindly way of opening the conversation. "With those bare legs of yours you'll freeze. It's like being at a Highland gathering to see all you young things with your kilts above your knees. I don't know how you stand it. In December!"

"One has to wear what one can buy," Joan murmured meekly.

"Quite so. And, of course, the less stuff they give you for your money, the more dressmakers and tailors put in their own pockets," the old lady said tartly. "I refuse to be swindled." Certainly her garments left no seamstress anything to hope for in the way of spare breadths or inches off the hem. "I won't look as though I had jumped out of bed on an alarm of fire. But now about your sister. I liked Joan. She's quite unlike you."

Joan laughed. She could not help it. Miss Norreys pricked up her ears.

"You both laugh alike."

"Our voices are alike," Joan said equably. "No one can tell us apart when we're talking."

Miss Norreys nodded absent-mindedly.

"What's she going to do?" she asked bluntly. You could be blunt on Miss Norreys's income.

"I know what I'm going to do," said Joan with spirit, "and that's clear her."

"Easily said, but easily done?" Miss Norreys asked a trifle grimly.

"How would you begin?" Joan asked after a pause that had something a little forlorn about it.

"By getting the best private detective down, or by insisting on the Chief Constable putting the affair into the hands of Scotland Yard," the old lady replied decidedly.

"I'm not in a position to do either," Joan said, biting her lip. "Not money enough for the first—not influence enough for the second."

"I'm ready to help you to do either. I mean it," the old woman replied to Joan's little look of inquiry. "I'm very sorry for your sister. It's an awful position for the poor child."

Joan's eyes filled. She always responded to sympathy. "You—you are kind!" she murmured brokenly.

"Not at all—merely just. I've had an easy life myself; I don't say it's been any the happier on that account. There's lots of fun to be got out of winning a stiff fight; but I've never had one, and, illogically enough, I'm always sorry for young women who are up against things. Now which will you choose? The finest detective in England, or the affair in the hands of Scotland Yard?"

Joan took plenty of time to think over her answer. There was something to be said both ways. But at last she made up her mind.

"I think Scotland Yard is cleverer than any private agency."

"Of course they are!" Miss Norreys agreed. "But"—she cocked a very shrewd eye, bright as a blue glass marble, at her companion—"not all the king's horses nor all the king's men can stop them once they start. Have you thought of that?"

Joan sat up rigidly.

"Tut-tut!" Miss Norreys laid a plump white hand on the nearest silk knee under the fur rug. "Now, now, don't get cross! After all, you're only Joan's sister, you know, not her soul. And only the soul of Joan Ingilby knows whether she did kill my niece or not."

"*I* know she didn't!" Joan said with a conviction that brought another squeeze.

"It's natural that you should feel like that. But what I want you to think of is this; would Joan be equally sure? Mind you, frankly, I shall get the Yard into it in any case, but, at least, you wouldn't be the one to have set the hounds on your own sister's trail; they're bloodhounds, my child, after all. You and I, thank God, are apt to think of the police as protectors, helpers—I'm sure I don't know when we fat old women would get across a street but for them—but they're not protectors nor helpers to the evil-doers."

"My sister isn't an evil-doer," the girl beside her said indignantly, but in a voice that quivered, try though she would to keep it steady. The bloodhounds were to be set on her own trail, and it had seemed a very straight course to Blair's reasoning. They, too, might follow that article. But, on the other hand, they might help her. In any case, she must chance it, for Miss Norreys had just said that she would bring in Scotland Yard in any case, and Joan felt that she would. No one could rest until the murder was cleared up, let alone a relative of the murdered woman.

"Miss Norreys, surely you don't believe that Joan had any part in a murder?" she asked piteously, cowering away a little from the word.

"Certainly not," was the reassuring and instant answer, "but one has to speak of possibilities. And now we'll never refer to that as one again. So it's to be Scotland Yard. I'll drive straight to Captain Parry's house. I hoped you would choose as you have done."

"But, Miss Norreys," Joan said slowly, "what about... The Amcotts are all relatives of yours, aren't they?"

"Distant. I hardly know 'em. Yes. Well?"

"Well, doesn't what you said to me—about putting the bloodhounds on the trail of one's own people—apply to the manor too? Someone in the household killed Mrs. Amcott, so the police maintain. I know that Joan didn't. Then who did?"

"My dear," the old lady said in a very quiet voice, "there's no murderer at the manor house. Belonging there, I mean. Take each one. The squire? What does he gain? Nothing. He loses the weekly six guineas which Ralph and Doris Amcott paid for their wing. As to Mr. Hilary Amcott, he strikes me nowadays as quite incapable of thinking out a clever murder. Once he had brains enough for anything, but now—. Could he have juggled with that bath-chair and so on? No. I'm afraid not. I mean afraid form the point of view of brains. No, it wasn't Mr. Hilary. Then there's my other niece, Felicity de Maricourt. She gets nothing out of Mrs. Ralph Amcott's death, except an emerald necklace the like of which she could buy—well, if not every year, then every two years. Nor is she fond of jewellery, no Norreys is; personally I always wear imitations, and not too good imitations either. I don't intend to be robbed or killed because a man mistakes cathedral glass for the real thing. But where was I?"

"Going through the people at the manor," Joan said with a glint in her eye.

"Well, that's all there are, apart from that quiet young Frenchman, Mr. Hilary's friend. I talked with him before the funeral. Really, for so young a man, a foreigner and a Roman Catholic—poor fellow—his ideas on the revision of the Prayer Book are quite sound. He shared with me my feelings about the omission of the King's name. But, apart from his own character, like Mr. Hilary it seems that he was away from the manor house the night of my niece's death. No, my dear child, I think the crime is the work of a servant, perhaps of a discharged one. Someone who knew of the emerald necklace, and did not realise how impossible such things are to sell. Or else—I don't think the police have dwelt enough on the point after all, Mrs. Amcott's husband is in the Sudan. Doubtless he has antagonised some of the natives there, perhaps a priest of one of their fanatical religions, and I've understood that they never forgive, and will go to any lengths to revenge themselves. I remember when I was young how *The Moonstone...* But here we are at the Chief Constable's."

Captain Parry listened quietly to Miss Norreys.

"We are quite satisfied with our present arrangements," he said finally, and, to the old lady's amazement and indignation, not all her rather peremptory requests could get a more definite reply.

"And we will see about a private detective at once," she said to her companion on coming out.

"I think the Chief Constable has something up his sleeve." Joan said wisely, and counselled patience because of that.

Blair had paired with the Inspector, as soon as Joan had been whizzed off by Miss Norreys. The two men tramped back. in silence to the station. Blair was thinking of the look of sorrow on Joan's face as the coffin was lowered. The Inspector broke the silence.

"That sort of a funeral is a reproach to us, and we feel it as that. Shouldn't have happened. Should have been prevented somehow."

"Couldn't have been," Blair said comfortingly. He liked Armstrong.

"No. But should have been, just the same." The Inspector pulled at his moustache.

"No clues turned up yet?" Blair asked. He had already told the Inspector of the strange incident of last night.

"Clues? There aren't any in this case, Mr. Blair. All other ideas but the one you first worked out end in smoke. The parson knows nothing. I never thought he did. I wish we could lay our hands on Miss Ingilby—the real one, the governess. This one hasn't written her a line, nor sent her a message of any kind, as far as we know. I thought at first we should soon run the other sister to earth by means of this one. To tell the truth, that's why I welcomed her coming down here, but she's too clever!"

"Or too frightened," Blair said softly.

"No need to be frightened unless you're guilty," the Inspector said cheerily. "If Miss Joan comes forward and gives us a clear statement that we can verify of her actions from Saturday to Tuesday, she would be out of all trouble, and we should have one suspect, and in my opinion more than suspect scratched. You get that idea into Miss Lucy's pretty head, Mr. Blair. Nice young lady, Miss Lucy. You see if you can't get her to pass what I've said on to her sister. Oh, not as a trap! If Miss Joan can't come forward, then it's because she can't think of anything to say that'll hold water."

Blair was silent.

"Unless, of course, that other theory of yours is strong enough to be let out?" The Inspector eyed him hopefully.

"That coat last night smelled exactly like one that is hanging in a cupboard outside the manor smokeroom. I got a chance this morning to lose my way a bit," Blair said after a pause.

"And?"

Blair did not continue. He must have something more to go on than a coat. But there was a suspicion growing up in his mind that might yet give him a real basis on which to work.

"There's the rector! I'll press him again as to any suspicious characters that he's seen about here. Though mark you, Mr. Blair, Miss Ingilby, the governess, is the clue we're after by rights."

"You might ask him at the same time if he poisoned the dog at the manor house and doped the one at the inn," Blair suggested casually.

The Inspector gave his hearty laugh.

"I think I see Mr. Grimshaw doing either! Miss Dallas, that's a young lady friend of Baroness Maricourt's, told me just now that she was coming in to see me at my station as soon as she can get there on the quiet—has something to say. So you might drop in too. I'll hurry back."

Miss Dallas did not keep them waiting long. The Inspector had barely got back and reported another blank as far as the rector's observations were concerned, when she arrived, looking both determined and uncomfortable.

"I heard a rumour at the funeral that Mrs. Amcott's emerald necklace is missing," she began hurriedly. "The Norreys necklace, I mean."

"It is," Armstrong agreed.

"And that it's said that Miss Ingilby, the governess, had something to do with its disappearance?" This last was a question.

"So we were told."

"Is it—I suppose it's important?"

"It's not the principal accusation, but it seems to point very definitely to her as Mrs. Amcott's murderess," Armstrong confided. He was looking at her very keenly.

"Oh, surely not!" Octavia turned an agitated face to his calm one. "Joan Ingilby never murdered Mrs. Amcott.

But isn't this the author of the article in yesterday's *Comet*, saying that she did?"

She had not noticed Blair before, and the Inspector had "forgotten" to introduce him. He repaired the omission with many apologies. Octavia looked at him with grave eyes.

"It was awfully clever, terribly clever that article of yours, but you were all wrong as to Joan Ingilby having anything to do with Mrs. Amcott's death."

"I'm sure I am," Blair said gladly. "I, too, know that now." She looked calmer.

"I'm so glad to hear you say that. I was afraid you might be prejudiced. And I know Joan Ingilby is innocent."

Blair liked her on the instant, liked her as much as saw that the Inspector did, who, as he rightly guessed, had known her from a child.

"You know she is innocent?" Armstrong asked. "How do you mean, Miss Dallas?"

"Because I know she wouldn't hurt a fly. But as to the emeralds—I have something to tell you about that necklace. It won't clear poor Joan, but you ought to know that I met Mrs. Amcott last Saturday in Salisbury, and we came home in the train together. She told me, among other things, that she had just that morning lent the Norreys necklace to Baroness Maricourt; had got it from the Bank in order to let her have it to wear at the French Embassy ball that night."

The Inspector asked a few questions, but she could add nothing material to her statement.

"Did you ever hear that Miss Ingilby was found tampering with the lock of the trunk in which the necklace was at one time kept?" the Inspector asked when the other matter was finished.

"I heard that she caught her scarf on it," Octavia said quickly, "and had to go down on her knees to get it free. I suppose that is the time you mean? But I never heard any suggestion as to her having... oh, how horrid of people to cook up such untruthful stories! Doris, Mrs. Amcott, told me herself that she had torn her stockings on it in passing more than once."

Again the Inspector went into details and dates and hours.

"Miss Dallas," Blair said, when this too was over, "I wish you could explain something that puzzles me. To what were the strained relations due that obviously existed between Mrs. Amcott and her brother-in-law, Mr. Hilary Amcott? They seem to have been barely on speaking terms."

Octavia hesitated. "You see," Blair went on, "I need every help that can be give me if I can put right the harm done to the absent governess by that unfortunate article of mine. And I consider this quite an important point. I do really."

"Well"—Octavia evidently was no gossip, but she obviously intended to help Blair to help Joan—"you see, neither her husband not Mr. Hilary Amcott wanted Mrs. Amcott to come down to the manor house at all this winter. Her husband expected her to stay in town at their flat. But Mrs. Amcott found she could let that very well, and besides..." She seemed to hesitate here.

The two men waited.

"I think she wanted some help or guidance from Mr. Grimshaw. He's so wonderfully certain of things, you know. He always can clear up one's doubts so well. I think that was really the reason why Mrs. Amcott cabled to Sir Christopher before he had heard from his brother about the flat in town, and asked him if she might come down for the winter. He cabled back the reply, I know, just before he got out of touch with civilisation, saying that of course she could have the rooms and was welcome to bring the dog. For some reason or other, Mr. Hilary disliked having 'Laddy' down this time, though the dog is, or was, devoted to him—followed him about everywhere. But, of course, you see now how awkward it was for Mr. Hilary, and for Ralph Amcott too for that matter, to have

Mrs. Amcott down there after he and her husband had separated on such bad terms out in Khartoum. Mr. Hilary couldn't stand the climate out there, any more than Mrs. Amcott could. But I think that he misunderstood her being at the manor. He chose to assume, so he told her more than once, that she kept her husband acquainted with all that he did. He had as little as possible to do with her for that reason; they saw no more of each other than if they had both been stopping at the same hotel, only Baroness Maricourt helped to smooth things over; she was down a lot. Monsieur Waddy, who is making a long visit with Mr. Hilary, was one of her late husband's greatest friends, and is her favourite dancing partner. He does dance divinely. However much one may dislike the man, he certainly can dance! But lately Mr. Hilary had grown so constantly and increasingly rude to Mrs. Amcott that she told me on Saturday she was leaving the manor house shortly, though not Elmhurst, I think."

That was all.

"Well, I'm off to see the Baroness." Armstrong put on his topcoat after seeing Miss Dallas to her car. "I shan't be long. By Jove! I do begin to wonder if you're right, Mr. Blair, and that I may have taken all these people too much for granted. I always follow blood in backing a horse, you see."

"And I go by form," Blair countered, as he too left the station. "I'll wait for you here."

Inspector Armstrong was not long, but he was very red in the face when he returned to his room.

"That Baroness is a slippery handful! She says now that the emeralds were stolen from her on the way up in the train, or in her hotel before dinner on Saturday. When I asked why she didn't report the theft—if there was one (I didn't say that, but I begin to think it)—to the hotel or station police, she said that she was so worried over, having lost the family heirloom that she hoped to get it back on the quiet, as Monsieur Waddy suggested. Oh, yes, he travelled up with her it seems. She says she didn't want her cousin, Mrs. Amcott, to learn of the loss. And she seemed to think that I had no business to know of it either. The trouble is that, as I remarked before, the emeralds do belong to her, and any cock-and-bull story she chooses to tell about 'em we're bound to accept. I cut the interview short," the Inspector went on with a wry smile. "Patience isn't my long suit, and patience is what we're supposed to have an unlimited supply of in the Force: they call it tact. Same thing. Where we're to get more from when it gives out the authorities don't say. Suppose we've just got to keep on producing it mysteriously like a spider's web. If I'd stayed much longer in the room with that cheeky little devil of a Baroness I'd have said something that wouldn't have come under the heading of tact. It would not!" Armstrong evidently half congratulated himself, half regretted, that he had got away in time.

"What line will you follow now?" Blair asked.

"I'll tell you when the telephone rings," the Inspector answered mysteriously.

The instrument obliged on the spot. As Armstrong listened to it his face brightened.

"Good egg!" he muttered to Blair as he hung up. "The Chief Constable asked Scotland Yard, before the funeral, to take over. They wouldn't reply at once; fussed as usual about being drawn in so late, but acknowledged, of course, that they'd been watching the case. You bet they have—with extra-powerful binoculars! But it seems they finally agreed that one of their brass hats should come along and take over; that is to say, that he'll arrive within the hour, for he's flying down to Salisbury. I must get my notes in order. It's Chief Inspector Pointer."

Chief Inspector Pointer! Blair said good-bye with a chill running down his spine, and yet with hope in his heart. Could Joan deceive eyes that were reckoned among the keenest in England? In a desperate case like hers every new factor meant a new danger.

But at the inn he found his fairy princess herself very pleased at the news.

"The case isn't getting anywhere," she said thoughtfully. "I mean, I don't think any but trained detectives can worry out the truth."

"But—will it be safe for you to meet him, Lucy?" he asked in a low voice. She flashed him a glance of not very stern reproof for his use of her assumed first name. "You think you dare?"

"I'm absolutely safe," she said confidently. "No one of all the people who have known Joan has even guessed it. I think I was quite wrong about Mr. Waddy. And before the funeral I spoke to several people—the doctor's wife, Miss Grimshaw, and so on—who had all known me. No one suspected me. Why, even I don't recognise myself in the glass, nor in my heart. I seem to've changed inwardly as much as outwardly. I'd no idea I could be hard and fierce and fight for my right as I'm ready to do. You need to be in the peril I'm in to learn to know yourself. Those who know me best would be the last to think this Lucy Ingilby could be that meek little Joan. I'm not meek. I'm desperate."

She had risen impetuously, and stood facing him for one moment, then she passed a hand across her cheeks and sank again into her chair.

"But tell me, what is this Scotland Yard man like? Is he clever? I hope he is!"

"I've never met him. But he used to be a professional foot-baller before he joined the Force. The best forward that his home county, Devon, ever had. He played for England." Blair spoke reverently of the ex-Internationalist. "That speaks for itself. You don't get the reputation he had without having quicker brains than other people. He used to be a wonder at guessing what the man with the ball was going to do before the man himself quite knew; it isn't quick legs, but quick wits that do that."

"I want a clever man," Joan said simply. "A stupid man would never save me..."

"From what a stupid dolt got you into," he finished bitterly.

The door opened. The waiter entered to say that the Inspector and a gentleman wanted to see Miss Ingilby.

Blair and Joan exchanged looks. The brass hat from Scotland Yard? It must be. Blair admired pluck; he thought Joan's quiet way of meeting what both knew to be a very terrible moment, a crucial moment perhaps, was superb.

She did not alter her position. Lightly, gracefully sunk in the deep armchair, she sat watching the flames, her chin on her hand until the Inspector's voice began:

"Miss Ingilby, this is Chief Inspector Pointer from New Scotland Yard."

Then Joan rose and came forward with something very winning in her eager face. She had the frank, friendly, utterly disarming smile of a child. She was but a child, Blair thought with a pang; a child that had been tossed overboard in a raging sea to sink or swim—and by him.

Her eyes softly shining, she shook hands with the new corner, he looked much younger than she had expected, and more distinguished too. As his fingers closed around hers there flowed through her a sense of his power. A man dangerous to a criminal, was her first thought, a difficult man to deceive. She had a definite impression of a fine, clear, cold intellect, a great personal dignity, and of unusual force of character—force that showed in his quiet manner, in the clean, firm lines of the lean face and figure. In a certain stillness about him that meant vast reserves of strength, physical and mental.

She tingled with excitement. Would he suspect her? Would he help her? This brown-faced man with the pleasant but very enigmatic grey eyes.

"Oh, I hope you will be able to clear up this terrible mystery," she said a little shakily. "I thought I might be able to help Joan by coming down here, but"—she shook her head wearily—"it seems like trying to catch hold of water or air."

Pointer nodded thoughtfully, then he looked at Blair.

"I understand that you have changed your mind about the closing paragraph in your article in yesterday's *Comet*?'"

"Where I hinted at the governess as the criminal? Absolutely," Blair said very firmly. "More so than ever by this time. The problem is more complex than I thought at the time."

Again Pointer nodded, then once more he turned to Joan.

"I'd like you, Miss Ingilby, to come across to the manor house and help me in my first look at Mrs. Amcott's rooms. You may have heard your sister speak of this or that which might puzzle us. Can you manage to come now?"

She went with them gladly, Blair, by tacit consent, making one of the party. Pointer looked over the rooms with apparently but a casual interest; then he returned to the bedroom and stepped up to the mantelpiece.

CHAPTER SEVEN

THE mantelpiece in Mrs. Amcott's room was of white marble, with a strip of black velvet stretched along it. On either end glittered a brass candlestick, and in the centre, on a carved stand, stood a small wooden figure. Pointer lifted it off and looked inquiringly at Joan.

"I see there's a Saint Anthony and several Buddhas in that cupboard over there. Who's this gentleman? I'm not up in the Roman calendar, nor in Eastern teachers, but he hardly looks a saint or a sage."

Everyone smiled, for a more vicious face than that carved on the little figure it would be difficult to find. The statuette represented a capering black man with gilt turban, loin cloth and huge earrings. There was uncommon skill in the balance and rhythm of his poise and the savagery of the face; his gloating leer alone was a triumph of craftsmanship which not even a ridiculous knot of coloured ribbon around his bulging waist could spoil.

"Do you know who or what he is?" Pointer continued. "Mrs. Amcott seems to have thought him worthy of the place of honour in her bedroom."

Joan had no idea what the statuette represented, nor why it was on the mantel. She explained that her sister had told her that Mrs. Amcott was very superstitious, and always had what she called a ju-ju on that stand. Some sort of a mascot.

"Joan told me once that she altered them constantly. She said they varied from penguins to elephant hairs."

"They don't seem to've brought her much luck," Armstrong said drily.

"Perhaps that's why she changed them so frequently," Joan said.

"I wonder if Monsieur Waddy or Mr. Hilary Amcott downstairs could name him," the police officer ruminated. "Both are up in everything about collections and bric-a-brac, I understand."

"I wonder if the little chap saw the murder done?" Pointer said slowly. "Very likely he was on guard here the night Mrs. Amcott went to sleep and never woke up."

Joan covered her face with her hands in a gesture of horror. Blair had not paid any attention to the statuette before, merely noting it as a bizarre ornament. He now looked at it carefully.

"Some Gold Coast or West African fetish?" he suggested, "or some Nigerian spirit?"

"The Spirit of Crime?" Pointer asked. "If so, he shouldn't be black. He should be whitey yellow, so that all races could have a share in him. But we've no time to waste." With that he asked a few questions as to this and that arrangement. Joan was very cautious and very skilful. She gave him all important information, but on non-essentials she remarked that that wasn't the sort of thing that Joan would have been likely to speak of. There was not much that she could tell, and, thanking her for her trouble in coming along, Pointer opened the door for her.

Blair followed her out. In the lounge below, in front of a blazing fire, sat Hilary Amcott and Waddy, the former looking very sleepy, the latter imperturbable as always.

"Assisting the law?" he asked, turning his head with its strange, walled-in eyes towards her as he rose. "I hope you have not misled it in any way? Or should I say her? The law is a lady, is she not?" He turned to Hilary, who only gave a silly laugh.

"Don't ask me anything to do with laws. Ask Grimshaw. He always says he's one unto himself, whatever that means."

"I don't understand you," Joan said coldly, dislike in her voice as well as in her eye as she turned to Monsieur Waddy.

"I suggest that it is hard to be impartial," he murmured. "Sometimes, owing to circumstances beyond one's power, it is impossible. Close relationship, for instance, or being in love, or—oh, many reasons. But I hear that the case of Madame Amcott's death is now in the hands of New Scotland Yard." Waddy turned to Blair. "How interesting! And how the criminal must be trembling," he added with a show of his glittering teeth.

Joan said nothing; Blair only nodded.

"I often wonder why a criminal is a criminal," Waddy went on, leaning an arm on the mantelshelf, from above which a Tudor Amcott regarded him with a ruminating stare. "Don't you too, Miss Ingilby? Or should I say Miss Lucy Ingilby? I am not sure whether you or your so charming sister is the elder?"

"I am much older than Joan," the girl answered composedly.

"Thank you so much. I should have taken you for— eh—twins," he said smoothly. "But don't you agree with me that a criminal's life can never be really worth while? Such tremors, such agitations, for, generally speaking, very little result."

"Whoever got those emeralds, which you and Baroness de Maricourt believed were stolen, certainly got something worth while," Joan said with a flash of her eye.

"You think so?" he drawled.

"I don't think they would have been taken otherwise," she countered, turning her back on him and walking on. Outside on the drive she turned to Blair. Her composure was gone now, her lips trembled.

"He means mischief," she whispered, and Blair felt her quiver. "Sometimes I think he is only biding his time, like a great cat with a mouse. And I daren't answer him as I would like to and as I could! One word might betray me."

A servant came hurrying after them. Would Miss Ingilby step back for a moment. One of the gentlemen wanted to ask her a question.

Joan went back at once. Intensely curious, Blair followed. Pointer had a pair of dark fur-lined gloves in his hand.

"Do you know if these belong to your sister?" he asked.

She looked at them carefully. They were old, suede outside and rabbit inside.

"They seem about her size, but Joan never wears lined gloves. She detests them. Why?"

"Because of this scrap of paper I found in the very, tip of the thumb. The gloves were lying on the bureau over there."

Joan had passed them by a score of times without any but a cursory examination. But Pointer now held out a little slip of paper about an inch long and half as wide. It was obviously part of a longer strip, for both ends were torn away, whereas the edges above and below the writing were cut. All that was on the tiny scrap was 'one mad.' in ink. It was torn so closely in front of the o that part of the letter was missing, though enough remained to show its identity. Behind the 'mad.' came a full stop and a fraction of a clear space, though then came the mark of the pen showing that some other word was following. What word or what letter it was impossible to tell.

"Gone mad!" Blair breathed, and looked at the Inspector, who also muttered "Gone mad" reflectively and tapped his moustache.

All three recognised the writing as Mrs. Amcott's.

"You're sure these wouldn't be your sister's gloves?" the Inspector repeated.

Joan could not betray too great a certainty. She could not be expected to know every detail of her sister's wardrobe. She only repeated that Joan never wore lined gloves.

"Mrs. Amcott, I see, wears the same size. So if not Miss Joan's, they would probably be hers." Pointer had a pair taken from Mrs. Amcott's things in his hand. And this time Joan was definitely thanked and speeded on her way.

"Gone mad!" she repeated to Blair when they were outside. Her face was very pale now. "What can 'gone mad' mean? To think of all the times I've hunted those rooms through yesterday and to-day, and never saw that dot of paper!"

She and Blair talked of nothing else until they were at the inn, without fitting anything sensible to the strange little tag. Arrived at their quarters, Blair spent half-an-hour or so sitting thinking in the empty lounge. Joan was upstairs. He needed quiet to collect his fancies.

That paper in those gloves—Mrs. Amcott's gloves. "Gone mad," if a statement or a message, to whom would it probably be made? It suggested a medical expert or a friend of the family—Mr. Grimshaw? Grimshaw looked as if he would have muscles of steel. As a boxer he must be sure-footed and deft with his hands... Blair was thinking of last night and the search through his room.

"Chief Inspector Pointer to see you, sir," he heard the waiter announcing. Blair looked hard at the ex-Internationalist; he had decided already that Pointer, if he so wished, could play as bold and as skilful a game as ever.

"I wonder if you would help me tackle Mr. Grimshaw," Pointer began in a very friendly tone. "I'll start him off, but he might run on to you more freely than to me, and my being there might bring home to him the importance of the interview. Two men, labourers, have just come to the police station saying that they saw Mr. Ralph Amcott coming out of the manor house last Tuesday around midnight. The men in question—they were doubtless off for a bit of poaching—are quite positive about its having been Mr. Ralph. They say he has a walk that's unmistakeable, a twist of the shoulder every time he takes a step, and the Inspector confirms this. Now Mr. Grimshaw was seen about that hour too, and to reach his rectory from the Institute, where we know he was, in the

late evening, may very well have cut across the grounds
of the manor. Armstrong tells me that you have all along
held that the rector was keeping something back. It's very
possible you were right, and that he has been. But leave
it to me to speak of Mr. Ralph Amcott."

"Ralph Amcott! The husband!" Blair jumped to his
feet. He was off beside the other on the instant.

"The Inspector says that Mr. Grimshaw agrees with
you in thinking that Miss Ingilby had no hand in the
murder," Pointer went on, lighting his pipe.

"Don't you?" Blair flashed.

"So far I don't see any motive that would explain her
taking such a fearful step," was as far as Pointer would
go, but even that much, coming from him, comforted
Blair.

The two found the rector in his austere study.

"It's about Miss Ingilby, Mrs. Amcott's governess,"
Pointer began. "I wonder if you could give us any idea of
where to look for her."

"I?" Mr. Grimshaw's stare was as chilly as the room.

"You went a good deal to the manor; I take it you saw
something of her. Of course we would give a good deal to
get our hands on her."

"Why?" the parson asked curtly.

"Why do the police ever try to capture criminals?"
Pointer said coldly.

"But Miss Ingilby isn't a criminal," Grimshaw said at
once.

"We've not been able to find any other person who
could as easily have murdered Mrs. Amcott," Pointer said
gravely. "And if we're right in assuming that Mrs. Amcott
had suspicions of her governess—she had asked her to
leave, you know—why, there's revenge for a motive, not
to speak of some missing valuables."

There was a silence that the rector seemed prepared
to let last indefinitely.

Pointer glanced at Blair.

"For God's sake," the newspaper man exploded, "if you know anything to clear up this dreadful affair I do beg you to speak out. Miss Ingilby is having the devil of a time somewhere, we may be sure—will have it till she's cleared. All my fault, I know, for that rotten article, but she deserves every particle of help that can be given her. If you have any knowledge or any suspicion that might help to clear her, then, as I say, for God's sake, speak!"

Grimshaw put his fingers together and bent them backwards and forwards—strong fingers.

"I've always considered Miss Ingilby innocent, chiefly because I know her, and believe her incapable of a crime," he began slowly.

"But the police don't!" Blair again burst in. "I—I..." He stopped and bit his lip. His emotion threatened to swamp him.

Grimshaw looked at him for a long second, then he turned away.

"I regret that I cannot be of any assistance. I deeply regret it," he said coldly.

His two visitors rose and took their leave. But Pointer, parting from Blair almost at once, made a swift loop and came back.

"Is there any strain of madness in the Amcotts?" he asked, when he was shown in once more.

Mr. Grimshaw said that he had never heard of any taint. His eyes had narrowed.

"Of course, I have no right to say anything," the rector went on, "but I feel morally certain that the criminal was that French half-caste, that Monsieur Waddy, as he spells it, though I feel sure that Ouadhi would be the right way, for he's mongrel Arab by every supple joint of him."

"The dog hated him," Pointer said casually. "He wouldn't go a step with him. It must have been a regular member of the household, or someone the dog liked."

"Information has just reached us at the police station," he went on, "that Mr. Ralph Amcott was seen last Tuesday night coming out of the manor around midnight. Higgins and Richards are the two men from whom we have the story. They are quite firm and unshakeable as to having made no mistake."

Grimshaw seemed to press his elbows to his sides, as though a stiff fence were coming. Something about his pose suggested that he was jamming his hat over his eyes and was prepared to get over with something to spare. He made no reply, however.

"Now, Mr. Grimshaw, you were seen not far from the manor last Tuesday night. Did you see anyone at all moving about the house or meet any member of the household?"

"I could hardly have seen a man who is lying desperately ill away off in Khartoum, Chief Inspector."

"You met no one at all, or saw no one, last Tuesday night except the constable, Budge?"

"No one at all," Grimshaw said very firmly.

Pointer then called in at the police station for Armstrong, who was making his notes of the two labourers' separate statements.

"Suppose we drop in at the manor house. They don't do much there but drink and play, I'm told."

About that Armstrong agreed. "But what does this mean, sir—this about Mr. Ralph Amcott? The two men seem quite certain. I had another go with them after you left. They stuck to it that they saw him, though only his back. But we know that Mr. Ralph is as ill as he can be, and ill in the Sudan." Pointer only talked of a big burglary that had been committed up in Scotland until they reached the manor. There they were told that Mr. Hilary was in.

"It's about some information that's reached us, showing that Mrs. Amcott's husband was down here last Tuesday night," Pointer began.

"Well? What of it?" Hilary Amcott gave him a surly glance out of red-rimmed, red-veined eyes.

"But surely the information at the inquest was that he was ill. Very ill in Khartoum," Armstrong pointed out. "You yourself, sir, have said as much."

"I repeated what I was told. I shouldn't be surprised if my dear, good brother, anxious at reports that I'm wasting my time, had let that idea be circulated in order to slip over here and have a look for himself. I certainly saw him myself last night; so did Monsieur Waddy. He was walking down a passage upstairs. We chased him, but he got away. Have a cocktail, either of you? I've just christened my latest the Safebreaker."

Pointer and Armstrong declined rather curtly.

"What, not even a Fair Maid or a Mother-in-law? We are indeed in good hands. Shall we have prayers instead?"

"The point is this." The Chief Inspector spoke very gravely, very slowly, so that the drink-sodden man opposite him could follow. "Mrs. Amcott's husband is reported to have been seen here—here—on the night after his wife was murdered! You must see for yourself what that means."

Waddy had entered; he had a way of entering when callers came. He was listening intently, his head turning now and again, first to Hilary, then to Pointer, then to Inspector Armstrong.

"Well?" Hilary asked again with a bibulous cough. "Suppose I do see? What then? If you can connect my prating sobersides of an elder brother with a crime, Chief Inspector, I'll put you up a purse. But don't believe it easily; it's too good to be true."

"Too good that he should have murdered his wife?" Pointer asked.

"Too good that he should be tumbled from the high altar on which he delights to sit," Hilary Amcott said with a snarl. "He's a hypocrite and a canting, psalm-singing pussyfoot already, and if you can add worse to that list, so much the better!"

There was a note of almost mad ferocity in the grating voice that caused Armstrong to look closely at him. This was a new Hilary Amcott indeed. Yet in some odd way he seemed like some revelation of the inner, the real man. Something about a tag of Dr. Pearson's—in *vino veritas*—floated through his startled mind.

"But the nursing home, the medical certificate?" the inspector asked.

He had the latter cable in his safe.

"D'you suppose they would blab if he told them to hold their tongue?" Hilary asked, with a look of contempt at the speaker.

"Mr. Ralph Amcott was seen, actually seen here last Tuesday night?" Monsieur Waddy inquired. His face was a curious mottled colour.

"Here at the manor house." Pointer turned to him as though he had not noticed his entrance. "So that, since you saw him again last night, he may have been, or in the village or near here at least, since then."

Waddy passed a long, pointed tongue over his lips, lips that writhed when he spoke.

"Is someone impersonating him?" he asked rather unsteadily.

"Both the men who gave us the information are prepared to swear that it could have been nobody but Mr. Ralph Amcott himself."

The two officers took their leave.

"Drink is killing Hilary Amcott," Pointer said in a tone of pity. "I give him another six months at the outset before he breaks up, if he continues this gait."

"He was half-drunk, of course, or he would never have spoken as he did. He's a sorry wreck now, but you should have seen him only five years ago—the picture of health and energy, and keen as mustard."

"Now, Armstrong, supposing it wasn't Mrs. Amcott's husband whom those two men saw, taking the two men there at the manor and the rector, which of the three could best make himself up like Ralph Amcott, especially from the back?"

Armstrong thought carefully.

"The parson could do it best. He's Ralph Amcott's height and rather his build. But, on the other hand, Mr. Hilary Amcott's not unlike his brother either. Only he slouches, and the other has a back like a drill sergeant's. All the three Amcotts resemble each other a bit. The only one who couldn't do it is that monseer. He's too weedy."

There followed a long silence as the two walked back to the station.

"You've not traced the emeralds yet?" Pointer said next.

"No, sir, not yet, though we're hard at it, of course. I can't make up my mind about that necklace. Are they gone—the stones, I mean—or aren't they? Well, time will tell. Did you notice the look on that monseer's face when you spoke of Mr. Ralph at the manor last Tuesday night? That did put the wind up him. I think..." And Armstrong proceeded to repeat to Chief Inspector Pointer those reflections of his that so infuriated Blair—Blair who just now was fast asleep, making up for the previous night. But he did not have his usual length of rest, for towards morning a bell rang on the ground floor. Years of a reporter's life had made him as quick as a doctor to hear that summons. It might be for him, from the police, he thought, as he ran down the stairs.

It was an automatic exchange. He picked up the receiver. "Red Oak Inn. Who's speaking?" he asked.

"Martin!" His name came in a whisper of incredible gratitude, unhoped for joy, that seemed to tingle along the wire. "Oh, help! Come, London. Fourteen Kennington Park Mews. I'll be killed if the police get on—" Silence, sudden, absolute, awful. Blair's hair rose, and little prickles went up and down his spine; he did not dare hang up for fear of a click at the other end. Joan's tone as well as her words had told him that only some unforeseen stroke of luck had enabled her to get for a second to an instrument.

He leapt upstairs to her room, tried the door, opened it, and found the room empty, the bed untouched.

He flung on some clothes as though the last boat were leaving the ship, snatched up an automatic and an electric torch, and ran to the garage. He knew where the key hung. It would take too long to wake the inn's chauffeur-mechanic, sleeping in a distant attic. But he got out the inn's one car, rang up a good garage at Salisbury and ordered their fastest roadster to be waiting ready for him to drive off. He rushed to it as fast as the clogged old car would rattle. When he showed his papers, he found that the people at Salisbury had heard of him as down here to help with the Amcott case. A moderate deposit gave him the fast Bentley, and Blair drove her splendidly, but like a man possessed. He knew his London well.

He knew West Kennington Park Road; he had an idea of where the Mews must be. It only needed one glance at the map to show him finally, after three hours at the wheel, where he should stop his car and climb down. All around him was a maze of not too well kept streets, some of them quite respectable, some with reputations far worse than their looks. The Mews was a small deserted alley. Number fourteen was a garage at the end, with what looked like backs of shops and warehouses on either side. Blair knew that appearances were particularly deceptive on this side of the river, but the place seemed uninhabited. He looked at the door of the garage; it would have taken a stick of dynamite to force it, but the side showed a window that he opened without undue difficulty, so that he thought it had often served as an entrance. He. climbed in. All was silent. He would have said that the place was as empty as the houses around, but for hearing the gurgle-gurgle of a running tap somewhere. His torch in one hand, he looked about him with desperate keenness. In the further room he found

Joan's overcoat in a heap on the floor. Apparently it had been trampled on. And always the sound of the water as though running slowly into a bath. In the same room with the coat was a trap-door, not bolted. Opening it, his torch shone on water; it seemed to be within an arm's length of him. And then his heart seemed to stand still, for there, floating on the surface, was Joan's white face. She was gagged. The water was not far below her chin; her eyes met his at first dully, as might the eyes of a person already done with life—then with a wild hope. He seized a bar lying on the cellar floor and sounded. He was Joan's only helper. Rashness might leave her with no one, and Blair could not swim. The depth was five feet. He snatched off his overcoat and shoes, took his automatic between his teeth—he might yet need it in there—jumped down, and felt a cement floor beneath his feet. In a second he was beside her. With one hand he untied the cloth with which she had been gagged, and got her to take a drink from his flask, which he had transferred a moment ago to an inner pocket.

"I am chained," she murmured, trying to move the lips which had been crushed against her teeth till they were white There was blood on the lower one. "Mr. Waddy padlocked me and threw the key out of reach. If you're careful you ought to find it."

Blair trod the surface of the cellar's floor until he stepped on the key. Another second and he had turned it, and was lifting Joan to the floor above. She put her arms around his neck and kissed him.

"Thank you, Martin. Thank you, dear."

He held her close.

"As I thought he's after the emeralds," she told him, her teeth chattering. "Fortunately they tore off my thick coat before they carried me down there. It's here somewhere."

He put it round her. Suddenly she gripped his arm again.

"He'll be back any minute. He said he would be back just before the water reached my mouth, so that I could tell him where those emeralds are. If not, I was to drown by inches where I was chained. I told you he was mad on that point." She shrank against him. "Oh, Martin! He was such a brute when they carried me here. Look"—she showed the scarlet mark of a hand on her white damp arm—"but for wanting those emeralds he would so have liked to kill me. He said so. Hush-h! He's coming back!"

A step sounded outside The same window which Blair had used was opened none too noiselessly. Blair swept her behind him and picked up his automatic again. He was in a mood that was new to him—the mood of the killer. He would have Waddy's blood for this; his life for the all-but-taken life of the girl behind him. He was quite cool—quite determined. Let Waddy come in to finish his work and he would kill him, and leave him where he would have left Joan Ingilby.

But the steps coming quietly but firmly down the passage stopped outside the door.

"Don't shoot, Mr. Blair. It's me, Chief Inspector Pointer." And Chief Inspector Pointer it was. He helped Blair carry Joan into his own car, and Blair most unwillingly drove his own car, while Joan sat beside Pointer and talked to him. She was quite herself again by now. The only thing she would not do, she told them, was to stay overnight in town and go down to Elmhurst in the morning.

"I'm afraid of being left by myself," she said wanly. "Down there with you all about me I feel safer."

"Do you mind telling me what happened," Pointer asked gently, "or would you rather not talk just now?"

"There's so little to tell. I found a note lying on my pillow last night when I went to bed saying that the writer—a woman —could tell me how to clear my sister if I would meet her alone at the north end of Lovers' Lane. I was to bring the letter with me, and I was not to tell the police or bring a friend, or the writer would not come, and

I would not learn something of the greatest importance to me."

"As always," murmured the man from Scotland Yard.

"At the lane I wafted a few minutes, and then something was thrown over my head—I had heard nothing whatever and I was bundled into a car. The cloth was kept over me; someone fastened it and my arms to my sides by a strap. At last I was hauled out into a house—where, I have no idea—and dumped, tied up, into a room. I heard the key turned in the lock. A corner of my rug was loose, and I could see a carpet and what looked like a sort of office desk. I could hear the murmur of three men talking, or it may have been only two. The cloth over my head kept me from being sure. But, at any rate, I heard men's low voices next door in the next room, and one of the voices was Mr. Waddy's. I heard someone say rather sharply, 'You mean fourteen Kennington Park Road, or do you mean the Mews?' And someone say, 'Sh-h! The Mews, of course.' Then I caught sight of the lower part of a telephone off in one corner. Monsieur Waddy came in and asked me where the Norreys necklace was. I said I didn't know. He threatened me for a while. Then he went out and locked the door again, and I think they talked in a further room. I could only hear the barest sound of voices this time. There was a hook on the door meant for coats, I suppose. I managed to use it to lift the blanket around my head a little. My hands were strapped to my sides, but I joggled the receiver off its hook with my shoulder and turned the disk with my tongue. I set it to Red Oak Inn and chanced anyone hearing. I kept my ear down to the receiver on the desk top until I heard someone say 'Hello! Who's that? What's wanted?' And you can't imagine what I felt when I heard Mr. Blair's voice." Her eyes looked out of the window for a minute as though her heart were too full for speech.

"I managed to get the receiver back into place by picking it up in my teeth. The men came in very shortly after and bundled me out into the car again. When they carried me out once more, it was to put me down on the edge of that trap-door you saw when you came in just now. But the cellar below was dry then. They took me down. It was all dark. I thought I was going to be killed." Her voice faltered for a moment. "But they only chained me to a pipe running up the wall and padlocked me to it. Then they turned on two taps. I don't know who was there. I think it was three men. But it might have been two men coming and going. It was all so dark. Also—well, frankly, I was too terrified to notice things much. All I heard was Monsieur Waddy keeping up an interminable request for those emeralds; I think he must have sat with his watch on his knee and timed himself. Finally, when the water was up to my waist, he dropped the trapdoor and told me he would come back just before the end and either watch me drown or take me out if I told him—what I can't tell him, Chief Inspector, what I don't know."

"You recognised Mr. Waddy?" Pointer asked.

"I know he was there," Joan said promptly and decidedly. "I dislike him far too much to be mistaken about him."

"But did you see him?" Pointer pressed her.

"Not actually see him," she agreed reluctantly. "The rug was over my head at the first house in town, and the cellar was all dark when he chained me." Her voice broke off in a little tremor. "And when he spoke up on the floor he stood out of my sight. There was a small light up there, a gas light, I fancy. But I feel absolutely positive that it was Monsieur Waddy."

"Still, that won't help us to bring it home to him," Pointer said after a pause. "Only a face-to-face recognition, something to which you could swear, would be of any use. Besides, the puzzling thing is that you should be attacked; if you were your sister one might understand it easier."

Joan's heart missed a beat.

"I don't see that," she said instantly. "Why should they attack her?"

"Monsieur Waddy maintains that she took Mrs. Amcott's emeralds; that he wants to get them back for the Baroness. Don't misunderstand me," Pointer said carefully. "I don't think so, but that is what he claims."

"Pretends!" she flashed out.

"Claims," he repeated in a tone that said that if he were not an official he, too, would prefer her word. "But the question remains, why should he attack you?"

Joan hesitated. Should she or should she not tell him who she was? With him on her side she felt that she would indeed be safe.

"I'm not concerned with the answer," Pointer said quickly—so quickly that it conveyed a warning, "but if we try to bring this outrage home to him, we shan't be able to prove it; we shall only give him an opportunity of asking, and getting others to ask, why he should be supposed to want to attack you. And there is such a thing as forcing a step on the police, Miss Ingilby, that they really don't want to take."

Joan gazed attentively at him. She felt fairly sure now that he suspected that she, Joan, was masquerading as Lucy; that he was giving her a friendly warning, telling her that unless forced to act he would do nothing about her presence down at Elmhurst.

"He might think her interests and mine are one," she ventured with a timid but friendly glance at him.

"Naturally they are," and for the ghost of a second their eyes met.

"I—I do so want to clear her!" she said passionately.

"Joan is innocent, Chief Inspector, and yet that dreadful *Comet* article brands her in front of all the world as a criminal. Even though Mr. Blair wants to take it back publicly, they won't let him. His article has to stand, with its dreadful concluding paragraph!"

"Those words that distress you may be proved all wrong any day," he reminded her.

"By you?" she asked with a most engaging smile. "Are you on her side? Oh, if you are, I'm not afraid of the issue!"

"Scotland Yard is always on the side of justice," he said reassuringly.

She drew a deep breath.

"I hope so. But isn't justice blind?" she asked, her eyes dancing a little.

"I never did care much for that as a symbol," Pointer confessed. "especially when they put a sword in the lady's hand as well. A sword nearly as long as herself."

Joan said no more all the rest of the long drive. She seemed to doze a little. When at last the two cars pulled up at the inn and Blair ran to the door to help her out, she looked absolutely spent. It was now nearly ten o'clock in the morning.

Mrs. Black, who came running out, was told a rather incoherent tale by Blair of a fall into the river off a slippery bank that Miss Ingilby had been investigating.

Joan insisted on being able to get to her room unaided. She remembered the untouched bed. And Mrs. Black hurried off for hot bottles and a cup of hot milk with a dash of rum in it.

Blair made for the police station, where he found the two officers busy with notes and telephone inquiries.

"What about that infernal brute, Waddy? And the cellar?" Blair asked.

Pointer only looked grave, very grave.

"Shooting Monsieur Waddy wouldn't have helped to solve Mrs. Amcott's death, Mr. Blair," he said firmly. "No murder ever helped to clear up a murder. But for my coming into the room, I think you intended to kill him?"

"And who wouldn't!" Blair asked, "if they had blood in their veins and had seen that girl's face all but under water?"

"It wouldn't have helped the search for the murderer," Pointer repeated. "As to this Monsieur Waddy, I certainly would like to catch him, so would Inspector Armstrong, but he can't be caught with this night's story. There's no evidence against him; he tells us he was in his bed all night. He certainly didn't use an Elmhurst car. That cellar belongs to a brewer who is trying to sell it—never uses it now. Miss Ingilby doesn't, can't, know to what house she was first taken, nor whose was the other voice or voices that she heard."

"Except this Waddy's," Blair said hotly. "I believe he killed Mrs. Amcott."

"But the theatre, the stall at the theatre where he was seen with Mr. Hilary Amcott?" Pointer asked, with a tiny spark far back in his grey eyes, eyes that were so keen, yet could look so casual.

Blair made a gesture, rather like one Joan often used these days—a hopeless, almost a helpless gesture, and went off.

CHAPTER EIGHT

POINTER meanwhile took out of a shed hardly bigger than a small garage, but standing at one end of a field belonging to a friend of his, an old single seater fighter, an S.E. 5a on which he had flown down. He replaced its wings, and was off with the little carved figure from Mrs. Amcott's mantelpiece in his bag, the statuette which Joan had not thought of connecting in any way with Mrs. Amcott's death.

To her it was but one silly mascot rather than another, but to the Chief Inspector it suggested a possible clue to something, as yet unknown, for which Mrs. Amcott had selected this particular blackamoor as a luck bringer. Else why had she troubled to place him in the post of honour?

Pointer had learnt from a housemaid that it had been put on the mantelpiece only this last Saturday. She was certain of that, for on Saturdays she "did out" Mrs. Amcott's rooms, and on that morning "a fat old man" had had the post of honour—she meant a Laughing Buddha, one of the thirteen Buddhas in Mrs. Amcott's possession. But in the afternoon of last Saturday Mrs. Amcott must have taken out this figurine, for the maid had found it on the ju-ju stand on Sunday morning, ribbon bow and all, and there it had remained since.

Mrs. Amcott's late maid, on Pointer going over to see her, ostensibly about the glove in which the paper had been found, said that she had only once seen the statuette put out. That single occasion was a year ago. They had gone to Scotland to spend Christmas. It was on December 20th that they had arrived—the date had remained in the maid's memory as it was her birthday—and Mrs. Amcott had at once placed the same little monstrosity on the same carved stand, making a place for it on her already overcrowded dressing-table. She had not seen the "little nigger" since. As to the knot of ribbon, it had not had it last year.

December 20th... Pointer had eyed his shoetips reflectively as he stood talking with the young woman. This year it was mid-December. The same month both years...

He asked Miss Turvey about the Christmas before last? But she had not then been in the employment of Mrs. Amcott, who had spent it with her husband in Spain. As to the glove, the maid could not identify it, beyond stating that Mrs. Amcott generally wore lined gloves in winter in the country.

Pointer next spoke of Mr. Ralph Amcott. She seemed to be in a considerable awe of him. But as she was both by nature and inclination a very silent woman, and very distrustful of the police, Pointer fared no better than had Armstrong in trying to wheedle out of her any gossip, any talk about the dead woman's character or life with her husband. For the moment Pointer was not concerned with that. The ugly figure set out so conspicuously on Mrs. Amcott's mantelpiece was what he was trying to "place."

Now, as he flew towards town, he was thinking over the little that he had learnt of it. It was little, but intriguing. For, though there might not be any connection between the two dates, yet the fact remained that each year the month had been the same.

On landing in the small aerodrome in Regent's Park which belongs to New Scotland Yard, Pointer, thinking of Blair's guess that the idol—if one came from the Gold Coast, went first of all to a curator familiar with ju-jus and tangible spells from every land. He inspected the little polychrome figure closely, then he shook his head.

"African work apparently. Probably a fetish of some kind. But the carver must have been thoroughly in touch with Europeans, though the figure itself is pure Arab. Carved from life, I should say."

In fact, in this instance, the curator could only do what Pointer could do, and that was, guess. Pointer went on to the South Kensington Museum. Here he had no better luck. The experts "inclined to the belief" that the workmanship, which they agreed was of a very high kind, was European, but if so, the sculptor knew the lower Arab type perfectly.

So far Pointer had only wasted his time. He lost still a little more of it at the British Museum. Finally he had another look at the little man himself. He was made of wood. That much was certain. Kew Gardens have experts who at a moment's notice can identify a splinter for a puzzled timber merchant. To the Botanical Gardens he hurried, and there he was told his first definite fact. The statuette was made of olive wood, of a kind that grows only in the south of Europe. In this particular instance the wood had grown in a very dry region, and had been cut and carved about four centuries ago.

South Europe... Pointer first thought of southern France or Italy as the possible home of the little blackamoor. But the very word gave him another idea. Moors—what about Spain? Spain, with the dryest regions in South Europe, the country that most of all others had had to do with the Arab race...

Instantly came the recollection of the maid having said that Mrs. Amcott had spent the winter before last in that country.

Pointer went to Lord Barlock's private secretary. Lord Barlock has the best collection in England of Spanish *objets de vertu*. Not even that at Apsley House is finer.

Pointer's hopes rose from the very way that the secretary in question picked up his little man and studied him with it faint smile. The Chief Inspector had at last, he told himself, come to The Man Who Knew.

The secretary put the little carving down with reluctance. "If anyone wants to sell him, I should certainly urge Lord Barlock to buy him. It's a *Paso*, a miniature *Paso*."

Mr. Wilton went on to explain that the statuette was one of the carved figures used in Spain at a *Paso*—a scene illustrating the Passion—the whole series of which are carried in procession during Holy Week in every village and town of the peninsula. As a rule the figures are life-sized, but now and again small ones were used at court or in some secluded monastery. Owing to the occupation of the land by the Moors, the Spaniards often depicted the most cruel figures in the Passion series as Moors, as had been done in this case apparently.

"Here's a family relation of his." Wilton went out of the room, and came back with a very similar statuette. "Supposed to be one of the attendants of King Herod. So is yours probably."

Pointer asked if the figures were ever used as mascots.

"The small ones are, very often, but their powers are purely local. A Cadiz *Paso* wouldn't assist anyone living in Seville, for instance," Wilton warned with a grin. "Where did this little man come from?" He thought that he was one of several small sets made for Ferdinand and Isabella by Arrigo of Madrid, and used there. When the figures got shabby they were sold to the devout or the superstitious.

Pointer thanked Wilton and hurried back to his rooms at Scotland Yard. So the little black demoniacal-looking figure was a Madrid mascot, out of commission in other parts of the world. Yet Mrs. Amcott had placed him in the point of honour this year as she had last year—both years in December, though not on the same date.

What could there be, two years running, in Madrid in the same month, that the figure could be supposed to influence?

Suddenly Pointer altered his step, a sure sign of mental excitement. The Gordo!

The drawings of the big permanent European State lotteries are dates that every Scotland Yard man knows approximately. Spain has three every month, drawn in

Madrid on the 1st, 12th, and 22nd respectively. And on December 22nd the Gordo—"the fat one"—is drawn, the great annual Christmas prize of fifteen million pesetas, or, roughly, four hundred and eighty thousand pounds. Moreover, this year, for the first time since the lotteries were started by Royal Decree in 1763, it had been drawn not on the usual date, but on the 12th, to coincide with the State opening of the Madrid International Fair. The 12th had been last Monday. And Pointer believed with Blair that Mrs. Amcott had been killed that night. Certainly, so far, no one had come forward who had definitely, unmistakeably spoken to her face to face since that afternoon.

On Monday at noon the news of the winning numbers would have been broadcast from Madrid, and would be posted up in every Spanish newspaper shop and library of any size throughout the world.

The statuette had been placed in its position of honour last Saturday—two days before the drawing. And the year before, when the drawing had been as usual on the 22nd, it had been put out on the 20th, and taken away on Christmas Eve.

The dates fitted the idea. So did Mrs. Amcott's words about it never yet having brought her luck. So did the fact that the dead woman had spent the winter before last in Spain, where Spanish lottery tickets are hawked incessantly in every café, along every street. The lotteries are only too popular.

And with this idea came another about the knot of ribbon—ribbon that by its look had probably come off a box of sweets, but a dark purple ribbon for all that.

Pointer telephoned to the secretary of Ranelagh Club, a man he knew.

"What are the colours of the Spanish polo team that did so well last August? I mean the Duke of Peneracla's *El Gordo*."

Pointer loved to watch polo. He loved to play it too with the mounted police down on their own big polo ground, though he took an outsize in ponies.

"Colours? Dark purple vest and ordinary regulation breeches and hat," came the reply, which he had expected.

Pointer thanked him and rang off. Dark purple that fitted, supposing that the mascot was for the Gordo, the ribbon might have been twisted around it, probably in some gay moment when the Gordo team had had a particularly good day, as an additional luck-bringer.

And that scrap of paper found in the lined glove... That "one mad."... Mrs. Amcott's writing had the peculiarity that certain of her capital letters, such as m's, n's and o's, among others, were practically the same size as her small letters. Gone mad... The cut edges of the scrap of paper found showed it had been a narrow strip, such as one might pick out for a message, a memorandum, or an order, but which would not seem to admit of the explanations those two words would need, one would think, where there was no known case of madness. What if the half words had been "telephone Mad." The last word an abbreviation of Madrid written with a capital that looked like a small m?

He thought that, so far, the bits fitted quite well, though, beyond the mere possibility that Mrs. Amcott was interested, like many other people, in Spanish lotteries, his inference could not and did not go.

It might be connected with her murder, but the gap between "it might be" and "it is" is as great to a detective as to a chemist.

The Chief Inspector's thoughts now turned to the *Paso* and an odd fact that he had noted about the little figure. The odd fact was, that though the figure which Mr. Wilton had brought to show him was made from the same kind of wood and smaller than Mrs. Amcott's, yet it was considerably heavier. Wood varies, of course, in weight, even the same kind of wood, but not, he thought, to such an extent. He now examined the little Moor more closely. There was nothing to suggest a join, even when looked at through a magnifying glass. But his loincloth was carved in deep folds around his tubby waist. If there were a join at all, if the inside of the figure were hollow, it could only open there. There, too, was where the ribbon had been tied.

Carefully Pointer twisted the body in opposite directions. Finally it turned, unscrewing in the middle.

In a second he had it apart, and in the hollow inside he found a rolled piece of paper. He opened it out, looked at it for a moment, and then picked up his telephone.

He telephoned to a foreign bookseller and news-agent, where he knew Spanish journals were sold. He, the speaker, gave no name, but asked what the winning number of the Gordo was this year. The answer came back at once, and Pointer heard the number called that was on the little piece of paper—about the width of an average cheque, but square, which was what he had taken from the wooden figure—for the paper was a half ticket in the Gordo. It represented, therefore, a sum of two hundred and forty thousand English pounds, if presented in Madrid within the space of one calendar year. It was, moreover, a bond to bearer. For a lottery ticket is cashed without any inquiries, even though the man who presents it has stabbed the previous holder of it on the bank steps and snatched it from his dying hand.

Investigations are for the civil authorities. The motto of the Government lottery is pay on sight. That being so, more than one lottery ticket has meant at the same time a prize and a burial certificate for its winner.

Pointer asked over the 'phone when the news had reached London. The numbers, he learnt, had been broadcast from Madrid last Monday at noon. Yes, the proprietor had, of course, placarded them in his shop.

Had anyone asked for the numbers to be telephoned to them? Pointer now gave his official position. A list of nearly fifty names and addresses was read to him, none of which interested him. But that meant nothing—even though the man whom he at once sent off to every similar shop in town should also draw a blank. If she had spent a winter in Spain, Mrs. Amcott had very likely had the ticket sent direct from there—probably under an assumed name.

Who had won the Gordo this year? Pointer asked next. One half had been won by a bank official, and, since no names had come in as having won any small parts of the remaining half, it looked as though either someone had bought that too in its entirety, or it had not been drawn.

Pointer thanked the speaker and hung up the receiver. He picked up the ticket thoughtfully. Here was one tremendous incentive to Mrs. Amcott's murder. It might not be the real one. Strange conjunctions are found in murder cases—as though sucked in by the crime. Mrs. Amcott might yet turn out to be murdered for a reason far afield from any Spanish lottery. But two hundred and forty thousand pounds, paid to whoever should present this scrap of paper, could not but rank as the probable cause until something that negatived it was known. And so far, not only did nothing do that, but he thought that the idea that she had been killed for it, and for it alone, explained much that had happened, and was still happening down at Elmhurst.

Pointer felt quite sure that Mrs. Amcott did not know of her win, or she would not have left the ticket, unlocked, in that figure. There was no wireless at Elmhurst. No cable seemed to have reached her from Spain. It looked as though she had gone to bed on Monday night ignorant of the large fortune that was now hers. But others might have been quite aware of the fact, and had seen to it that she should not wake on Tuesday to receive a list of the numbers, or read them in an easily obtainable paper.

While Pointer was busy in town, Blair spent the morning trying to think things out, since he could not sleep. But he found reasoning as difficult as resting. In

the afternoon he learnt that all the village was talking
about the visit of Mr. Ralph Amcott to the manor last
Tuesday night. No information could be gathered as to
how he had come or how gone. The villagers were divided
in then minds. Some, headed it was said by the rector,
inclined to the belief that the husband's spirit had come
to warn or protect his wife in her hour of peril, but come
too late. This idea was very popular. Gross materialists
thought it simpler to believe that the two men who
claimed to have seen the figure were either drunk at the
time or lying now. But there were those, Blair amongst
them, who wondered whether there might not lie the
solution of the mystery concerning Mrs. Amcott's death.
There was talk of Mr. Ralph having sent his wife home
because of a flirtation with a fellow-official, of her having
kept up a forbidden correspondence, and even—of
course—of a proposed elopement, which the husband,
hurrying home secretly while he had been himself
announced as lying ill, had prevented in a way more
common in Latin countries than with us.

It was in the early afternoon that Joan motioned Blair
to come into the deserted drawing-room.

"I've been over the manor," she said softly, "and while
I've been out someone has been through my things here
in the inn—again! I knew it as soon as I got back by the
position of the suitcase—my only piece of luggage—on the
side table. Inside it I keep my money. No, no! Not gone at
all. Wait!" as Blair made a quick, involuntary motion
towards his own pocket-book.

"Now I happen to keep a very close account of my
money, naturally." She gave a faint smile "It's not
difficult. But I found two ten-pound notes too many. I
have no ten-pound notes, but I got a cheque cashed for
Mrs. Amcott on Saturday when I went to the bank for the
emerald necklace, and these notes were among those
handed me for her. When I was hunting among her
things the day before yesterday I found a slip with the
numbers jotted down, and by luck I knew where it was

still. I got it, looked at it, and found I was right. Those two notes put upstairs among my money are two of Mrs. Amcott's notes."

"Where are they?" Blair asked quickly.

"I put them in an envelope, printed Monsieur Waddy's name on it, and dropped it in the manor letter-box a little while ago, along with a note, also printed, to Mr. Hilary Amcott, which stated that two ten-pound notes which the sender believed belong to the late Mrs. Amcott had been found and returned to Monsieur Waddy."

"Good for you!" laughed Martin. Joan laughed too—for the first time since that meeting on the boat, like a happy child.

"Oh, Martin!" He had been promoted for bravery on the field, she told him; in other words, for his efforts to rescue her last night in the flooded cellar. "Oh, Martin, I've been talking to Mrs. Black. She told me that Mr. Ralph Amcott was seen here in Elmhurst last Tuesday night, and if Tuesday, why not Monday? Mr. Ralph, whom everyone thought in Khartoum."

"I doubted that much-credited item," Blair could say truthfully enough. She looked at him admiringly.

"Up at the manor all the servants are talking of it too. The maid who spoke to me about it says that she and two other servants have seen Mr. Ralph too, but thought, of course, that they were mistaken. It was only from a distance, and they thought up till now that it must have been Mr. Hilary in a dim light. But to think that at last there's a hope of the truth being found out! It really looks as though Inspector Armstrong, with his talking of time as telling everything, is going to turn out to be true after all. And it got on my nerves so!" Then suddenly her face grew very grave. "I met Monsieur Waddy as I was coming down the stairs." She shivered.

"And he?"

"He looked at me as though he would have liked to fling me down them," she said with a shiver. "'Still here?' he said in a quiet indescribably mocking and yet very terrifying way. Oh, I don't pretend that he doesn't frighten me, Martin, for I feel that he's got some plan, and is only waiting for the right moment. Now more than ever, now that I seem about to be cleared."

"You ought never to have come down here really," Blair said at that.

"I felt that I had to! I hoped so much to find something out, to help clear myself, but I've found nothing. Why, I had even passed by a score of times that 'gone mad' that the Chief Inspector found at once. I wish I knew what that means..."

"So do I," Blair agreed, "though one can link it up with her husband's arrival. Like Ralph seems to have gone mad about so and so. Something like that... But what are you thinking of doing?"

"Of getting away before Waddy springs that trap of his. After his attempt last night on my life, and just now on my liberty—for, of course, be would have seen to it that I was accused of stealing those notes—I'm more terrified of him than ever. I have a sort of feeling"—she paused—"that it's touch and go," she finished under her breath. "You foiled him the first time, I've avoided the second plan, but the luck may be with him next time. And in some way this news leaking out about Mr. Ralph's arrival seems to be hurrying him up. That's how I read those bank-notes planted in my case, and his face and manner on the stairs of the manor. You know, I shouldn't wonder if his belief that I have those emeralds is my salvation in a way. But for believing that I've got them, I think he would have pointed me out to the police at once."

Blair on the whole was inclined to agree with her.

"You don't think it's something else that he may think you have?" he asked. "Somehow the emeralds don't seem to me to quite explain it."

"But what else could it be?" she asked him, round-eyed. "What else can it be? Anyway, I want to get away until everything is cleared up. Thank heaven, that seems to be near at hand now. But for the police, of course, I'd go openly. But they still want Joan Ingilby—poor, hunted Joan Ingilby" She spoke with sorrow, but with no bitterness. "At least, the Inspector does. The man from Scotland Yard is on my side. He's like you. He's got brains. The trouble about getting away is that I'm watched all the time. Unfortunately for myself, I gave their man the slip last night, and since then, for my own sake also, they're watching me closer than before. We shall have to be very clever and very quick. I suppose I can count on you?" She asked it with a roguish little smile that told of how certain of the answer she felt. There was a soft light in her eyes. that made his heart beat fast...

"Nothing need keep me here now. The case, my case, is in good hands, and I want to escape before Waddy strikes, before his net closes around me finally."

"*My* net!" he put in remorsefully.

"I don't believe I shall escape it, or him, next time." She was speaking very soberly now. "Premonition perhaps."

"Superstition!" he corrected on the instant, but his mind was racing to help her. "We've got to escape from the police, you think, as well as from Waddy..."

Both were silent for a moment; both trying out plans. She spoke first.

"The rectory might help. It's a house out of which it's easy to slip unnoticed. Part of the cellars are Plantagenet. There's one that runs ever so far under the ground and comes up in a little tool-house near a gate in the orchard. Mr. Grimshaw's sister showed it to me once some time ago. They don't often use it, but it's convenient for wet Sundays, as it cuts off a windy corner by the church. The door leading up into the shed is bolted only on the inside. I know that Mr. Grimshaw is always at the Institute later on this afternoon. If I went to his rectory I could easily slip down into the passage. His front door is never locked. That's a rule with him. Day or night it's only latched. He has only one woman as a housekeeper and servant. If I met her I should explain that I had stepped in to write a

note after ringing in vain. People do, you know. He keeps
literally an open house, and the same old woman who
was there in his father's time. What was that?" Joan
clutched Blair's sleeve convulsively.

Blair had heard nothing, but he had been listening
very intently to her.

From the point of view exclusively of the suspicions
against Joan, it seemed a pity to do anything now to
jeopardise herself. If discovered, if anything went wrong,
she would indeed be in a parlous state. At the same time,
he thought she was wise to get away, just as she had been
foolish, or at least too daring, to come. There was a very
real and a very terrible danger still hanging over her
head, and there was Monsieur Waddy and the
incalculable menace that he seemed to represent. That
flooded cellar rose before Blair's mind. Had he been half-
an-hour, a quarter of an hour later!

"Wasn't someone in the passage?" With a gesture she
slipped to the door and flung it suddenly open. The wind
seemed to howl at them, but the passage was empty, so
was the landing, so seemed the stairs.

"I thought the door creaked as though someone leant
against it," Joan said when they were once more beside
the fire, the door shut. "It must have been the wind, I
suppose. But now, to go on. I will chance getting into the
passage unseen and out of the shed. So meet me by the
gate"—she described exactly where it was—"and we'll slip
away on foot to Salisbury. It's a glorious afternoon for a
walk, not too light, and yet light enough. I've got my
things all packed. My bill is settled. I said I didn't like it
to run on. If you telephoned to a discreet garage in town
to send down a car to meet you at a given place on the
Salisbury road, you could take me on too, and all would
be well."

"Would you go far?" he asked wistfully.

"Anywhere where Waddys don't grow," she said
wearily. "He's got on my nerves. If only that wretched
necklace would turn up he'd cease to take an interest in

me. But as it is, I thought of one of these sea trips." She pointed to an advertisement in the Morning Post. "'A trip to the Canaries and back for seventy-five pounds.' It seems a fearful sum, but I'm quite wealthy. I've had no expenses for three years back, and when I left Countess Gérode she gave me fifty pounds as a parting keepsake. I think a cruise would be a delightful souvenir, don't you? I should think of the dear soul every hour, and wish to heaven I'd never left her. But for the fact that the kiddies were to go to a convent, for they said I spoiled them, I should never have left her."

"I haven't had a holiday since the unforgettable day when I met you," Blair said, staring at the paper.

She touched his sleeve with one of her rare, friendly pats. "You stay here and work, Martin. Work for Joan. Clear her name for her. I can't. That much I have learnt at last. I might stay down here all my life, and spend every hour at the manor, and yet be no nearer the reason for that murder. But you're different. You're clever. I'm such a hopeless fool. I don't know where to begin."

Blair went over the plan carefully. He did not care for the underground passage part, but Joan insisted that it was the only way that she could avoid the man who always followed her, by orders of the police ostensibly to protect her. Perhaps really for that reason, she agreed. The man would suppose she was waiting to speak to Mr. Grimshaw, or was writing a note to him.

It all went off well. The car picked them up at the spot agreed on, though Joan was a little belated.

It was getting dark when they ran into Salisbury. Blair had decided, on talking it over with her, that they would pass through that busy town to confuse the trail. They were almost in the outskirts when Joan turned to him very quietly.

"We're being followed. That's a car from Elmhurst— Mr. Hilary Amcott's Sunbeam. You can't hope to outrun her. I know that car. She easily does seventy without going all out."

Blair saw that the big car behind them, purring like a great cat, was closing up.

"There's a turning near here. Our one chance is to shoot into it and have them think we've gone on." She still spoke quietly, but her face was tense. Her eyes burnt. "It's downhill. The engine's off. You can turn her silently..."

Blair did. Like a mouse his car crept around the curve. It was twilight now. They heard the big car hum past. Their own lights out, they saw Waddy at the wheel, that cruel chin poked far forward, his all but invisible eyes raking the confusing grey as he turned his head from side to side like a blind adder.

"He'll be back in a moment," Blair said softly. "Now then, out of the car!" He swung Joan out and jumped down beside her.

"There's an open gate back there," she said, "I think if we went towards him he wouldn't look for us in that direction."

"He'll give up the hunt when he finds that empty car," Blair said, confidently. "It's one thing to follow a car, another to hunt out people on foot."

"He'll hunt me!" Joan said between her set teeth as she hurried towards the gate that she had seen standing open. They were in a street of what house agents call semi-detached villas, each standing back from the road in a little garden.

"Let's hide in the porch here."

Blair hurried in her wake. He thought that she was taking too serious a view of things, but he was not sure. There was a street lamp not far away that might show them up by the gate. For the trouble was that this was a danger where no personal courage or devotion on his part could be of the least use. Blair was very good with his fists; he had plenty of pluck; he would have faced long odds at any time; and for Joan he would have faced them gladly. But Joan's danger was something so all-enveloping, yet so subtle, that he could only hold his breath and watch with, and for, her.

The dazzle lamps of a big car came into sight as they swung two half-circles. The car was turning in after them. Then she stopped. After a second a figure got out, locked the car, and moved silently down the street, past them as they stood in the porch.

"It's a cul-de-sac," Blair said, peering at the lamps at the farther end. "Better slip out now and into the main road before he turns back."

"There's another man back there, waiting behind that pillar-box." Joan was peering over his shoulder. Then she stiffened.

"Monsieur Waddy is turning round." She backed against the door behind them. The porch was shallow, a mere foot or two in depth.

"The door's not fastened!" Joan gave a gasp. "What luck!" She caught his arm and pulled him inside, closing the door behind them noiselessly. The hall was dark. A thin carpet was under their feet. Blair guessed that some servant left in charge had slipped out for a trifle, and had left the front door conveniently on the latch.

It was odd, standing in a strange house, in a street whose name he did not know, waiting for he knew not what... Blair thought Joan was taking the wrong course. But she left him no choice, and he dared not make a suggestion or question any suggestion of hers in a hurry.

It was surely time now to open the door and slip out to their car and be off. His hand was turning the little knob of the lock, when he stopped. It did not need Joan's touch on his wrist to tell him that someone had come up the short path and was outside in the porch. He heard no key inserted, but the door was opened with a sudden, soundless push for which he was unprepared. Also, subconsciously, he was at a disadvantage. This was undoubtedly someone who had a right to enter the house. Blair had none. There is no sensation more laming, that more makes for hesitation, than an uneasy conscience. It was all done in a second. As he gave ground, so did Joan behind him. Following her pull, he found himself in a room just by the door. Joan drew the door shut.

"The key's this side!" she gasped half hysterically, turning it without any effort to do it silently—speed being her one aim. "Now, out through the window!"

"No, no!" he said soothingly. This had gone far enough.

"That was Waddy who came in—who opened that door! It's a trap. He's caught us where he wants us. Martin, I've found something since we parted—a sealed envelope slipped behind a bureau drawer in Mrs. Amcott's room. That's what made me late. I didn't want to speak of it till I had had time to see what was inside it, for it's marked 'Important' in Mrs. Amcott's writing. Mr. Waddy came in just as I slipped it into my handbag, but he came in with such a rush that I wondered if he hadn't been watching me in some way. He looked—oh, extraordinary. His eyes were like coals of fire."

"Sparks," corrected the user of the written word automatically. "You can't have coals as small as his eyes."

"Fortunately a maid was passing down the stairs to post a letter, and I let her show me out, and kept beside her for a while. There must be something tremendously important in that envelope," she went on eagerly "I think I am justified in opening it under; the circumstances—don't you?"

Through her whispered words Blair heard something stir even now outside the door.

"Hand me over that envelope," he said in tones loud enough to be heard outside, and yet subdued enough to suggest an effort at secrecy on his part "They'll never think of looking for it on me. It'll be much safer than with you. Trust me, dear." he said. He had—a plan to divert to divert the hunt from her to himself.

"But they'll suspect at once that I've given it to you to keep," she whispered with an admonitory frown to him to talk lower He did not heed it If anything, he raised his voice

"Not they! And if they do, I shall know how to keep it safe. Let me switch on the light"

"But why?" With the look of one who is none too pleased at the incomprehensibility of suggestions showered on her, Joan handed him, on his urgent gesture, a sealed envelope. On it was the one word "Important."

"Now then, out of the window with you!" he whispered, switching off the light and glancing out into the street. "I see that the house, outside of which I left the car, has lighted up. A couple of women are having tea in the front room. I think you might make it unnoticed. I'll be here in the window covering you And as I have the paper—you ought—"

"You can't do anything against that awful man" She hung back.

"Can't I?" Blair's pride was aroused.

But she wheeled "No! Give me the envelope back I know him, you don't. He'll trick you in some way and get hold of it. I have a feeling that it's vital in proving who murdered Mrs. Amcott. It's the only thing I've found in all these days. Let me have it back, Martin. I can run across and be in the car before they know I've gone, if you stay and call out to them."

Had it been possible for Blair to be angry with Joan, he would have been so now. The idea that she, or any woman, could hold what he could not, or that he could not keep what she could! That he could be easier duped than a girl! It would have rankled from anyone but her. Even as it was, he flushed deeply.

"Waddy or anyone else will only get this paper over my dead body," he said curtly, if somewhat melodramatically.

"But I don't want..." she began with a little cry.

He stopped her. "Now let me help you out."

He watched her slip across the road and into a car opposite. After a second's pause he saw the car turn and rush off into the darkness of the road beyond the lamp-post.

CHAPTER NINE

BLAIR looked around the room. His back to the window, he studied every inch of floor and wall and furniture for some good hiding-place, if need be, for the paper.

As he stood so something banged. For a moment he thought that it was the front door, and meant a hasty pursuit of Joan. Then he saw that the outside shutters to his window had closed. He threw up the window to fling them wide again, but they would not budge. Shaking them, he felt that they were fastened on the outside by some stout bar that had been shot up from below. They were of stout oak, and effectually blocked that way out.

As he wrestled with them, there came a sharp rat-tat! rat-tat! on the front door. Blair heard the front door opened.

"Registered letter for Mr. Blair," said a businesslike voice. "Marked 'urgent.'"

"No one here of that name," said a voice that Blair did not know, speaking as though closing the door and turning away.

"But he's in the house all the same," the postman retorted. "Saw him just as I passed. In that front room where the shutters have just been closed. I know Mr. Blair well. That's why I stopped here, seeing as the letter is marked 'urgent.' Mr. Blair!" came his voice, raised in a hearty call. Blair had already unlocked his door. It was amazing what that familiar uniform meant. A moment before very sinister things had seemed stirring, and stirring close by. But with his door open and that stalwart, business-like-looking man holding out a letter and a slip for him to sign. Blair felt once again back in familiar surroundings.

"Knew I wasn't mistaken" the man said in the same cocksure way that he had spoken from the first. "Just sign here, will you please, sir? Letter for you. Registered and marked 'urgent.' So as I caught sight of you in passing, why not bring it in, I thought, and save time?"

"I'll walk on with you, postman," Blair said after signing. "I want a chat with you on your views on the abolition of Christmas boxes," and with a keen glance at the man who stood back in the shadow of the hall, a man whose face was unfamiliar to him, Blair passed out beside the postman, who swung his heavy bag over his shoulder with a practised twist of the linen, and looked at a small bundle in his hand.

"Got another letter, registered, for next door but one," he muttered as though only on duty bent as they passed out of the gate together.

"Who lives in that house—the one where you found me?" Blair asked lightly enough.

"Mr. Waddy, sometimes," a familiar voice replied. "Yes, it's me, Mr. Blair—Chief Inspector Pointer. You gave my men the slip, you and Miss Ingilby, but I was following Mr. Waddy. I felt sure that I should meet Miss Ingilby again if I kept on his trail. What was going on in there?"

"Is Miss Ingilby safe?" Blair asked instead of answering.

"She is," Pointer assured him, leading the way towards a car some distance down. "One of my men was on the lookout for her. We were following Monsieur Waddy. I hung around to see what was going to happen." Pointer motioned Blair to take the wheel, while he stepped into the closed car. A few minutes later he spoke through the tube. Blair stopped, and the Chief Inspector, his quiet, good-looking self again in tweeds and felt hat, drove on with Blair beside him.

"When I saw those shutters close I thought it was time to take a hand. What was happening?"

Blair told him. "What would have been the next move if you hadn't come along, Chief Inspector?"

"What do you think yourself, Mr. Blair?" Pointer asked in a very level voice. "They evidently think, or Mr. Waddy, let us say, has reason to think, that you hold something he wants. It was after the discovery of the tag of paper in the dog's kennel, you know, that the poison was put in the coffee you and Miss Ingilby nearly drank. I think Mr. Waddy and his friends would have searched you, and after that?" He left his sentence unfinished for a moment.

"Look here!" Blair said, "I want to understand this. Is that chap Waddy still in that house?"

"I don't think so," Pointer said, faintly smiling. "When I asked for you by name I fairly felt the cold air on my feet from the opening and shutting of the side door. I think we shall find Mr. Waddy at Elmhurst when we get back—quite astonished at the idea that he was supposed to be anywhere near this part of Salisbury this afternoon. But the fact that they let Miss Ingilby escape makes me certain that it is you, not she, who has, or whom they think has, something that interests them. One moment; that's a police car's horn." He gave a sudden toot of his own. The two cars approached, slowed down, and drew near. Inside the one coming to meet them sat Inspector Armstrong.

"Just got a 'phone message from Miss Ingilby. She seemed in a rare taking. Thought you were in danger, Mr. Blair. Begged us to fly to you and save you from Mr. Waddy. I think she's got Mr. Waddy on the brain," and with a laugh the Inspector pulled in behind Pointer's car.

"Let's see what it is that you have on you that interests Mr. Waddy so greatly, Mr. Blair." The Chief Inspector stretched out a hand.

"There's nothing of mine that can interest Mr. Waddy," Blair said casually. He had no intention of handing over the letter given him to keep to anyone but to Joan herself.

"That's highly likely," Pointer agreed, "but what about something given you by Miss Ingilby? Something she found in Mrs. Amcott's rooms, say. Something like a paper, for instance. I should expect it to be something in an envelope."

Blair looked at him. "So you were on the lookout too?"

"No." This time Pointer laughed. "Did you ever read *Zadig*, by Voltaire, Mr. Blair? I take it it's the first detective story we have, and certainly he out-Sherlocks Holmes in it. Well, along those lines I deduced an envelope."

Pointer meant that believing him to know about the Gordo ticket, he thought it highly likely that Waddy would keep an intensely keen eye out for anything that could be, or contain a lottery ticket. But Blair, not knowing that simple clue, only drew his brows together.

He knew better than to question Pointer. There was something about the Scotland Yard man that did not encourage probing. At the same time, he had no intention of handing over the letter that Joan had given him to keep, a letter marked "Important"—in Mrs. Amcott's writing. He put his hand into his inside waistcoat pocket and gave a sort of hoarse cry.

"Lost it?" Pointer said, turning on him in

"Yes." Blair was equally brief. "Turn round and drive back to that house we've left, will you, Chief Inspector? I've had a valuable letter stolen from me, or I've dropped it while wrestling with those outside shutters. I nearly stood on my head trying to get at a catch that ran down out of sight below the window."

Pointer drove back at once.

"Come now, Mr. Blair, confess. The letter was handed you by Miss Ingilby, wasn't it?"

Blair told how it had come to be given to him.

The door was opened by the same man whom Blair had seen on leaving. He stood aside stonily when the newspaper man said that he had dropped something in the room beside the front door. Blair searched the room in vain. He could have beaten at the walls in his rage. Joan's one find gone! If he had dropped it, how long would it have taken those dark, dull eyes of the man in the hall to find it? He himself, when he heard the unexpected voice of the postman at the door, had left the room without another look around. It was natural enough under the circumstances of intense excitement, but the fact remained that the letter was gone.

Still without speaking, the man let them out again when Blair gave up the hopeless search. As he closed the door Blair saw that he was of some Levantine mixed race like Waddy himself, so Blair believed.

In the car again, Pointer turned to the young man sitting white-faced beside him.

"I don't think there was anything of value in that envelope, Mr. Blair. Even if Monsieur Waddy now has it, it won't be of any assistance to him, any more than I think it would have helped Miss Ingilby to clear—her sister."

Was it Blair's fancy, or was there the hint of a pause before the last word? He told the Chief Inspector about the bank-notes in "Miss Lucy's" suitcase. Joan had decided that this should be done if she was not able to get away at once. Blair went on to give the conclusion that he and she had arrived at, which was that Waddy was evidently trying to discredit the elder sister as well, or at least to frighten her away from Elmhurst. He thought the latter quite possibly was the true motive.

Pointer listened attentively, but he said nothing as he stopped the car at the inn.

Joan took it with very great magnanimity when Blair had to confess what had happened. She did not even look "I told you so."

"It must have slipped out while I tugged at that bolt. I ought to have looked around the room before leaving it, of course. But I confess I was so surprised by the turn events were taking, my name asked for by the postman, as I thought him, that I stepped out into the passage too hastily," he finished unhappily.

She leant forward and laid a hand on his sleeve. Joan rarely touched people.

"I don't suppose for a moment it was of any value." She spoke with resolute cheerfulness. "If it had been, Monsieur Waddy would certainly have found it long ago. Also, after all, it was Mrs. Amcott's letter. I felt a frightful sweep at the thought of opening it. Besides"— her face showed a look of relief—"perhaps if he has got hold of whatever it is he wants —something to do with the emeralds, I know it is—he may now let me be in peace."

That was all very well that night at dinner, but next morning Joan came down looking very pale and disturbed.

"Monsieur Waddy was outside my window all night; at least, every time I looked out he was there—under some trees. I saw his face when he lit a cigar."

"Cigar? I thought he smoked..."

"Cigarettes? He does. I think he lit a cigar only to let me see him. He played around with the match so long before he got it to draw right."

"Was your window shut?" he asked swiftly.

"Rather!" she assured him emphatically. "Rather! but even so, I couldn't sleep. Each creak I thought was a jemmy. Are windows opened with jemmies? Well"—she shut her even teeth and her eyes showed sudden fire— "yesterday was an absolute fiasco, but to-day won't be. I'm going to go openly, by train. I've dropped Chief Inspector Pointer a note that he'll get later, to say that I'm off for town, for the hotel where Mrs. Amcott and I used to stay. I'm going to stop there for a while, and see if I can come on any trace of the motive or the criminal among Baroness Maricourt's circle. Also, I ought to be looking around for a job later on. They're not jumped into in a week as a rule." She stopped. Three figures were walking up to the inn door. They were Baroness

Maricourt, Hilary Amcott, and Monsieur Waddy. The frost that prevented hunting all this week made the days glorious for walking. The Baroness barely nodded, but Waddy gave as usual his exaggeratedly deep bow. The three sat down in the hall lounge and ordered cocktails.

Joan bent towards Blair.

"He wants to see where I'm going. Well, let him!" Her chin high, she rose and walked out into the hall.

Waddy showed his teeth at her. "What is this? A suitcase? Does that mean that we're losing you, Miss Ingilby?"

"For the day," Joan said curtly. The boots stepped forward to carry it to the train, but Waddy, with an "Allow me!" took it in his hand. Then something happened. The case went hurtling down the front steps. It opened—which was strange, considering that Joan knew that she had locked it. Out tumbled a few articles of underwear, and a jewel-case which shot out as though it had been put in last of all. It, too, must have been unlocked, for from it tumbled a quaintly twisted gold chain set with large cabochon emeralds that winked like green lights in the winter sunshine.

"The Norreys necklace!" screamed 'Ty Maricourt, who either was, or pretended to be, absolutely dumbfounded.

Joan whirled on Waddy. "You—you..." She bit her lip to keep some semblance of self-control. "You did this!" she said finally.

He smiled in her face—a long smile of intense enjoyment. His tiny, eyes really closed by his merriment.

"What does this mean, Miss Ingilby?" Baroness Maricourt spoke with composure now. "What does this mean, please? The necklace which was stolen from me last Saturday, here in your suitcase?"

"You identify the necklace?" Waddy asked her, holding it out on a long yellow finger.

"Of course I do. It's the Norreys necklace. Miss Ingilby, you must explain things."

"Ask Mr. Waddy," Joan said passionately. "He can explain it. I can't! There was no necklace there when the suitcase was packed by me this morning. Unfortunately I let it be put in the corner over there while I waited until it was time to go to the station. It has been unlocked and tampered with."

She was very pale. Suddenly she turned to Blair, who now came hurrying down from his own room, where he had gone for his greatcoat, and had consequently heard nothing of the tremendous happening. She turned to him a face as though she were drowning, so white and tragic that he sprang to her. Then he saw the emeralds in the hands of Baroness Maricourt. She showed an indignant, yet very troubled face.

"Will you please telephone for the police." She spoke coldly. "I would have settled this quietly, of course, but after the accusation brought against Monsieur Waddy by Miss Ingilby it is impossible. The matter can't rest here."

"I have just telephoned for the police," Waddy said, with his eyes glittering and dancing like iceflakes in the sun. "They'll be here on the instant."

The waiter and a couple of maids stood gaping at the scene. The landlady, to her great regret afterwards, was out.

Blair followed Joan into the deserted coffee-room, where she sank into a chair. She looked ghastly.

"Done for!" she breathed. "I knew it! Didn't I tell you I had a premonition? Now I shall be locked up, tried, and how can I prove anything?" She was shaking from head to foot with deep, shuddering breaths. "And they'll find out at once that I wear a disguise. That I am..." She put her hand to her heart in a wild gesture of despair.

Blair would have given ten, twenty years of his life to have knocked the truth of the plot out of Waddy. But what of Joan, if as she, and he too, believed, the man knew or guessed her real identity?

He strode out again just as Armstrong arrived in his car, with the tall figure of Chief Inspector Pointer beside him. The two listened with imperturbable faces to the tale told them, at Pointer's request, in the coffee-room instead of on the front steps.

"The point is," the Chief Inspector said gently and quietly, "the question is, how did this necklace get into Miss Ingilby's suitcase?"

"Why, she put it in, of course, to take it up to town with her." Baroness Maricourt spoke impatiently. Her eyes showed that she thought the remark more than silly. But Joan caught her breath. She leant forward with parted lips. Hope shone in her white face.

"But why did she put it there?" Pointer asked again. "Why did she bring it down here at all, back to Elmhurst, in a suitcase which any key might open, and which apparently she had not even locked this morning? According to you, Baroness de Maricourt, the necklace was stolen last Saturday, either on the way up to, or in London, where there are literally hundreds of safe hiding-places for such a thing. Do you really think that anyone who stole that necklace, such an easily identifiable piece of jewellery, would deliberately bring, it down here—here to Elmhurst where everyone who saw it would recognise it? Where there are no practical places of concealment compared with town, and no means of disposing of it at all?"

Joan looked as though a respite from a death sentence had arrived. Baroness Maricourt seemed startled. She glanced at Waddy, who leant back, turning his head slowly from Joan to the Chief Inspector. As for Hilary Amcott, he stood watching the scene with his light, red-rimmed eyes and his silly smile.

"Then how do you account for the necklace being in her suitcase?" 'Ty Maricourt asked finally. Her tone showed some hesitation.

Pointer made no reply. Inspector Armstrong made none. The Chief Inspector had been standing throughout the short interview.

"I certainly refuse to arrest Miss Ingilby on any such insufficient evidence," he said now, turning away, as though the matter were finished. "But if you wish us to investigate the theft of your necklace, the Inspector here, or I, will be only too pleased to do so." Pointer spoke a trifle grimly.

Monsieur Waddy looked up; at least, he raised his head. More than that was guesswork.

"What it is to be young and beautiful!" His evil smile gleamed out for a moment whitely. "I think, Baroness, that you can hardly show yourself less tenderhearted than your own police, though, naturally, you are less susceptible to a lady's charms. However... suppose you let the matter drop? At any rate, you have recovered your necklace. May I have a look at it? What pretty stones!" Waddy made a pretence of languidly examining the chain. "Don't you think so, Amcott?"

Hilary Amcott only laughed, a curious cackle, which was a blend of malicious amusement and contempt. Without a word in reply he turned on his heel and walked out of the gate.

"Perhaps he's right," Waddy murmured. "Luncheon will be late if we do not hurry." And he and his companion followed him.

"Aren't you going to arrest anyone over those emeralds?" Blair asked the police officers in great disappointment. Joan looked almost imploringly at Pointer. But the two men shook their heads.

"You have to have proof before an arrest," Armstrong reminded Blair. "I'm sorry to say, this isn't Italy."

"Cheer up, Mr. Blair. Give a man rope enough—you know the rest."

The gate opened again. The Baroness Maricourt had come back.

"I owe you an apology if I've made a mistake," she said to Joan, biting her lip, "and apparently from what the police seem to think, I have made one. But seeing the jewels tumble from your case... you must allow that appearances were against you, Miss Ingilby."

"Appearances, possibly, but not facts," Joan said with fire in her eyes. "You didn't take the trouble to inquire into the facts, did you, Baroness de Maricourt?"

"I can only say I'm sincerely sorry for having misjudged you, or anyone, in such a matter." The Baroness hurried after her companions, evidently glad to get away from the burning indignation in the face of the girl whom she had so promptly and so definitely called a thief.

Joan went up to Pointer. She held out her hand. A lovely flush was on her cheeks now.

"I owe you my life!" Her smile robbed the words of bombast. "Arrested for theft! And my poor sister... With this murder charge still unsolved hanging over her! It would have been the last blow. How can I ever thank you enough! I only wish" —she gave a deep sigh—"oh, if only you could clear her of the charge of murder as easily as you did me of having taken those jewels!"

"You're leaving us?" Pointer asked.

She gave a little smile and shook her head ruefully.

"I seem doomed to spend the rest of my life in Elmhurst. The train has gone by now, and the next one would get me into town later than I care to arrive. I shall try again to-morrow morning. I shall leave my address," she said almost pleadingly. But neither Pointer nor Inspector Armstrong were prepared to detain her. Pointer thought that if she would keep them posted as to her movements they would have no objection to her leaving the New Forest. He said as much.

When the two police officers had gone on, Joan turned to Blair, her eyes still alight.

"Lucky for me that Scotland Yard is in charge of the investigations! I believe somehow that that man is on the right track."

"He's on Waddy's track then?" Blair said hotly.

Joan shook her head.

"Unfortunately I saw Monsieur Waddy at the theatre both nights. Sometimes I'm tempted to wish that I hadn't. But as I did—it couldn't have been he who murdered poor Mrs. Amcott."

"You think it's the husband? The police seem absolutely certain that he's really ill in Khartoum; that if anyone was seen, it was someone only made up to look like him."

"If I tell you something—" she spoke in the tone of one who has thought a good deal on the matter—"will you promise not to act without very careful thought? What I want to tell you is important, perhaps—but dreadfully misleading."

Blair promised. She told him of Mrs. Amcott's diary, which the rector had taken from the tallboy.

"Now, of course, Mr. Grimshaw himself is quite beyond suspicion. I didn't tell you before, because I hoped to get it back myself. I like to do things by myself, you know," she confessed, "but I've failed there too. In a way, I didn't want the diary found. Certainly not by the police, for heaven only knows what Mrs. Amcott wrote about my leaving her in it. But I feel more and more that I've no right to let the matter slide. The clue to the murder may lie in that book. Yet I can't, I simply can't believe that Mr. Grimshaw would willingly shield a murderer."

Blair said nothing. He had Joan repeat every incident, and, as far as she could, every word that had passed between her and the rector when the diary was taken.

"Miss Dallas and I are going to the rectory to-day," Joan said finally. "I may get a chance to speak to Mr. Grimshaw alone. If I do, shall I tackle him about it again, or shall I leave the whole matter in your hands?"

Blair thought she had better leave it to him, but keep her eyes open for the diary's possible whereabouts.

"And now"—she tucked a hand into his arm—"let's not say another word about the whole sorrowful, terrible affair. Let's turn back the calendar for this my last day in Elmhurst for a while."

"For how long?"

"Until Joan is cleared," she said more hopefully than she had ever yet spoken of that longed-for day. "Oh, what it will be like to come down openly—myself—once more, and know that I am really free from this nightmare! Come, Martin, let's go for a walk in the Forest."

Winter to the trees spells a time of peace and withdrawal. Impressive, bracing, symbols of self-reliance, they stand awaiting the spring. The sharp, cheerful, eager call of the nuthatch to its mate now and then broke the stillness as he hunted in some crevice of oak or split hazel. Now and then Joan and Blair caught from some deep recess the peevish note of that recluse the woodpecker. They saw ponies, shaggy as young bears, and squirrels a size larger in their winter coats. Once a snow-white hare scurried past, its black ears level with its back. As they stood watching the swift dash of Mr. Hare, a robin redbreast, appearing with consummate woodcraft from nowhere like a competent gamekeeper, came to investigate them. This was evidently his estate. He condescended with alacrity to share a crumb from Blair's pockets. A wren passed by without a glance at them—wrens care nothing for humans —but a hedge-sparrow who thought of lingering caught Robin's pugnacious eye and hopped past.

The rest of the woodland creatures were wrapped deep in sleep. Even the adders slumbered. But the tufts of wild honeysuckle like fairies' fans were here and there. A crimson-tipped daisy peeped at them from a sheltered nook. Spring would come in its own time, it said to those who had ears to hear.

In the next few days Blair was often to remember this walk. Joan was again the fairy princess of the boat—charming, gentle, with a certain radiant sweetness. She was in high spirits—so high that the word "fey" occurred to him more than once. He thought it, as it was partly, the reaction from the morning's terror.

Hilary Amcott dropped in before Joan and Octavia Dallas left the rectory that afternoon. He devoted himself quite especially to Joan. It was apparently his way of making amends for the scene about the emeralds.

"Look here," he said finally, "I've got a collection of Arabic amulets you might like to see. Suppose you come along with me and have a look at them?"

The talk had turned on native charms.

"I collect them, you know."

Joan was sure that he had some motive for the invitation. She was curious to learn what it was.

"I shouldn't care to meet Baroness Maricourt again, or Monsieur Waddy," she said frankly.

Hilary looked awkward.

"Small blame to you! The Baroness has left us. She's gone up to town, and is going abroad. Waddy's away for the day. I'm all alone, if you care to come."

Joan did care to come, because of that conviction that he had some reason for the request.

He really had a collection, and a good one, though he told her that Mrs. Amcott had taken two of his most interesting bits. Then he suddenly closed down the case and said, glancing at her from his weary-looking eyes:

"Speaking of Mrs. Amcott, I've had rather an odd letter, from a woman in Marseilles who believes she knows all about her death. She's Madame Cadmeia, the well-known clairvoyante. She says she'll tell what she knows, but won't write it. Of course, it may be stuff, but I'm rather a believer in such things. Would you care to go and hear what she has to tell? She says she 'saw the murder done' in a dream; that there's two men in it. That's all she's willing to put on paper. But, knowing how you feel, I wondered—what about your hearing her tale?"

Joan sat very silent. She looked at Hilary very intently. Was this a trap or a genuine offer? Hilary's ravaged face looked very amiable this afternoon, his silly smile seemed good-natured itself. He had seemed before this awful affair genuinely attracted by her.

"Like to see her effusion?" he asked, and produced a sheet of letter paper on which, in a dashing, pointed hand, which seemed all pot-hooks, the famous seer invited "M. Hilaire Amcotte" to come and see her, promising a vision of his sister-in-law's death that would settle definitely how the crime was committed and by whom, and so clear the child's governess.

"Well, what say?" he asked, when she still said nothing, only sat thinking.

Suddenly he went to the door at the further end of the long room, tried it to see if it was caught, and came back to her.

"Miss Joan," he said in a very low voice, "I think I'd clear out while the going's good. Oh, of course I knew you; at least, I knew from Mrs. Amcott that you're an only child. Now look here—that scene this morning about those emeralds —'pon my soul, it sickened me. Waddy made me think that you—oh, dash it all, what was a chap to think! Those emeralds—and a girl loves jewels—and, of course, he believed if himself—but your face showed me that someone had planted them in your bag. By Jove, that put a different complexion on things. Made me think. I don't often think these days. Jolly hard work thinking. But I've been doing it this afternoon. And the point is, why not accept the old lady's offer, go to Marseilles, and hear what she has to say?"

Joan decided that he was honest, that there was no snare concealed in the offer.

"But—how can I?" she breathed. "Oh, if I could! You know, Mr. Hilary, a crystal gazer once found a bracelet of mine when I'd lost it. Told me to look in a slipper toe in my wardrobe. And Madame Cadmeia! She's said to be a marvel. They say kings and queens consult her."

"Just so. Well, why not hear what she has to say?"

"But the police won't let me out of England," she reminded him. "Even though they think I'm Lucy Ingilby, they won't let me go abroad, or, rather, I think that if I tried to go, they might wonder if I weren't Joan. It's only been because I'm here at Elmhurst they don't suspect me."

"Jolly plucky of you to come!" he said. "By Jove, I couldn't do it."

"Oh, I had to. I hoped to clear myself, to find out who really killed poor Mrs. Amcott. But now that Scotland Yard is looking into the case I feel safer. I don't mind leaving my name in their hands to clear. Theirs and Mr. Blair's."

"I tried to give you a leg-up about talking to Doris on Tuesday afternoon," he said a little shamefacedly, "but it was no good. And you see Waddy was honestly mistaken about those emeralds, and I can't quarrel with him. He's got some I.O.U.'s of mine I shouldn't like to have hurried, so altogether but about getting away to Marseilles"— Hilary changed the subject with the air of a man throwing open a window in a stuffy room—"I think I can help. I've worked out quite a plan this afternoon. Oh, I used to be a demon at plans once—but that was before I got tired of life, and found it only bearable when I'm drunk. Fact, my dear. I have the most wonderful feeling then of being a prize-winner and all that. I only begin to live towards evening."

"Oh, don't!" she begged with infinite pity in her voice.

"Sorry, but it's true. However—about my plan, it's this. Grimshaw is sending a packing-case full of books to an institute in town. It's going off to-morrow morning by the milk train, leaving here at four. He's off by car to Southampton himself to-night, due to preach there Sunday morning early. He asked me if I'd mind leaving word for him at the station —I had told him I was sending down to inquire about the changed hour for the afternoon express—to be sure and send a cart for the case. Well, here's my plan. Grimshaw has another empty case at the rectory, which he got to send an upright piano of his to a boys club next week. Suppose I leave word to-night at the station, after he's safely departed, saying that two cases are to be carted to town to-morrow—the one with great care. And suppose I arrange, in his name, of course, for one to be delivered at his private address in town. The railways do that often, and won't be surprised. He shifts his furniture back and forth a good deal. Miss Grimshaw left yesterday for the Riviera. The house is in charge of a caretaker, I happen to know. The case, with you in it, will be delivered without any bother. I come along after a few minutes, say that there was a mistake, and cart the case and you to my brother's house in Holland Park. There you get out, and I'll see about a passport for you. There's a chap in the passport office who only knows me as my brother's secretary. He'll hurry up things if I ask him. We'll get a photograph of you as you are now, and call you by some other name. I'll be sponsor, and it'll be rushed through in an afternoon. Trust me. Meanwhile you give out down here that you're ill, or on a holiday near-by, or whatever you like. You can fly to Marseilles and be there the next day, and a couple of days to get back. You'll do it in five, and can bring home Madame Cadmeia's version of the murder, if it was a murder, which I doubt, that'll clear up everything. Now I call that a jolly good plan. Don't you?"

"I call it a very risky plan," she said thoughtfully. "If I'm discovered in that packing-case..."

"But you won't be. Why should you be? It's not going through any Customs. It'll be marked Fragile and This side up with care, and so on. We'll put a couple of eiderdowns in for comfort and to soften corners, so I don't see how the plan can fail."

Joan sat for some time thinking it over. It might succeed with any luck, provided the man was playing fair and she thought he was.

"And you won't let Monsieur Waddy guess where I am?" she asked earnestly. "Do you think you can keep it from him, Mr. Hilary?"

"Trust me!" he said confidently.

"I do trust you. But Mr. Waddy is very clever. If I'm not here, he may wonder... and suspect..."

"I shall know nothing. Look here, Joan, I really do want to help you to get to Marseilles. Like you, I've heard wonderful things of this woman over there. And, besides, after this morning and those emeralds—well, obviously someone has it in for you. We both can guess who. And a devilish trick it was to play."

"It was Monsieur Waddy," Joan said bitterly.

"Not he!" Hilary said with warmth. "There was a woman's spite in that! But you take it from me that I shall tell no one where you've gone. I shall know nothing, as I said, and who would think of connecting me with your absence?"

"That's true," Joan murmured. "I should love to learn what Madame Cadmeia can tell me," she said finally, "and if you can work it as you suggest, it's a tremendous temptation to try. Of course, I can't let the police know, but I'll drop Mr. Blair a note saying where I have gone. He might worry otherwise. He's away for this evening until late."

She looked very straight at Hilary as she said this. He nodded.

"Right-o! Ask him to keep it to himself. He would anyway. But don't let him find it until to-morrow morning after you've gone I know that type of fearfully clever chap, they always want to row stroke. What will you say to him? As I shall have to back it up, I had better know."

Joan went over to a table and wrote for a minute She handed him the sheet when she had finished the letter.

"Dear Martin,
I have had a wonderful piece of news. The famous Madame Cadmeia has seen Mrs. Amcott's murder in one of her visions. She says two men were in it. I am leaving at once for Marseilles to hear the rest. Mr. Hilary Amcott is helping me to get out of England... There's no reason why he shouldn't but the police would try and detain me if they knew... So I am going inside one of Mr. Grimshaw's two packing cases to his town address by the milk train on the

*day you get this (to-morrow, as I write). There Mr. Hilary
is going to 'collect' me and take me to Sir Christopher's
house in Holland Park where I will be unpacked and
provided with a passport in the name of Lucy Jenkins. I
hope to leave England next day, and be back here in town
in four or five days at most. I will send you a wire from
Marseilles, signed Tom, saying when to expect me back
and, oh, wish me the best of luck. I very much hope to
bring back some news worth having.*
    'Sincerely yours
    'Lucy INGILBY"

"Ask him to burn it," was Mr. Hilary Amcott's only
suggestion; and Joan added a postscript. They arranged
all details, till finally she rose, and began to say good-bye,
thanking him very prettily for his help. Suddenly she
started.

"That's Monsieur Waddy's step outside. No! please,
don't trouble to open the door." Joan was out in the hall
before Hilary could stop her. She stepped swiftly past
Waddy, apparently without seeing him.

"Been entertaining angels unawares?" Waddy asked
with a curious glance at his host as he came in.

"More or less. Why? Look here, Waddy, I suppose you
heard something—that door leaks noise like a piece of
cardboard. But don't try to prevent that poor girl from
leaving England. I've told her something that she ought
to investigate. Besides, I think, after this morning, that
'Ty has got her knife into her, and you never know what a
woman will do under those circumstances. You're not
going to stop the little Ingilby girl, are you? If so, I warn
you that I'm on her side."

"What a threat!" drawled Waddy. "But as to stopping
her —like you I'm sorry for her, and would help her if
she'd let me. I begin to think, too, that that affair of the
emeralds this morning was a plant. As you say, women
are cruel cats. Where's she going?"

"I promised not to speak of our plan, but if you're on her side, there's no reason why you shouldn't know. She's off for Marseilles. I've had a letter." Hilary repeated about Madame Cadmeia's invitation.

"Surely she isn't going alone?" Monsieur Waddy said as he handed back the letter which his friend produced for his inspection. "Marseilles is a funny place. I only know it as a Parisian knows a provincial town, of course, but for a girl..."

"Just what I've been thinking," Hilary said puckering his face as though in an effort to clear his brain. "But there isn't time enough to get hold of any woman going that way."

"There's 'Ty!" Waddy gave his white smile and Hilary his silly giggle.

"I'd offer to go," the former said smoothly, "but I don't think Miss Ingilby would care for me as a courtier."

"Frankly, my dear chap, I don't think she cares for you in any capacity," Hilary said, with again that silly crow of his. "But there's a lot in what you say—Marseilles, I mean, and a girl who doesn't know her way about. I think I'll go with her myself—there and back—just to see that she comes to no harm. I won't tell her, but I'll just happen to be there if she needs a helping hand," Hilary finally decided after another interval of thought.

"No offence, but you generally need a helping hand yourself, Amcott, especially towards bedtime," Waddy said with his smooth but rather biting voice.

The two men laughed as though at a good joke.

"Still, I can make myself useful even so," Hilary said finally. "I don't remember a thing about last Monday night, but you tell me that you were with me all the time, and I made a most excellent bolster-up of your statement to the police; and desperately keen they are on drawing away that bolster," he finished meditatively.

"I know. I heard you and the Inspector at it again this morning. You kept your end up splendidly, old chap." For once Monsieur Waddy's voice sounded genuinely pleased.

"Your answers were models. They were really. And, of course, you and I were together all Monday evening till we turned in at milk time rather than cockcrow, into my rooms in St. James's Street. But now about this little girl. Is Miss Ingilby going by train or 'plane?"

"Oh, train, of course; as soon as she can get a passport, which takes a day or two even though I shall try to rush it through for her."

Waddy nodded carelessly. His face, with its all but invisible points of eyes, was turned towards the fire, as though he were reflecting.

"I might come along too," he threw out casually, "and we could cut over to Monte and have a flutter while Miss Ingilby is having her fortune told."

"You mean the fortune of whoever killed my sister-in-law," Hilary said with his unfeeling chuckle. But Miss Ingilby wouldn't go if she thought you a part of the luggage; and I want to hear what this Marseilles woman has to say. I suppose the letter is genuine. Miss Lucy is going to pass herself off as Miss Joan to Madame Cadmeia. Did you speak?"

Waddy had given a strangled snort. He shook his head now.

"I confess to being curious to hear what will come of it," Hilary went on, "so I'll escort the girl. But look here... that idea about Monte... you can fly there in an hour, weather permitting, from Marseilles. You go on ahead of us, and relieve me after we get there. I'll take Miss Ingilby out there, and you take her home. How's that? That would halve the fag of squiring the lady, and give each of us a turn at the tables. You first, and me afterwards?"

Waddy reflected for some minutes. The idea found favour in his sight, great favour.

"When and how do we transfer attendance?" he asked finally.

"Give me an address and I'll 'phone you when we arrive," Hilary suggested.

Waddy sat silent for some time.

"I shall stay as usual at the Paris in Monte," he said finally. "Ring me up there. I'll leave at once—if the police have no objections," he added sarcastically.

"The police? My dear chap, we Amcotts have fallen pretty far, but at least our guests are still allowed to come and go," Hilary said fatuously. "It's only Miss Ingilby who isn't allowed to leave England, and that only because of that fool's scrawl about her sister. Where the one is, they think the other may go."

"What an absurd notion," Waddy said smoothly, turning his face towards his host and apparently staring hard at him. A minute later, as Hilary was silent, he sauntered out of the room with his beautiful glide.

Hilary sat on for some time, staring into the flames, and there was something as fierce as they in his face, as though some fire, burning in the man's heart, leapt out to meet the one upon the hearth.

Then he too went to the station, there to make very careful arrangements about two packing-cases which were to be fetched from the rectory the next morning— one of which, in particular, the one for Mr. Grimshaw's own house in Eaton Square, was especially fragile, and must on no account be jolted. A handsome tip ensured that this would not be forgotten. At dinner he heard that the police had no objections to the dispersal of the party at Elmhurst any more than they had had to Baroness de Maricourt's departure earlier in the day. Monsieur Waddy left for town at once.

Hilary, after an all but untouched solitary dinner, strolled down to the inn, so late that Joan had gone to bed. It seemed he wanted to make some inquiries for a friend about rooms and stabling for next week. That done, and a couple of cocktails shifted, he drifted out— apparently. But Hilary knew the house from childhood, and within five minutes was in by a roundabout way and outside Blair's room. Here he poked a long bent wire in the gap which the sagging floor had left beneath the door.

A very skilful manipulation of it, not the first clearly, scooped out a letter—a letter in Joan's writing addressed to Martin Blair. Hilary slipped it into his pocket, and in its stead pushed under the door one that he had written himself before he left Elmhurst, but which, to a casual glance looked as though written by Joan Ingilby. A moment later and he had slipped out of the inn and was making his way home to the manor.

CHAPTER TEN

BLAIR had spent the evening in Salisbury receiving reply cables from Egypt. Ralph Amcott certainly seemed to be genuinely in the Sudan, honestly ill. Returning very late, as he had told Joan he would, he found a note thrust beneath his door. It ran:

"DEAR MARTIN,
"Don't worry if you don't hear from me for a few days. For I'm off to follow up a clue I've found at last. I shall be quite all right. Best of luck to both of us.
"Sincerely yours,
"JOAN INGILBY."

He eyed the paper with great disfavour. Joan's other ventures had not been of a kind to let him think, without the gravest misgivings, of her as off on her own. And on that he fell asleep, to wake very early in the morning with his thoughts still full of her and her letter. What clue had she found. Where?

Had she come on something of real importance? That was what this letter looked like. He knocked at her door after dressing quickly. The room was empty, but the bed looked as though it had been slept in. All seemed as it should be. But she had gone to tea yesterday afternoon with the rector. With Mr. Grimshaw... The clue must have been found there... Why had she said no word in her note about the diary of Mrs. Amcott, since she was leaving for a few days?

Was she after it? Blair made his way at once to the rectory. He knew that the rector was away, or supposed to be away. The woman who answered his ring told him as much.

Had Miss Ingilby called there, early though it was? She had spoken of leaving a note for the rector. No, Miss Ingilby had not been yet. Blair, asked if he might wait for her. He was shown into the study. The housekeeper left him to his own devices and continued her work upstairs. Blair looked round him keenly. Looked for the possible hiding-place of Mrs. Amcott's diary. He sniffed. There was a something in the air... a fragrance... a faint perfume... he started. It was the fragrance of damask roses. Sweet as though the sun shone on a bank of them on a warm evening. He glanced around him. Nothing that suggested roses was to be seen. The room looked very Decemberish. Then where did the smell come from? He moved to the table. The perfume was gone. He stepped back to where he had first stood, beside the room's only armchair, and caught it again. He remembered chaffing Joan only yesterday about her habit of stuffing her handkerchiefs into the depths of any armchair where she sat, like a dog with a bone he had ungallantly averred. He felt in the chair, and pulled out a little wisp of heliotrope lawn. From it came the rose perfume. So Joan had been here this morning already. The strength of the perfume suggested this and the colour confirmed the idea. For yesterday she had had on a navy frock when she left for the rectory, and with that dress she always used light blue handkerchiefs. She had but two frocks with her. He stared around him intently. Under a bookshelf he found a couple of long straws and litter, such as comes out of packing cases, or goes into them.

He rang the bell. "I don't think I'll wait for Miss Ingilby. She may not come after all. Is Mr. Grimshaw leaving for a holiday?" he asked, flipping the straws that he had raked out.

"No sir. Only sending off a couple of cases to town." The woman picked up the bits. "One case was packed in here by the rector yesterday evening."

Had the diary gone? Was Joan following it up?

"Oh, have the cases left?" he asked in tones of deep disappointment. "The rector promised to show me some of the things he was sending off."

"There now!" said the woman vaguely. "They left by the milk train. Round about four o'clock."

"Do you mean to say you're up and about at that hour?" he asked in amazement.

She smilingly shook her head.

"Oh no, sir. But the front door is never locked. Mr. Grimshaw, he won't ever allow that. So the men from the station, they just same and fetched it away. Or rather fetched them. There was a second case to go, it seems, from down in the cellar. They just called their instructions to me up the stairs and saw to it all themselves. Nice, respectable lads our porters are."

"Were the cases big ones?" Blair asked. "I'm thinking of sending some things to town that way. Will they take large sized ones?" A strange, mad notion had come into his head.

"Any size as far as I know. One was as tall as that table. But the other was one that the rector had intended to send a piano in. So you can think how big that was. They'll take any size, I think, sir."

Blair said he would immediately inquire at the station as to limitations.

What had become of Joan supposing that she had wedged that little slip of lawn into that chair? Had she followed the cases to town on the train? And that mad idea of his that refused to be scoffed away... At the station he could not learn of her having gone up yet. An inquiry at the garages around was equally blank. He turned his attention to the cases themselves, and learnt that two had been fetched this morning according to directions and sent up to London. One was for an institute. One for Mr. Grimshaw's own house in town. Blair explained that he had promised the rector to accompany them to London himself, but had overslept.

"You mean accompany Mr. Hilary Amcott, sir. He had to go up early and so promised the parson to keep an eye on un," said the clerk.

Blair nodded. Hilary Amcott... promised Grimshaw.

A few questions that seemed like idle talk and he learnt that one weighed about nine stone. That was about Joan Ingilby's weight. Ridiculous thought. But it stuck. Finally he went into Salisbury, got an air taxi there that flew him up to town, where a car raced him along to Eaton Square. There he rang the bell. Yes, a packing case had arrived. But it was a mistake. It, too, was meant for the Institute. A friend of Mr. Grimshaw's had fortunately come for it almost at once and taken it off, for which Mrs. Jones was duly grateful, as it was a huge, heavy thing. It was labelled fragile on every side, too.

Blair explained that he too was from the Seamen's Institute in question and that it would have been his painful duty to have carted the case off, had not some brother-worker forestalled him.

"What was the gentleman like who took it away?" he asked, as though wondering which friend had done him the good turn.

"I don't know his name, sir, but I've seen him here at the house before. Looks like he has one leg in the grave."

"Fair?"

"Very fair, sir. Seems hardly able to keep his eyes open."

While he chatted, Blair looked very, carefully over the floor of the hall where the case had been deposited for a few minutes, until fetched by Hilary Amcott. Stooping down, he tied his shoe. No, there was nothing on the floor. But again, and this time strongly, he caught the same fragrant otto of roses smell as in the rectory study. Joan generally carried a tiny phial with her, he knew. Had she spilled it as the only clue she could leave him? Was the handkerchief, a forlorn S.O.S.?

"How sweet it smells in here," he said, rising. The caretaker had not noticed it.

"Big case, wasn't it. How did the gentleman get it into his car? You didn't help him, surely?" Blair asked, slipping half a crown into the woman's hand.

Oh no, Mrs. Jones had not helped. The street porter had done that. Who was this individual?

She pointed out through the door and said, "That's Burton. He's always about here on the chance of a job. Burton helped the gentleman."

Blair had a talk with Burton. The man described Hilary Amcott fairly well.

"Didn't the case feel funny?" Blair asked, offering the other some tobacco. "As a matter of fact, there's a mistake been made. It's not fully packed."

"That's what I said to the gentleman!" the porter broke in. "I felt the weight shift as I slung it into his car. 'Better have a look and see if it's fill right, what's inside,' I says. 'When the cargo's shifts, you never know what you will find.' But he said as he hadn't the authority to open nothing."

"What sort of a car was it? Yellow car? The gentleman you described isn't the one I expected to find had come down about the case." Blair seemed puzzled.

The porter told him that it was a yellow Delage car, and her number was—he gave it after a glance in a thumbed note book. The porter was a man of sense and always kept tally of car numbers, he told Blair.

Which way did it go? That way. The man pointed around a corner. Blair seemed to find everything in order, and drove on after tipping him.

Further down, around the corner in question, a young constable was on point duty. Blair asked him a few questions too. By mistake, a wrong packing case had been given a gentleman, a collector who had insisted on taking off a bargain himself. "And when he gets home, and finds that he's got a bureau instead of a gate-legged table, there'll be trouble." Had the constable noticed the yellow car that had driven down this road with a packing case in it. The constable had. He had seen it turn that corner there to the right at a speed which he thought careless, considering the main road just beyond.

Blair drove on. From point to point he traced that small yellow car with the large packing-case to a house in a dreary square on the outskirts of town. From the house again he followed the same car, but without the packing-case and with a woman as well as a man inside it. A woman... could it be Joan? Suppose his vague fears were right, Hilary Amcott, if he knew that Lucy and Joan Ingilby were one, could force her to accompany him where he liked. She would feel, and rightly, that almost any risk was less than the risk of being handed over to the police before they had their hands on another suspect. True, both she and Blair fancied that hour to be close at hand, but neither could be sure of this. And that suspect... Blair was sure that Armstrong at any rate, and therefore probably Chief Inspector Pointer, was wondering whether Hilary Amcott had not played the part of his brother. As far as Blair knew, there was no motive yet found to account for Mrs. Amcott's murder, but he felt sure that some such idea of an impersonation by either the brother or the rector was in the police mind. And the latter was hardly tenable.

He crouched behind the wheel and whizzed on. It was a devious route, this second one. But at last he saw where it had made for, and that was Croydon. Croydon with its aerodrome. He was very close on the car's heels, he thought, but at the aerodrome he learnt that a man, who answered to the description which Blair gave, had crossed in a plane to Le Bourget about half an hour ago. A "special" of course. He had had a lady with him. Name of Bartram, was that it? Mr. and Miss Bartram?"

Blair said that that was it. The civil aviation traffic officer went on to say that it seemed to be the lady's first flight. He thought she got into the plane as though she dreaded the flight. People did, you know, sometimes. What was the lady like, asked Blair. The manager could not say. She was wrapped up as though for a polar flight.

Blair set his teeth. His fairy princess helpless in the power of the dragon. For he did not believe that Joan would have willingly left with Hilary Amcott without leaving him word, and with such secrecy.

He knew that Amcott must have his false papers in apparently perfect order, or he, would never have tried flying. Leaving a country by air is simple. Landing is another matter.

He made for the telephone. A couple of years ago, a man had crashed in a Moth, and died next day. Blair had been sent to report the case, and had done what he could for him during the last hours. To his surprise he found that the stranger had made a will leaving him the plane. She had been very little damaged, and was a good little machine. The fault had been in the pilot. Blair had promptly joined a club and learned to fly. He had passed the Royal Aero Club's test for a private pilot's license, a license that he rarely used, for flights have a way of entailing unexpected expenses should things go wrong in out-of-the-way places, or in crowded ones either.

"Mabel" was housed at Brooklands. In a little over an hour he was climbing into the scat, and fastening up his safety belt. But even so, the short winter day was almost over.

The weather was fine and clear. The mechanic filling up his petrol tank began to sing the national anthem of the flying man during the war. A cheerful ditty with a take-off of "A brave aviator lay dying?" He got as far as:

> *"When the Court of Inquiry assembles,*
> *Please tell them the reason I died, I died,*
> *Was because I forgot 'twice Iota'*
> *Was the minimum angle of glide."*

when the traffic officer of the aerodrome had a brainwave.

"By the way, if you are going to see the lady again, you might hand her this. She dropped it just as the plane started. Luckily it didn't hit one of our mechanics in the eye. Ask her to be more careful another time. A gilt powder-box can be dangerous."

Blair looked at it. It was Joan's little box. It was still one more message for him, should he be on his way to help her.

On the box were the intertwined initials J and I He had questioned the wisdom of her using it. But, as she had pointed out, the J was so very like an L that she had chanced it. So he was right. He was not following a will-o'-the-wisp, but his princess. And she in some deadly peril.

He began to taxi up wind, with the throttle open. He knew "Mabel". She always wanted to soar at a forty foot length. But Blair ran her on to fifty. Fainter came the words:

> *"Ask the staff officer for a school bus,*
> *And bury me out on the Plain, the Plain,*
> *Get Randall to write on my tombstone*
> *Some formulae out of Duchesne"*

To an all but inaudible last verse of:

> *"So when I'm dead I'll be joining*
> *The flying corps up in the sky, the sky,*
> *Lets hope that they've studied 'Iota,'*
> *And the wings that they give me will fly."*

Blair let her up, and the seventy horse power little engine bit the air. Ninety miles an hour was "Mabel's" best, but Blair loved her. She mounted in huge leaps higher and higher, as a panther might leap, with life in every bound. Like a sentient creature she turned, obedient to every touch of the sticks. She was splendidly fitted for night flying. "Mabel's eyes" were better than any night creature's What would Hilary Amcott do when he landed in France? He must have wonderfully forged documents, or his real ones must have been altered to include Joan in some clever way. Wherever he went Blair would follow. He had utilized part of his enforced hour of waiting to tap his paper for funds.

He flew on "fast and high." Over the French coast the sky grew cloudy. Croydon had told him that there was no need to warn the night staff at Le Bourget to be on the look-out for him, as some important trial flights were going on. True enough, he soon sighted a great glow of light—the aerodrome. There, enormously powerful electric cables laid in straight lines, some distance apart, connected by curving ends, discharged currents which lit "Mabel's eyes"—tiny glow-lamps on the instrument board in his cockpit. By their brightness, their fluctuation, he could make the aerodrome in any weather —a change in the "eyes" telling him when he was off the path. There was another little set of lights that told him the altitude. How bright the wide levels of the aerodrome were to-night. All the navigation lamps were lit, even the flood-light batteries must be working.

Finally he swooped down, with engine shut off, making for the great central flare.

And then he saw disaster.

Barely thirty feet ahead of where he must land was a car. There were two men in her. A crash seemed inevitable. He had not time to start his engine up, and leap up and away from danger. A parachute is no use under a hundred feet. Nor would it have saved the occupants of the car. He leant far out and bellowed to those busy with it to stand clear. But some repairs were going on in a welding shed that drowned all the noise he made.

He saw to it that the petrol was turned off, braced his body in the seat, and put his goggles inside his coat. Fortunately the wind was head on. Now he was racing along the ground at forty miles an hour, straight for the car ahead. Still no one looked round. Still the noise in the shed drowned his. He kicked the rudder hard over, and his machine slewed round, whipping off the under carriage Then it tipped. It was his one chance to avoid a collision. For one fluttering second the field rose up in a huge wave, spun around as a swirl of black and green water with many lights floating on it might swirl. He covered his face with his arms. Thank God, he had missed the car. Was this the end? If so—crash! The wing took the shock first, and buckled, then broke.

Men rushed towards him. There were shouts— confusion. Blair leapt to the ground unhurt. The car which had been ahead was already out of sight.

"A Mr. Bartram and his sister landed a little while ago, from an 'Imperial' plane, didn't they?" he asked the French official in charge of the landing ground, to whom he hurriedly handed out his papers, those papers which would be scrutinized so carefully.

The official did not reply. Later, if everything was in order, he might. But "suspicion" is a word far below the attitude of mind of those in charge of landing places, especially at night, especially with solitary flyers.

But a mechanic was human. An Inquiry, not unaccompanied, received the reply that a gentleman and a lady of that name, had landed two hours ago from an Imperial Special. They had wirelessed a request for a car to be ready to meet them, and had driven off at once

Blair asked for the fastest car that the nearest garage stocked to be there within five minutes. The mechanic said that the car taken by the couple in whom Blair was interested, came from the same garage. Blair asked for details of the machine supplied to Mr. Bartram He explained that he was Bartram's business partner, and it was an unexpected affair of thousands, that was at stake. He must catch up with him on his holiday.

The official with his papers seemed to take an eternity. But finally Blair was authorized to land on the soil of France. He had meanwhile given instructions as to "Mabel's" stay in hospital.

Then the car arrived, and he settled about the deposit. He learnt that the one sent for Mr. Bartram was the mate to his. A Renault, capable of doing ninety English miles on the level—police permitting. What sort of a horn had the car. The same note as his. Had the garage supplied a driver? They had. There had been some mistake, unfortunately. Someone had sent the wrong message, or it had been wrongly written down. It appeared that the monsieur had wished to drive himself, but of course, once a chauffeur had been assigned them, the garage could not take him back without considerable trouble. Finally, however, when the monsieur had grasped the fact that to hold out would entail a delay till morning at least, everything had arranged itself.

Where had they gone? They pointed out the road—the Paris road. And with that Blair drove off. It was close on midnight. From Le Bourget to Paris by car is about an hour's journey. But if Paris, why had Amcott not used one of the regular cars supplied by Imperial Airways?

Just in front of Blair ran the marks of the car that he was following. Like two ribbons they wound ahead. He could tell by the freshness of the tracks, that nameless look of sharp edges when the road was muddy, that he must be very close on the man and girl in front. As he was following, he could drive faster than they. Fortunately, his car had a spotlight with a universal movement to enable the motorist to read unlighted sign-posts. Blair kept it trained down on the car tracks. How he blessed that appliance. It saved his alighting to peer at the ground at every cross road. Soon, not altogether to his surprise, the tracks turned abruptly to the east—at right angles to the road to Paris. Then they bore off to the south, and south easterly they remained mile after mile. He drew in nearer to the car. There came a moment when he heard its horn. Blair did not use his. What a noise his car made. This aspersion on a really good engine was most unfounded. Fortunately the wind was rough... And it came on to rain. Rain that slashed viciously like steel filings. Once he had to slow down. The car in front had stopped. It was in front of an aubeige; the chauffeur was doing something to the wheel. Only a few minutes did the delay last, but the man and woman came out to watch. The man had his hand affectionately tucked under the woman's elbow. The woman constantly turned her heavily veiled head up and down the road. His glasses told him that the man was Hilary Amcott, but the woman? He could not be certain of her. When they drove on, Blair searched the ground. He found a little gold pin, a little knot brooch that he had often seen. So it was Joan in the car as in the aeroplane. Poor little Joan. How hopeless she must be feeling, how abandoned to her fate, for he dared not give her even as much as one signal that help, or at least a friend, was at hand.

It was getting light now. He could not venture to keep so close behind them without being seen, unless—he eyed a motor-cycle leaning against the auberge wall. A tall young man, obviously an American, was coming out of the door and preparing to mount. Blair had a good look at him. There was something attractive about his clever, lean face.

"Look here," Blair said, going up to him, "I'm a newspaper man, rushing to get hold of a stunt. Here's my passport." He handed it out, photograph open. "I'm not an escaping criminal. Nor is this car stolen. Here's the receipt for the deposit for her paid back at Le Bourget. It's all O.K. But I want to exchange this car for that bike of yours for a while. I've got to catch up with someone, and your machine can beat this car."

"You bet she can," the man agreed, "but—" He looked Blair very sharply over. He saw the passport, the deposit note.

"Be quick," Blair urged, "every second counts."

The American nodded.

"Guess I'll risk it. Is this a permanent exchange, or just for the time being?"

"Just for the time being."

"Where am I to drop this, then?"

Blair said he would telephone. The other gave him an address in Paris, and Blair told him he could investigate at the British Consul's. That busy man knew him well from only a few months back and a very complicated business swindle that the journalist had ferreted out. With a hasty thanks Blair flung a leg over the cycle and tore off up the road.

"Gee whiz!" the American murmured. "The only adventure I've had in France, and that with a Britisher."

Blair now drew in quite close behind the car, which had no window in the back. He shut off his own engine, and hung on to the car by a stout strap which had carried the American's bag, and was now passed through the car's luggage grid, and around his own handle bar.

The tandem drove on and on, always south-easterly. It was close on five in the morning when they slowed down. They had been running along a railway line for some time. The day was too wet to see much of the landscape, or, Blair might have recognised the rich plain of Burgundy.

As it was, he guessed from his map that they must be approaching Dijon. Soon they were in that quaint little town, with its winding main street, flanked with shops stuffed with Dijon ginger-bread in incredible quantities, or else with rows on rows of Dijon mustard in pretty little faience pots.

The car began to slow down. Blair detached his strap, and dropped back as it drew up at a garage. A moment later, its two occupants got out, and disappeared into the office, to come out shortly with the manager who pointed out the street. Blair, bending over his cycle, with his back to them, heard the man say in French.

"He's due in half an hour, Monsieur. But he's late. Only stops two minutes. There won't be many passengers."

Half an hour—two minutes—Blair looked at a time-table. A train for Mentone was due in half an hour, and

would stop two minutes. Blair swallowed a cup of coffee
at a café near by. The average French coffee was one of
the first disillusions of his travels long ago. But even so, it
was warmth and food in one as no other beverage is. He
felt in his inside waistcoat pocket, a pocket that buttoned.
Luckily he had a large sum on him. No circular notes for
Blair, with their need of signatures on signatures, and
verifications, and banks shut over Sundays, and on the
unexpected holidays of the continent.

He walked his, or rather the American's bicycle to the
station. There he made out the necessary papers for it to
be sent on as soon as possible to the address given him in
Paris. Then he telephoned to the American. He was in,
and glad to hear of his machine's expected arrival. He
had already left the car at the garage which Blair had
given him.

"Say, did you catch up with your girl?" the man asked.
"Shucks! Of course it was the girl. I saw her just before I
went into that 'oh berge.' Say, she wasn't smiling at the
other chap. I thought she looked at the chauffeur once, as
he tanked up with petrol, as though half-minded to fling a
match in, and send him, and her, and the man with them,
all up together, and damn the conflagration. She did that!
I tell you..."

Blair had to drop the receiver. The bell for the express
had rung. He hurried on to the platform. There in front of
him were the two figures whom he had ridden behind for
so long. As they climbed into the train, Hilary Amcott
first, but always keeping a hand on his companion's arm,
as though to assist her, Joan dropped her handkerchief.

Blair retrieved the little crumpled bit of lawn. He
himself got into the next coach.

In his seat, he took out the little powder box that Joan
had dropped at Croydon. When the ticket collector came
around, Blair tipped him, and asked him to give this to a
young lady with fair hair who had got into a carriage—he
gave its number, and added that if the collector would
seem to have picked up the trifle himself, it would save

an appearance of trying to make the lady's acquaintance. The lady had dropped it in the corridor, but he had been in too much of a hurry just then to stop and hand it her. The man obviously thought him most discreet, but a trifle lacking in the right spirit of adventure.

Blair lit a cigarette and watched him on his way. Then he buried himself in a newspaper. Joan would understand. It was the only message he dared send. He would have liked to scratch a B on the surface of the powder, but he did not dare. Lyons was reached about ten. A restaurant car was put here. He put his head out of the window, deaf to the shivering expostulations of his fellow travellers, and waited. Once a man's head began to emerge from the window of the compartment where Joan was. He felt sure that it was Amcott, but he dared not look. Then, after an interval, when he looked again, he saw Joan glancing up and down the train. Their eyes met. She looked at him for a long second, her face immobile., then she put her hand to her felt hat, and drew in her head. Nor did she look out again as far as he could tell, though he rigged up a small mirror on a cane as a sort of periscope

The first lunch was served at twelve. Blair was sure that Hilary Amcott, and therefore his prisoner, would go to it. They did. Would an officious guard, he wondered, lock their compartment door?. Fortunately it was between stations, and the door was open. The compartment too was empty. Blair saw Joan's little close fitting hat crushed into one corner. She had twisted the veil from it around her head. Newspapers littered the floor. He picked them up. There was nothing written on them? He turned to the hat. She had put her hand to it. Did that mean anything? He remembered that she had placed her hand on the band. And there, under a cockade of ribbon he found a scrap of paper. He stepped into the next compartment, also empty, and opened it. On it was scribbled in pencil:

"How dear of you to follow after us. Everything is all right. But of course you're coming on to Marseilles. I'm putting up at the Hotel Noialles. You might happen to drift in there too and then you could come on with me to see Cadmeia. I won't let on I've seen you en route. H. A. might think you were keeping an eye on him."

It was not signed

Blair stared at the words. What new riddle was here? But he scribbled a line, "I will keep near you," and tucked the message into the place where he had found hers. Then he slipped back to his own compartment, wrapped himself in a newspaper as before, and began to think.

What mare's nest had he stumbled on? The letter was not that of a frightened prisoner. Nor of a prisoner at all. And yet... Blair was out of his depths for the time being. He could not feel solid ground try as he would.

Marseilles came next. It is a town that emphatically needs sunshine and its gay flower stalls ablaze with colour, or piles of its fruit, tomatoes or oranges, or great mounds of purple and green grapes. Seen on a wet and cold day—and it has its full share of both—it can be a peculiarly repellent town. Its mud can seem muddier, Blair thought, its rain wetter, and its smells more oriental than those of any other town, along the "Blue Coast."

He kept close on Amcott's heels. As close as he dared, though he wore motoring goggles and a flap cap which passed muster with his leather jacket.

At the big entrance portal a man jumped out of a car. It was Waddy. He came towards Hilary Amcott, hand outstretched.

"Got your wire just in time. Sorry to hear you must turn round at once and go back to England. How d'ye do, Miss—ah—Bartram."

He held Joan's hand in his. Patently held it. Blair would have stepped forward, but Hilary Amcott said languidly, "See after our friend here, will you, Waddy.

The police want me at home. Miss Ingilby has disappeared, it seems. And they think I can help them out with information. Such a silly notion! As if I would— lightly. Nothing but absolute necessity would make me take such a step. Absolute necessity," he repeated, and he squcezed the elbow that he still held in one cupped, bony hand.

Blair stepped behind a near-by pillar. His heart was pounding. What was best to do? How to help her most usefully? There was danger in the air. This was touch and go. Joan knew he was at hand yet she made no sign. She did not even look behind her. Even though he felt certain that she was in desperate straits. Something in her figure had suggested a start of terror when Monsieur Waddy, with all his teeth showing, had stepped forward.

Now she spoke. And Blair knew by the sound of her voice that he was right, that she was terrified and trying to hide it. In God's name, what ought he to do? Joan, not he, would pay for but one mistake—for but half a blunder.

"Mr. Hilary!" she begged, clasping Amcott's skinny arm with both hands, "please don't leave me! I don't know Marseilles. I don't want to be left here all alone with Monsieur Waddy."

"Oh, come now," grinned Hilary, and his smile was like a shark showing his teeth, Blair thought. "Waddy will only help you, you know. He knows his way about a lot better than I do. You'll take good care of her, won't you?" he asked with a note in his voice that made Joan flinch away.

"Now, don't make a scene," he suddenly added in a harsh whisper. "You go with Waddy, my girl! And no nonsense! Or I call that policeman there and give you in charge. Do you forget who you are, Joan Ingilby?" And wrenching his arm free of the hands that would have held him, Hilary Amcott walked off like—Blair clenched his hands—like a man who had tossed a bone to a dog.

Without a word, however, Joan was following Waddy to his car.

Blair signalled to 'a taxi. "Follow those two, and send me word at the station buffet where they finally stop. Take this." "This" was some money. "Don't let them guess they are being followed, and don't lose them. You will be content with the day's work if you don't slip up on the job."

The man, a typical Marseillais, with round black eyes and plethoric red cheeks, winked and moved off. An empty cab can loiter where one with a fare would be noticed at once. Blair sent another cab off with the same instructions. There followed a terrible wait. At last the second driver returned.

"The monsieur and the lady have gone to the carpet shop in the Rue Mazagran. Behind the Quai de la Joilette. They were still there when I left. It is a short distance from here."

Blair abandoned his meal, and let himself be hurried to the shop, a dingy spot in a dingy street. The Quai de la Joliette is in the most unsavory part of the old town and that adjective means something when speaking of Marseilles. The shop in question was one of those fly-blown Eastern places that abound along its length The only window was pilled high with carpets and rugs. Dust lay, thick on them. Dirt grimed the window pane.

Blair saw the cab which he had first despatched at the entrance to an alley nearer him. He got out, paid the second man, and walked to it. The chauffeur came forward.

"Your two birds are in that cage there, Monsieur. They have not come out this way, but all these houses have at least two doors. At least. There are supposed to be some down into the water. But I take it that that would not be where your friends are bound?"

Blair paid him, told him to wait at the end of the street, and stepped into the shop. There seemed to be no one inside. But it was bigger than it looked. Apparently it had at some time been a warehouse stretching to an unexpected length behind, narrow and long. The air was furry with the carpets hanging everywhere, or stacked in thick rolls around the walls. Stairs led up with a landing on each floor. Blair mounted carefully. He heard voices on the first floor. Walking up to the far end of an upper hall, the duplicate of the shop below, he heard them now as men's voices. His foot struck a narghile with a slight jingle. Inside a room at the end a voice, Waddy's, said sharply, *"Uskut!"*

Now Blair's knowledge of Arabic was less than little, but "Be silent!" happened to be one of the few words which it included. There followed a command to open the door, but Blair was down the stairs and out of the shop before the heavy key, that badly needed oiling, had turned.

He told the taxi drivers, each from separate sides, to keep an eye on the front door, and if the couple they had followed came out, to follow them, or at all costs to follow the lady. Blair would go on to the station buffet if he found the cabs had gone when he came into the street again.

He found the back of the house looked on a sort of open place where women were selling bits of young squids, tit-bits to your true Marseillais when stewed with plenty of olive oil, garlic, tomatoes and herbs.

He was in great doubt as to what was best to do. Would his interference precipitate a vague danger into something concrete? He stared up at the house. It looked unspeakably dilapidated.

Suddenly a window opened. Out of it came a little cream coloured close-fitting felt hat with a floating veil, a hat and a veil that he had followed for many an hour. A hand signalled.

It signalled urgently. Blair ran around to the front again. He entered the shop. This time a hunchback was bending over some bales of rugs. He looked up as Blair hurried in.

"I have business upstairs with the patron. I'm late," was Blair's only, remark as he ran up the flight in front of him. The hunchback looked after him. He had eyes as expressionless as a painted mummy's. Blair rushed up to the second floor. He hurried to the door which should lead into the room from which Joan signalled. It was unlocked. He stepped in. There, her back to him, buried in a high armchair; only her head showing, sat a familiar figure. "Joan! I'm here!" he said quietly shutting the door behind him. "It's me. Martin."

The figure jumped up. With a sharp cackle of a laugh the veil was thrown back. He stared into the face of Waddy.

CHAPTER ELEVEN

BLAIR looked a calmness which he was far from feeling. "Monsieur Waddy! What brings you to Marseilles? You were in Elmhurst when I left."

"The same thing that brings you here," Waddy replied with his key-board grin. "Watching over Joan." As he spoke, he leapt to Blair's side, and, with a deft pull, brought the other's coat down to his elbows, thus pinioning his arms to his sides. Blair was amazed at the steel of those flexible arms and fingers. Another second, and a woman, who apparently had appeared from nowhere, had tied his ankles together so swiftly, so dexterously, that one motion of her hands seemed to have done the trick. Then she tied his wrists, using hand-spun rope, strong as wire, that yet did not hurt or mark the skin. It was a kind that threw a terrible light on the house where it could be found, for, had Blair known it, it was the kind used in the East with which to tie up valuable but disobedient slaves.

"Better gag him," Waddy said, lighting a cigarette, and speaking as though to a servant. Yet Blair knew that there must be a close relationship between the two. Both had the same strange effect of a face without eyes—like an unpierced wall. A gag was skilfully inserted into his mouth. It did not hurt, but it blocked speech.

"Ialla!" Waddy gave the Arabic word with an effect of cracking a whip. The door opened. Two lascar-like men entered. They lifted Blair as though he had been a carpet, and swinging him gently in rhythm to their step, carried him up the stairs.

"Don't hurt him," Waddy murmured in the careless tone of one whose lightest word is law. Blair noticed that he gave no instructions as to where to carry him. The men seemed to have done this work many times before. They carried him to the top of the house, and put him down, not ungently in a large, low attic bedroom. Blair was surprised that they set him down on his feet. He soon saw why. Still smoking his cigarette, Waddy came up with something that clanked in his hands. A stout dog-collar was padlocked around Blair's neck, and again to a pillar in the centre of the room, with a fair length of chain between the two. A band was fastened around his wrist in the same way, and—in the same way—attached to his left ankle. It was a very effective arrangement. Waddy smoked on nonchalantly, puffing his smoke into Blair's eyes whenever he would have had to turn his head to avoid doing this.

"I suppose you know that if I am not out shortly, my taxi driver has instructions to go for the police," Blair said when they took out his gag.

"Indeed?" Waddy said in his throaty voice, a voice that always had suggested potted figs and *kousskouss* to Blair. "They will be delighted to meet Miss Ingilby. And she, no doubt, will be charmed to see them. Come, come, Mr. Blair," Waddy made a sign to the men who left the two alone, "you and I ought to be friends, but I'm afraid of your discretion. Hence these chains. But only for a few short hours. We both want the same thing—to find the murderer of Mrs. Amcott. You for the sake of Miss Ingilby, to save her from the consequences of that very interesting article of yours you wrote. I—for other reasons. By the way, may I offer you one of these cigarettes? No? Well, to resume, there is a man here in Marseilles whom I have been following. He intends to meet someone—I regret to have to be so vague—whom only Miss Ingilby can identify. A person whom I believe was outside the bank when those emeralds were handed to her."

"The emeralds found so miraculously in her suit-case?" Blair asked equably. He must not let the anger flaring inside him get the upper hand. For he did not trust Waddy, and if he was not telling the truth, he and the Devil between them only knew what was in store for the girl.

Judging by Waddy's position, he was looking at Blair, but in the dim light the other only saw the glitter of his teeth, not the glimpse of an eye.

"That was not the Norreys necklace, Mr. Blair. As we are alone, I will confess that I dropped a good replica into our friend's suit-case. I did it, not to have her arrested, as I am afraid she still believes—but to make her join forces with me and find out the thief. She has brains, has that young demoiselle! Also she alone has the clue to the whole affair. To the theft of the emeralds, certainly. To the murder, possibly. Once she has identified that certain person, of whom I speak, then I can act. For that person knows—must know—who murdered Mrs. Amcott. And Miss Ingilby will be free to return to England—and its so delectable winter climate. And you will be free to return with her—unless, of course, the idea of the shock to Madame Grundy?"

"But why these gyves?" Blair asked, still in the carefully good-tempered tone in which he had spoken before.

"It is so hard to keep an enterprising person a prisoner, Mr. Blair," Waddy explained in an apologetic tone. "I do you the justice to think you as clever as myself, and there is nothing else that would keep me a prisoner an hour after I had decided to leave. When Miss Ingilby has helped me out, you too will be set free. Till then— patience. It is only a matter of a few hours, and no calls, please, or I should be obliged to re-gag you. *A tantôt*" And Waddy negligently slung out of the room.

Blair looked after him with burning eyes. What was he to believe of this story? Much? Little? Or nothing? He decided to get rid of his ridiculous prisoner of Chillon chains as soon as possible. He looked about him eagerly for the means. An hour passed, and he had found nothing. Another hour passed and he knew that he could find nothing. His neck chain was long enough to let him move fairly freely in the centre of the room but not reach the walls, door, or the skylight in the roof.

About eight o'clock, the bolts outside his door were withdrawn, and in came one of the dark-skinned men who had carried him up the stairs. He had a large tray in his hands and it certainly exhaled a most appetising smell. He set it down on the table and showed Blair an untouched bottle of wine, of a very good vintage. Then he showed him the corkscrew, running his fingers along its curves several times. Blair was not to suspect the wine of poison or dope.

Blair looked the tray over.   If Waddy had meant either fate to be his, he certainly would have sent the hungry man some rich Marseilles stew, not the simple fare he saw under each cover as it was lifted.

There was no soup, but a fine grilled sole that had swum to someone's hook only that morning. There was a roast chicken that kept up the honour of its commune of Bresse, with it was a salad, and a pile of golden puffballs that once had been potatoes. A slice of cheddar, that certainly had not been tampered with, was under a glass lid, and a jar of English biscuits and good Isigny butter filled up odd corners of the tray. Blair ate with a will, the man cutting up his food and carefully collecting every knife and fork and spoon when he had done. Then he carried everything away except the wine and a glass, and brought in another tray. On it were magazines, French and English, and a box of cigarettes—unopened—as well as a little petrol lighter that only needed one hand to use. His mate now appeared with a pair of new pyjamas. They unchained Blair, helped him into the suit, rubbed and kneaded his right arm and left him in bed, with a reading lamp beside him, but with the left arm and right leg chained together.

Blair found that the chain bothered him in bed. He could not be so that it did not irk. As for the magazines—

was it possible that people actually read such stuff? Wrote it? Paid for it?

His mind was on Joan, and on the riddle that eluded him. Think over it, puzzle over it as he would, he could reach no solution.

Suddenly he sat up, stilling his clanking chain. Someone was outside his door. Very cautiously he heard the bolts drawn back—so slowly that it seemed hours to his tense ears, and must have been full minutes.

Someone was in the room now. The door was closed with the same precaution Then a low whisper reached him "Martin—"

It was Joan He turned the switch and looked at her. Her face showed very pale and determined, with her fair hair like a halo around it. She stepped up to his bedside and murmured, "I have the key to your chains. I guessed they had treated you as they did me in that cellar in town."

She unlocked his padlock, letting the chain fall with the greatest care. "Join me outside as soon as you've dressed. Don't speak. Just touch my arm. But put out your own light first."

She slipped away with the same precaution as she had used in entering.

A couple of minutes later, Blair opened his door noiselessly. All was dark outside. He extended his hand and touched a soft, round arm.

On the instant, Joan moved back with him and closed the door.

"Take this!" She handed him an automatic. "I found it with the keys in Waddy's desk. He's lying asleep. Drunk, I think. Or if not, he's been drinking heavily. But we must make no noise. We may want it." She spoke with a certain hard tenseness that her next words explained. "Don't let me fall into Waddy's hands again, Martin! Promise me that if things go wrong, you'll keep a bullet for me! So far, I've been lucky. He wanted me to help some plan of his. But when he learns that I've fooled him,

and I have fooled him, he won't spare me. Come! I have
no idea what we shall find downstairs, but we must
escape. I've promised Waddy to sail with him to-morrow
at dawn." She gave a mirthless smile.

"We've one extra helper," she told him. "He's been able
to get in. It's the chauffeur who drove us to Dijon. But
even so, you'll only be two against at least two Arabs, and
Waddy and his father. Though there was some sort of a
secret meeting here to-night... That may help us."

Blair turned out the light, felt for her hand, gave it a
squeeze, and pushed her behind him as he reached for the
door handle. She stopped him.

"Remember, Martin, don't fail me! Keep one bullet for
me. Waddy means to carry me with him, if I'm still here
to-morrow morning, or hand me over to the police. He
gave me my choice."

"If necessary I'll shoot you," he replied steadily, "but it
won't be necessary. I'm a good shot, and I think it'll be
Waddy who'll stop any bullets that go flying."

Again he opened the door carefully. Outside he felt
rather than saw in the blackness a man standing
listening intently. He was too big for any of the Arabs, or
for Waddy.

"A la bonheur!" he heard a hoarse whisper, "I've just
tied up *le pere.* I think the way is clear. If we make no
noise." He turned. Blair followed, feeling for the
bannister. Joan came last of all. They reached the landing
below them, then the one below that. They were now on
the first floor. Here a faint gas jet burned, showing a tiny
flicker of light. Blair was half across the landing when
Joan touched something that slipped. There came a thud
of a toppling bale and, as though it were a mechanical
device, the whole landing was illuminated by a strong
electric light, and there facing them was Waddy, another
automatic in his hand. But his face was yellow enough.
His snarling lips were twitching.

"Trapped! Shoot, Martin, shoot!" Joan called, in a
voice of terror and agony.

Blair pressed the trigger. Nothing happened except that the chauffeur, who had doubled to the ground as the light went up, now caught Waddy round the knees, bringing him down with a jolt that left him lying stunned. Then he turned and caught up Joan. *"En avant!"* he called, rushing down the stairs with Blair at his heels. Someone opened a door beside them. For the barest second a face stared at Blair, then he was in the street. Joan was calling him.

"Martin! Martin!" Her voice was panic-stricken.

"It's all right, darling," he answered, quite unaware of his words.

"Put me down. You're in the plot. I don't trust you!" Joan was speaking to the man who had carried her out.

The chauffeur set her down at once.

"Did I hurt madame?" he asked in the "fat" Midi accent of Marseilles.

Joan drew a deep breath and, managed a smile. She had been badly frightened.

"Let me see your automatic, Martin." She took it. "I thought so!" She turned on the chauffeur. "You took the cartridges out that time when I handed it to you for a second to hold. You must have!"

"Eh bien, I did. A loaded revolver is not for a young lady."

"We might all have been killed."

"No, no! I was there, madame. But we must hurry. Where to, madame?"

"To the station."

The man had a car waiting. He jumped on the seat, Blair tumbled in beside Joan and they were off, taking the first corner on two wheels. A shout came from the house behind them. It sounded like *"Au voleur!"* Blair would have drawn Joan into his arms but she pushed him away. She wanted no one's arms about her. She wanted to feel free—to taste her escape.

"Not now, Martin! I can't yet realise that I'm away from that house—from that man! Oh, I thought all was over when I found that he had got me!"

"What clue was it that brought you here?" Blair asked in the tense silence that followed.

She echoed his words in amazement. He showed her the note.

"I never wrote this!" She could not believe her eyes. She stared wildly at Blair as though he could explain the riddle. "Monsieur Waddy must have imitated my writing!"

"Waddy? Why not Hilary Amcott?" After those brutal words of his to Joan, Blair believed that the man, whom he had considered a negligible sot, was capable of anything.

"Mr. Hilary wouldn't forge my name," Joan said promptly. "He's never in two minds long. That's the danger in dealing with him. He takes on whatever colour Waddy wants him to, and talks him into. But it was Waddy who changed my note for this." And with that, she poured out her story in a quick rush, beginning with the talk in the library at Elmhurst, and Hilary's suggestion of her going to Marseilles, and starting off as far as London in Grimshaw's packing-case.

"Of course, it was quite true that the police wouldn't let me leave England. And I confess I do want to hear what Madame Cadmeia has to tell me. She really is marvellous. Incredible."

So was Hilary's tale, thought Blair.

"Mr. Hilary and I slipped into the rectory about three in the morning, and I let him help me into a large packing-case intended for an upright piano, that he lugged up—all by himself, I had no idea he was so strong still—into the study."

"Where I found the handkerchief!" Blair murmured to himself. She told of the care with which the case had been put on and off the train, of how endless the journey had seemed to her.

"And Mr. Hilary was so odd. He was always most considerate. So much so that I was glad—in a way—to have him always at hand. Yet there were moments when he quite frightened me," she gave a smile at her folly; "when he seemed to me more of a jailer than an escort. He really was like a machine, not a man. I tried to slip away once, just after leaving Le Bourget, but he was out of the inn in a flash and had his arm tucked under mine and led me back as though I were a child. Of course, I thought you had my real letter, so I wasn't half as alarmed as I should have been had I known that you only had that forged thing to go on. I don't see yet how you traced me by it!"

"That story is for later," Blair said. "Do go on!"

"I felt sure you would be close behind, if there was anything wrong. So just as I had emptied my phial of attar through the cracks in the case's boards in Eaton Square, and dropped my powder-box at Croydon, I dropped my brooch along the road to Dijon."

"I got it." Blair was proud of himself at that moment.

"You wonder-boy!" She gazed on him with an admiration that warmed him like wine.

"And then I saw you on the train. I was glad. Yet somehow I thought it would be as well not to say anything to Mr. Hilary about your being there. He seemed all right, and yet I felt that he was acting a part. What has happened, is that Waddy has been getting him on his side. He always could twist Mr. Hilary around his little finger, and because of something Waddy must have said, some lie, Mr. Hilary was absolutely changed. The further we went on the more he changed. And then that awful scene on our arrival." She shivered at the recollection.

"Monsieur. Waddy drove off with me and bundled me into a house, the house where you found me. Where was it? I mean what street?"

He told her.

"He didn't say a word while going there, only kept his arm linked in mine! In the house I was hustled upstairs between him and an old man who looked just like him, and there, in a room, Waddy said that first, before I saw Madame Cadmeia, I was wanted to identify someone for him, here in Marseilles, who had talked to Mrs. Amcott outside the bank in Salisbury on Saturday morning when I brought her out that case with her emerald necklace in it. But Martin—" Joan broke off her recital to say with wondering eyes, "I saw no one talking to Mrs. Amcott outside the bank. No one except Mr. Grimshaw, who was passing on the other side of the road."

They were at the station now, a noisy, but safe place. The chauffeur got down.

"And now?" he asked cheerily. "Name of a pipe, but that went off well, that little engagement back there, eh? But where next?"

Joan said she could not tell him where to drive her until she had been to the telephone. Blair took her to one in the station. She rang up a number, gave her name, and asked whether Mother Saint Joseph was still Mother Superior? If so, she would remember a Miss Ingilby who came there several times last autumn with the Countess de Gérode and her little girls? Evidently the name was familiar to the sister answering, for after it Joan seemed to need no more introductions. She explained that she had been stopping in a house in Marseilles which turned out to be a kind that she should not stay in, even for the remainder of the night. If she came on now, would the sisters give her a bed? Anything would do. Safety was all she wanted. There was a little quiver in Joan's voice as she said that, that made Blair's heart bleed for her.

Evidently the answer was cordial, for she hung up the receiver with many thanks, and hurried with him, back to the car.

"Do you know the church of Saint Louis at Hyères? Good. Have you petrol enough to get us there? You have? Well, there's an Ursuline convent just before you get to the church. A long grey wall with trees showing over the top. Stop there, please."

The man said he knew it, and they were off again. At this rate, Joan should be safe behind convent walls by two in the morning.

"And in that house, what happened to you there?" Blair asked, while the car sped on.

"I was locked into the room, and—well—somehow I grew dreadfully frightened. Oh, nothing happened to me, it was just fatigue and nerves. Then suddenly I heard your voice. Oh, I knew it at once!"

Martin pressed the fingers that slid into his so confidingly.

"And then I heard a frightful struggle. And something heavy being carried past my door. I—oh, I thought it might be your dead body!" She freed her hands to hide her face in them for a second.

"Did you care?" Blair asked softly as he took them again. She only looked at him, and then away. This was not the time for love-making he too felt.

"But after awhile, Mr. Waddy came in and he talked to me again quite—I really think—honestly—except that he spoke as though he had nothing to do with letting me go, or stay, as if he merely had to obey orders. Which is nonsense, isn't it?" Blair could not say.

"However, he said that the plan had had to be altered. That now we were to go on to Mogador. That Madame Cadmeia was there too. Mogador! I don't know where the place is except somewhere in Morocco, but he spoke of it as though it were Clapham. I refused at first. He told me that I could choose between going on board with him early to-morrow, or being given up to the police! He meant it. So, of course, I gave in. I—I flirted with him, Martin." She turned a pair of mischievous eyes like a kitten's on Blair. "He's frightfully vain. I let him think he'd made quite a conquest."

"A dangerous game, my dear girl," Blair said very gravely.

"Oh, I was desperate. I felt that I must find out what had happened to you. We had dinner together. And whenever I got the chance, he was called three times to the 'phone—I emptied my glass of wine into his. He talked quite freely about you. Said you'd be left in good hands until we got to Mogador, when you'd be set free. According to him, this person whom I'm to identify had got away, and we were to hurry after. The same old man came in, he called him father now. I said goodnight, and went into my room, locking my door on the inside. I was so afraid they'd locked it on the outside. But they were both fearfully worried about this someone having given them the slip, and besides, by this time Mr. Waddy felt quite sure of me. He and his father talked on and on, but about some sort of a meeting. Whether it was safe or not. Whether 'they' would suspect there were outsiders in the house.

"Finally they stopped, and I heard Mr. Waddy stumble to his room. He could hardly walk. I listened with my door open to hear where he went, and gave him an hour by my watch. Then I went after him. His door wasn't locked. He was snoring frightfully—divinely I thought. I had a box of vestas which he had handed me after dinner for my cigarettes, I wouldn't let him light them for me—and striking one, I saw, just by his bed, two keys on a hook, and under his pillow the gleam of something bright. His head hung far down the other side, so I slipped out the automatic, took the keys and crept from the room. The rest you know."

"By Jove!" Blair said admiringly, "you've the spirit of a dozen men. But the chauffeur, where does he come in?"

"He had noticed my effort to get away, it seems. And as he is a Marsellais, and on his way home, he was on that same train with you and me, he kept an eye on us when we got out. And to-night, he forced a window and got in, because he had heard of such dreadful things happening in that house, and thought I was in some way being kidnapped. He told me that he had known of more than one girl who had been lured there and never seen again."

She shuddered. "He tapped ever so softly on my door tonight. I opened it, thinking it was you—I knew monsieur Waddy wouldn't tap like that—and there was this good fellow. Even though he wasn't you I was thankful to see him. The house had begun to frighten me. It seemed somehow wicked. I began to think I had made a most frightful mistake in coming at all. But who wouldn't have come! To hear who really murdered Mrs. Amcott!"

"I suppose you never thought of Hilary Amcott in connection with her death?" Blair asked after deep thought.

"But why should Mr. Hilary have killed Mrs. Amcott? But then, why should anyone?" she asked wearily. "That's the question that always stops one's thinking."

It stopped Blair certainly. He was not proud of his brains in this case. They seemed to find a dense fog in every direction. He would so dearly have liked to pierce the mystery with a few brilliant inspirations from his usually adequate brain.

"Even that would be easier than to explain why he should be one of your kidnappers," he said finally, "unless..."

"There's no unless," she said cheerily. "Mr. Hilary is many things. He drinks. He gambles. He hasn't any spine. But the poor dear never got together enough will-power for a crime in his life."

"He seemed to be able to summon enough to make himself a bully to you when he fairly threw you to Waddy?" Blair's eyes flamed. Joan pressed his arm.

"If you hadn't been there, and if I hadn't known you were there, I think I should have died of fright. But don't be misled. I'm sure I can't be all out in my ideas about Hilary. He's a very sick man. And evidently Waddy made him change his mind about me, and think—what you thought in the beginning. He swings to and fro lately like a broken sign post."

Blair did not agree with her but he said nothing. For the face that had peered out at the three of them on leaving that house in the Rue Mazagran had been Hilary Amcott's. Hilary's, who had spoken of being summoned home to England in a hurry. Blair's thoughts hovered around the dead woman's brother-in-law, feeling, knowing, that there was more here than he knew of, and yet unable to grasp any thread that would lead to the explanation of all that puzzled him.

"I learnt from Inspector Armstrong while you were having tea in the rectory, that Mr. Hilary has practically beggared himself," Blair said thoughtfully. "He was never wealthy, it seems, and has sold out every security he has in the world, and mortgaged the life interest in Elmhurst that his father left him, and raised all the money he can at ruinous rates on some expectations he has from an elderly relative. But for his pay, he's dead broke. And all in three years! Doubtless Monsieur Waddy's bank roll would be found to be increased by just about that amount. He may very well have some powerful lever that makes Hilary have to give in to him, be afraid to come out, like a man, against him."

"He did say something to me about some I.O.U.'s which Waddy has of his." Joan had forgotten the point. "I didn't pay much attention. I was so keen on the idea of Madame Cadmeia. You see," she went on apologetically, "I wanted to go alone. Well—I did!" She finished on a sombre note. The perils from which she had escaped, but by the skin of her teeth rushing back over her.

"And what about that diary you saw the rector take out of Mrs. Amcott's drawer?" Blair asked.

"I looked about me at the rectory, but I saw no sign of it. But, of course, in an afternoon call—" she finished with a little laugh. "Besides I have Madame Cadmeia now. She's worth twenty diaries. Oh, she is really!"

They were slowing down now. Soon they were in Hyeres itself. Blair knew the town with its long avenues of dusty, sandy palms, looking very much the worse for wear, its general air of neglect and decay, and of suffering from that blight peculiar to French *villes*. It reminded Blair of Pau, and of many another place in France, with its air of having no real life of its own, of being a parasite town living on foreigners. Cannes would have it to-morrow if fashion left it. He turned again to his companion.

"And now, what are we going to do?" he asked. "The convent, I take it, is only for to-night?"

But Joan shook her head.

"No, Martin. I want to stay there two or three days. Just quietly there. You've no idea how I long for peace—and silence—and real safety." Her voice faltered a little. Suddenly he saw the look of strain in her face. It had grown much thinner these last days, thinner even than when she had come to him for safety in town. She looked like a girl who had been under a tremendous strain. As she had been.

"As you will," he said instantly. "And then?"

"I suppose I had better make for Paris by way of Digne and round by dreary Nancy. It's a way I've been with the Countess of Gérode once, and is quite off the main line. In Paris I'll go to one of the G.F.S. Lodges there. I know an awfully nice one. I'll telephone you every stage of the way, and write to you as soon as I get there. No, no, you mustn't come with me now. For if Monsieur Waddy can put me in a bad light he will. After last night he will! I have plenty of money for the journey. Or at least enough."

But Blair had ten five pound notes ready, and Joan finally accepted them as a loan. Blair then came out with another suggestion.

"I don't want to take advantage of your helplessness, God knows," he said urgently, "but, what if we were married? If we got married here, or in Nice?"

"I shouldn't like to think I was married from pity," Joan murmured softly.

"Pity! I loved you the first time I set eyes on you. On the boat... in that blessed fog..." Blair began hotly, but Joan was too practical to debate the point now. Her first aim was to get clear of Waddy.

"Later on, Martin, dear. When everything is cleared up. Then, if you still feel as you do—and if I still feel as I do—" she added with an adorable glance up into his eyes. "But not now. Why, I couldn't even give the clergyman my name! Let alone show my papers at the Maine."

Blair had to acknowledge the weight of this objection.

"And while you are making your way back to Paris, where I suppose you won't mind my looking in to see you?" he asked.

With a laugh she said she would not mind—not in the least.

"I shall have a little clearing-up here in Marseilles. A clearance I hope. But a settlement, at any rate!"

"Oh good!" she breathed. "Good! I've grown frightfully bloodthirsty of late. I don't feel as though any fate could be too bad for Waddy!"

"But we can talk that over at the convent to-morrow or the next day. What hotel are you going to in Marseilles?"

Blair named one of those caravanserais where there would be pretty sure to be room, or where, at any rate, failing that, any telephone to him would be passed on.

"Then I'll telephone to you whenever I wake up, morning, noon, or night, and we'll arrange an hour for a talk. Heaven, how I long for a sleep!"

They had reached a long grey wall now, behind the old, old church. She got out, rang the dangling handle of a little door, and after a few words to the sister who peered out with such a lantern in her hand as Noah might have used in the Ark, came back to the car and the waiting Blair.

"It's quite all right. I shall be safe enough here, but they've got a Retreat on, which will last another two days. That means that I may not be able to 'phone to you or arrange to see you for that length of time. But meanwhile you'll know I'm resting. And oh, how I long for that!"

She held out her hand to Blair, and then to the chauffeur.

"Thank you for all you did for me, monsieur. You helped magnificently. Believe me, I shan't be ungrateful—even though you did take those cartridges! Meanwhile monsieur here, has promised to settle a little of the debt I owe you."

She and Blair had agreed on a handsome sum on the way down.

"Do not think of it, mademoiselle. As I told you, I knew a girl once, she went to that house and no one, no one ever saw her again. What became of her? Doped, and put on board some eastern-bound boat. Sold, as we sell cattle. Ah, but I thought of her and others such as her, when I saw you pass behind that ill-fated door. That was why I acted as I did. Not again, I said to myself, not again, Michaud!"

Joan pressed his hand without speaking, and with a farewell glance to Blair, followed the sister into the convent. The door was locked and bolted behind her. Blair could understand how that secure world in there would appeal to storm-driven Joan Ingilby. The chauffeur suggested refreshment at a little all-night café he knew of near the Old Port of Nice. Blair stayed him. He wanted to go at once back to Marseilles.

"And when am I to sleep?" the man asked with a grin. "I am not in love, monsieur. I need sleep."

Blair prevailed on him to drive back at once, however, and climbed up beside him.

"And let me warn you, monsieur," the man went on, "it is no business of mine, but do not lay out that monsieur who took that young lady into the house as you would like to, as any man would like to. I could tell you strange stories of that place, monsieur! It has passages, and doors in walls through cupboards, that no one knows of. Wait until this monsieur leaves the house and then!

Then you will fight equal. For suppose something happens to you, then what of mademoiselle, eh? What of her? You out of the way, this man would only get her into his power again. Or the other one who brought her down here. The one with eyes like badly boiled fish."

Blair felt the truth of the man's argument. He liked the fellow, he would have liked to take the man on but Michaud explained that by the terms of a contract which he had with the Citroen firm, he must do a certain number of days', and part-days' work for them, each week. But he promised to report morning and evening to the hotel, also he gave the other the telephone number of the Citroen garage which could always find him.

CHAPTER TWELVE

BLAIR hurried first of all to an American acquaintance of his. Mr. Rimington ran a night and day detective agency in the great seaport. He himself always took night duty. Now, in the hush of the very early hours of the morning, he listened, with a smile that suggested amusement, to Blair's request that a certain Waddy be kept under constant surveillance. It deepened as Blair showed him a snap-shot of the man, copied from one taken by Armstrong.

"Want us to keep an eye on this chap? Have to be a swivel eye. Say, I'll see about ordering it done at once, and then hand you some very interesting private reading matter on that young man's past. Where is he hanging out now?"

Blair mentioned the carpet shop. The man whistled.

"Gosh! That means he's some business on. That address's his factory, his workroom, his what these Frenchies call his *atellyer*. He never stays there for his health."

He went out to give a few orders and then came back, lit a cigar and laid down a volume on the table. "This is chiefly that friend of yours. But he's had his fingers in some mud-pies. And I'll tell you something, Blair. Your Scotland Yard is after him too. I've had word from there lately to supply all information known. I nearly had to charter a special plane to carry it, but I sent it. You bet they're still reading it."

So Scotland Yard had "placed" Waddy here at Marseilles. Blair wondered how? He asked particulars of when this had been. The date given was the day after Mrs. Amcott's murder.

"Well, boil some of it down for me," he suggested. "Who is he?"

"Supposed to be the son of an Arab lady of high rank, lady-in-waiting to an Egyptian princess and a French officer. Sounds fine, eh? Boiled down it comes to a French sergeant who was half Senegali or some other nigger, and a Cardiff washerwoman. Name is really *Ouadhi*."

"Cardiff?" Blair had often wondered at Waddy's perfect English.

"Yep. She did up the undies of the Egyptian princess. But Waddy, your friend, made his appearance on the Riviera about five years ago as a professional dancer. He certainly could dance. Got all the ladies wild about him. Used to stay in hotels all along the coast wearing one of those little red carnations and dancing with anyone who chose to take a lesson. Collected enormous tips. Then he took to giving a series of cabaret entertainments at night clubs. Say, you surely have heard of the *Le Mort et La Morte* dance? Shook even the Riviera. You bet that takes some shaking too. He used to paint himself black, and outline his bones with phosphorescent oily stuff, till he looked like a skeleton on fire and she—well—it couldn't have cost much to dress her for that dance. They used to do it in front of a black curtain with lights down and she had a black velvet bag drawn over her head so that it looked as though she had none. There was a red mark around her neck, and she carried a pretty wax head with long fair hair under her arm. Supposed to be her own. It dripped blood. The only light was the phosphorescent gleams from the skeleton, which, considering the fact that she had nothing but tights on, was maybe as well. But it certainly was some dance!"

Blair remembered it. And the horde of surmises as to who the woman was. So Waddy was a professional dancer.

"Who was the woman?"

"Not known. She never showed up with him by day."

"And when did Waddy leave off being Death?"

"He became very pally at Aix with a weak-kneed sort of chap, Baron de Maricourt. He had danced a lot with the Baroness down here—I don't mind telling you that there were a good many who insisted that she was the lady with nothings on but the black bag. The Maricourts had left Cannes by then, and as I said some whispered that the lady was back here incognito. However, after Aix, he said the Maricourts took to going about together. The Aix police don't think the Baron knew who the man was. They both gambled a lot—Waddy with tremendous luck—genuine luck. But it was noticed that 'Everywhere that Mary went a lamb was sure to go.' By 'lamb' you are to understand a valuable piece of jewellery. We had made the same unkind remark down here and been equally unable to prove anything. So Waddy was asked to try another resort. He seems to've carried the Maricourts off with him, or else the Baroness carried him off, anyway they all made their appearance in London together. Then the Baron died, and since then Waddy hasn't come over here for any length of time and we've sort of forgotten him."

"And that Marseilles carpet shop?"

"The Waddy family mansion as one might call it? Pa Waddy lives there. So did Ma, the lady-in-waiting." The American laughed. "Say, you ought to've seen her! And heard her! She could swear in nine languages and not get 'em mixed. Well, Ma's dead now... Pa is still alive, and keeps the gambling hell going."

There was a pause. Then he moved his chair closer to Blair.

"I'll tell you one thing, old son. Keep it to yourself, mind. But if you're after Waddy, drop it. You won't get him."

"How do you mean?"

"Wa-al—" the other shifted his cigar to the other corner of his mouth—"I don't know as I knows myself," he said humorously. "But it's a fact nevertheless. I'm like old man Franklin studying a phenomenon and trying to see how to explain it. I have an idea of how it could be explained though."

Blair only looked his question this time.

"Say, there's no other explanation possible but government support. Like the Belgian franc, he's pegged, in my opinion. Not officially, of course. Gosh, no! Officially Waddy is anything you like to call him, but all the same you'll find he'll slip through. He's warned off from places for a while. Then he reappears and the French detectives grin and have to bear it. When you ask them, as between two of a trade, why this thusness, they shrug the windows out of the walls and say that he must have a powerful protector. But a little chap I helped once gave me the advice three years ago that I've passed on to you. Not to set my heart on Waddy. I shouldn't be allowed to get him."

"You think he's a French government spy?" Blair asked.

"I never think anything but what I'm told," the other retorted, "but maybe some such thought passed through my mind before I caught sight of it and chased it out. Either a spy, or working for them in some way. And that's why, I think, he never changes his name, and also why that den in Marseilles is allowed to run on. Of course they try to keep it in order, but I think they say that tourists will disappear, do what they will, and pretty girls get shipped off in other towns too, and meanwhile that shop is a rendezvous for the Arabs and Levantines all the world over. Waddy *père*, and *fils* too, when he's at home, draw them. They like the place. It has a dozen secret exits. It's dirty too. That must make them think of home."

There was a pause. Blair rose. "Well, then," the American summed up, "information wanted about Waddy as soon as possible. You look as if you could do with some sleep. How about nine to-morrow morning? If anything turns up we'll telephone you to your hotel at once."

Blair hurried away. He knew he needed a sleep. But before he dropped off, he turned, and tossed, and thought.

Joan was safe, thank God, but what was the key to the riddle of her kidnapping, of her being held here in Marseilles? Of her being about to sail to Mogador? What had Hilary Amcott to do with it all? Hilary, who had peered out from behind, that door. Hilary, who had taken up sides against Joan, what ever she might still think. Hilary, who had not gone back to England, yet who had not shown himself when she was in such appalling peril—alone in that house. Hilary, the silly ass who giggled at Waddy's dullest jest.

And thinking of that swift, sinister, glimpse of his face through the door, something else sprang forward in Blair's mind that had for the time being been rammed down.

He saw again the car into which his plane had so nearly crashed. He saw again a face turned to speak to one of the men on the field. That vaguely familiar face... it came to him now whose it was. It was that of the rector of Elmhurst. So Mr. Grimshaw was on the continent too—at Le Bourget.

Did this mean anything? Suddenly it occurred to Blair that all of the circle closely associated with the crime at the manor house were now abroad. It was but a passing thought, without significance to him. And on that he dropped into a deep sleep. But a short one. His nerves were on edge. He must be up and doing. He hurried into his clothes, then he made his way towards the front door.

"Could he have a taxi?"

"Oh, certainly." The night porter would telephone for one, but the man eyed him doubtfully.

"Monsieur knows Marseilles?" he asked as he opened the door to the telephone booth hesitatingly.

"Not well. Why?"

"It's not a town to go walking about in, in the dark. Just for exercise," the porter said meaningly. "A taxi is good, but if one leaves the taxi and goes for strolls, èh? There are certain quarters that I would not care to stroll in, and I am a Marseillais."

"Are you?" Blair looked interested. "I bought a rug in the town yesterday afternoon. In a shop down behind the Quai de la Joliette. Burian was the name over the door. Are their things any good? Do you know the place I mean at all?"

The porter grinned and said that if he told half what he knew, he would be had up for slander.

"*Allez*, monsieur, with your talk of carpets!" He laughed knowingly. "The only carpets ever sold there are of the diamonds, hearts, clubs and spades pattern, eh? Oh, I know, I know! And let me tell you, monsieur, that of all the tripots in Marseilles, there is none worse. None more dangerous. They have a pull somewhere. That, of course. But they also have luck. Raided? Nightly for a time. The Prefecture is not of their admirers. But what would you? The police might as well raid a Trappist monastery. They were warned, those ones! Always. Cunning foxes. We had a gentleman staying here in the autumn, going on his yearly rounds. He was a wine merchant. It was the time of vintage tasting. And as monsieur knows, our wine-merchants carry big sums on them at such a time. They pay in notes. This man had heard of the carpet shop—as a carpet shop. He went there one afternoon with his daughter. Monsieur—" the porter thrust his pointed beard almost into Blair's eye—"neither the man, nor his daughter, nor the money he was carrying, were ever seen again! What could we do? We went to the police. They at the house said that no such persons had ever been there. Well, what could one do? To this day I know what happened. So do the police. But there is no proof. So I entreat monsieur not to—let us say buy his carpets—at that place. They come too dear, monsieur."

He so obviously intended to notify the police if Blair did go there, that the latter stage-managed a yawn as he looked out at the night. It was a true southern night. The sky was like the inside of a vast blue-black hive with golden bees all quivering at their posts, and twirling where they clung. Blair went upstairs again. He had hardly shut his door when a knock came on it. A telegram had just arrived for him. Marked "Urgent. Night delivery." As he tore it open and read it Blair's hair bristled.

The telegram ran:

"Inquire at once at Marseilles Prefecture for young lady you accompanied here. She was arrested half-an-hour after her arrival, and charged with murder in England. Charge made by someone in Marseilles. She asked me to telephone you at once but telephone out of order. She does not wish facts laid before Consul until you have seen her. No one was allowed to accompany her in car except the undersecretary from the Prefecture and two policemen.

MOTHER SAINT JOSEPH
Ursuline Convent, Hyères."

It had been sent off from Hyères at three this morning. Joan had only arrived at the convent at two. It was now five, and as dark as midnight. The sun would not rise till eight.

Blair leapt for the dial of the telephone by his bed, twirled it with a tense forefinger to the Prefecture's numbers. The bell at the other end rang. He heard a gruff "'ello! 'ello!" and replied that he had been informed that a young English lady had been arrested at the Ursuline convent at Hyères and driven to the Prefecture here in Marseilles, doubtless to be formally charged later on this morning. Where was she now? He, the speaker, represented the head of the family—always a trump card for a man to play in France when making inquiries—and would like particulars.

It took some time before he and the official whom he had rung up understood each other, for no arrest had been made last night at Hyères. No English lady had been charged with anything at all. No information laid against her by anyone in Marseilles.

Blair tried to get Michaud on the telephone, but the man was out with his car, so Blair ordered a taxi through the hotel porter instead. He told him to drive up to the famous viewpoint, the Madonne de la Reserve, explaining that he would like to watch the sunrise from there; but once away from the hotel, he told him to drive as fast as he could to the Rue Mazagram behind the Quai de la Joliette.

For this was Waddy's doing without a doubt, or Hilary Amcott's, or both of them. Joan must have been followed—there had been a great deal of traffic on the roads around. Toulon—or else they must have heard her refer to the convent at Hyères sometime, and guessed that she would make for it as her safest refuge. They might even have inquired by telephone, before that instrument went out of order, or was put out of order.

Blair's thoughts were like separate hot skewers thrust through him. At the entrance to that squalid street another taxi stood waiting. Blair saw a familiar figure half-way through a weird-looking piece of sausage. He flung his chauffeur some money and rushed to meet Michaud.

Just as he got to him he stopped as though shot. An awful scream rent the air, that chill air of before six on a December morning, a scream like a trapped animal's, a man's by its violence, its force, but otherwise sexless. Then came a shot.

Up and down Blair's spine ran a horrid feeling as though it were sand and crumbling away, for a window blind in the blank, dark house that they were watching had been pulled aside, and a face had looked out. By the light of the lamp in the street it seemed to look straight at Blair. It was Joan's face, but such fright, such terror— so ghastly a fear, so horrible a terror—was stamped on it, that had not Blair's heart and mind been full of her, he would never have recognised those distorted, blanched features.

Blair saw Joan now pull up the blind, a tattered affair, and open the window with what was evidently the greatest care to make no noise. They saw her shoot a fearful backward glance behind her, then she looked down. She was on the first storey. She evidently measured the jump. The floor was low. Blair and Michaud with one accord rushed across with the cushions from the taxi and spread them on the cobble stones. Blair had his stout topcoat off, and he and the chauffeur stretched it like a net to break the fall. Blair would have called to her to jump feet first, but she made an imperative gesture for silence. They were all alone in the street. She climbed out on to the window-sill, took a look below her, and then in another moment she was safely beside Blair, clinging to him for the briefest of seconds before she ran to the taxi.

"Get me away, quick! I had to ring for the police to stop murder being done, but I wasn't in time. Mr. Grimshaw's killed Monsieur Waddy, or Mr. Waddy Mr. Grimshaw. I don't know which. But anyone the police find in there will have to explain themselves. I daren't risk that, yet I had to telephone, if only to stop the quarrel. Oh, Martin, to look out of the window and find you here! As soon as you've seen me off for somewhere—anywhere out of this horrible town—go back and see if you can help. Though that awful cry! It sounded past help. Where are we going? To the station? But I'm afraid of trains. I'm afraid of everything since last night."

She looked a wreck.

"What about the aerodrome and a plane?" he suggested, holding her cold and trembling hand.

She nodded. He gave the order through the speaking tube.

"Oh, Martin, last night I thought everything was over! When they arrested me at Hyères was bad enough, for I never suspected that the men weren't what they made themselves out to be, any more than the reverend mother did. But when they drove me to that carpet shop and hustled me inside!" She began to shake from head to foot. Blair would have had her rest awhile, but she would not, could not be silent.

"They locked me up in a room, the room I climbed out of just now. I couldn't hear any sounds in the house, but suddenly the door opened and Waddy came in. Oh, Martin!" She clung to him. "I thought he would kill me then and there! He wanted to. I think he meant to, but someone called him away into the adjoining room. There's a door between. He didn't lock it, only shut it, and I heard him talking in low tones at first. Then the voices grew louder, and there was a most awful quarrel. I opened the door between. I had to see what was going on; it sounded so dreadful. I saw Mr. Grimshaw shaking Mr. Waddy by the throat like a rat, and then Waddy seemed to twist away and rushed out on to the landing calling 'Achmed!' Mr. Grimshaw rushed after him, and I could hear the thud, thud of their blows and the dreadful sounds they made. It was horrible! horrible! And then I saw that one of them, if not both—they were twisting round and round on the floor so that I can't be sure—had a revolver and was trying to get the hand free that held it. And then came a dreadful scream and a shot!"

"I heard both," Blair said, holding her close.

"And then someone tried—oh, so softly—the door of the room I was in. But I had bolted it, and I was telephoning for the police. Oh, Martin, I thought I was signing my own death warrant."

"Yet you did it, you plucky darling!" he breathed against her hair. Her real hair, soft and golden, not the neat little Byzantine wig.

"Not plucky. I was terrified, almost too terrified to get the words out, and I seemed to have forgotten all my French. But I couldn't let murder be done and not lift a hand to stop it in the only way I could. And then to look out and see you below... To know that I was saved again!"

The, car was slowing down. Now it stopped. It was the Marignan aerodrome.

"Nous voila!" Michaud opened the door and helped Joan out.

"Where shall we go?" Blair asked her in an undertone. Wherever she went this time, he was coming too. Joan had only squeezed his arm when he said as much in the car. She wanted him to come, to be with her after what had just happened.

"I don't care where," she whispered.

"It musn't be England; not yet," he said regretfully.

They read the notices placarding the ticket bureau of the aerodrome.

"How about Paris? You meant to go there originally, and it's the next plane off."

She nodded. "Good. I suppose we shall have it all to our selves in weather like this."

"Have you your papers as Miss Bartram on you?" Blair asked.

She nodded and stepped towards some hoardings that formed a discreet corner.

While she wrestled with hidden pockets, Michaud touched Blair on the shoulder. He pointed to the passport that Blair was taking out of his pocket.

"'Monsieur is not leaving Marseilles?"

"He is," retorted Blair, "and as soon as he can get off with mademoiselle. Why?"

Michaud looked worried. He turned his cap around on one ear and scratched his thick black curls.

"I'm summoned. The Citroen Company is making trouble. That is the real reason why I was not at the garage, monsieur. It seems I should have notified them when I took the car out for all night long last night, and I left it in the street, which was contravening law nine thousand and ninety-nine of the town. That was the real reason why I was sitting outside that house there now. For it seems to be a law of *le bon Dieu* that one has to be somewhere. The garage people here would have made

some fuss about my driving off in the car again, but—
well, after all, there are some things one can stand and
some one cannot! Is it not? And, after all, a blow with the
knuckles kills no one. But the fact remains that I must be
at the Prefecture at eleven this morning without fail. And
you are the only person, monsieur, who can be my
witness when I tell my story of how pressed for time I
was last night. I can keep mademoiselle out of it, if you
will pass as the fare whom I was driving. That story will
do for the police. As for my character—it stands by itself!"
Michaud twirled a moustache that seemed also to stand
by itself. "I would have asked mademoiselle here, but—
well, it says itself that there is some delicate affair on
hand. You will do as well, if not better."

"Martin, don't leave me!" Joan looked on the verge of
tears.

A newcomer appeared on the field—a rather
scholarly-looking, white-haired man with a well-trimmed
beard, who glanced around him uncertainly.

"Excuse me." He spoke in English. "Could you tell me
where I get my ticket? I want to take the first plane that's
off."

Blair showed him the bureau and answered a few of
his questions about necessary papers.

When he came back to Joan he was glad to see that
the respite had given her time to recover her nerve. She
even managed a watery smile at him.

"Forgive me. Hysterics due to lack of breakfast." She
tried for a light note with only semi-success. "Of course
I'm not a pig! This man needs you. Of course you must
stay and see him through, after all he's done for me! But
don't go to that dreadful house without the police, Martin.
Promise me you'll be careful of yourself. As for me, I'll
wire you when I arrive."

"I'll send word to Cooks' to meet the plane," Blair said,
"but in case it arrives after you get in, though they
generally keep you an unconscionable time at Dijon,
promise me you'll do so yourself."

They both laughed, she still rather hysterically, at the promises and counter promises each wanted from the other.

A crowd of laughing young people arrived next with a bride and groom, also bound for the supposedly gay capital. Blair was relieved of his worst fears. Joan would be safe enough now while on board.

He and Michaud watched the take off, and saw her handkerchief flutter a good-bye to them.

"Now to the British Consulate to swear an affidavit," Blair began, for that was what Michaud had explained must be done. But that good man now shook his head lugubriously when Blair would have made for his car.

"I have been talking to a friend of mine, that thin little gendarme over there, monsieur." He pointed to a quite sufficiently large and stout person. "He says it would make a better effect, be *plus correct*, if you would go to your Consulate in another taxi. If we were as strangers until this *sacré* case is over. So, monsieur, if you will put yourself to the trouble of taking some other cab, I will drive away alone, and wait for you at the Commissariat de Police, Rue Gambetta, at eleven precisely."

There was no help for it. Blair could not let the man down, and, taking the first cab on the rank, he told him to drive as fast as possible to the British Consulate.

Outside the aviation ground a private car passed them. The chauffeur jumped down hurriedly and came to Blair's window.

"Did you see who that was? That's Count Incantevoli, the Italian aviator, who's making the flight around the world. He arrived here last night, and continues his journey to-day, I knew. Aha, we are in luck! He has given the reporters the slip. Of course you wish me to drive back to the areodrome. It would be a thousand pities to miss his departure. He never comes down until the last moment. It will be over in ten minutes, and his machine is a beauty."

Blair too, felt that ten minutes in seeing the great airman take-off would not be wasted. The driver jumped for his seat, and turned the car to rush back the way they had come.

Facing them came a taxi on whose seat Blair recognised the overflowing form of Michaud. Behind him came a long, silent racer.

"Tiens!" muttered the chauffeur driving Blair. "They are running well those two, and yet one would say—" He was puzzled. Blair, who had not had the top of the cab shut, was on his feet in an instant. The first oncoming car, the one driven by Michaud, was flying, and something in the set of his head and shoulders told Blair that the driver was listening to the car behind him. The speed was terrific. Now, the road out to the aerodrome at Marignan, a temporary one, has a deep drop on one side of it, protected by a low but adequate wall, but not a wall that was intended to stop such a speed as that of these two cars. The road is none too wide at its broadest. Just here it was at its narrowest. Two cars could pass with ease. But this second car, the long, silent racer, was keeping exactly behind the first, yet coming on at a tremendous pace—gaining but not swinging out. It was almost touching it now. Still it did not swerve. Michaud was racing, not with another car, but with death. The car behind him seemed to leap forward at a spot where the road makes a sharp turn, it missed the one in front by the narrowest of inches owing to Michaud's skill, but the car, the grey racer, seemed to slide crabwise. There was a crash, and the Citroen taxi had been literally shoved off the road down the embankment.

On flew the grey car. Blair and the chauffeur driving him were more concerned with the fate of the man who had been rammed. The taxi lay on its side in a ditch below them as they ran to the edge of the road and peered through the gap in the stones which had been its wall. Scrambling down, they found Michaud very silent and still lying some distance off. Evidently he had leapt as the car overturned. Blair raised his head. It fell back inert on the grass. He put a hand within the coats to feel for his heart. Heavens, how many garments did the man wear? It was like exploring in a feather bed. But the lids flickered. The other taxi-driver was pouring brandy down the injured man's throat. "It's his legs, the poor devil. But what an escape! Luckily we have the car's number... He must be drunk?"

Michaud sat up, only to fall back with a curious grey showing under his tan.

"Water!" he gasped in French. "Drinking water!"

The chauffeur hurried off to a nearby house. Michaud made a sign to Blair to bend down closer.

"I'm not much hurt," he said in English, "but every moment is valuable."

At the language and at the voice Blair's eyes narrowed. Where had he heard that quiet voice before?

The man with the hurt leg smiled.

"I'm Chief Inspector Pointer." He had drawn out a packet of cigarettes from an inner pocket. "I want you to take this packet to a Mr. Brown at the Hotel Noel here in Marseilles. It's the next door but one to the hotel at which you stayed last night. Say to him 'Hello, old top!' If he says 'Top yourself!' give him the packet. That's all. But it's important. The case is where it can't stop even for a minute. Now as to me, I can't go to a hospital. My indiarubber pads and manifold beauty aids might arouse too much interest. Will you take me to your hotel as your brother? I'll get to the lift and along to your room somehow. No bones have been broken. It's only a sprain and surface cuts."

"Your boot's full of blood," Blair remarked inconsequentially.

Pointer did not waste a glance on the foot.

"I ought to have jumped sooner, but I couldn't find a sandy spot on which to land." He did not add that because he expected some attack to be made on him, he would not let Blair accompany him in the taxi. He explained to the returning taxi-driver that he was a member of the *sureté* on the look out for a gang of international swindlers, and requested the favour of a shut mouth as to his little attempt to clear him out of the roadway. The young man, greatly interested, promised absolute silence.

"You're on Waddy's track, I suppose?" Blair asked, helping to get him into the taxi and prop his leg up on the opposite seat. Then they were off.

"I followed him from Elmhurst," Pointer explained, "but as Mr. Hilary Amcott seemed to be stirring too, I transferred my attention to him as the darker horse. While he was getting his tickets at Croydon Aerodrome, I got myself taken across in one of our new fast bombers, so as to be in waiting for him when he arrived. His wanting a car to meet him gave me a splendid chance, of course."

"One moment! Have you actually got that infernal brute, Waddy, or did Grimshaw kill him? And what about Hilary Amcott? It only needs the Baroness to have the Elmhurst circle complete here in Marseilles."

Pointer gave a little moan of pain.

"Miss Ingilby is safe," he gasped. "As to the rest— sorry, but I need all my strength for getting to the hotel. And on the way, will you stop at the Citroen garage, where I hung out, for me to pick up a bag I must have before I can see the doctor? I'll muffle up going into the hotel. The cold day will excuse that."

"There's no trouble with the Citroen Company?"

"None whatever. I asked you to stay behind because I didn't want to lose you just now. But I don't want to talk..." The voice trailed off weakly.

The programme was followed without a hitch. At the garage Pointer called a mechanic, who at a word from him came out with a bag. As he made no comments, Blair guessed, and rightly, that he also was not entirely or merely what he seemed. "Brown" received the cigarettes after the interchange of the right words with a "Thanks awfully" and turned away.

Pointer was got without much difficulty to Blair's room and there made comfortable. While Blair telephoned for an English doctor, the man from Scotland Yard busied himself with a small flask and some powder, which, followed by plenty of soap and hot water, soon altered his face back again to the appearance that Blair had seen in England. His wig, a masterly wig, discarded, he looked himself again. Yet in the cab, and now while waiting for the doctor, Pointer sat as in collapse, hardly able to articulate. Blair was not callous, but he suspected this extreme debility. He hinted as much now. "There are such a lot of things..."

Pointer let his head droop further forward on his breast. "Not now," he whispered feebly. "I need absolute rest until the doctor can patch me up."

Blair snorted.

The doctor came on the scene very quickly. The, leg was badly cut and lacerated, and had had a severe wrench, but, bandaged into a splint, Pointer declared his intention of going for a drive.

"Alone," he added with a placating look at Blair and a twinkle in his grey eyes. "Talking is still the one thing that seems to make my leg hurt."

Without a word the newspaper man helped him into the taxi which he had had summoned.

"There is such a thing as a day of reckoning, brother," he said darkly as he shut the door.

"And for more than either of us, Blair." The words were grave. Pointer looked very stern as he drove off.

CHAPTER THIRTEEN

BLAIR himself hurried to Rue Mazagran. What had happened there? What was still happening there? A crowd, thick as his own wild surmises, surged around its entrance. A cordon of gendarmes kept the people back. Blair picked out a big fellow, head and shoulders above the rest, who stood In a vantage place just beyond the turning. He managed to reach his side. Blair's experience was that fat men—and the man was huge—were always big talkers.

"What's happened?" he asked him breathlessly.

"A murder, monsieur," the man replied with gusto. "Some say two murders. Ah, at last the gendarmes are able to get their claws into this house! But the birds have flown, of course. Still, without doubt it will now be shut up, as it would have been long ago but for the protection of some of the Royalists."

"Not at all!" snapped a thin man a yard away. "These people were in with the Centre."

"With the Left!" hissed another man indignantly. "I ask you, does the Centre..."

"Who was murdered?" Blair inquired anxiously.

"Don't know yet. One stretcher has left, apparently for the hospital, which is quite close. But I think that was only a blind. I think he will go on to the mortuary. And it's said that there's another chap, dead too, still inside. The Sub-Prefect is taking a deposition from the police."

Blair got out of the crowd. He hurried to the hospital, "which was quite close." There he asked to see the injured person who had been brought from the Rue Mazagran. He. believed that he knew him. He handed in his card.

A gendarme hurried in.

"Your Inspecteur General de Scotland Yard thought you would soon be here! This way, monsieur."

In a private ward Blair saw first of all Chief Inspector Pointer, his leg propped on a chair. Beside him, writing at a table, was "Brown" of the cigarette package. The man in the bed turned his head. It was Mr. Grimshaw. There was also a French official present, very much *galonne*, who would be able to assure himself and others afterwards that the translation sent in of the interview was correct. The gendarme, after placing a chair for Blair, sat down himself with his back against the door.

The rector of Elmhurst looked very pale. His breast and one arm were swathed in plaster bandages. He did not look pleased to see Blair.

"Another newspaper hunt?" he asked coldly.

"On the hunt for truth. Quite a different matter," Blair assured him. The talk continued. He had to pick up the threads as best he could. Pointer was speaking.

"I would like to spare you bad news for the moment, sir, but we're a bit pressed for time. I assure you that there is no possibility of a mistake. We have it from the authorities out there. Mr. Ralph Amcott died early this morning in the nursing home in Khartoum where he has been lying ill since Tuesday—since just a week ago."

Mr. Grimshaw turned his face to the wall for a second. "Dead! Poor Ralph! Blood poisoning, wasn't it?"

Pointer said that it was. "Therefore," he went on, "any fears that you may have had that he murdered his wife are quite groundless. Your silence is only protecting the murderer, not helping your friend."

"What makes you think that I thought or feared he had killed his wife?" the rector asked after a pause in a rather muffled Voice.

"Your taking Mrs. Amcott's diary for one thing. The diary that had been written by a woman whom you had just been told was very fond of writing about other people, among whom, one might well think, that her husband would take first place. You evidently knew that any references to him would be the reverse of flattering."

"So you have the diary which I've been chasing," Grimshaw murmured. "And so Hilary Amcott hasn't gained anything by trying to help Miss Ingilby to get to Cairo with it. I don't blame her, mind you. But I'm thankful that his insane hatred of his brother hasn't turned out as he hoped, that Ralph is beyond his worst efforts to harm him. Ralph..." Mr. Grimshaw sighed. "he looked the picture of perfect health and fitness when we parted last year."

"You didn't see anyone made up to look like him on the night after Mrs. Amcott was murdered? I mean the man whom the next night the two labourers mistook for Mrs. Amcott's husband?"

Mr. Grimshaw said nothing.

"Come, sir," Pointer repeated, "did you or did you not see Mr. Hilary Amcott dressed up in his brother's clothes that night?"

"Have you any warrant for such a question?" Grimshaw's large, rather fierce eyes snapped at Pointer.

"Certainly. The warrant of being in charge of Mrs. Amcott's murder."

Pointer's tone was very calm. Blair felt a sudden sense of the man's powerful personality. Looking for them, he saw now the immense resolution of the pleasant grey eyes, the iron will of the firm lips, the indomitable energy, of the high cheek bones. Lean and vigilant, there was a certain quiet confidence about Pointer, a knowledge of his own ability, that again impressed the newspaper man immensely. He was thankful that the Chief Inspector was on Joan's side, that he had helped her to escape. This man would not let anyone slip from his grip except of his own free will.

Grimshaw shot him a very alert look.

"I see," he said ruminatingly, but he left it at that.

"Leaving that question on one side for the moment, sir," Pointer went on, "was I right in my idea as to why you took Mrs. Amcott's diary in the first place?"

The rector seemed to ponder deeply. His subtle, flexible mouth pursed up.

"Yes. It was because of the absolutely untrue portrait of Mr. Ralph that I knew would be in it," he said finally.

"But you took it before you could know the tone of its contents," Pointer said at once.

Grimshaw's features relaxed into a faint smile.

"I forgot to whom I am speaking. Mrs. Amcott had favoured me with her confidence in large measure." He paused. "I think she hoped first of all to get me to persuade her husband to make her a larger allowance. He had sent her home to England rather in disgrace, and drawn the purse-strings tighter than Mrs. Amcott liked, but not tighter than was fair, especially as she had installed herself against, his wishes, rent free, at the manor. She claimed that only by so doing could she make ends meet. I refused to be drawn into the matter at all. Like all the Amcotts, Ralph has a hard side to him, but he is emphatically a just man. I should not have dreamt of interfering in his arrangements for his own wife's stay in England. When she realised as much, Mrs. Amcott tried to change my feelings towards her husband by making the most outrageous charges of cruelty and neglect, and yet of jealousy against him. Mad jealousy, she called it. It was a ludicrous idea to one who knew Ralph Amcott as I did. I tried to smooth matters out between them. But Mrs. Amcott refused to see any but her own side. When, on the very morning that I learnt of the possibility of a murder charge in connection with her death, I heard that she had left a diary behind her, and was told that she habitually wrote down in it her impression of people, as you rightly guessed, Chief Inspector, I decided that I must get possession of the diary at once—at all costs. And it cost me something," he said, pressing his lips together tightly, as at some most unpleasant recollection.

"Then you had lately seen what you took to be Mr. Ralph Amcott," Pointer said very sternly, "else even so you would not have thought him in any danger."

"Eh—yes." Grimshaw conceded with apparent reluctance. "You're right, Chief Inspector. What a redoubtable cross-examiner was lost in you. As I cut through the east corner of the manor park last Tuesday about midnight I saw what I took to be Ralph Amcott let himself in by a side door."

"The side door leading up into Mrs. Amcott's rooms?" Armstrong, for he was the "Brown" of the cigarettes, asked. He had not yet had time to take off his make-up.

The rector nodded with some hesitation.

"Just so. Letting himself in very quietly. I was surprised, but I expected to hear all about it from him later in the day, of course. When I did not, I knew that something was wrong. But I imagined it only to be in the relations of the couple to each other. However, obviously it was none of my business, and was not for me to seem to know anything about it. I had to be away from Elmhurst until Wednesday morning, the day of the inquest on my friend's unfortunate wife. At that inquest I was, I confess, on tender hooks. One incautious word from me, and the idea of domestic unhappiness might rouse some idea of suicide on Mrs. Amcott's part. She was the very last woman in the world to take her life, but you know what country juries are. On Wednesday there was, of course, no idea of foul play. That only came next morning with the appearance of your article, Mr. Blair, in the *Comet*."

There was a little silence. Mr. Grimshaw sipped some medicine and wiped his forehead wearily. The interview was a strain on him.

"And why did you think Miss Ingilby had taken the diary away with her?" Pointer broke in to ask.

"Obviously it was she, while she had tea at the rectory. I had locked the book in a despatch-box which stood under a pile of papers. The key was in one of the table drawers. While I was showing Miss Dallas a piece of

early Italian majolica which I had picked up, Miss Lucy
must have abstracted the book. Oh, I'm not blaming her.
Her need was desperate. But I had written to Ralph
Amcott at his club address in town asking his permission
to open and read his wife's diary because of that need.
When you and Mr. Blair came to see me I had just posted
it. I did not feel at liberty to speak frankly; in fact, I
thought it my duty in the interests of my friend to—lie
like a Spartan," he finished honestly.

"Because you had seen him on Tuesday night?"

Grimshaw nodded. "Returning, as I thought, to make
some overture to Mrs. Amcott with an idea of starting
their life together afresh, or possibly to give her some
stern word of warning. But certainly not to murder her!"

"But when he did not come forward at the inquest?"
Pointer asked.

"I thought he must have returned at once to the
Sudan; thought that he had not yet read the awful news.
Understand me, I was extremely puzzled by the reports
that he was ill and still in Khartoum, but to anyone who
knew Ralph Amcott the idea of associating murder with
his upright and high principled character was ludicrous.
Even the poisoning of the dog could not alter that, though
it placed him in a very dangerous position, I thought."

"But what about the diary?" Armstrong, whose pen
had been dashing along at great speed, pulled up to say
as he adjusted a fresh sheet of zanetic paper between the
leaves. "I want to get this down clearly, sir. You thought
Miss Ingilby had taken the diary..."

"I knew she had," said Mr. Grimshaw, quite unaware
that he was speaking to the man who really had taken it,
for Chief Inspector Pointer, on going over the rectory on
Saturday night, when the owner had gone away—the
night when Joan and Miss Dallas had had tea there—had
recognised Mrs. Amcott's writing, and abstracted the
purple-bound book, to learn of its original purloining later
on from Blair. Pointer had found more than a diary in Mr.
Grimshaw's house that night. In the garbage tin had been

a twisted-up ticket for the Spanish Christmas lottery, the same as that in which Mrs. Amcott had drawn half the great prize. This meant at least that Mr. Grimshaw would have had a list of the winning numbers sent him, and might mean much more.

"When I got back," the rector continued, "after preaching for a brother priest, and found the book gone, I realised that Mr. Hilary Amcott would like nothing better than to throw suspicion on his brother. He was, I knew, the danger. My housekeeper met me at the same time with a tale about two cases having gone, and of Mr. Hilary Amcott having been in before daylight to superintend their removal. Hilary Amcott, who nowadays never gets up till noon! If then! She had seen him let himself in, and was quite certain about it, considering it most kind on his part. I could not understand the affair of the double cases and Hilary's presence at all, but for the moment I was concerned with Miss Lucy Ingilby and the diary. I went up to town to get into touch with Ralph Amcott, and stepped in at my house in Eaton Square for some papers. There I was told that Mr. Hilary Amcott had been in, and had taken off a case that had been sent to my house by accident.

"Hilary again, and again a packing-case. I realised that something was on foot. I decided to find out what it was, and traced the car quite simply to Croydon Aerodrome, where I learnt that a man answering his description had left with a lady by the Paris plane. It was some time before I got there, of course. But my brother Fulke is in the R.F.C., and soon whizzed me across the Channel to Le Bourget. There, a friend of his met me in his car and drove me into Paris, where I spent the night. I tried to reason out what Hilary was at—who the lady with him could possibly be. And suddenly the explanation came—it might be Miss Ingilby. We all know now that it was. I reasoned—correctly—that she had read the diary, and been misled by its wild hatred of Mrs. Amcott's husband, and intended laying it before the authorities in

Khartoum. That was why she had left England, and that was why Hilary Amcott would assist her as he was doing. His presence proved my theory right. That meant that they would probably make for Marseilles, the port by plane or ship for Cairo.

"I wired for a good detective in Marseilles to make every inquiry, and had one doing the same in Paris in case of a mistake in my deductions, and learnt from the former that Hilary Amcott and Miss. Ingilby had arrived that noon, and had been met at the station by a Monsieur Waddy. There all trace of Hilary Amcott vanished. He had, I feared, got away on some small steamer to another port with the precious book, leaving Miss Ingilby to her fat. The detective's report wound up by saying that Monsieur Waddy had driven her to a house whose reputation as a gambling-house was of the worst. That poor child's fate drove even the thought of the diary from my mind. I hurried down to Marseilles, and made my way as soon as possible to the place. That was this morning. I saw a light in the house. I rang and gave my name to the Arab who opened the door, and said that I must see Monsieur Waddy at once, that I had an appointment with him. He led me upstairs I had an idea he took me for someone else. He seemed to be expecting someone. A moment later and Monsieur Waddy rushed in. At sight of me he actually jumped. Clearly I was not the man whom he expected. I thought he seemed rattled when I asked him for Miss Lucy Ingilby at once, as though he wanted time to think. He left me 'to see what he could do,' were his rather odd words. In another moment I heard a most awful scream. I rushed to the door. It was locked. But he shot at me from an eyehole in the door. His shot only grazed my arm, luckily, but I fell against a chair and went down like a log with a tremendous clatter. I think that fall saved my life. But I confess I was thankful to learn from you, Chief Inspector, that it was not that poor child Lucy Ingilby who screamed like that."

"No. It was one of the men in the carpet shop," Pointer said. He had listened throughout Mr. Grimshaw's story of what had happened with the absorbed but peaceful air of a man listening to a sermon.

"You know," he now went on casually, "there was an idea in some quarters that you yourself impersonated Mr. Ralph Amcott at the manor on Tuesday night, and again on last Thursday."

The rector only gave an incredulous smile. Pointer got up with difficulty. "Here," he said, laying a book on the bed, "is Mrs. Amcott's diary, Mr. Grimshaw. I read it in the course of duty. If you look at it you will see that your fears are groundless in this case also. I never read more touching expressions of a wife's love for her husband and hopes for a happy reunion with him."

Grimshaw, as though unable to believe his ears, opened the book and turned a page or two. Then he looked unable to believe his eyes.

"It shows," he murmured in apparent amazement, "that you never can tell! Not with women, and rarely with men." With which cryptic utterances he closed his eyes.

"Did Mrs. Amcott ever send you a lottery ticket?" Pointer asked next.

Grimshaw opened his eyes with a look of great fatigue.

"Lottery? Yes, she sent me a ticket for a Christmas lottery in Spain. I've no objection to lotteries, and I want a new organ badly for our church."

"Did you win anything?"

Grimshaw rolled his head in weary negation on his pillow.

"Do you know if she took a ticket for herself?"

"I'm very tired, Chief Inspector.—"

"I know, sir. I'm done in a minute. Did she take a ticket for herself?"

"I think she told me that she took two half-tickets every Christmas since she had been in Spain, but I can't be sure."

"Just a couple more questions and I'm done." Pointer said apologetically, "When did you learn that your ticket, or half ticket, was worth nothing?"

"She telephoned me Monday afternoon that neither of us had won anything. So I threw mine away."

"Do you know how she had learnt that?"

Grimshaw said that he did not. And this time he closed his eyes in a way that showed that he did not intend to open them in a hurry.

Pointer glanced at the gendarme and at the sick man. The former moved to the Englishman's side. Pointer and Armstrong both said a word to the gentleman with the stripes and decorations, and, followed by Blair, tiptoed from the room. Outside the two officers climbed into a taxi.

"I'll meet you at Pascal's in time for dinner if you like, Mr. Blair. Just now every second is valuable," and with a wave of the hand the Chief Inspector drove away.

Blair found Marseilles, bathed in warm sunshine this December morning—the champagne sunshine of the Riviera, golden and exhilarating, but nearly as unhealthy to sit out in as the Mistral. The great broad streets hummed and buzzed around him, for Marseilles is a city of perpetual motion. He heard many an English voice as he roamed the pavements almost unseeing, all but deaf, his thoughts on this baffling problem. Many an Indian civil servant, or Australian, or South African stops here on a journey and never finishes it, but lingers on in some charming villa between the great port and grim Toulon.

Blair strolled up the Cannebière up a broad lane of hedges, festooned with innumerable bunches of flowers, past the railway station; he mounted the slopes to the great Corniche surmounted by the beautiful church of Notre Dame de la Garde, between houses of white and coloured marble.

Then, still with the riddle unsolved, he descended by steep little back streets and steps to the old town, and finally wore the day down till it was time to fetch up in the famous eating-house just off the old port, than which there is none better in the whole town—no, not even in the Restaurant de la Reserve. There, waiters in snowy shirt-sleeves flitted to and fro, the great kitchen glowed copper and shining steel. But Blair saw none of these things; he only saw Pointer installed in an inconspicuous corner with his leg stretched along the wall.

The journalist took a chair facing him with the determination not to part from him without learning the secret of this puzzle—supposing that Pointer knew it.

The very way he snapped his napkin open said as much. Pointer nodded.

"When dinner's over, Blair. When we're safely back in our hotel. Though I chose Pascal's because there aren't so many of our countrymen around. What shall we have first? We would insult the house if we didn't start off with bouillabaisse."

Blair neither knew nor cared what he ate or drank. No effort of which he was capable would turn him into a conversationalist this day. Finally he and Pointer drove back to his hotel, where a telegram was handed him. He tore it open and read it thankfully. Here was a load off his heart. Joan was safe in Paris—really safe at last, in one of the G.F.S.'s hostels. He handed the slip to Pointer. Now for the answer to the questions that were fairly scorching his brain.

"Hilary Amcott! What was his part in the murder?"

"Hilary Amcott..." Pointer repeated thoughtfully, "the man who impersonated his brother down at Elmhurst the night after that brother's wife was murdered, and again a second time when he and Waddy 'saw' him? Waddy, of course, saw Mr. Hilary's back made up to look like Ralph Amcott's back. And Mr. Hilary—saw nothing."

"But why? And if he murdered his sister-in-law, why again?"

"His is a long story. But to begin at the beginning. You know, of course, that Mr. Ralph Amcott is Civil Secretary in Khartoum?"

Blair said that he did.

"And you know, I take it, better than I do, that there's a not inconsiderable stream of trouble running all through Africa, and that in every part white and black men who care for the country are trying to keep it from broadening into a river and then into a vast swamp in which all that makes for civilisation out there would go down. Mr. Ralph Amcott is one, or was one, of the men most particularly keen on seeing due there's no spread of the evil unrest. Now there's a secret society in North Africa called the Scorpions of Allah; not unlike the Leopard Society of the Gold Coast in its savagery. These Scorpions are found throughout the length and breadth of the land, though they're supposed to come from among the Touaregs.

"The Egyptian 'Vengeance Society,' the Masri, that murdered Sir Lee Stack years ago was an early offshoot of theirs, so at least the Egyptian C.I.D. tell us. The headquarters of the Sudanese Scorpions is at Khartoum, and with it Mr. Ralph Amcott came into contact, and determined to stamp it out, not merely the Sudanese branches, but the roots as well."

Pointer paused again for a moment.

"You heard, I suppose, that Mr. Hilary went out as his brother's private secretary, and how he got slacker and slacker, and how finally Mr. Ralph Amcott suggested a return to England and a change to work in some other part of the Empire? You know that Mr. Hilary, besides drinking far too much—in his case drinking himself to death—is passionately fond of gambling, and how through both these weaknesses, he and that Franco-Arabo-Cardiff washerwoman's son seem to have become the closest of pals?"

Impatiently Blair said that he had all this part of the story at his fingers' ends.

"Well, wipe it all off your fingers, Blair. Forget all that you've heard, or seen, or thought about Mr. Hilary Amcott, and meet him for the first time, for it seems that in all Ralph Amcott's labours he had no keener, or better, or more selfless helper than his brother, this same Hilary."

Blair stared at the Chief Inspector incredulously. He was not going to swallow such a story without one gulp. But the man from Scotland Yard went on in a quiet, almost dreamy way.

"It seems that the two brothers worked together, but each had his own field, and there was no outward harmony between them. It was a slow business because of the sudden deaths that overtook those who mixed themselves up in the Scorpions' affairs. But finally the two brothers got hold of the main root, and Hilary Amcott came to Europe to follow it up, or down rather, from this end, according to his own ideas. These ideas of his finally had made him decide that a certain notorious ex-cabaret dancer and present gaming-hall proprietor named Waddy was one of the chief and most dangerous go-betweens of the Scorpions—dangerous not in the least from any personal character, but from his opportunity of meeting with all classes, and his knowledge of the underworld of at least two continents—his and his mother's. His beliefs, I may add, were shared by the French Secret Service of Morocco, which was why blind eyes were always turned to happenings at the carpet shop. They were after worse criminals yet, and had to be patient. But Mr. Hilary arranged to meet Monsieur Waddy in such a fashion that not even the wariest Scorpion could have any suspicion of him. He played the part well and thoroughly of a lazy drunkard with but one thing that really interested him, and that was gambling. The drink was because of his previous reputation for brains. He knew that the Scorpions would be afraid of a man with keen wits, so Hilary Amcott threw his away, poisoned them deliberately. Not even Mr. Grimshaw was allowed to guess the truth. He has sacrificed every farthing he has in the world and every chance of a cure in order to become friends with Waddy, on the chance of securing the

men or the names of the men responsible for the trouble
among the blacks. All went well. But the Scorpions
suddenly decided to make London their headquarters.
This did not suit Hilary. He had laid his plans in and for
their old rendezvous here in Marseilles, the carpet shop of
the Rue Mazagran, where Waddy has been so long
tolerated just because Hilary and the French hoped to
make this grand coup. Also, he thought London too big to
be a safe place in which to snare them. So he decided to
stampede them here by letting Ralph Amcott be seen
slipping into Ouadhi's flat in town. He himself, Hilary,
was not considered in the least as a menace. On the
contrary, the Scorpions believed that from him they
learnt of his brother's intended steps against them. But
that brother himself was quite another matter! Mr. Ralph
Amcott, whom they had hoped they had got out of the
way by poison, to be apparently well, and apparently not
wanting to have it known that he was in England,
therefore doubtless on their tracks, or at least on the
track of Waddy, the go-between! Unfortunately, Mr.
Hilary picked on the night after Mrs. Amcott was
murdered for Ralph's first appearance down at Elmhurst
Manor. He had flitted through Waddy's flat the night
before in town and found him gone.

"That murder, or rather your article publicly stating it
to be a murder, plunged Mr. Hilary in despair. It had
been bad enough having Mrs. Amcott down there at such
a critical time. He knew well enough who the criminal
was, but he was within a week of what he and his dying
brother believed to be the end of their long and desperate
work. He would still like to shoot you, Blair, for having
written it! He hoped to squelch the idea of murder—until
he had brought off his coup. When that was impossible,
he decided to stand in with Waddy in every way, even in
his false alibi, pretending to the man himself that he had
been too fuddled that night to remember whether. Waddy
had been with him or not, and whether he himself had
been at his rooms or at the theatre."

"You don't think he also impersonated Waddy at the theatre? Or did Waddy manage to show up there for a little while and then slip down to the manor afterwards?" Blair asked eagerly. He had felt all along that there lay Waddy's weak point.

"One fence at a time, Blair, or we'll never get home! Mr. Hilary decided not to take the police into his confidence. He believed that we would not hold our hands. And, above all things, Waddy must not be arrested—then. And I think Armstrong would have arrested him at once, but for Mr. Hilary's bolstering up of his story. To Hilary Amcott the most important thing in the world was to get hold of the men in Marseilles whom he believed would meet Waddy in a few days to give him the orders which he would afterwards pass on. So once more Ralph Amcott—in reality already half-dead in Khartoum—was made to appear again—this time at the manor itself. As both brothers hoped, this sent the two men who head the League of Scorpions off to Marseilles. But not Waddy. Mr. Hilary found that he wouldn't leave Elmhurst. He might be frightened, but he would not budge, and Mr. Hilary hunted for the reason. He finally guessed that Waddy still believed that Miss Ingilby—we know that there is but one Miss Ingilby—had the Norreys necklace, and that until he had the emeralds—that which was put into her suit-case was but a copy which Mrs. Amcott had had made for an exhibition loan once— Waddy would not stir. So Mr. Hilary decided to get Miss Ingilby to Marseilles—by fair means or foul."

"The unspeakable blackguard!" Blair jumped up. "Oh, damn his fine motives! Where is he?"

"Patience, Blair. As I warned you, we'll never get all this untangled if you let feelings come in."

"You're right." Blair sat down again, clenching his hands.

"He let the plan which he and Miss Ingilby had decided on for smuggling her out of the country leak out to Waddy, who, as he hoped, was delighted at the idea of getting the girl into his power off in that house in the Rue Mazagran."

Blair bit back an explosive comment with difficulty.

"Waddy went ahead of them to Marseilles, and thither the chief Scorpions collected, only too thankful to be there in safety from Ralph Amcott. And there Hilary brought Miss Ingilby. But..."

"And left her there, friendless and alone!" Blair burst out. "He changed a letter she wrote me in which she told me where she was going so that I shouldn't follow her and be able to help her. Thank heaven, I did get on her track almost at once by sheer luck!"

"He didn't leave her alone in Marseilles, Blair. Apart from his own reasons for staying, he would not have left her in Waddy's hands. He was hiding all the time in the house, and knew all that was going on. He, too, had an inside helper. Once he saw we had her safely out, he went about his own business."

"Selfish brute! We needed his help. But for you, Miss Ingilby needed it frightfully!"

"But he knew I was there helping you. I had slipped him a paper when he looked out from behind that door. I guessed then, only then, a little of his game, and if there was one of us who was playing with death it was Mr. Hilary Amcott in that house, Blair. As to openly helping Miss Ingilby, he would have undone the work of patient months, he would have shown his hand, and never been able to finish his self-appointed task. I think, whatever the fate of the rest of us, seeing how momentous was the game he was playing, that Mr. Hilary would have done the right thing to stand aside."

Blair emphatically did not agree. Pointer did not expect him to.

"Once she was out of the house he decided that the pincers should close. But Waddy sprang a surprise on him by getting hold of Miss Ingilby again. How Hilary Amcott cursed that emerald necklace! He and the Prefect were actually arranging the final touches at the police headquarters when her telephone message came through, saying that there was murder being done in that house. As it happened, in accordance with his plan, he had telephoned Waddy in his own person a little while before, saying that he was back in Marseilles from Monte Carlo, and would drop in with a friend for a little game, his friend being, like himself a man who liked to go the limit. The friend, of course, was to be a disguised French official.

When Mr. Grimshaw appeared he was mistaken for Hilary Amcott's friend, or for Mr. Hilary himself, by some stupid servant, and this very much upset Waddy. I think he saved Miss Ingilby from torture, and possibly from death. Grimshaw, of course, was quite mistaken about her having taken the diary away with her, or of Hilary Amcott's having the slightest interest in it."

"Was he really mistaken, Chief Inspector, or was he lying?" Blair asked almost in despair of ever getting this thing clear in his mind.

At that moment the door fairly burst open, and Armstrong was in the room with a bound.

"Here are the cables for you, sir."

Pointer took the papers calmly, though there was a glow deep down in his eyes. He opened them, read them, and nodded to the police officer.

"It's all right, Armstrong. They're in cipher. But the faked ticket which I had printed at the Yard and substituted for the real one has just been presented this afternoon at Madrid. They made an immediate arrest. Detective Inspector Watts was on the spot to take over. He's already got the confession he wanted, and has started back for London with his prisoner. You're free now to help Mr. Hilary round up the last of his splendid catch. I'll be there, too, within the hour, and so, I'm sure, will Blair be."

"Right, sir, and well played again!" Armstrong, with a wave of his hat as on a football field, was off. He had not taken any notice of Blair.

That young man had risen to his feet. He felt the thrill in the air that had swept through the room with Armstrong's entrance—and had not left with him.

"Faked ticket? Madrid? You've got Waddy?" he asked tensely.

Pointer was still on his chair, and Blair after a glance at him sat down again, and heard, for the first time, the real reason why Mrs. Amcott had been murdered—the, possession of the ticket that had won half the Gordo, that stood therefore for a sum of two hundred and fortyr thousand pounds if presented in Madrid before the year was over.

"We printed one exactly like it, except that in one corner we added the letters S.Y. for Scotland Yard. I felt sure the murderer wouldn't notice them, or know that they weren't on the original. And I placed this new ticket, instead of the right one, in the body of the little black chap, and stood him, as before on the mantelpiece in Mrs. Amcott's room."

CHAPTER FOURTEEN

AND you've got Waddy!" Blair asked, rejoicing. "His body, yes," Pointer replied. "We have had that for some hours. He was killed before the police got to the carpet shop. That was what I meant when I said that he had escaped. He was stabbed between the shoulders as he stood bending forward, sending off a telephone message—killed by a very firm neat stroke. No bungler's work, but done by the same hand that intended to kill Mr. Grimshaw, as it had first of all helped to murder Mrs. Amcott."

"Hilary! Hilary Amcott! But you said just now—" Blair stopped himself. He was only impulsive, not an imbecile.

"No, Blair, not Mr. Hilary Amcott, but Joan Ingilby. Yes, Joan Ingilby. As you heard me tell Armstrong, she was arrested at Madrid on presenting that faked ticket. She got out of the aeroplane at Dijon and into one going into Spain. The telegram you had was sent off by one of her friends in Paris.

Pointer was talking on to give Blair time. He needed it.

Joan Ingilby! Blair felt as though lightning had struck close beside him. There was a sound of many waters in his ears. Dimly he heard Pointer's voice; the Chief Inspector's eyes were on his shoe-tip.

"Your reasoning was quite right. The crime *was* committed just as you thought. Your mistake was to let your judgment be swayed, changed, reversed by an uncommonly pretty face and the most taking manner of one of the very cleverest actresses I have ever met."

Pointer did not say, as he might have done, that in the pretty face and beneath the taking manner, and behind the accomplished actress there was yet a something that would have warned an acute observer not to trust the girl, that if her eyes were crystal clear, they were, to an unbiased watcher, hard as crystals, and in their depths was at times a curious flickering gleam that did not belong in the eyes of an honest man or woman.

The Chief Inspector was concerned only with facts just now.

"Joan Ingilby, as she called herself for the purpose of getting into the Countess de Gérode's household, is as abandoned a young woman as exists in the ranks of the criminals of to-day. She belongs to the Madame de Brinvilliers type—cowardly where her own self is at stake, ruthless everywhere else. She and Waddy were old friends, though now they hate each other. Both of them are Paris apaches. She and he used to dance all through the Riviera as *Le Mort et la Morte*. You must have heard of that macabre dance, often suppressed, but always a draw? When Waddy started gambling dens in every large town in Europe, she was his decoy. Many a girl, Blair, had been taken by her to that carpet shop in Marseilles, and taken by Waddy the devil only knows where. That was what I meant when I, as Michaud, spoke as I did. Naturally, they did well. He also went in for jewel snatching, and for blackmail. For the later reason he got her into the Countess's household. Poor Madame de Gérode to this day does not connect the theft of some very incriminating letters with the presence of the charming young English nursery governess they happened to have just then. Waddy just after that successful venture was offered ten thousand pounds by a South American magnate's go-between if he could secure him the Norreys necklace. He had seen Baroness de Maricourt wear it on one of the many occasions when Mrs. Amcott had lent it her. For that reason Miss Ingilby proceeded to enter Mrs. Amcott's employment. She bungled badly in the

beginning, though she managed to avert suspicion by
talking about her scarf having caught, and she stayed on
solely for the purpose of getting those emeralds in the
end, though Mrs. Amcott sent the necklace to the bank
after that. Then last Saturday Mrs. Amcott, who went in
for the Spanish Christmas lottery since she spent a
winter in that country, asked her little girl's governess to
find out in town on Monday at noon what the winning
numbers were and telephone them to her. 'Telephone
Madrid lottery winning numbers,' was the note she
handed her, of which such an odd fragment remained
behind in Miss Ingilby's glove. It was Joan Ingilby's glove.
The marks of pushing the child's go-cart were quite clear.
When Joan saw the list, she learnt that Mrs. Amcott had
won half the Gordo. Instantly she telephoned some other
numbers to Mrs. Amcott and then sent a summons to
Waddy. She could not manage Mrs. Amcott's murder
alone. They only had that one night, for next morning the
true numbers would reach Mrs. Amcott by post. Together
the two planned and then carried out the murder exactly
as you reasoned had been done. But when Joan opened
Mrs. Amcott's jewel case, in a secret pocket of which she
always kept her lottery tickets, she found it empty.
Pleasant shock for her—Joan, who had told her
accomplice that she had the ticket in safety! However,
there is a year's allowance before the ticket expires. Both
she and the man thought the murder a perfect crime, and
she believed that before the funeral she would have
ample time to hunt quietly and find it. Then came your
article next morning. It was a thunderbolt."

"One moment!" Blair said hoarsely. "Are you guessing
this, or are they facts?"

"It's Miss Ingilby's confession, Mr. Blair. Made at once
when she thought Waddy had confessed and given her
away. She knew that he would, if he were ever arrested
for that murder! Just as he knew that she would do the
same. Which was why each of them insisted that the
other had not committed the crime. I'm afraid," Pointer

said sadly, "that Detective Inspector Watts, who's over in Madrid—he was the stout gentleman who accompanied Miss Ingilby to Dijon yesterday and then flew on with her as a horsey-looking English groom—made Joan Ingilby think, when he arrested her, that he did so on evidence sworn to by Waddy, who was not really killed by her knife thrust... who would, in fact, recover and had already turned King's evidence... Joan and he hate each other nowadays. Each has tried to kill the other more than once. But each knows so much about the other that he or she can always force that other to help. But to go back to your article. They had made a perfect affair of the murder, they thought, but if you had detected a capital blunder—that of the clean slippers—what about the police? What about clues? In fact, what about themselves? Joan and probably Waddy had the usual idea about our brains. Hence her preference, I feel sure, when you told me that that old lady gave her her choice of getting Scotland Yard called in or going to a private detective, and her relief when the Chief Constable had put the matter in our hands. Still, even a poor detective is a danger. She must get down at once and look for clues, and also for that lottery ticket, now that any return on her part openly to the manor house is out of the question. But how could she venture out into the streets, let alone down to Elmhurst? It was the merest chance that she got as far as the station. She decided to do what I thought she would do—go to you."

"You thought she would come to me? Why?" Blair asked almost savagely.

"Because she had no one else to whom she could turn. Waddy might be already watched, or soon would be. As a matter of fact, he thought she went to you to give him away, or, rather, he thought that you would see through her at once and have her arrested. He almost fought her to get her away from your door. He wanted her in his power—and the ticket; especially now that a word from him would mean life or death to her. She, of course, drew your attention to the scuffle, didn't she? I was sure she would. It would create just the right atmosphere. 'Young Girl Attacked by Unknown Aggressor.' I saw her come to your room. You see, I was that watcher standing in the doorway opposite. I didn't try to make myself invisible. Fright drives criminals to hasty deeds sometimes. I hoped it might her."

"Or did you expect I would hand her over to you?" Blair asked with a mixture of pain and anger in his voice.

"No; I was sure you wouldn't." Pointer had not lifted his eyes from his shoe. "She was a young and pretty girl. You were young, and therefore impressionable." Pointer did not know of that enchanted day in the fog. He never knew of it. And Blair, therefore, never learnt that that poor rug was one of Joan Ingilby's—to give her a name she had used for some time—stock-in-trade in winter. She had mistaken Blair for young Lord Mountserrat, and had planned her approach accordingly. When Blair told her about himself finally, she left him with a good impression—Joan always did that if possible —especially as he was connected with the press, but she took no trouble to return him his rug, or to meet him again, or to have him see her home in the 'car, as had first been planned.

"She was a trained decoy," Pointer went on. "I felt sure she would throw herself, as an innocent dove, on your chivalry."

"You were so certain from my article that she was guilty?"

"Your article had nothing to do with starting the wheel to turn, Blair." Pointer was glad that he could say that truthfully. "Inspector Armstrong had already noticed those shoes, and we at the Yard had come to the same conclusion that you had. The night you were writing your article, the Assistant Commissioner and I were tabulating the facts of the inquest, so that, should the Yard be called in, we could arrest the governess on the instant, should she try to get away. A hint to that effect went to Armstrong by the morning's special telephone. Naturally Joan Ingilby stressed the effects of your article. It made you still more anxious to help her. Just as she doubtless must have seemed to you over-anxious as to its consequences. You see, she knew that, once arrested, her past would practically do for her. Certainly if she were implicated in a murder charge, it would hang her. She really was terrified of arrest, though she couldn't always give you the reason for her fear. As for us, the trouble was the lack of any adequate motive, or even of any motive at all. That was my only concern from first to last—the motive—and that she should not get away. For she was the real criminal. Waddy was only her assistant. And, incidentally, Hilary Amcott knew that. Though he thought they had killed his sister-in-law for the sake of the emerald necklace, and that Joan had done her fellow-criminal out of his share. He had overheard them once when they thought him far away. And because he knew of their being linked, he tried first of all to get into Waddy's confidence by making love to Joan. He thought she, too, was in the Scorpions' secrets. And when he found that she and Waddy were on opposite sides after the crime, he, of course, sided with Waddy, until the affair of the emerald necklace in the suit-case gave him a chance of seeming to come over openly. He knew that if she or Waddy suspected that he even thought, let alone knew, that they were guilty, his life would be snuffed out in a moment— and his work left undone. It was that last alone that counted. But because he knew that she had murdered his sister-in-law, he had no qualms about treating her as he did until he was prepared to give her and her helper up to us; though we must remember that, even so, he did not hand her over to that Levantine crew without being at hand. That hunchback in the shop was in his pay, it seems."

"You take his story very much for granted surely," Blair broke in chokingly.

"Every fact told us has been tested and proved."

Blair buried his face in his hands.

"And you, too, knew all along that she was guilty?" he asked dully.

"I could not imagine any other reason that would make her go down again to the manor house, running the terrible risk she did run, unless she had left something vital down there. I rather thought it might be some jewel or money, until that little Paso figure pointed to Spain and Madrid. That slip in her glove wouldn't fit many things. If it was Madrid, then 'telephone Madrid' was hardly likely. Mrs. Amcott would have gone up to town herself for anything important enough for that, one would think. It seemed as though Madrid must be an adjective; that the sentence must have run: Telephone Madrid. What? News? Results?"

He went through the steps again of his reasoning and the final finding of the ticket. It helped to relieve the anguished tension of the room. He did not add that the absence of the ticket would not have made any difference; that he had deduced the possibility of it from the Paso figure and the one mad., and would have had a watch kept on the winning Gordo numbers just the same.

"That was why that effort to poison you was made when you had found what you doubtless spoke of as a Spanish ticket to Joan Ingilby. She, of course, poured the contents of both cups together into one bottle and destroyed the cups so as to prevent any one finding out that there had only been one poisoned drink—yours. That of the man who had what she believed from your vague words might be the Gordo ticket in his possession. What I would like to know is how her end was defeated."

Blair made no reply. He remembered with horrible clearness that at the moment of drinking, when she had been summoned from the room by a telephone message from the vicar's sister, he had noticed that the cup on her tray had a crack in it, and knowing that she disliked to drink from cracked china, had changed the poisoned cup for hers.

"The poison must have been put in by her when she was alone in the room, before she joined you at the telephone. For even as far off as that you would have heard anyone comming into the drawing-room, the boards outside creaked so badly. It was an escape. She had it in for you from the time you wrote your article, of course. But she wanted you to save her first, then to be useful generally, but not to be allowed to live a moment once you became a danger. When her attempt on your life went wrong she was indeed almost mad with fright—of detection by you or the police."

Blair thought of that afternoon. Of her terror—for herself! All, all for herself!

"As for the diary that Mr. Grimshaw took, her first thought was certainly that it might mention the Spanish lottery. That was why she wanted it back, and yet did not speak to you or anyone of the book's disappearance until she had the ticket. By that time I feel sure that she had looked through the book when Mr. Grimshaw was absent. I feel sure of that, or else she would not have told you of having seen him take it."

But Blair was still thinking of the poisoned coffee.

"She must be mad!" he said hoarsely. "Demented! Insane!"

There was a silence of utter dissent on the part of Pointer.

"Waddy, of course, wanted the ticket from her," Blair went on. "Was that why he almost drowned her that night?" Blair asked after a pause.

"That little scene was none of his doing, Mr. Blair. That was stage-managed by Joan Ingilby herself for one sole reason. Can't you guess it?"

Blair could not have guessed his name during this talk.

"You must understand," Pointer went on—he thought that the best way to help Blair from a cruel blow was to explain all that there was to know and leave the cure to time—"that we have been watching a fight between two tigers—Waddy and Joan Ingilby—each wanting to have the other killed. She intended to have him killed, because she had had to promise halves to him. He not daring—yet—to go as far as that, for he hadn't any idea where she had put the ticket, but he desired above all things that she should be arrested, and if possible sent to prison for more than a year. By that time the ticket would be useless, and she would have had to take him into her confidence at once. Hence his efforts with the emeralds. Joan would have done exactly the same if she had had them. That was what infuriated her so—that she could not bring the theft of the Norreys necklace home to him. She was quite right. He had stolen it from Baroness Maricourt, probably in the train. We found it on his dead body. But once he heard of this ticket, he decided not to sell it to the South American, but to keep it for possible eventualities. Joan never gave Waddy away because she couldn't. If he were arrested for Mrs. Amcott's murder he would have given her away at once, and she had made no arrangements for such an emergency. What she wanted, just as he did, was that he should be imprisoned for over a year. Failing that, she decided that she could not venture to arouse suspicion by killing him herself. The only thing to do was to get you to kill him. That was the meaning of that cellar scene, Mr. Blair. And I assure you I trembled for fear I should be too late, and find that you had done what I think you meant to do had Waddy entered the cellar—shoot him. Fortunately he was quite aware of his danger, and when she telephoned him to come at once to a house which the whole gang used, he very wisely stayed in bed. The police station was linked with his 'phone, and I went instead. By the way, didn't you—but of course you didn't"—Pointer's eyes were very kind; he was desperately sorry for Blair—"notice that her shoes were barely wet instead of sodden? She could only have stepped into the water the moment before you climbed in at the window. The marks on her arm were done with strips of mustard plaster. But that's by the way. That second time you and she were in danger, as you thought, that time when I turned up as a postman, she had handed you over to Waddy, hoping that you would act just as you did act—ask for a paper which Waddy would think was the lottery ticket, and to get which he would kill you. Once he had killed you she would have seen to it that he was at least detained for your murder. Because of the money, Waddy would not have given Joan away unless she had implicated him in Mrs. Amcott's murder. The day after the baulked cellar effort, she found what she thought was the ticket. I had twisted the little black man half around on his legs so as to catch her eye—hers or Waddy's. I knew that whichever presented the faked ticket would be arrested, and once arrested could be made to tell on the other by the old police dodge of being assured that the other had given him or her away. Neither of these two had the pluck of a frightened cat when it came to themselves. If all's fair in love and war—which it isn't—all certainly is when trapping man-eating tigers.

"Now she had the ticket, Joan's one thought was to get away. The difficulty was how. She was nearly caught out by Waddy with those emeralds. Little she knew that nothing would have made me let her be arrested—not until she had had time to give in that lottery ticket of ours. Then Mr. Hilary made her his proposal about the packing-case and Marseilles. It suited her to perfection. Even when it went a little wrong, and Waddy met her at the station, she soon recovered her wits, though it must have been a jar. From what Mr. Hilary Amcott has told me, she completely hoodwinked the incredibly vain semi-Oriental into thinking that she was as fond of him as she had been in the days when they danced all along the coast. She did not dare kill him—in that house. She knew that it was full of his friends, though she knew nothing as to who or what those friends were. Then you came to her rescue. In more ways than one, she hoped. She had left that message in your room because, though she thought him a fool, I take it she was not quite certain of Mr. Hilary. There would be times when what was in his heart—contempt and loathing of her and of Waddy—would peep out. It nearly always does. When you came, she decided that if in stealing with you from the house, Waddy, whom she had very lightly drugged, should wake and interfere, you would shoot him. At the convent Waddy scored over all, of us, quite unexpectedly. He arrested her. And this time he was really dangerous. He meant to have the ticket. It was only Mr. Grimshaw's bewildering appearance and his request for her that upset Waddy. Could this be Hilary's friend? Hilary, too, was at hand, as he had just telephoned. He forgot for one' moment the dangerous nature of the creature in the room with him as he turned his back to telephone to another member of the gang. She had a knife, snatched it from the table as he turned to telephone probably, and struck or threw it—the doctor thinks the latter. So do I, for her father had earned a respectable livelihood for years as a knife-thrower at the Paris music halls. He and her mother were both strolling jugglers —but decent people all the same. After she threw the knife she shot Mr. Grimshaw, so as to make it seem like a quarrel between the two men. Then she looked out and saw you—and, though she did not know it, me. For the reason of her reputation with you, she took the daring step of telephoning then, when she stepped back from the window, to the police. You were at hand to save her. And even you—I mean anyone, might have wavered in their faith in her if they had come upon her in that shambles. You see, the difficulty for her was that she wanted to return to life in England, to keep the most respectable circle that she had entered. Dr. Pearson's wife liked her, so did Miss Dallas. Returning with some tale of a legacy from some wealthy relative who had died abroad, she would have been able to take up her residence there quite pleasantly. For that reason, I think, she kept a tolerant eye and tongue on Hilary Amcott. Failing his brother Sir

Christopher, he might do for a stepping-stone... But you were a great difficulty. You knew a great deal. Had you found her out in one lie, your idea of her character would be changed. In that case you might even have reverted to the cold and logical reasoning of your article."

There was a long pause.

"And the Baroness..." Blair said at last. "I had at one time an idea..."

"I think she's just a silly woman infatuated with a worthless man. Waddy doubtless tried to frighten her into silence about the emeralds being missing by some story of the danger of being supposed to be implicated in her cousin's death. Only her dislike, her hatred—for she felt that there was some tie between her and the man—made her want to attack Joan Ingilby. Waddy told Hilary Amcott that he would be suspected if he let it be known that he had been drunk on Monday night, so Hilary pretended to be terrified into standing in with him, and also claimed not to remember things clearly himself. By the way, Waddy poisoned the dog when he and Joan had arranged that she should go down at once to the manor and look for any incriminating clues. Waddy couldn't have the free access to the suite of Mrs. Amcott that she had. Hilary Amcott was thankful the dog was gone, though he wouldn't have hurt the poor beast, but he was greatly in the way when he spied on Waddy—just as Mrs. Amcott was. But the dog had a habit of following him about that was decidedly dangerous. Waddy's reason, of course, was that the Airedale might have greeted the 'sister' as an old friend."

"Was Hilary in the room when I was searched? That night at the inn?"

Pointer shook his head.

"Probably Waddy wore his coat so that if you tore a piece off it wouldn't incriminate him. He wanted to be sure that Joan hadn't handed you the ticket to keep for her, without telling you what it was, naturally. By the way, when you lost that envelope she had handed you, the envelope that was to induce Waddy to kill you to make you hand it over, she probably took it herself from your pocket when you helped her out of the window. I need hardly say that there was nothing in it, nor that she had not found it in Mrs. Amcott's room, nor been seen putting it in her handbag."

"I wonder Waddy didn't do for me in the carpet shop," Blair said after a silence.

"I don't think he minded your being there. You see, he thought she was in love with him again"

Pointer did not add that Waddy had probably had the most profound contempt for the intelligence of the man whom Joan had duped so completely.

"What he didn't realise was how gullible he himself was in thinking that he had fascinated her afresh."

Pointer bit his lip. His spoken words were too closely linked with his unspoken thought, but Blair was staring moodily at the floor.

"I shouldn't wonder if he had been the cause of all her downfall," he said somberly.

Pointer was honest. Truth is a wonderful medicine.

"I doubt if there was much lower that she could fall than the plane on which she chose to live her life. Joan Ingilby, Blair, is incurably vicious. You see, I'm thinking of the girls who really were young and innocent whom she decoyed to that house out of which we watched her climb. She saw to it that there should be no escape for them."

Blair felt sick. But these terrible words buried for ever what the Chief Inspector's revelations had already killed. He visualised something of the real woman—that dreadful harpy that wore so fair a shape.

Yes, there was a net around Joan Ingilby, but it was the net of facts—evil facts. And rising, he put on his hat, and followed the Chief Inspector.

THE END

Other Resurrected Press Books in *The Chief Inspector Pointer Mystery* Series

MYSTERIES BY ANNE AUSTIN

Murder at Bridge

When an afternoon bridge party attended by some of Hamilton's leading citizens ends with the hostess being murdered in her boudoir, Special Investigator Dundee of the District Attorney's office is called in. But one of the attendees is guilty? There are plenty of suspects: the victim's former lover, her current suitor, the retired judge who is being blackmailed, the victim's maid who had been horribly disfigured accidentally by the murdered woman, or any of the women who's husbands had flirted with the victim. Or was she murdered by an outsider whose motive had nothing to do with the town of Hamilton. Find the answer in... **Murder at Bridge**

One Drop of Blood

When Dr. Koenig, head of Mayfield Sanitarium is murdered, the District Attorney's Special Investigator, "Bonnie" Dundee must go undercover to find the killer. Were any of the inmates of the asylum insane enough to have committed the crime? Or, was it one of the staff, motivated by jealousy? And what was is the secret in the murdered man's past. Find the answer in... **One Drop of Blood**

AVAILABLE FROM RESURRECTED PRESS!

GEMS OF MYSTERY
LOST JEWELS FROM A MORE ELEGANT AGE

Three wonderful tales of mystery from some of the best known writers of the period before the First World War -

A foggy London night, a Russian princess who steals jewels, a corpse; a mysterious murder, an opera singer, and stolen pearls; two young people who crash a masked ball only to find themselves caught up in a daring theft of jewels; these are the subjects of this collection of entertaining tales of love, jewels, and mystery. This collection includes:

- **In the Fog - by Richard Harding Davis's**

- **The Affair at the Hotel Semiramis - by A.E.W. Mason**

- **Hearts and Masks - Harold MacGrath**

AVAILABLE FROM RESURRECTED PRESS!

THE EDWARDIAN DETECTIVES
LITERARY SLEUTHS OF THE EDWARDIAN ERA

The exploits of the great Victorian Detectives, Poe's C. Auguste Dupin, Gaboriau's Lecoq, and most famously, Arthur Conan Doyle's Sherlock Holmes, are well known. But what of those fictional detectives that came after, those of the Edwardian Age? The period between the death of Queen Victoria and the First World War had been called the Golden Age of the detective short story, but how familiar is the modern reader with the sleuths of this era? And such an extraordinary group they were, including in their numbers an unassuming English priest, a blind man, a master of disguises, a lecturer in medical jurisprudence, a noble woman working for Scotland Yard, and a savant so brilliant he was known as "The Thinking Machine."

To introduce readers to these detectives, Resurrected Press has assembled a collection of stories featuring these and other remarkable sleuths in The Edwardian Detectives.

- The Case of Laker, Absconded by Arthur Morrison
- The Fenchurch Street Mystery by Baroness Orczy
- The Crime of the French Café by Nick Carter
- The Man with Nailed Shoes by R Austin Freeman
- The Blue Cross by G. K. Chesterton
- The Case of the Pocket Diary Found in the Snow by Augusta Groner
- The Ninescore Mystery by Baroness Orczy
- The Riddle of the Ninth Finger by Thomas W. Hanshew
- The Knight's Cross Signal Problem by Ernest Bramah

- The Problem of Cell 13 by Jacques Futrelle
- The Conundrum of the Golf Links by Percy James Brebner
- The Silkworms of Florence by Clifford Ashdown
- The Gateway of the Monster by William Hope Hodgson
- The Affair at the Semiramis Hotel by A. E. W. Mason
- The Affair of the Avalanche Bicycle & Tyre Co., LTD by Arthur Morrison

The Middle of Things
Ravensdene Court
Scarhaven Keep
The Orange-Yellow Diamond
The Middle Temple Murder
The Tallyrand Maxim
The Borough Treasurer
In the Mayor's Parlour
The Saftey Pin

R. Austin Freeman

The Mystery of 31 New Inn from the Dr. Thorndyke Series
John Thorndyke's Cases from the Dr. Thorndyke Series
The Red Thumb Mark from The Dr. Thorndyke Series
The Eye of Osiris from The Dr. Thorndyke Series
A Silent Witness from the Dr. John Thorndyke Series
The Cat's Eye from the Dr. John Thorndyke Series
Helen Vardon's Confession: A Dr. John Thorndyke Story
As a Thief in the Night: A Dr. John Thorndyke Story
Mr. Pottermack's Oversight: A Dr. John Thorndyke Story
Dr. Thorndyke Intervenes: A Dr. John Thorndyke Story
The Singing Bone: The Adventures of Dr. Thorndyke
The Stoneware Monkey: A Dr. John Thorndyke Story
The Great Portrait Mystery, and Other Stories: A Collection of Dr. John Thorndyke and Other Stories
The Penrose Mystery: A Dr. John Thorndyke Story
The Uttermost Farthing: A Savant's Vendetta

Arthur Griffiths

The Passenger From Calais
The Rome Express

Fergus Hume
The Mystery of a Hansom Cab
The Green Mummy
The Silent House
The Secret Passage

Edgar Jepson
The Loudwater Mystery

A. E. W. Mason
At the Villa Rose

A. A. Milne
The Red House Mystery
Baroness Emma Orczy
The Old Man in the Corner

Edgar Allan Poe
The Detective Stories of Edgar Allan Poe

Arthur J. Rees
The Hampstead Mystery
The Shrieking Pit
The Hand In The Dark
The Moon Rock
The Mystery of the Downs

Mary Roberts Rinehart
Sight Unseen and The Confession

Dorothy L. Sayers
Whose Body?

Sir William Magnay
The Hunt Ball Mystery

Mabel and Paul Thorne
The Sheridan Road Mystery

Louis Tracy
The Strange Case of Mortimer Fenley
The Albert Gate Mystery
The Bartlett Mystery
The Postmaster's Daughter
The House of Peril
The Sandling Case: What Would You Have Done?
Charles Edmonds Walk
The Paternoster Ruby

John R. Watson
The Mystery of the Downs
The Hampstead Mystery

Edgar Wallace
The Daffodil Mystery
The Crimson Circle

Carolyn Wells
Vicky Van
The Man Who Fell Through the Earth
In the Onyx Lobby
Raspberry Jam
The Clue
The Room with the Tassels
The Vanishing of Betty Varian
The Mystery Girl
The White Alley
The Curved Blades
Anybody but Anne
The Bride of a Moment
Faulkner's Folly
The Diamond Pin
The Gold Bag
The Mystery of the Sycamore
The Come Backy

Raoul Whitfield
Death in a Bowl

And much more!
Visit ResurrectedPress.com
for our complete catalogue

About Resurrected Press

A division of Intrepid Ink, LLC, Resurrected Press is dedicated to bringing high quality, vintage books back into publication. See our entire catalogue and find out more at www.ResurrectedPress.com.

About Intrepid Ink, LLC

Intrepid Ink, LLC provides full publishing services to authors of fiction and non-fiction books, eBooks and websites. From editing to formatting, from publishing to marketing, Intrepid Ink gets your creative works into the hands of the people who want to read them. Find out more at www.IntrepidInk.com.

www.ingramcontent.com/pod-product-compliance
Lightning Source LLC
Chambersburg PA
CBHW070832250626
47159CB00003B/752